"Sizzling. . . . *Shining Through* explodes more than one myth about being as American as apple pie."
*Los Angeles Times*

"Susan Isaacs can sure kick-start a novel. . . . Witty, literate soap opera with some derring-do . . . a feisty heroine, a reluctant lover, the girl you love to hate, and an intriguing older man playing out their personal dramas as the world goes to war."
*New York Daily News*

"Laced with heartbreak, drama, and thrills . . . marvelously readable. . . . *Shining Through* is a dandy book, with a smile, a tug at the heartstrings and an insight on every page."
*Philadelphia Inquirer*

"A down-to-earth Cinderella story that is a totally captivating and unexpected blend of action, adventure, romantic fiction and spy thriller. . . . Keeps readers hooked from first page to last. . . . The wonderfully wrought characterization of Linda Voss shines throughout this novel. Isaacs has hit her stride."
*Chicago Sun-Times*

"Extravagant. . . . As witty as she ever was, but her imagination has gotten wilder, and the story she tells is bigger."
*Cosmopolitan*

# RED, WHITE AND BLUE

"Isaacs delivers."
*Cleveland Plain Dealer*

"A passionate page-turner. . . . Should earn the allegiance of her countless devoted fans."
*Entertainment Weekly*

"Isaacs excels at keeping the reader entertained."
*Seattle Times*

"Superior entertainment. . . . A funny, suspenseful, true-to-life novel. . . . Who the heck is our best popular novelist? The nominee from this quarter is Susan Isaacs. . . . Isaacs is a comic realist, an astute chronicler of contemporary life in the tradition of . . . Anthony Trollope. . . . During the course of her career, Isaacs has produced eight novels that, with their humor, suspense, and equal grasp of male and female psychology, are unlike anything else on the bestseller lists."
*Ft. Lauderdale Sun-Sentinel*

"The jauntiness and frothy exuberance of Susan Isaacs's style in her eighth novel carries you along as if on a wonderful joy ride. She is superb at quick character sketches, the deadly battles between fathers and sons, family frictions and generational antagonisms. Her effervescence convinces you that everything will turn out all right in the end. Which it does. But just barely."
*Providence Sunday Journal*

# LILY WHITE

# AFTER ALL THESE YEARS

"Entertaining and imaginative. . . . Isaacs scores again with this relentlessly funny portrait of the rich, old-line and nouveau. The plot rewardingly twists, the characters charm and Rosie carries the day. . . . A delightful summer cooler."
*People* magazine

"Bursts with energy, razor-sharp dialogue and memorable characters."
*Detroit News*

"Fabulous beach reading."
*McCall's*

## MAGIC HOUR

"Vintage Isaacs. . . . *Magic Hour* is like polishing off an entire box of chocolate-covered chocolates. . . . Fun."
*New York Times Book Review*

"Clever, unexpected, drum-tight. . . . The plot is streamlined and the time-frame is short and the voice we hear is witty and coming-at-us real."
*Washington Post Book World*

"A delightful blend of obsession, comedy, romance, movies and murder."
*San Francisco Chronicle*

# CLOSE RELATIONS

"Jane Austen brought up to date. . . .
Highly amusing."
*Atlantic Monthly*

"An entertaining novel by a witty, wry observer of
contemporary life."
*New York Times Book Review*

"A delightful read."
*Publishers Weekly*

"The gritty political detail and the fairy-tale ending in
this page-turner are equally appealing."
*Library Journal*

"Both a witty analysis of big-city politics, family
relationships and the singles scene in Washington and
New York, and a fairy-tale love story in which the heroine
finds her Prince Charming almost despite herself."
*Publishers Weekly*

*Books by*
**Susan Isaacs**

COMPROMISING POSITIONS
CLOSE RELATIONS
ALMOST PARADISE
SHINING THROUGH
MAGIC HOUR
AFTER ALL THESE YEARS
LILY WHITE
RED, WHITE, AND BLUE
LONG TIME NO SEE

# SUSAN ISAACS

# SHINING THROUGH

**HarperTorch**
*An Imprint of HarperCollinsPublishers*

HARPERTORCH
*An Imprint of* HarperCollins*Publishers*
10 East 53rd Street
New York, New York 10022-5299

Copyright © 1988 by Susan Isaacs
Library of Congress Catalog Card Number: 87-45630
ISBN: 0-06-103015-5

First HarperTorch paperback printing: July 2000
First HarperCollins hardcover printing: August 1988

HarperCollins®, HarperTorch™, and ◆™ are trademarks of HarperCollins Publishers Inc.

Printed in the United States of America

Visit HarperTorch on the World Wide Web at
www.harpercollins.com

10 9 8 7 6 5 4 3

In memory of
Gloria Safier

She <u>lived</u>.

# ACKNOWLEDGMENTS

I sought help from the people listed below; they gave it freely and cheerfully. I appreciate their generosity:

Arnold Abramowitz, Consuelo Saah Baehr, Jonathan Dolger, Sheldon Elsen, Janet and Robert Fiske, Phyllis and Milton Freeman, Helen Isaacs, Inga Joseph, Rita Kashner, T. Barry Kingham, Edith and Herbert Mendelsohn, Otto Obermaier, Frank Perry, Mary Rooney, Angelica Rosa, Cynthia Scott, Jeff Stolow, Hilma Wolitzer, Hon. Inzer B. Wyatt, Susan Zises, and the staff of the Port Washington (New York) Public Library.

My assistant, AnneMarie Palmer, deserves commendation not only for her loyalty and good humor but also for the formidable amount of work she did. Tim Guzley was a great help with research and translations.

Owen Laster more than lived up to his celebrated reputation. He is a talented agent, and a wise, congenial and kind man as well.

Larry Ashmead, my editor, offered me reassurance, guidance, sound criticism and a lot of great jokes. As usual, he was wonderful.

In addition to their warmth and support, my children, Andrew and Betsy Abramowitz, gave me valuable editorial comments. They also, on occasion, pulled me away from my word processor. I thank them for their impatience, as well as for their patience, their love and the pleasure of their company.

And after four novels, two screenplays and twenty years of marriage, Elkan Abramowitz continues to hold on to his title: Best Person in the World.

# SHINING THROUGH

# 1

In 1940, when I was thirty-one and an old maid, while the whole world waited for war, I fell in love with John Berringer.

An office crush. Big deal. Since the invention of the steno pad, a day hasn't gone by without some secretary glancing up from her Pitman squiggles and suddenly realizing that the man who was mumbling ". . . and therefore, pursuant to the above . . ." was the one man in her life who could ever bring her joy.

So there I was, a cliché with a number 2 yellow pencil: a working girl from Queens who'd lost her heart to the pride of the Ivy League.

And to make matters worse, John Berringer bore absolutely no resemblance to the typical Wall Street international lawyer, the kind whose gray face was two shades paler than his suit. Sure, a girl could wind up losing her heart to one of those dreary men. There's nothing quieter than an old maid's bedroom, and in that black stillness it's so easy to create magic: A lawyer with the profile of a toad— Abracadabra!—is transformed into an Adonis, pulsating with passion under his pinstripes.

But John didn't need any of that midnight magic to turn him gorgeous. The big joke in the law firm was how could I *not* have a mad crush on him. "You've got to be made of iron, Linda," one of the girls said at lunch, "not to go nuts for those blue eyes. They're blue like—" Someone at the far end of the table called out, Twilight! And someone else chimed

1

in, No, like a clear lake . . . but with a funny kind of depth, like on a cloudy day. John Berringer made poets out of stenographers. Someone else piped up, Come *on* . . . blue like pansies, and Gladys Slade, my best friend, called out from the head of the lunch table, "How can anybody even *think* of the word 'pansy' in the same sentence with 'Mr. Berringer' in it?" Everyone giggled.

In private, Gladys said, "Listen, Linda, don't kid a kidder. I'm the first person to understand your not wanting to make a public announcement, but even if you didn't care about looks, think about brains. I mean, you're always reading the papers and wanting to talk about—oh, God, you know— English naval power. Or French politics. So aren't you attracted to someone brilliant like him? I bet he loves all that boring stuff."

"It's not boring. Three quarters of the world is—"

"He's *so* charming," she cut me off. "Like a blond Cary Grant."

"Gladys," I explained, "when you sit across the desk from this guy day in and day out, you realize he's *always* charming. It kind of wafts up from him, like B.O. Don't you get it? It doesn't mean anything. And his looks . . . Yeah, he's handsome, but what's behind it?"

"That's for you to find out," Gladys ho-ho-hoed.

"I've got to tell you," I said, "there's something deep-down unappealing about a man who knows he's stunning and uses it. You know, like it's six-fifteen and you're so tired all you want to do is suck your thumb, but he has forty-seven letters he still wants to dictate. So he flashes that five-thousand-watt smile and that's supposed to brighten up your life and make you want to go on. But see, a guy who pulls that sort of thing isn't . . ."

"Isn't what?"

"Isn't masculine."

"Oh, come off it!"

"I'm serious, Gladys. And he's *much* too blond. Girls are fair. Guys should be dark. And with those big blue eyes. It's like some artist made him up to illustrate 'Cinderella.' Can't you just see him, with green stockings and those bubble shorts, holding a glass slipper?"

"I can see him *with* green stockings . . . and *without* green stockings." This was a very racy remark for Gladys, whose idea of wild sex was Fred Astaire loosening his tie.

"He's Prince Charming," I said. "Who needs it? I've got to stay late when he asks me, even if he looked like a pile of you-know-what. It's my job. But he thinks: Ha! I've charmed her. I've got her where I've got *all* the girls, in the palm of my hand." I looked Gladys straight in the eye. "You know why he doesn't do a thing for me? Because he's a woman's man. Not a real man."

Naturally, I was lying through my teeth. But I kept my secret love a secret. I would not let myself (as his secretary) be honorary president of the John Berringer Fan Club. What I felt for John wasn't meant to be shared with the girls. It was precious, and different.

Because even way back then, I felt *I* was different.

But was I (am I?) really different in any way from all the women from Brooklyn and Queens and the Bronx who trekked up the stairs from the subway every morning and got lost in the dark canyons, the gloomy buildings that loomed over Wall Street? Well, I'm not in Queens anymore. I'm certainly not a secretary. I'm not the girl I was.

But how did I get all the way here from there?

Because when America finally did go to war, the other subway secretaries fought Hitler by saving their bacon grease in tin cans and putting makeup on their legs instead of silk stockings. My fight, though, was different—perilous, real. I wound up in the middle of the Nazi hellhole. Me, Linda Voss.

So what I did during the war: Was it my fate? Was it courage? Or was it inevitable? Did I finally realize that all those people in Europe could be me, so that I *had* to be responsible? Or did I just take so many small, stupid steps that I slipped over the edge, into an abyss where I had to either do—or die? Would any girl in my shoes have done the same?

Now they say I'm a hero. But who are the heroes, anyway? The brave? Or the terrified ordinary?

I still don't know. The only thing I do know is that when I start going over all that happened, the first thing that pops into my mind is not one of those major moments, which proves: Hey, that Linda! *So* special. I had more than enough of those major moments. If you saw them on a movie poster—PASSION! BETRAYAL! WAR! DEATH! LOVE!—you'd assume you were getting one hell of a double feature.

But when I look back, it's funny. What I remember first is just a regular day—the last before my life slowly began to change.

At home that morning, I put the old, dented coffeepot on to perk and looked out the window. Nothing unusual: a dull white January sky, like a bleached-out sheet. The attached houses of Ridgewood, six in a row, were as lifeless as cardboard cutouts: no hyacinths popping up, no maple trees turning red, no kids on roller skates. My down-the-street neighbor's cocker spaniel, Champ, came and did his business on a Christmas tree that had been lying on the curb all week; then he trotted off, leaving drippy tinsel and a yellow stain on the dingy snow.

At work, the view of Manhattan from the forty-sixth floor wasn't what you'd call thrilling, either: not at all that exquisite jagged line of skyscrapers you see in those turn-me-upside-down-and-I-snow paperweights. I glanced out at the narrow streets and overpowering buildings. New York looked gray, tired of itself.

In the office, the radiator clanged, reheating the air it had already overheated. My face flushed hot and red. My lips were so chapped it would have hurt if I smiled. And my sweater had fuzz balls.

But who cared? John Berringer, the man I loved, was there. He sat at his desk. Naturally, he didn't bother to look up.

"Are you positive you gave me the Kunstadt contracts?" he asked. I stood up, put down my pad and pencil, walked around his desk and stood by his chair. His hair gleamed gold and soft under the light of his desk lamp. I imagined touching it.

Was this one of those magic moments they're always singing about on the radio? Did I somehow *know?* No. But still, looking back, that ordinary day in January 1940 is lit so bright that I can see everything about it: even the streaks of bronze and platinum that shot through John's beautiful fair hair.

"The contracts are right here, Mr. Berringer." I tapped the pile of papers with my finger, and it slid back the quarter inch into his line of vision.

"Oh. Thanks." He paused, then looked up and smiled. "What would I do without you?" Probably get up, go to the men's room, then come back, pick up the telephone and call the employment agency for another bilingual secretary. "You're the best there is, Miss Voss. You know that, don't you?"

I thought to myself: This guy is so full of it that it pours out in an endless, effortless stream. I knew that what he was saying meant absolutely nothing to him. But guess what? I still believed it.

He picked up the contracts and, of course, forgot me. That was the end of my excuse to stand close to him. I went back to my seat and picked up my pad.

I can see myself sitting there, like in a spotlight. Pretty. Really pretty if you bothered to look close, but if you didn't—a secretary.

But in one way maybe I actually was different: I wasn't just some girl worshiping her boss from afar, cherishing the very impossibleness of her dream. See, I was a true democrat; I honestly felt I deserved John.

He may have known the difference between an ode and a sonnet, but I had no doubt, even then, that I was as good as he was. If it hadn't been for a few twists of fate, you could have seen our engagement announcement and my picture (with pearls) in the *New York Times*. And the reason you didn't was just a few not-so-giant twists.

Twist one: John's father's family had made it out of Germany three or four generations before my father's family did. And so the Berringers had plenty of time to drop their lederhosen and lose their accents. To become real Americans.

Twist two: John Berringer did not seem to know I was alive. Well, in a way he did. I mean, he wouldn't have allowed a dead secretary to hang around his office. But although he was always charming—with the wide smile that showed both rows of teeth (perfect and white, but with one slightly crooked front tooth, to prove he was human, flawed) and the wink that said: This is our private joke, Linda—what he offered me was really no more than he gave the bookkeeper or the shoeshine boy: reflexive enchantment. I wasn't really real to him in the way, say, lawyers were; I was less than a person but more than a typewriter.

And I don't know if this was a twist or not, but John was all that Americans are supposed to be (Protestant), and I was only half. My mother's family, the Johnstons, had been Americans—Brooklyn-Americans—for a hundred and fifty years. But my other half happened to be Jewish. Granted, John didn't seem like the prejudiced type, but how many people are there in the world who jump for joy over a Jew? Not that he, or anyone else in the office, knew. I wasn't an idiot. Wall Street law firms didn't hire Jewish secretaries (to say nothing of lawyers), so since I didn't look it, why volunteer? Besides, no one in my family had anything at all to do with being Jewish. So the couple of times people said, Um, what kind of a name is Voss? I'd look them right in the eye and tell them the truth: It's German. Well, it was.

Oh, and finally, twist three or four (depending on how you count): There was a Mrs. John Berringer.

But still, I knew I deserved him.

If I'd gone to college, we could have had brilliant conversations.

If my great-great-grandfather Ludwig—or whatever his name was—had come to Manhattan around 1800 instead of hanging around a Berlin butcher shop flicking chickens, John would be getting me my coat instead of vice versa.

If only John knew what I really was inside, he would love me. I was positive. He would want to kiss me exactly the way I wanted to be kissed. He would get up, walk around to my chair, pull me up and hold me so tight against him that I would feel the itch of his worsted trousers through my skirt. Oh, Linda, he'd practically moan, and before I had time to say, Mr. Berringer! and try to push him away so he wouldn't think I was cheap, his hands would be all over my—

Enough! I fought to keep those thoughts out of the office.

I was almost always hysterically busy, and I couldn't allow myself to do what I really wanted to do: retreat into a world without houses or trees, without anything except me and John, a world of desire. But to tell the truth, taking dictation in two languages, typing, and filing tons of paper kept me from creating ten thousand different sizzling scenes of our coming together. When you've got an inch-thick contract to type in German, and it's seven o'clock at night and your boss wants it by seven-thirty, it doesn't help to imagine his muscular, hairy thigh rubbing between yours. For real lust, you need leisure.

And another thing. I was usually too nervous around John to relax enough to let those thoughts rise up: nervous just being so near to him, nervous that I'd make some stupid slip of the tongue that would let him know the score. I could actually goof and call him John. Oh, God, less than a month before, I was saying, I want to wish you a Merry Christmas, Mr. Berringer, and I couldn't believe it, but I almost said, I want to kiss you a Merry Christmas. Every time I thought of that I got the shivers.

He said, "I want those letters to Frankfurt to get out today. I know it's asking a lot . . ."

"Oh, it's no problem, Mr. Berringer."

He started to dictate again. His hands, holding the contract, shone in the circle of light made by the fancy modern desk lamp his wife had picked out. The lamp was long and skinny, like Alice in Wonderland's neck, but with a bulb instead of a head at the end.

I sat up straighter. If nervousness wasn't enough to keep steamy thoughts away, his cold, modern office could; it was the talk of the law firm. But because of who his wife was, the talk was very respectful: Oh, what sublime taste! She'd picked out everything for him. Black furniture so shiny, every time you lifted a pencil it looked as though another hand, trapped inside the desk, was doing the same thing. Ultra-ultramodern design. His carpet and chairs were somewhere between brown and gray, the color of new sidewalks. The walls were such a bright white that even if you worked forty-eight hours straight, you couldn't doze off.

Like the office she'd designed, Nan Berringer had no soft edges: no lace around her neck. I'd only seen her twice, but both times she'd worn those severely plain, fantastically expensive dresses classy fashion magazines call simple. But if that makes her sound hard, she wasn't. Even if you're like Nan, aristocratic and intellectual, it's hard to be hard at twenty-one. And besides, she was terrific-looking.

John stopped dictating and cleared his throat. "I have to be away from the office this afternoon. And probably tomorrow as well." He sounded a little stiff, but that was because he was still talking German; sometimes when he finished dictating in it, he'd forget he was still speaking it. "I hope you will have time to finish all the work I have given you." Was his accent great! Before law school, he'd spent three years at the universities in Cologne and Heidelberg. He spoke the language as if he'd been fraternity brothers with Goethe.

My accent was nowhere near so hotsy-totsy. It was pure *berlinerisch*, courtesy of my grandmother. People always say that *berlinerisch* is to German what cockney is to English. For all I know, they could be right; I never met a cockney. "Is there anything special you'd like me to do?"

"No. Nothing special," John answered. What did I expect him to say? Take off your clothes? "I know I've given you too much." When he smiled his eyes crinkled, so you couldn't see their glorious dark blue, but the smile made his face glow; it made you feel you had your own sun to warm you.

I popped back into English, where I sounded as well-bred as I had in German (that is to say, as far from being a Vanderbilt as a human being can get), but in which I felt much more comfortable. "Really, that's okay, Mr. Berringer. I'll try to get everything done by the end of the week."

Fat chance. We'd stopped being swamped six months earlier. Now we were drowning. The great thing about being one of the top Wall Street firms is you have the top clients: the biggest corporations and banks in the world. The bad thing is that before they pay you, you have to do work for them. Since John's work was representing their interests in Europe, they all wanted ninety-seven times more work done than had ever been done before in the course of legal history.

Half of them said, Get us (and our holdings) out of Germany. Now. The other half said, Hey, look at what those Nazis are spending! It costs a fortune to conquer Europe. Get us a piece of it. Now.

"It would be great if you could catch up," he said in English. "Oh, I forgot. Mr. Leland wants to borrow you this afternoon. He has a letter to go to Germany. Very simple. You can translate it yourself and send it off. Could you fit that in—without hating me forever?"

"Yes, Mr. Berringer."

"And still be caught up by Friday?"

"Sure."

"Wonderful!" He looked up at me. "Miss Voss . . ."

He stopped for a second, maybe to think what else he wanted. I didn't care. I'd wait. While his mind was someplace else, I could study him. His mouth was open, just a little. What a mouth! Beautiful, not one of those thin, mean men's mouths that look like an appendix scar. Full, but not too full. He'd be on top of me, roughing up my face with his, but then he'd bring his mouth over mine and—

"Miss Voss."

"Yes, sir?"

"Thanks. You can go back to your desk now."

\* \* \*

My dream world was like all those European countries in the papers: Poland, Czechoslovakia, Albania. One minute beautiful. The next, destroyed.

Listen, the Voice of Reason would probably butt in here, what you're talking about isn't love. It's a crush: a common enough occurrence, *n'est-ce pas?* (The Voice of Reason sounds a lot like the executive secretaries, Vassar girls who work for the senior partners.) A working girl from Ridgewood, Queens . . . bright enough for what she is, but a suitable match for John Berringer, Esq., *magna cum laude*, Columbia College, editor in chief of the *Columbia Law Review?* How *marrrvelously* droll. (You get stuck in a booth in the ladies' room a few times when the Vassar girls come in to powder their noses and you get to be an expert on how Voices of Reason talk.) *Delightfully* piquant. And a trifle touching too, this secretary's dreams of "love" with a married man.

Well, it may have been droll, but as I said to myself, over and over: Hey, this is love! Although not at first sight. I'd seen him for nearly ten years in the firm's international department, from the time he was out of law school.

We'd talked about John even then. He was ridiculously handsome, I told the girls, like a young movie star playing the Big Man on Campus role in one of those *Cubby Cooper Goes to College*–type movies. He was meant to be fifteen feet tall and black-and-white; he was too good to be real. I remember he'd worn white shirts so starched they could carry on a life of their own. He'd shared a secretary with three of the other young lawyers. When he had to write a letter in German, he dictated it to himself.

Way back then, I was twenty-one years old and a secretary to one of the middle-level partners, P. Louis Tracy. You'd think there was something a little wrong with a guy who answers his phone, "Good ahfternoon. P. Louis Tracy." There was: not his head, though; his heart. Nine years later, on the Fourth of July, 1939, P. Louis Tracy joined his wife at the bar of their country club after playing eighteen holes and dropped dead over his third Rob Roy.

Even before P. Louis Tracy played his last hole, John had been made a partner—the only other member of the firm really fluent in German. Back then, the fact that he was about thirty times smarter than P. Lou hadn't been a secret around Blair, VanderGraff and Wadley. But since, despite his brains, he was also about thirty years younger, he hadn't been considered one of the important international partners. But suddenly he was; less than a week after July 4, John inherited P. Lou's office, cases, percentage of the profits—and me.

At first I looked at John and thought: Another pretty face. In fact, the prettiest. I can live with that. It definitely beats working for a guy with four chins. Okay, he dictates like a snail, but at least he gets it right—doesn't make me retype fifty thousand times. John Berringer was going to be a good boss. But fall for him? Not me. Even though he was supposed to have a brilliant legal mind, all I could see was the gleam of the surface: eyes, hair, teeth. John shone—for everybody: Hello. You're wonderful. I'm gorgeous. Life is grand.

But late one January afternoon, when the sky outside looked like a thick black velvet ribbon, I glanced across his desk and realized he was *beautiful*. Deep-down beautiful—and more.

Let's face it. He was hot. Beneath his gloss, under his charm, he had it. *It*. John Berringer was one of those men on fire. It took a while for me to feel that heat beneath the cool impersonal brightness. But that afternoon, just watching his thumb flick the pages of a memorandum of law (dumb, but true), I suddenly *knew*.

Unfortunately, from the way he flew out of the office the second he finished work, it was obvious Mrs. John Berringer knew too. Knew, and was waiting, because she loved everything he had to offer.

\* \* \*

On that last normal day, Hitler sent endless cables to his generals, Mussolini had several recorded temper tantrums, Neville Chamberlain took a long, silent walk, and the secretaries of Blair, VanderGraff and Wadley ate lunch. After all, this was America.

Like just about every other day, the partners strolled out to their clubs around twelve-thirty. At twelve-forty, making sure the elevators had time to empty out so the partners couldn't see their stampede, the young lawyers—the associates—made a mad dash for their restaurants. Five minutes later, the Vassar girls tippytoed off to their tearoom, where they met other Vassar girls from other law firms, probably to talk about what they were always talking about, like what Schubert had been played at last night's symphony concert and who the *really* top-drawer Princeton men were.

Exactly two seconds after they left, the regular secretaries raced to the conference room—ten or twelve of us, with lunch bags, at that giant rectangular table in that giant wood-paneled room. It was like eating inside a mahogany tree. Suddenly it was as if somebody yelled, *On your mark . . . Get set . . .* But instead of a gunshot, one enormous crinkle—the noise of ten or twelve sandwiches being ripped out of waxed paper.

"Why I even bother to mention this, girls, is beyond me," Gladys Slade began, her voice slightly muffled by Spam on white, "but Mrs. Avenel called *four* times this morning!" Gladys put on her haughty, high-class voice: " 'Gladys, my deah, *do* hate to disturb you, but *would* you get my husband on the line for one *tiny* second.' " Gladys shook her head. "She probably wanted his permission to flush." Her boss's wife called at least ten times a day. We nodded in sympathy because our mouths were full, and huddled in our sweaters.

It was always cold in the room. We had to keep the windows open so the lawyers wouldn't sniff out secretary-lunch smells and know we were eating in there.

Gladys was Queen of Lunch. Better, actually. Gladys Slade—with beginning-to-gray brown hair cut into what was meant to be a neat Dutchboy but frizzed into crazed curlicues when the humidity was more than five percent, with hazel eyes a little too small and a little too close together—looked absolutely ordinary. Well, except for her nostrils: They were so immense she could have hidden two salamis up her nose. But she was a born leader.

Her being forty didn't hurt, either. Gladys had been at the law firm longer than any other secretary, twenty-two years, and no one knew more about what was going on at Blair, VanderGraff and Wadley than she did. Someone—Shakespeare, George Washington—once said, Knowledge is power. She'd seen it all: Mr. Blair becoming under secretary of the Treasury, Mr. VanderGraff going bald, Mr. Wadley dying of a stroke while waiting for the elevator. She hadn't actually seen him die—no one had—but she was one of the first afterward, while he was still purple. Gladys knew everything. And not just the big stuff. She knew who was doing what to whom, and probably how, when and where, but Gladys being Gladys, she never let on about the really sizzling stuff. She probably tuned it out; all Gladys thought about were clothes and hairdos and innuendos, not bodies. For her, life did not actually exist below the neck or under the vest.

But for good old-style gossip, she was better than anyone. My dears, she would begin, like we were whispering in a corner at a society cocktail party, did I tell you who the widow Carpenter brought with her to the reading of the late Mister's will? Her 'financial adviser'! With a pompadour! I thought Mr. Avenel would have a stroke, because she insisted . . .

Since I was Gladys's closest friend, she turned to me first. "What about Mr. B, Linda?" It was just a regular lunch question. No one in the office, including Gladys, had a clue about what I felt for John. "Anything new?"

"Who has time for anything new?" I answered. "We're going crazy trying to keep up with Europe."

"What's with Europe?" Wilma Gerhardt called from down the table. Her voice was so horribly nasal that every time she opened her mouth it was like listening to a bad vaudevillian attempting a Brooklyn accent. God knows no one else from that borough ever made you cringe like that at the wrongness of the sound, worse than the *eeeeek* of chalk on a blackboard. But she was saved from total awfulness by a single grace: her looks. Wilma was a knockout. "You going to Gay Paree or something, Linda?" She patted her dazzling dark hair; she was the only girl in the office who wore an upsweep every single day. Luckily for her, she had plenty of time for hairdos. Her typewriter was untouched by human hands.

"What's with Europe?" I repeated. I had to lean past Helen Rogers—who as usual was dribbling onto the shelf made by her bust (this time the shelf was dotted with little yellow dabs of egg salad)—and past Anita Beane, who was nineteen, dewy and engaged. "Wilma, you ever read a newspaper?"

Gladys interrupted: "Linda, you're not going to give us your Growing Nazi Shadow speech, are you?"

"I'm just asking Wilma a simple question."

Wilma gave me a simple answer. "Why should I read a newspaper? The ink gets all over your hands!" For a second, Wilma was so thrilled by her brilliant, witty comeback that she forgot she was with the girls and actually broke into an acutely adorable giggle. It was a technique, like her eyelash-batting, she wouldn't ordinarily have wasted on women. She saved her talents for men, and they were talents not sneezed at; they'd helped get her a job eight or nine years earlier, in the pit of the Depression, while lots of inky-fingered readers of the *New York Times* and the *Herald Tribune* were stretching their hands high above their heads and taking swan dives off skyscrapers.

"Haven't you ever heard of Adolf Hitler?" I demanded.

"So is Mr. Berringer dictating letters to him?" Under the Brooklyn accent, her voice had a nasty edge. She could be tolerant of homely girls like Rose Guthrie in Trusts and Estates, who looked like Winston Churchill (or, more accurately, Winston Churchill's bulldog), but anyone who had a chance of attracting a man's attention—like me—was a threat.

I'd always been intrigued by Wilma. Her entire life was dedicated to men and to getting them. She made no pretense that she cared about who the mayor was, or what Gladys had thought of *Gone With the Wind*. She never looked beyond her own cleavage. Did she choose to be that way? Or did it come naturally? Was her selfishness just self-protection, a byproduct of hard times?

Sometimes I wished I could be like her, absolutely, contentedly selfish, not having to smile, not being forced to listen to Helen Rogers go into her umpteenth recounting of her Uncle Gus's brother-in-law's funeral, where they'd botched up the makeup on the late lamented, and it formed globules under the heat of the lights, so it looked as if the guy in the satin-lined box was sweating. Helen would recount: "His wife *screamed*, 'Mickey! Mickey! You're hot!' And they had to grab her because she fished out her hankie and was going to—"

Wilma had turned to Helen one day and snapped, mean and hard, "Hey, shut up with that vomity funeral crap, would ya?" And Helen had. What would it feel like, being free to say something like that?

Gladys's theory was that Wilma could say anything she wanted to; all she had to do was show up at the office. Her job, her life, would always be safe. Why? Because she had someone to protect her. See, she and her boss were friendly.

I agreed. Very friendly. Only for a very special kind of friend would an influential partner in a major law firm sneak in early in the morning to do his own typing. (Helen had once come in early and caught him typing a letter on the firm letterhead with two fingers, *very* slowly.) You got to figure, I'd told Gladys, that Mr. Post was catching the 5:37 A.M. from Garden City just to catch up on his correspondence. He was no spring chicken, either. Another few months of the ebony-haired Wilma by night and the 5:37 by day, and we'd be chipping in for a wreath and writing letters: Dear Mrs. Post, I'm only a secretary at Blair, VanderGraff, but I was so sorry to hear about Mr. Post's sudden demise. His late hours were a measure of his devotion . . .

"What does Mr. Berringer write?" Wilma kept going.
" 'Dear Adolf: How are you? I am fine.' "

She would have babbled on, but Gladys turned to her:
"Can it, Wilma."

That's all Gladys said, but it worked. Even Wilma showed
deference to Gladys. She mumbled, "You can it," but it
wasn't a challenge; her words had no heart. She just took a
vicious bite of what actually looked like a steak sandwich
(old Mr. Post kept her in protein) and chewed ostentatiously,
as if to say, I got something to bite into, not like you girls
with your crappy cream cheese.

Gladys turned back to me. "Anything new?" she asked
once more. "I am *desperate* for gossip, Linda."

"Well, nothing scintillating," I began. "Mrs. Berringer
called late yesterday. Didn't even want to speak to him. Just
left a message that she was having cocktails with her
museum committee and wouldn't be home for supper."

"Dinner, Linda," Gladys corrected. "Where's your class?
Ditchdiggers eat supper. Attorneys dine."

"Okay, she wouldn't be home to dine."

Very daintily, Helen Rogers picked her egg salad drop-
pings off her bosom as she asked, "You think the lovebirds
had a fight? Her just leaving messages, I mean."

"All married couples fight," Gladys pronounced.

I noticed Anita Beane flashing a fast look down the table
to Fay Landon. They were the only engaged girls, and the
look said, Would you listen to these old maids pretending to
be marriage experts? But naturally, being nineteen and
twenty-one and not complete fools, they didn't challenge
Gladys. What did they have to gain? By June, they'd be married, and free from Blair, VanderGraff forever.

"Mrs. Berringer went to Smith College. Right, Linda?"
Gladys asked me. I nodded and took a bite of my meat loaf
sandwich, which would more accurately be described as a
bread-crumb loaf sandwich, the price of meat being what it
was. "Smith College sounds so average," Gladys explained
to the group, "but it's *the* poshest. Every year, they have one
or two graduates who become duchesses or . . . earls' wives

or . . . Anyway, it's *much* better than Vassar. Now describe Mrs. Berringer, Linda." Gladys was bossy, but she was fun. Well, not a bundle of laughs herself, but at least she was able to find fun for us—in the lives of lawyers. "Every single minuscule detail," she added. "Give us the works."

Everyone leaned forward. There were a lot of reasons why everyone in the room was interested—no, fascinated—with Mrs. John Berringer.

All that attention on me—and on that tender topic—made me a little nervous. I had to put my sandwich down; I was squeezing it so hard, pretty soon I'd have a fistful of mush. Questions would arise: What's with Linda? She was talking about Mr. Berringer and she squished her sandwich. . . . Oh!

"You girls know what I know," I said, fast. "And what I know is that Mrs. B must really be something. Mr. Berringer would do *anything* to make her happy." Everyone nodded. They loved it. "He spent *six hundred dollars* on some oil painting she fell in love with at an art gallery. He gave me a certified check, sent me over to this art gallery, to some skinny guy with one of those nipped-in-waist suits, and the guy there says, 'Oh, for Mrs. Berringer. So young, but such a discerning eye.' "

When I went to the gallery that day, all I could think was John was buying her a birthday present that cost half what I earned every year. And he was taking her out to dinner besides. I knew; I'd made the reservations.

Helen Rogers said, "Six hundred dollars for a picture! Can you beat that?"

"For *art*," I said.

"Was it pretty?"

"How should I know?" I answered. "Did I go to Smith College? It was modern. Mostly red squiggles with a little black—like old chopped meat."

"Linda," Gladys said, "at least *pretend* you have some taste."

"For that much money I'd get emerald earrings," Wilma said. She massaged the lobe of her ear. I had a feeling Mr. Post was going to buy her a present in the near future. "Not the dangle kind. You can't wear those during the day. Just give me big, fat emeralds that go right smack on your ear."

"I'd take a mouton jacket," someone else called out. "And with the change . . ."

Anita Beane twisted her engagement ring round and round and said, "I'd buy a house for me and Herbie."

"I hate to say it, Anita," Gladys said, "but you can't buy a house for six hundred dollars." She was tired of hearing about Herbie, who worked as an assistant in a beauty parlor in Washington Heights and had another year to go before he could be called Mr. Herbert. "You'll have to move in with his parents. But you'll save up."

Then Gladys opened her thermos of coffee with the pads of her fingers. It was the ladylike way, but there'd also been an article—"How to Avoid Nail Tragedy"—in the *Mirror* the day before. She took her time pouring, and that was a signal for all the others: free-play time. Ten or twelve soprano voices started squeaking at once.

But over all of them I heard Gladys, talking in a voice just meant for me: "I don't know, Linda. Sometimes when a man does too much for his wife, she gets to not appreciating him. Sometimes . . ." Gladys deliberately drowned her voice in her coffee. Then she turned—fast—to Winnie Curtis, at the farthest seat down the table, and called out: "Doesn't Mr. Nugent look like Ronald Colman with pockmarks?"

Edward Leland's face looked wrong. But he was so close to being normal-looking, you were dying to get up close and examine precisely how off his face was. But of course, you didn't get anywhere near Edward Leland. He was the most senior of the senior partners.

He was a genuine war hero too. In 1917, he'd taken his rifle, crawled on his belly through a forest in France, and mowed down a platoon of German soldiers. He'd saved his men. He might have gone on, gotten more Germans, or gotten killed, but he crawled over a mine. His face and his shoulder had been blown up.

There were so many rumors in the office about how many operations he'd had to get put back together, it was impossible to ever know the truth. The only thing we did know was that half his face was flatter than the other half, as though one or two pieces were still missing. Someone swore he had lots of little scars, but I couldn't see any. What I could see— what nobody could miss—was that the left half of his face was paralyzed. It didn't move; it didn't show expression. He was very scary.

As the cold afternoon light slanted through the big window behind his desk, Mr. Leland's heavy black brows, like twin awnings, cast shadows; you couldn't see what was in his eyes, although I had no doubt it was strictly cold, hard business. I was on loan because he had a letter to send to Germany. I'd been on loan before, but never to Edward Leland.

Despite his position, he was not where he was because of his age; he was actually younger than most of the senior partners, in his early fifties. But whatever he had that the rest of them lacked—intelligence, cunning, courage, personality: who knew?—had made him extraordinarily powerful. The strings he pulled were tied not only to the law firm but to government. Anytime a New Dealer decided to talk to a Republican, guess whose phone rang? And did he ever bring in business!

I stood across the room from him, my back flat against the door. His secretary, Katherine from Vassar, had told me to go in, but not how far. His desk seemed half a city block away.

"Come in," he called. I began. The trek along his rug seemed forever. Each time I looked at Mr. Leland, he appeared just as far away; the rug was an eternal Persian stretch of dark red and blue. And the worst of it was not making my way across that vast space but knowing he was watching me. He made me a nervous wreck.

At last I made it to his desk and stood before him. My left ankle wobbled, and I had a hideous picture of my leg giving way, and me crashing to the floor and trying to lift myself up

by holding on to the edge of his desk, but instead pulling
down his blotter and inkstand. "I've forgotten your name,"
he said, interrupting my nightmare.

"Linda Voss." I was amazed I still had a voice.

I made myself look straight at him. There were only two
things right about his looks: his chin—tough, squared off—
and his nose, an ordinary nose, although inappropriately
upturned for such a man, daring to suggest that he'd once
been a cute little boy.

"Linda Voss. That's right." He paused. I snuck a fast peek
around. Actually, his office wasn't as big as I'd thought—
nowhere near what you'd expect from such a big shot. To be
equal to Edward Leland's clout, though, the room would
have had to be the size of Radio City Music Hall. But it was
medium-sized, with the kind of seedy leather furniture you
see in *The Adventures of Sherlock Holmes*—lots of cracked
old leather chairs with fat feet, and scratched tables. That
was the point, of course, the rattiness of it. If he'd gotten
nice new slipcovers, everybody would have thought he was
an upstart.

"Please sit down," he said. No big deal, right? But just go
into some lawyers' offices to take a letter and they keep you
standing for half an hour. Even if you fainted on the floor,
they'd just keep dictating, as if they came out of the
Gestapo, not Yale Law School. Mr. Leland not only said,
"Please sit down," he said, "Please sit down, Miss Voss."

Look, I knew he knew I wasn't one of the executive secretaries, but he treated me as if I was. For someone like that,
I'd take dictation till my fingers fell off. Because even
though he was scary, you knew he was decent.

Okay, the real truth? The decency, but mainly because
Edward Leland was John Berringer's father-in-law. And
Gladys, who'd filled in a few months before when Kat from
Vas was out with whooping cough, had told me about a picture of John and Nan—their wedding portrait—Mr. Leland
kept on his desk. As I flipped open the pages of my pad, I
noticed an oval silver frame angled so that if I leaned forward a little, I could get a glimpse. So I leaned forward.

Nuts. In the frame was a picture of an old-fashioned-looking young woman. She was pretty, with hair that reached her shoulders and curled in little commas over the lace of her dress. Her neck was long, what they call swan-like, and she wore a locket. The picture must have been taken years and years ago . . . and then I realized. It was Mr. Leland's late wife. Very late. She'd died from some terrible liver disease when Nan was two, nineteen years before.

But where were John and Nan? I was dying to see the wedding gown. I'd imagined it as something airy and beautiful, like chiffon or tulle—the stuff gowns in fairy tales are made of. But then I thought, no, nothing airy for Nan. She'd wear satin, with a tight bodice and bell skirt, and everyone in church would whisper, Ooh, look how tiny her waist is!

"Dear Herr, uh, Doktor Uhl," Mr. Leland began. "Herr Doktor? You'll do all that for me, Miss Voss? Keep the 'herrs' and the 'doktors' straight?"

"Yes, sir," I said. "It's easy. Lawyers are always 'Herr Doktor.' "

He leaned toward me. It looked casual enough, but when Edward Leland was leaning in your direction, it didn't feel casual. You were too nervous to begin with because he was so important, and then you were extra nervous because you didn't want him to catch you staring at how *still* half his face was, and, even worse, you were afraid he'd know you were trying not to let on how you couldn't stop looking at him—

"Were you born in the United States?" he asked.

I started to take it down in shorthand until I realized he was asking me a question. "Yes," I said, a little too loud.

I knew why he was asking that; people at work, hearing that I was a bilingual secretary, often spent months waiting for me to slip and say, *Guten Morgen* . . . oops, good morning, or—if they were real anti-German—to goof and, instead of a friendly wave, give a fast *Heil Hitler!* At least Mr. Leland had the sense to realize that the English you learn in German schools is not spoken with a Brooklyn-Queens accent.

"Were your parents born here too?"

"Yes. My father's parents came from Germany. Berlin. My grandmother lived with us."

"And it was she who taught you German?"

Gladys would have swooned with pleasure over the way he said "And it was *she*." She'd say, See, Linda, class will out. Mr. Leland wasn't even tempted to say, "And it was her"; you could tell.

"Yes, she and my father and I"—I made sure I said *I*—"all spoke it at home, and I took it in high school too. That's where I learned to write it, and learned the grammar. Well, whatever grammar I know."

"But you practiced it with her?"

"It wasn't really practice, Mr. Leland. She never learned English. She never had to. See, we lived in Ridgewood—that's in Queens—and there are loads of Germans . . ."

God, was I ever running off at the mouth! I was mortified. But Mr. Leland smiled, a nice half smile. At least I didn't feel like a prize imbecile, even though I knew that he knew I was feeling funny about talking so much. I managed a small smile back. I mean, you just don't sit there and give a powerhouse like Edward Leland a big, fat grin.

"My clients have just completed reviewing the most recent versions of the proposed contracts for your clients' acquisitions of the specified industrial components," Mr. Leland began suddenly, "and it would appear that with the exception of two points, all matters have been settled."

Nan Berringer hadn't gotten her looks from her father. I realized, as I tried not to peek over at the picture again, that Nan resembled her mother: good-looking in a clean way. Even though they were Society, the Leland ladies didn't look like the sleek, snooty Merle Oberon type. But still, you could tell they were for real, with far more than passably pretty faces. And then there was their background; it added an extra glow, like candlelight. If I'd been born rich, I wondered, would I have been in the same league as the Leland ladies?

"We have considered at great length your requirements for assurances of the delivery date . . ." Mr. Leland's voice was so deep that there were moments when it made you shake inside; it was almost a growl.

"My client obviously cannot assume the risk of commitment for dates of delivery at Port of Bremerhaven."

Boy, I thought, comparing myself to Nan Leland Berringer! Still, it was interesting to think about what a couple of million could do for a girl.

"Inasmuch as both of the above points have been previously discussed at some length and you had indicated that your clients would probaby have to agree . . ."

Unlike ninety-nine point nine percent of all lawyers, Edward Leland did not lean back and close his eyes while he dictated. Instead, he looked straight at you. Not at you, but it wasn't off into space, either. So you couldn't stare at him. And you couldn't give the Life Saver you were hiding a fast suck during pauses; I had a puddle of lime Life Saver juice under my tongue.

But in one pause, he seemed to be looking away, thinking about something else, so I took the opportunity to really check over his desk. Maybe John and Nan's wedding picture was just a teeny one, and I'd missed it. But it wasn't there. I felt so sad, as if I'd just had a loss.

"Miss Voss."

"Oh, sorry, Mr. Leland."

". . . We are assuming that all terms have been met and appropriate contracts including purchase orders will be forwarded within several days for execution by Volkswerke A. G.," he went on. "On behalf of both my clients and myself, I would like to thank you for your courtesy and efficiency in helping to bring this negotiation . . ."

My pencil was going fifty miles an hour; I could have gotten the Billy Rose Stenography Prize for 1940. Because I *knew* Mr. Leland had definitely been onto exactly what it was I'd been looking for on his desk—and hadn't found. You don't get to be Edward Leland, talking to presidents of Chase Bank and Ford Motor and the United States, for nothing. So I wrote like mad, which nudged him into dictating faster.

But Edward Leland wasn't in business to miss a trick. I think he knew what my sudden speed was about. And not only did he know what I'd been looking for, but he probably even knew why I'd been looking.

My hands got so wet my pencil almost slipped, but I kept on writing. Yes, he knew. But he wasn't going to make a federal case of it. Why should he? He saved his federal cases for when he had dinner with his dear old chums, the justices of the Supreme Court of the United States.

But just for a second, Mr. Leland looked me straight in the eye. A kindly look on that messed-up face. A little sad for me. And then he just kept talking.

As we left the office that day, I waved a copy of the *World-Telegram* in front of Gladys's face. "Look at this. You think Hitler's playing games? He's just given Goring total control of the whole German war industry."

Gladys said, "Quiet! I have *real* news. You're going to die when you hear it. And not a fast heart attack. A slow, painful, hysterical death."

"Oh, sure," I said, positive it was going to be some gossip about Mr. Hastings in Litigation.

Gladys clutched her coat around her. A little dramatic. Although it was January, with that cold dampness that makes your toes ache, there wasn't even a snowflake swirling under the streetlight, much less the blizzard she seemed about to brave. But that was the wonderful thing about Gladys's theatricality. How many old maids are there who can watch life from behind a typewriter and find passion, thrills and chills in a law office? Me, you say? No. I didn't just want to watch. I wanted to *have*. Gladys didn't. She savored it all, but from a distance. "When you hear this, you're going to say, 'Take me to the hospital. I'm having a stroke from shock.' "

"Gladys, tell me!"

"When you were in Mr. Leland's office today . . ." She smiled for a moment. I knew what she was doing: remembering when she had started at Blair, VanderGraff, when Mr.

Leland had gone from being a loving husband to being a young widower with a small child. *That* had been great drama. "Right after his wife died," she said, "Mr. Leland turned gray. His hair, I mean." She paused. "What do you think he looked like when he was young? Before *it* happened with the land mine."

"I don't know. Forget Mr. Leland. Tell me: What's the big secret?"

"How was Mr. Leland today?" Gladys insisted.

"The usual. He wanted to gossip about Carole Lombard and Clark Gable and—"

"Come on. Didn't he seem at all funny?"

"Yeah, Gladys. He told me three jokes. *Very* dirty. About filthy things you never even heard of."

"Linda, listen!" Gladys slowed down, but the crowd wanted to get home. It forced us faster along the street, toward the subway. "Mr. Berringer is Mr. Leland's son-in-law, right? Well, you may think you know all there is to know, but hold your horses!"

It was what they say happens in an awful accident: Time slows down. Not slow motion, but in the terrible moment just before awfulness, you're more alive than you've ever been before. Everything matters. I felt my scalp tighten. I could smell the soggy wool of Gladys's tweed. Coal soot made my eyes water. The wind whooshed down the street, and a flyaway page of the *Post* slapped against a lamppost.

"I'm holding my horses," I said, cool, a regular cucumber. Like, what could there possibly be about Mr. Berringer that would surprise me for more than a tenth of a second? Like, come on, Gladys, let's get this over with so we can get on to something *big*.

"How long have they been married?" Gladys demanded.

"Mr. Berringer and Nan Leland?"

"Oh, don't be cute. Tell me. Two, three years?" I nodded. "Well, that was enough for the young Mrs. B!" Gladys proclaimed.

You'd think I'd have dropped dead right there on Rector Street. But all I said was, "Oh, Gladys!"

Gladys was stunned—and peeved—at my disinterest. "Linda, this is a *fact*."

"Har-har-har," I answered. Look, I wanted to say, if there was anything going on with John Berringer, wouldn't I be the first to pick it up? But I didn't trust my voice enough.

"I have proof," Gladys said.

"What? A mysterious stranger's fingerprints on Nan Berringer's you-know-whats?"

"Would you please get your mind out of the gutter and *think*. What would be final proof?" Gladys was having fun. This was nothing more to her than office drama—but the most supreme, the richest, the juiciest.

"I give up."

"Why are you giving up so easily?"

The crowd swept us on, a great force that stopped at nothing, down the gritty stairs to the subway, past the overhead "To Brooklyn and Queens" sign, past a giant Nestlé's Cocoa ad. I felt out of control. Halfway down, my foot skidded on the cellophane from a pack of cigarettes, and if I hadn't grabbed the banister I would have gone crashing down. My body was finally comprehending what my mind had learned.

"Linda, are you okay?" Gladys asked.

"Fine." I swallowed, although all that made me do was realize how sick I felt. "So," I managed, "is this what you were talking about at lunch? About a wife not appreciating?"

"Linda, don't you realize . . . ?"

"No. I really don't. Listen, it's some ridiculous rumor. I'd know if there was anything with anything."

"For your information, it just so happens I was slumming today." That means she was hanging around Marian Mulligan's desk. "Who does Marian work for?"

"Mr. Wilson."

"Mr. Wilson who does *matrimonials*." Oh, God, I thought, oh, God! I managed to shrug. "Guess who Mr. Wilson was writing to?"

"A sob sister. 'Dear Penelope Potts, I am a creepy attorney with so much hair hanging out of my nose people think it's a mustache and—' "

"Linda, listen! Nan Berringer is going to Reno! Mr. Wilson was writing to a Nevada divorce lawyer, giving him *all* the details of who gets what." Somehow I had gotten down the flight of stairs and was on the platform, waiting for the train. "Do you believe me now?" I nodded. "Are you shocked? Linda, are you shocked?"

She would have been heartbroken if I wasn't, and, of course, I was. So I gave her something for her trouble. "Yeah, Gladys, I'm shocked."

"Good. I mean, you should be." The subway roared through the tunnel into the station and screeched to a stop. As the doors opened and we pushed our way on, she said, "You should *see* the list of what she's getting. Stocks. Bonds. And much more. One hundred and fifty-seven pieces of sterling-silver flatware. With all their friends and family who shop at Tiffany, you'd think they'd have more, but . . ."

Dear God. John was going to be free. My dreams were dangerous.

# 2

"Linda, honey, put on some rouge, stick your boobies in his face, and bingo! He'll be kissing your feet." My mother was great at advice to the lovelorn. "What are you waiting for? Mistletoe? *Now's* the time to grab Mr. Whosis. That John guy you work for."

"Why would John give me the time of day?" Why would any normal, rational human being take me and John Berringer seriously, even for two seconds? The answer: They wouldn't. They'd say, Snap out of it, Linda! But this was my mother, and the normal and rational categories were not the places you'd go looking for her.

"Angel, if he wanted some rich Manhattan snot-nose, Mrs. John wouldn't be in Reno, Las Vegas."

"Forget it, Mom," I said, "I'm living in a dream world. Men like him don't marry girls like me."

Instead of saying, Hey, what about Cinderella and the prince? my mother merely sighed; she was too drunk to give me a fight. Then she lowered her still-gorgeous eyes and gazed passionately at her plate. An outsider would have thought she'd fallen in love with her salmon croquette.

Last night's booze still sloshed inside her. She looked the way she usually looked on any typical winter Wednesday night—or any night: half drunk, half hung over. She didn't even make a stab at her salmon, but then, my mother hardly ever ate anything. I worried about her; gin and ginger ale wasn't carrots and peas. The booze drowned not only her beauty—and my mother had been so incredibly lovely—but

28

her health. Her clear white skin, with its faint glimmering of pink—like a seashell—had turned yellow. Then the tiny crisscross lines on her face deepened until, under the glare of the light that hung over the table, her skin resembled those terrible pictures of the Okies' dry, cracked land, desperate for rain.

She'd bought that light herself, soon after she'd gotten married. It dangled from a once-white wire; the bulb was half covered with a glass shade painted with pink, blue and purple bunnies. Cute, silly, meant for a frilly boudoir—like my mother. The light didn't belong in the kitchen, and neither did she. It was a useless room as far as she was concerned. She couldn't cook and she wouldn't eat.

Even if she'd been starving, my mother wouldn't have picked up a fork. Eating interfered with drinking. Two spoons of mashed potatoes could soak up a shot of gin, and my mother liked to get sloshed as fast as possible. That she held off till I got home from work, so we could have dinner together, was proof of her love. She needed a drink so badly; she had d.t.'s nearly every night: not near-convulsions, but gentle, feminine d.t.'s. Pale, trembling hands. She kept them in her lap, hoping, I guess, that I wouldn't see them and get upset. She honestly tried. Though she was no prize as a mother and she knew it, she loved me as much as she could.

But she wouldn't eat to save her life—not even for me. Eating smudged lipstick, and, even plastered, my mother managed enough self-control to keep her makeup perfect. Well, almost perfect: I noticed she'd drawn one of her eyebrows into a higher arch than the other, so it looked as if she had doubts about everything I said.

Suddenly, she sat straight up and smoothed the front of the pink duster she was wearing over her dress to protect it from the dinner she wouldn't touch. She'd remembered we were having a conversation. "Linda, dollface, why do you keep thinking Wall Street lawyers are different? Sweetie, men are all alike. There's only one thing makes them happy. You know that. You wanna hook this John? Clue him in you're ready to . . . I'm not shocking you, am I? You're over twenty-one."

"By ten years, Mom."

"Men aren't like girls. They *need* it. He'd probably give his right arm to have your company tonight. Unless you think the reason Mrs. Whosis took a walk was because he has a chippy on the side."

"No, he's not that type." That was my worst fear: Nan getting a divorce because John was in love with someone else.

"Sweetie, they're *all* that type."

"Why don't you try the croquette? Just a bite. It's not bad."

"I bet it's great! You're a wonderful cook, lovie. But I'm just not hungry tonight. Now listen to me about men. I *know* what puts a smile on their face."

I (obviously) didn't. Maybe my mother was right. After all, Betty Johnston Voss had been born to please men. She was beautiful. Huge, limpid brown eyes instead of the predictable blue. Blond hair so soft that it looked like the froth on top of an ice cream soda, and if that wasn't enough (and it wasn't), the world's deepest dimples. My father had pulled a fast one, beating out the competition by eloping with her the day she turned sixteen. I'd been born nine months later.

"Now's your chance, Linda. I know you're more like your father than like me. Real smart, listening to the news, reading the papers. You could get yourself a lawyer if you weren't—well, you know—such a stick. Get your hair out of that old-lady bun. Wear red lipstick. Give him a little thigh."

"Mom, that's not law firm etiquette."

"Baby doll, you use your brain. So what's wrong with using your legs too?" My mother smiled encouragingly, then belched. "I wouldn't tell you this if you was a kid, but now . . . Listen, if he wants a virgin—you'll pardon my French—he's gonna find a young one, so you might as well . . . What the heck. Live a little."

It was so hard being a brainless ex-beauty. There she sat—in a chair upholstered in faded red oilcloth at a creaky oak kitchen table—behind a wall of makeup, forty-seven

years old. She'd started boozing soon after she'd lost my
father, when she suddenly realized it was impossible to be a
child bride when you were no longer a child—and when the
groom was kaput. A bride was all she'd ever been or wanted
to be.

When I didn't want to scream at her for stealing food
money for her boozing or for throwing up in her bed or—
once—for carrying on with three men in a car parked right
in front of the house, my mother broke my heart.

"Don't be afraid of a little fun, Linda," she went on. Her
eyes were made up to look wide and girlish, and she'd
painted her mouth into a young pink kiss.

My mother was the youngest and prettiest of five sisters.
Her father, a subway maintenance man, had died of a heart
attack when she was six or seven, and her mother had kept
the family going by taking in boarders, and from a few
things my mother had said ("Mama had her favorite boarder,
and Lucille had *hers*, and Meg *hers*, a trolley motorman with
a peg leg, and . . ."), I guessed they'd managed to supple-
ment the family budget a little above and beyond the rent
money. They'd had to. My mother's father's family—the
Johnstons—hadn't helped out at all after he'd died. The
Johnstons weren't a close-knit group, although for some
peculiar reason they could always be counted on to show up
in droves for a funeral. As far as I knew, my mother's
mother's family—she thought their name was Dunstan or
Duncan—were all dead, although there might be a cousin in
California.

My mother gave her hair a tender, loving pat, checking to
see if it was still fluffy. "Let loose. Like I do. Live a little!"

Six nights a week my mother let loose. She traipsed from
bar to bar along the Brooklyn-Queens border. Nearly every
night she wound up with the first man who gave her the eye.
Usually she was home before dawn, but sometimes she
didn't show up for days at a time.

"Why don't you give old John baby a try? You two got a
lot in common, working together on law stuff, talking German. How many girls speak it? I'm not talking about those

Kraut piggies with earmuff braids. Your father could've had
a million of them, those fatties. It would have made his old
lady happy, but he wanted an all-American girl, not some
frowline. But I admit, I used to think it was so nice, your
father saying sweet nothings to me in German—when we
were alone, if you get me. Not that I got what he meant, but
it was *so* Continental."

That my mother could have spent almost thirty years living in a German-speaking house never caring enough to
even learn the meaning of the word *ja* explains what she was
like. That her mother-in-law, my Grandma Olga, could have
come to America in 1884 and spent fifty-four years in
Brooklyn and Queens—until she died in 1938—refusing to
understand a simple *yes* explains what she was like too. My
mother at least had an excuse. Like many born beauties, she
had been allowed to concentrate on her own loveliness;
skills like speaking foreign languages, scouring bathtubs
and shopping for groceries were things she could get other
people to do for her. My Grandma Olga, on the other hand,
would not learn English because it was a waste of time;
she'd truly believed it was only a matter of a year or two
before she'd go back to Berlin in a fur coat. And when she
no longer believed that—that America was the land of
opportunity—she refused to listen to its language.

My mother rested her elbow on the table. It creaked. The
table had been Olga's choice: plain wood, straight legs;
cheap but serviceable. She'd bought it in the late 1880s or
early '90s, after she'd come to America. Throughout the
house, her no-nonsense chairs sat stiffly beside my mother's
flamingo-and-palm-tree wallpaper; her white iron bedsteads
were covered with spreads that my mother picked, with
flower, kitten and bird designs in every single pastel shade
ever invented by man.

"Lookit, Linda," my mother said, as I brought the dishes
over to the sink. "I got an idea to help you loosen up. Make
believe you're me! Come on, don't laugh. It'll work. Flirt
with that John a little, call him big boy in German. Play your

cards right and before you know it, no more typing for you. He'll set you up real nice someplace."

"Mom, I don't want to be set up."

I went back to the table, swept off a couple of crumbs and put the ketchup in the icebox. It was just as well my mother didn't even try to help anymore. Dishes flew out of her hands, then crash-landed on the floor. And her idea of an interesting use for leftovers was to dump everything into the garbage. I went back to the sink and wrapped her salmon croquette in waxed paper. Her dinner was almost always my next lunch.

"So maybe he'll set you up legit. What's the matter, you never heard of a boss marrying a secretary?"

"I've heard about it, but . . ."

"Listen, for the time being get what you can out of him. A good time, satin nightgowns. Some girls get diamond watches, even. And then who knows? Maybe a wedding ring." For a second, a mist came over her eyes. She blinked it away before it could ruin her mascara, but when she spoke again, the mist was in her voice. "Maybe he'll be your Herman, honey!"

Was my father something! To hear his name—Herman Ernst Voss—you'd think: Big deal, another Heinie. But would you have been wrong! My father was a real American. Tall and strong. And smart.

Right from the start, my father was good in *everything*: sports, math, history. And so all-American he could have been Andy Hardy's taller, handsomer big brother. If he hadn't quit high school to get a job, he could have gotten a scholarship to any college; that's what the principal told him. But he had to.

His father, Otto, had died of influenza when my father was little. Otto had been a butcher, but he never got to own his own shop. When he went, all Olga had was a little insurance; it was enough to cover the casket, but not the hearse or the hole in the ground. Some German-Jewish charity paid for that, although they wouldn't have been too thrilled if they'd heard Otto Voss's claim to fame had been his pork patties.

For the next eight or nine years, my Grandma Olga went back to the work she'd done in Berlin as a girl. She got a job in a button plant in Brooklyn, operating the press that made the holes in the buttons.

She worked till she couldn't. Her arthritis got so bad she could hardly lift her pocketbook much less heavy machinery. So my father had to leave school and support her.

But my father. When he left school, he told his mother, "I'm not going to get stuck making sausages the rest of my life. This is temporary." By the time he was eighteen, though, my father was the master sausagemaker of Ridgewood, a prince among butchers, and he was making the wages of a man twice his age. And he seemed content. He was always having fun, something Olga (being German) was slightly suspicious of.

Fun was something that happened on Sunday afternoons. If you came from Berlin, sure, you were much more lighthearted than the average potato-dumpling German, but you were not exactly a fluff-headed fool. You knew real fun was for the people who could afford it: business tycoons who kept cabaret singers as mistresses; barons who threw huge post-boar-hunt bashes. It was the job of the rich to have fun. The *berlinerisch*-speaking lower and middle classes were supposed to be the happy masses. But it's an effort to be a happy mass, and Olga couldn't manage it a lot of the time. She was too busy trying to figure out why she'd been born poor and plain and Jewish—why life had shoved her into three slots she wouldn't have chosen for herself—to let loose and go whoopee. Olga had wanted to be a grand German lady, and she never even came close. And so while she kept her solid *berlinerisch* ability to laugh at the guys at the top, she couldn't laugh at herself too well; she had never realized a single one of her lovely dreams. That was no laughing matter.

But my father was an American. And was he a popular,

*happy* American! Olga used to say it was a blessing they couldn't afford a telephone, because it would never have stopped ringing; as it was, there was a parade of girls past the house every summer night. He was so handsome it didn't matter that he was a Jew. He was a catch for any girl. Olga said it a little wistfully, because any girl would have been better than what he got; my mother was not exactly what Olga had in mind as daughter-in-law material.

But my father wasn't having anything to do with the local Helgas; he wanted a girl as red, white and blue as he was, and sure enough, he found one. He was twenty-three years old, keeping company with a girl named Annabel Johnston. Could you get more American than that? It seemed so, because to both families' amazement, my father dropped twenty-year-old Annabel and eloped with her sixteen-year-old sister. Her name was Betty. My mother. The all-American girl—dumb blonde variety.

Truly dumb. Smart dumb blondes marry sugar daddies with limousines and fat cigars. But my mother was the real McCoy: absolutely magnificent, genuinely dim; she picked a guy who worked ten hours a day in a two-bit sausage plant, who came complete with a live-in mother who didn't speak English. And smart dumb blondes keep their figure; my mother got pregnant with me a couple weeks after the wedding.

But big deal: they were crazy for each other. When I was a kid, my mother would leave Olga and me with the dishes and lead my father toward their bedroom. He wouldn't look back, but my mother would give us a wave. "Nighty night," she'd call. "We're so-o-o sleepy." Even then, when I didn't understand, I knew.

It wasn't just in the bedroom, either. They were more in love than Romeo and Juliet. When the Depression came and the meat business got bad and my father got laid off for almost a year when his plant closed, a lot of beauties would have taken a hike. Not my mother. She loved having him around the house, and even though for a while there things got very bad—to keep us going, we had to take scraps from a butcher my father knew who was still working—she was blissfully happy. (To be fair, my mother only looked at the pictures in the Sunday paper, and since we couldn't even afford the paper in those days, she probably didn't realize there was a Depression on.)

There was only one thing my mother couldn't give my father: companionship. But that was okay. All she had to be was his "little girl." That was enough. That was wonderful, in fact. His mother had been smart and hardworking, but so German. Finally he had someone who wasn't ambitious for him; he had a dumb, happy American, not an ambitious immigrant. If it wasn't for *her*, Olga told him, you'd own a string of butcher shops by now. My father grinned at his mother and said, Who needs butcher shops? I have my family. What he meant was, I have my little girl.

And so what if my mother couldn't give him companionship? For conversation, he had the guys at work. And then he had me. Since "little girl" was taken, he called me his pal.

"Hey, pal, I'm gonna take you to the plant Saturday. Show you what a real, prime pork belly looks like." Boy, did we have great times! Going places, or just talking. "What are you, a parrot? Don't tell me what the radio says. Tell me what *you* think." Naturally, we had our moments. If I was fresh, he wouldn't take any guff from me. "Shape up, Linda!" he'd snap, and a couple of times he gave me the back of his hand.

But most of the time was wonderful. Just walking to the hardware store with him to pick up a bunch of penny nails, I'd be so proud. All the other girls' fathers looked like fathers. Mine was tall and lean, with strong, manly features. He looked special, like someone famous who was just passing through the neighborhood.

We talked about everything—movies, baseball, politics. He was a Dodger fan and a Democrat. "Pal, there's only one group in the world richer and rottener than the Yankees— Republicans. They don't care about anything but holding on to everything they got. They don't give a damn about the little guy, and don't ever let anyone con you into believing different." He told me all about sausage casings, and I told him all kinds of dopey things about the kids in my class and, later, about the people at work. We talked about everything in the world—except two things: ragtime music, which he loved, which I didn't get . . . ragtime music, and my mother.

My mother did nothing except stay beautiful; at thirty, she still acted like the sixteen-year-old my father had eloped with. She listened to the Victrola, visited her girlfriends (they gave each other manicures) and went to the city, to the fancy department stores, to try on clothes. So my grandmother got down on her arthritic knees and scrubbed the floors. She did laundry, she cooked. Naturally, I worked alongside her. I guess I figured housework was something that skipped a generation. But once I finished high school and went to business, I wasn't much of a help. My grandmother was really the housewife in her son's home—which I guess made my mother, the dumb blonde, the kept woman.

Olga was smart. (My father didn't get his brains at Woolworth's.) She read every German-language newspaper and magazine she could get her hands on, kept up a correspondence with a couple of old relatives in Berlin. And so she was at least as well informed about what was going on in the world as the average U.S. senator.

By the mid-thirties, Olga and I started having fights about Hitler. She called him the Austrian, and she said he was an embarrassment. *An embarrassment?* I fumed at her. We stood on opposite sides of the table, stretching strudel dough. "An embarrassment is when you spill soup on the tablecloth. He's passing laws saying Jews can't be citizens. They have to have a 'J' on their identity cards." She eased the dough, coaxed it, into a paper-thin sheet. She was a great German cook. Her strudel technique was not only graceful, it was flawless. "You're the perfect German," I went on. "But not in their eyes. Don't just read what they say. *Believe* it. You're not one of them. They'd make you go around with a 'J.' They hate you."

She looked away and murmured: "And you also. You're half . . ." I lowered the dough so I could look her right in the eye.

"I know. You know what they call my parents' marriage? *Rassenschande*." Race defilement. I didn't rub it in by pointing out that her son would be considered the defiler and that his dopey wife would be viewed as Miss Aryan Purity. "You call all that an 'embarrassment'?"

My poor, smart, sweet, hardworking grandma . . . stuck in a foreign country she didn't understand, hated in her homeland, living with a birdbrained American daughter-in-law who, if she thought about Olga at all, considered her an old foreign thing attached to a mop.

I tried to talk to my father about it. I tried to tell him how hard it must be for Olga; she couldn't say a bad word about my mother to him because she was afraid he would get so angry he'd ask her to leave. And where would she go? But my father didn't want to hear about it. Listen, pal, your grandma's a good sport and she *likes* to keep busy. Anyway, if she had a gripe, wouldn't she tell me?

I tried to say, Hey, Dad, Mom will pick up a dust rag and spend a half hour admiring the fabric and then forget to dust. He wouldn't listen. I'd try again. She'll put down the dust rag, wander over to a mirror. She'll make a little face; she wasn't perfect. So she'll drift into the bathroom for repairs. Makeup. Eyebrow tweezing. He didn't want to hear any of it.

Whenever I started on him, my father would just shrug or stick his head back into the paper or smile. Love isn't blind. It's deaf. He wouldn't hear me. And he couldn't hear the weariness in his mother's voice, or the sadness. But he was all ears for his Betty, his little girl. The minute she warbled, "Herm, honey," he'd leave me in the middle of a sentence and rush down the hall to their room.

When I started working and got to listen to some of the lawyers, I realized my father was as smart as any of them. What he lacked was education—and ambition. But they lacked something my father had: a honeymoon waiting when they got home. They worked till all hours on Wall

Street, but in Ridgewood when the clock struck six, my father could have been sorting a new truckload of meat, getting his pay or talking to his boss. It didn't matter. He took off and ran home.

In 1933, when he was forty-six, he died when a fire caused by a sparking electric meat saw blazed out of control in one of the refrigeration rooms. The funny thing was, it happened about two minutes to six. Just a hundred and twenty seconds later, he would have been safe, rushing through the streets of Queens, back home to his little girl.

I know, I know. It may not have been a breeze to be the sole support of an arthritic grandmother and a lush mother, but it's no old-maid guarantee, either. Some smart girl could have landed a guy who'd buy a house with a couple of back bedrooms.

So why wasn't I married? Was I a prune-face, a blimp? Did my breath wilt celery? Did my small talk send guys into comas? No. What went wrong, I guess, was that I waited too long. I was looking for someone to love.

In senior year of high school, when the rest of the girls were grabbing up anything with hair under its arms, I said, Uh-uh, not me. I can do better. I was smart enough, and pretty.

While I didn't inherit my mother's true beauty, at least I had her fair hair and her eyes: big and brown. Depending on the light, they made men think I was either sad or intelligent or romantic. And I'd wound up with my father's good, solid German bones: definite cheeks, strong mouth. It wasn't a gorgeous face. People didn't pass me in the street and go Ooh! But if a guy looked twice, he might say, Hey, not bad.

So while I wasn't whistle-bait, I looked pretty nice in a dress and heels. And without; sometimes after a bath I stood on top of the toilet seat and angled the medicine cabinet mirror so I could see myself. It looked okay to me. From the front, anyway. I couldn't really see the back. So except for guys who insisted on a girl with a chest like two footballs, I could do fine. Then how come I didn't?

Nineteen, twenty, twenty-one, I was doing okay. There was always someone for Saturday nights; there even was a proposal. Willy Bauer was a bookkeeper for Con Ed and going to Brooklyn College at night to become an accountant. He had a friendly face—like the men in chewing gum ads—and there was nothing wrong with him. But at twenty, that wasn't enough, so I said no.

I had a half proposal too. Michael Donnelly, who was a steamfitter, asked me to marry him after knowing him three weeks. It was half a proposal because there were strings attached; our children would have to be raised as Catholics. Michael said "Catlicks," and that probably had more to do with my saying no than any worries about my future kids in a confessional. In any case, our romance happened so fast I never actually learned what a steamfitter was.

And then came twenty-two, twenty-three and twenty-four. Suddenly the phone got quiet. All of Queens, to say nothing of the other four boroughs, was married. And the few guys who weren't, the bachelors and the widowers, either had the brains or faces of cockroaches or were old enough for my Grandma Olga.

Sure, I could have kept busy with someone at the firm; in the history of the world, it is not unknown for lawyers and secretaries to be buddy-buddy. There was always some corporate partner from New Canaan who wanted to grab a couple of laughs (etc.) before grabbing the 8:38. They didn't tempt me, though, those lawyers whose wallets bulged with pictures of their kids. But even if my tongue had been hanging down to my knees for one of them, I would have said no. I was supporting Olga and my mother. Getting mixed up with a married man could mean a lot more than lonely Christmases. It could mean a pink slip when the fun stopped, and you'd have to be a complete fool to take such a risk during the Depression. The world was full of fast typists. So no married lawyers. And no unmarried ones, because what did they need me for?

It was then, right before my twenty-fifth birthday, that I

suddenly realized I'd missed my chance. I was so lonely. All my friends were married, and I was the old maid. I had reached the age when guys say, So what's wrong with her she's not married?

Well, she waited for someone wonderful to come along, and he never did.

George Armbruster walked back into my life when I was twenty-eight. As George said: "Hey, twenty-eight's a lot older than the last time I saw you. But you still got a pretty face." Then he gave me the once-over. "I bet the rest of you's not bad, either."

By Ridgewood standards, George was a very eligible bachelor. He was an electrician who'd moved somewhere on Long Island but who had his own shop on Metropolitan Avenue and his mother had just died. What could be more perfect? We'd gone to the same high school, and one Saturday when I was at the grocery store communing with a slab of Swiss cheese, he came up beside me. I said hello. Despite a hairline that had inched backward, the face was familiar; he was one of a pack of boys in my English or civics class— the sort of boys who laugh sneaky har-har-hars, and until you see who they're laughing at, you're always afraid it's you. But he was alone now, and seemed okay enough. He said, I forgot your name. Linda Voss. Yeah, that's right. George Armbruster. You were at Grover Cleveland, right?

He came calling every night. Olga had been thrilled. Holding down a decent job in 1937. So what if he was Lutheran. He was very attentive. And okay, no one would ever say, "Hiya, handsome" to him, but good looks don't pay the rent.

Even right after he shaved, George's beard looked dark, like the bully in comics. That wasn't so bad, but he had eyes, nose and a mouth just slightly less appealing than everyone else's; there was not a single thing about him to go Ooh, how nice! No great eyelashes or broad shoulders or even interesting ears. And while he claimed he was five eight, I was just under five five, and you could have drawn a straight line over our heads.

I said to myself, Well, it takes time to get to warm up to some people. What do I have but time? My front door didn't have dents from eligible bachelors pounding on it.

Besides, George wasn't awful. In fact, he was slender and even graceful, like Leslie Howard from the neck down if he'd been an electrician. And he traveled in style. No subway: George had private transportation, his own truck. On the door was painted "ARMbruster Electricals," and just below that, an arm with a grapefruit-sized muscle.

Every night, rain, shine or sleet, there was George at the door. Olga beamed and my mother actually risked her makeup to smile when George came for me and said Hiya.

Hiya, he said that first night, as we walked down the wooden stairs from the front porch onto the street. Howya doing?

Fine. I was a nervous wreck. I had a whole list of subjects to talk about, courtesy of the girls at the office. If he was going to be the strong, silent type, I would have to keep the conversation ball rolling all by myself. But conversation wasn't necessary. George talked all the time.

"Wanna come see my shop? Hey, I got this new job in Glendale. I'm telling you, one more day and the place woulda been on fire. Never saw wiring like that in my life. I turned on my flashlight and thought, Jee-sus, this looks like a plate of Italian spaghetti. And the fuse box! Lemme tell you, it . . ."

Maybe I'd watched too many movies. Maybe I was a romantic sap. But maybe I'd been alone too long. This was obviously the way men and women talked, and I'd better get used to it.

We arrived at his shop, that first night and every other night for the three months we went together. Oh, boy—went together. Well, what else should I call it?

"So that George is coming around a lot," my mother observed. "Guess it's serious, huh?" My mother, who generally went off drinking before George came to the door, passed him now and then on her way out, when she was still sober, so she remembered him. After the second time, she pulled me aside and said, "He certainly is . . . well . . . You know how they talk about good things in small packages. Not that he's *that* small. Having a good time with him?" Another time she giggled and started humming "Here Comes the Bride."

My Grandma Olga had the time of her life, telling the butcher, the grandson of the man my Grandpa Otto used to work for: Linda and George Armbruster are keeping company. The butcher said, Oh; he hooked up my refrigerator. Every morning at breakfast, Olga demanded, "Tell me about last night."

Well, I'd say, we had coffee with some friends of his. We went to a movie. The one I saw last week, but I sure didn't tell him that. Olga would nod, smile. We went dancing at the Trylon Terrace. We went to Coney Island and went on the rides. We went to the city, to a restaurant that had candles on the table. He's a real gentleman. Olga agreed. She could see that; George always got me home by nine at the latest.

But none of that was true. That first night and every night . . . three guesses. We never really needed the truck because we never went anywhere except to his shop. In the back was a couch with an itchy green afghan his mother had finished crocheting the month before she died.

"Come on," he said, and started to unbutton his shirt.

"George!" I couldn't believe what he wanted me to do, and boy, did I ever let him know it.

"Come *on*," he insisted. I shook my head no. "Hey, Linda, you're so pretty. I wanna see a pretty figure to match that face."

He turned on a light bulb hanging from an old electrical cord. And I let him see.

Me, who had never let a boy in high school do more than kiss me good night, and after high school, not much more. I let George take off all my clothes in that dim, flickering light. He was trying to unhook my brassiere, and I was look-ing at the light bulb and thinking: Some lousy electrician, some rotten connection. Me, who had the guts to tell one of the senior partners in the first law firm I'd worked for, Lis-ten, Mr. McCallister, I'm not that kind of girl. Well, I was.

For a little more than twelve weeks, I let George Arm-bruster do anything he wanted on a couch that smelled like it had gotten rained on two years before and never really dried. Not that George's anything was such a big deal. I thought: This is what people make such a big to-do about?

What went on between men and women seemed like Thanksgiving turkey: Everyone always says, "Great!" even though it's invariably dry and disappointing.

And then one night he stopped coming around. George has a real bad cold, I told my mother. He called me at work, still has a fever, I said to Olga. George is getting better, but he has a big job in Brooklyn. I kept it up for nearly two weeks.

I stopped because one night I came home from work and Olga pulled me aside and said, "The butcher took me to the back room, with the sink."

"What?" I figured, Oh, God, now we're in for it. It's bad enough with three fourths of the neighbors. Now the butcher's going on about my mother's being a drunk. Maybe she took off her panties again.

"He feels bad about you."

"About *me*? The butcher?"

"About you and that George Armbruster."

"What about George Armbruster?"

Olga kept her head down. She chopped an onion. She muttered, "About that he's married."

"Married?"

"Ten years." She chopped. "Right after school. He got married then. When everybody else did."

Olga died the next year. Her heart gave out. So many times in those two years since she'd been gone, I'd thought: Maybe she would have managed to hang on if she'd just had

George Armbruster to believe in. She could have been alive, believing in me and George, except for that damn big-mouth butcher.

Instead, she left me alone with the mop and my mother.

# 3

John Berringer could hardly bear the loss of his wife. He looked terrible, and boy, did that make me feel good. Dark gray circles appeared under his eyes, and their glorious deep blue glint died. His glow faded. It's not that he wasn't still gorgeous, but he was now gorgeous and in pain; you could see it. His skin was chalky. His lips were almost white. And you know what I thought, watching him suffering? Wonderful.

I know I sound like a monster, but I really wasn't that bad. I think I was just hoping that as John got closer to the end of his rope, he'd need someone to grab on to. And who better than me? There I was, only four feet away, in my good white blouse with the soft, floppy bow at the neck.

He rubbed his face. "We have about another hour," he said. "Can you manage?"

"Yes, Mr. Berringer."

It was after seven, dark, silent. Nothing is deader than Wall Street at night and—sure, corny—it was as if we were the only two people left in the world. He'd loosened his tie a little, so I got a bonus: a couple of extra inches of neck, the smooth part, where he didn't have to shave. I would have loved to kiss him right there. I smiled; if I was the only girl left in the world, maybe he'd let me.

He saw me smiling. *So* embarrassing. I couldn't decide whether to pass it off as a cooperative smile or, because it may have looked something more than cooperative, to make up a boyfriend: Sorry, Mr. Berringer, just thinking about, um, Joseph. Everyone calls him Big Joe. We're kind of engaged to be engaged, and . . .

"All right," he said, "let's get to work." I could have taken out my teeth and strung them on a necklace in a permanent grin; he wouldn't have noticed. "We still have the Hayn matter and . . ." His voice faded. For a second, he looked at the papers spread out all over his desk. He looked more than sad; he looked desperate, as if he knew his mind was somewhere in the room and his job was to find it.

That's how I knew what bad shape he was in. John's mind was always under control, whirring away like a perfect machine—even when all the other lawyers were sitting around looking like some lower, dopey form of animal life.

"We have Grunberg to take care of," I said, trying to help him. "And we're a little behind on the Schaaf matter too." He looked at me. His shadowed eyes looked empty, like the eye holes in the tragedy mask at the Roxy.

The work! It was too much. I felt as lousy as he looked. We came in before seven every morning and stayed late just trying to stop the clients' fright from turning into panic. It wasn't easy. There was no one terrible event that March 1940, but each night the world grew worse. Turn on the radio, pick up a paper, and the only names on earth seemed to be Hitler and Mussolini. One evil, one deranged, and they grew huge, thriving as Europe sickened. And as their blight spread, the clients wouldn't leave us alone. Those beady little corporation eyes that had been gleaming at the thought of the rich fascist war machine the month before were suddenly blinky, nervous; now all they wanted was to see their way out: Can you tell us what the situation is? What they really wanted to know was: Will everything be all right? And their only hope was that John Berringer— brilliant, calm, masterful—would tell them, Don't worry. What they all wanted to hear was, Everything's going to be just fine.

They probably would have paid him double to hear it, but he wouldn't have taken their money. He was too ethical. He was the best kind of international lawyer. He didn't just come up with a solid contract. He had the patience and the brains to explain to his big corporate clients how the German system worked. He didn't just speak its language. He understood its laws, its ways of doing business, its people. But every day John was making transatlantic calls that didn't get through. He was writing letters to people who no longer answered. Then he had to go back to the clients and say the words nobody wants to hear from a lawyer: I can't help you.

"Mr. Berringer?" I said softly. He jumped, as though I'd just come into the room and yelled Boo! "If you have a lot of preparation, I could come in real early tomorrow and we could finish the dictation then." Maybe I was no diplomat, but it was better than saying, Hey, listen, you'd better get a good night's sleep or you're gonna find yourself on a funny farm.

If a man has some pleasure in one half of his life—home, work—he can usually take pretty much what the other half has to dish out. But in those weeks, what did he have? Hysterical bankers weeping on his desk in the office—and a lot of extra closet space at home. No wonder he looked like Boris Karloff's first cousin.

And he just sat there, helpless. This had never been a helpless man. His face tilted upward, as if he was looking past me, at the door or beyond. Oh, how I could have kissed that neck, slipped my hand under the shirt and rubbed his shoulders, his chest.

"Mr. Berringer?" I whispered. Nothing. He'd forgotten he was handsome. He didn't remember he was charming. He closed his eyes and exhaled a sigh, not even trying to cover up how loud it was. He simply didn't know what he was doing. "About six tomorrow morning," I said. Nothing. "Six, Mr. Berringer?"

"Six," he repeated, but I wasn't sure if he got me.

"In the morning."

"Of course," he said at last. "Of course, Miss Voss."

*  *  *

Gladys smiled, but to me, Friday night did not signal freedom or fun. All it meant was the beginning of two days of being overwhelmed by the ordinary, two days without John to make my life come alive. So what the hell: I took a gulp of my whiskey sour, but since I'd spent lunch hour filing, the alcohol went straight north. Not that it made me silly. I didn't leap up on the cocktail table and begin a soft-shoe routine. The liquor just made the sides of my head sensitive; I was suddenly aware of the weight of my ears. It was the kind of feeling that signaled: You should be home.

So why was I sitting in the Blue Elephant, a cocktail lounge for third-rate lawyers and washed-up stockbrokers, a place so dark you couldn't see the last guy's greasy lipprints on your glass, even though you just knew they were there? To get whatever highly sensitive, top-secret information Gladys Slade had picked up on John or Nan or Mr. Leland. And also to keep her company.

The only company Gladys had at home was a radio and the *Reader's Digest*. A couple of times I'd been up to the third-floor room she rented in an area of Brooklyn with no name, south of Greenpoint. The wallpaper was so old the roses had turned brown. Even on Christmas, her landlady never once said, Come on, have a cup of eggnog with my family; Gladys had to mail her rent check because the family that lived in the rest of the house wanted "privacy."

Both her parents had died of TB by the time she was twelve, and she had no brothers or sisters, no cousins, even. All she had were the girls at work.

I can't say life with a mother who giggles in the bushes was anything *Good Housekeeping* would recommend, but still, it was family. She'd lost track of all her sisters except for Annabel, who had married a sailor and lived on a navy base and sent birthday cards. And there were still Johnstons left in Brooklyn. We got asked to all their funerals and—until my mother had started showing up drunk—to an occasional Thanksgiving or Christmas dinner. And I had a neighborhood. I knew Ridgewood's fruit and vegetable man, the dentist and the corsetiere. And on summer nights when we all sat out on our stoops, I knew everybody's business, and they knew mine.

But after Gladys's parents died, she'd been pushed off on a cousin, who died right away, as if to say, The *nerve* of such an imposition. So Gladys lived at the Sarah Stewart Mac-Dougal Home for Girls, run by some cheap Presbyterians, until she was eighteen. They found her the first of her furnished rooms the day she found her first (and only) job—at Blair, VanderGraff and Wadley.

Still, seeing her at the office, you'd never feel sorry for her. The law firm was all she had, but she made it hers.

Gladys took a long but ladylike slurp of her second whiskey sour. "Do you think Mr. Berringer is behaving"—she paused, and then found her word—"normally?"

"Normal for a lawyer who's so tired he's two minutes away from dropping dead." But there was something funny in her questions, a tightness in her voice that even the loudness of her slurp wouldn't ease. "Why?" I asked. She shrugged. "You know something I don't know, Gladys? I can't believe it. We've been sitting here for twenty minutes."

"Well, I know one thing."

"What's that?"

"I know you're in love with Mr. Berringer!"

My stomach flopped over; for a second, I thought I was going to give back my drink. But I just swallowed and said, "You talk about behaving normally? *You're* the one who's nuts." I tried to kid myself: Gladys is a great kidder. But Gladys was genuinely upset and very serious. She held her head high; her flared nostrils looked like two dark tunnels cut into a mountain. "When did you come up with such a crazy idea? Hey, and anyway, if I was gone on someone, wouldn't I tell you, of all people?"

"I always would have thought so, Linda. We're best friends."

Boy, was she ever on the alert. Her eyes were like two thumbtacks, trying to pin me to the wall. The possibility of me, Mr. Berringer, a secret crush: It was the stuff Gladys's dreams were made of. And if I did anything—sip my drink, twirl my beads—it would give me away. So I sat frozen. But there was terrible silence. I could hear the bartender squeezing out the sponge, moving a glass, cleaning up a spill. Then I made myself smile. I said, "Okay, you're right, Gladys. Mr. Berringer really swept me off my feet. I'm madly in love. It was his smile that got me. You know, the smile he only gives to seven million people every day. So deeply personal. So very, very private." But Gladys didn't let her guard. "Oh, come on. He's not a human being. He's a charm machine. You don't think—"

"All I know is, you say you're drowning in work, but you have time to run around the office, talking to this one, that one—"

"So what? Since when do you stay stapled to your desk?"

"All of a sudden you're best friends with Marian Mulligan, and you're asking her so many questions even she's getting suspicious. If *she* gets suspicious . . . And you never even told me you were talking to her."

"Gladys, I'm sorry. I've been crazy with work, and this is the first chance—"

She cut me off. "How come you have time to talk to that moron Marian?"

"Because I'm *very* curious. Okay? I admit it. I'm curious about Mr. Berringer, and her boss is handling part of the separation agreement. And Mr. Berringer's *my* boss. . . . How many bosses do you know whose wives leave them?"

"You're buttering up Marian, and then you're stopping off at Wilma's and Helen's, asking all kinds of questions, like you were Mr. and Mrs. North." She almost had tears in her eyes. With the other girls she was queen, but I was her *friend*. "I would have gone with you to ask."

"Gladys, what's the big deal?"

She banged her glass on the table. "Linda, the big deal is, all you do is talk about him. Someone says, Gee, there's a great glove sale at Ohrbach's, and you say, Oh, Mr.

Berringer, *he* wears gloves. Oh, and by the way, Mrs. B, when she walked out on him . . . do you happen to know what color gloves she was wearing when she left?"

"Gladys, what's with you? I didn't talk to you about Mr. Berringer for a couple of days, so it's a major felony?"

"I just don't want you to make a fool of yourself. If any of the partners get wind of it . . ."

What was she trying to pull? I thought. And then I realized: She wasn't only desperate for gossip; she was scared that if I'd fallen for John, I'd want to cherish him alone. I'd float up to the clouds, abandon her. Gladys wanted to keep me, and keep my crush for just the two of us. A Sunday special.

And part of me wanted to be kept. What a relief it would be, to talk about John, to have someone—a sober someone, my best friend—to take pleasure in all I'd gathered. Let me tell you about the veins in his hands, Gladys, about the way he holds the phone. But then what would I be? Just another girl with a cheap pash for her boss.

It burst out of me: "Listen, Gladys. There's a big, fat difference between worrying about someone—someone you have a lot of respect for—and going nuts over them. It so happens I *like* Mr. Berringer. Okay? He's a wonderful, decent man. And—"

"Linda, calm down."

"No. I mean, how would you feel if I accused you of holding back on me?"

"I didn't mean—"

Don't back down, I said to myself. "Gladys, I'm a human being. He's someone I see five days a week, and sure, I'm sorry Mrs. Berringer took a powder. More than sorry. Sad. But I'll confess something. I'm nosy. So sue me. I asked a couple of questions. You know damn well that if Mr. Avenel's wife packed her bags, you'd bring in the bloodhounds, and don't tell me different. I think you owe me an apology."

I waited. When she spoke, I could hardly hear her voice. "I'm sorry, Linda."

"It's okay."

I thought: What's the percentage in turning to mush under a little pressure? Like that British boob who gave away Czechoslovakia. The only time you back down is when you're dead.

Gladys lifted her glass. "Thanks."

I gave one of those conspiratorial winks that you see in the movies but never in real life, but we'd just had a very dramatic situation and, sure enough, Gladys not only fell for it but winked back.

I said softly, "A girl in my position can't be too careful. If I got tipsy . . ." I paused. "Who knows? I could start babbling my secret. About my grand *passione* for my darling, precious John."

Then I laughed, and my friend Gladys joined me.


I couldn't believe it!

I'd been trying to pick up the tiny little strings of eraser stuck way down between my typewriter keys with the tip of my pinkie, and there I was with my finger in my mouth, rewetting it, and who should walk by and stare at me but Nan Berringer.

Was I shocked! I thought she was in Reno! I started to say, "Good morning, Mrs. Berringer," but I was so nervous I hadn't taken the finger out of my mouth. And she was in such a hurry all she must have heard was "Goo—" By the time I pulled out my finger and got to "morning," she was past my desk, the heels of her expensive black suede shoes making snappy sounds on the brown tile floor of the corridor where the secretaries sat.

She'd swept right by John's closed office door, so she hadn't come to fling herself into his arms and say either, I forgive you, John, or, My dearest, my love, I'm so deeply sorry. No, she just kept going, and fast. Still, in that second when she passed, I got a chance to see her like never before.

God, was she pretty! I could see why John loved her. Her skin was so flawless it looked as if it was made out of the stuff that covers pearls. She wasn't actually beautiful, but what made Nan Leland Berringer a knockout was that everything was wonderful. Wonderful, nice eyes. Same with the nose and mouth. Her hair may have been a non-breathtaking brown, but somehow it was a richer color than anyone else's. It was styled in a perfect pageboy: longer than her chin, shorter than her shoulders, and unbelievably shiny, as though she'd been given sole access to the world's best shampoo. If God had worked in a beauty parlor, He would have said, Okay, *this* is what hair is supposed to look like.

Naturally, her figure was as superb as the rest of her. Lovely, but not lovely like the figures of other lovely women. Nan was about my height but built on a finer, smaller scale. Not skinny; just petite enough to make a guy feel she'd been custom-made.

Her clothes were like gift wrapping for her specialness. Her gray dress was superior to anyone else's gray—the softest color, and the fabric so fine it looked like someone had taken a steamroller and flattened out a couple of yards of wool. It was absolutely plain; this dress didn't even have a button you could see. Still, it was beautiful. On top it was politely tight; the skirt flared. The dress said, Look at the classy narrow shoulders and the delicate waist, and if you've got an extra five seconds, take a gander at the regal posture. You could see why John loved her.

It wasn't only the way she looked. It was Nan herself. She wasn't just a pretty twenty-one-year-old matron. Oh, sure, she was that, but she was more. Smart. It didn't only show in her eyes, like with most people. Everything about Nan was smart: the size steps she took, the way she carried her purse. Smart in a way I would never be. If I could have been anything in the world, I would have been Nan Leland Berringer.

And I thought: God, what a loss. How he must miss her.

Then I got up and trailed her.

I was definitely no intellectual, but I wasn't the class dunce, either. I figured if anyone caught me tippytoeing ten feet behind Mrs. Berringer, they'd think John had sent me to spy on her, and that wouldn't be so terrific for either him or me.

So I snuck into the supply closet and came out with a couple of boxes of typing paper, enough pencils to last till 1947 and two bottles of ink; then I didn't even waste my time looking where Nan had gone. Instead, I sauntered by Gladys's desk. There's that old joke about the three major means of communications: telephone, telegraph, tell a woman. The comedian had probably worked at Blair, VanderGraff and knew Gladys.

She was on the edge of her chair, talking a mile a minute to Lenore Stevenson, the bookkeeper, who everyone called Lenny, and I don't think it was just a nickname. Lenny looked like a man in a skirt. A big man, and she had a pair of hands that would have looked great on a Giants pitcher, plus a cigarette voice that came pretty close to being as deep as Mr. Leland's.

"Lin-*da*," Gladys said, "come here."

"Yeah," Lenny echoed, "come here." She was huge, but strong—not fat: a rhinoceros, but a gentle one. She was shy—she ate lunch alone with her ledgers, never with us in the conference room—and she hardly talked, except to Gladys, whom she practically worshiped. But Lenny had a good heart and was always doing sweet things, like slipping me my pay envelope Thursday night instead of Friday morning.

I rested my supplies on Gladys's desk. "I can't talk. I got to go and kill myself, because that's the only way I won't die from overwork." I sighed, putting a little quaver in it—"Boy oh boy"—and picked up my stuff.

"You must stay," Gladys said, in her Queen of England voice.

"I 'must' stay? You going to pull out a silver teapot and pour?"

"Stay, Linda," Lenny said.

"I can't."

Gladys added, "We'll make it worth your while."

Lenny nodded and crossed her arms. Gladys swiveled her head around, looking for lurkers; when it came to gossip, she trusted no one. Then she nodded at Lenny, like Go ahead.

"I was down by Mr. Leland's office—" Bookkeepers could go where secretaries fear to tread.

"And guess who just happened to dance into Mr. L's office?" Gladys butted in.

"The Rockettes," I said.

"Linda, be serious," Gladys hissed.

"Okay, I'm serious."

"Mrs. Berringer!" Gladys said.

"Mr. Leland's daughter," Lenny added.

"Thanks, Len."

"Yeah, sure, right," Lenny rumbled. "Anyway, guess what she told her father?"

"They invited you in to join them? You got an engraved invitation?"

"Aw, Linda, you're a card!"

"How come you got to listen in, Lenny?"

"She didn't get the door closed fast enough."

"What did she say?" I demanded. Ever since my drink with Gladys, I stopped pretending I wasn't curious; I'd come to realize that when you're trying hard to be something you're not, people think you're phonier than you are.

Lenny raised her eyebrows and looked upward, like the secret was between her and Him . . . and Gladys too, because the next second, Lenny looked straight at her. And Gladys was almost jumping out of her chair, like she had taken a double dose of Castoria. "Tell her," Gladys bubbled. "It's okay. Go *on*, Len."

"Awright." Lenny made circles with her shoulders, like she was getting ready to throw her world-famous fastball. "Mrs. Berringer walked in there and said, 'Daddy, I won't wait another day. I'm going to Reno *tonight*.' "

"Tell her what happened next," Gladys ordered.

"Mr. Leland said, 'Close the door, Nan.' " Lenny could

add and subtract like a genius but sometimes seemed a little slow at general thinking.

"*No*. After that," Gladys said.

"Oh. See, Mrs. Berringer came back to close the door, but the second she was doing it, you could still hear her. And you know what she said? 'I don't care what you say. I'm going to marry Quentin!' "

# 4

The window behind Edward Leland's desk was open, and the year's first warm breeze floated in; even Wall Street smelled sweet. But in that office on the forty-sixth floor, there wasn't a trace of spring softness.

Mr. Leland stared as I stood near the door of his office. Not a man's stare—no *Look at those legs!*—but a cold look, searching for something, and the worst of it was, I had no idea what he was after. Without thinking, I brought my pencil up to my mouth; when you're scared, there's nothing like a good, hard chew on a pencil for fast relief. But the way Mr. Leland's eyes were boring through me, he would have known the depth of the teeth holes. I lowered it.

Some men undress you with their eyes. Edward Leland did worse. He looked inside you. Sure, I knew he couldn't actually read my mind, but still, I would have felt a lot safer if that dark stare had been meant to burn through my yellow sweater, my gray skirt, to observe my most private of privates—instead of my mind.

"Sit down, Miss Voss," he said from behind his desk. Somewhere outside, a bird flying over the southern tip of Manhattan, not knowing it didn't belong in the corridors of power, tweeted. For that second, the half of Edward Leland's face that could move softened. Then it went back to its usual hardness, and I looked away.

His office was filled with the mess of an organized man: manila file folders in precise stacks on two cushions of the couch, a couple of cartons under the window. The glass doors of his bookshelves were open, and the gaps where books had been pulled looked like knocked-out teeth. The books themselves were piled on a corner of his desk. An open travel case—a big, black one, like a giant doctor's bag—rested on a brown leather wing chair near the wall. I gave a fast peek as I passed. The white of underwear. Shoes. A heavy sweater—beautiful, like Sonja Henie's ice-skating partner would wear.

I sat in another leather chair, right across the desk from Mr. Leland, opened my pad, flipped to a clean page and looked up, ready. But Mr. Leland wasn't. He wasn't ready to do anything except stare. This time it was not to examine my mind but to send a message, to let me know that he knew I had taken inventory of his travel bag. I shifted a little, but the leather seat was so slippery I nearly slid off. I thought about landing on the floor—splat—on my backside, my skirt flying up, and then felt my face flush. Edward Leland saw that; in fact, he seemed to see everything. He probably knew I was crazy about the sweater in his bag. (It was dark blue, with white starry snowflakes.)

"I suppose you're curious about why I asked you to stop in, Miss Voss." What answer did he want? Yes? No? I thought about it so long that when I finally decided Yes, it was too late to say it.

Edward Leland sat motionless, framed by the high back of his chair, never moving his eyes from me. He was like a scientist examining a new specimen: Note how these secretaries react under pressure. Their eyes dart around the room. Oh, and observe, they chew their bottom lip. I took a deep breath. I forced myself to sit as still as he was. Then, suddenly, as if there had been no silence, he went on. "You know, I've been out of the office quite a lot lately." I nodded. "Do you have any idea where I've been?" I don't know how I knew, but I knew this was not a moment to play dumb.

I told him what the girls were saying at lunch. "I heard you were in Washington."

"I see. Well, what are people saying I'm doing in Washington?" he inquired. Get me out of here, I thought. Never once moving his shadow eyes from my face, he asked, "Am I making you uncomfortable?"

No, I said to myself, this is my idea of a truly swell time. But out popped: "A little."

"I don't mean to, but I like to know what's being bruited about the office." His eyes were darker than brown. They were black disks; there didn't seem to be any difference in color between the irises and the pupils. "Now, what am I supposed to be doing in Washington?"

"No one really knows, sir."

"No theories?"

His voice was low and so growly; that's what made his questions scary. This great, important voice, the voice that accomplished whatever it wanted—it was being used on me. Oh, God, I was starting to sweat: down the back of my neck, then in front, dribbling from under my brassiere to my belly button.

That was the moment he picked to smile at me. It was a wide smile, kind, the sort lawyers never give out, except maybe to their best clients. Like his voice, his smile was a weapon. An effective one, all the more because it was off center in that damaged face. But it lit him up. It made him the most wonderful person in the world. I found myself flooded with happiness. Life was good—and Edward Leland was letting up on me.

"No hunches about what I've been up to, Miss Voss?" Okay, so he wasn't letting up.

"I guess you're doing something for your clients, Mr. Leland." His smile stopped. He turned a paper clip over and over, waiting, patient. He knew he'd get what he wanted. "Is there anything else, sir?"

"What kind of something, Miss Voss?"

"Mr. Leland, I'm sorry . . ."

He leaned toward me. The light reflected off his black eyes; they looked unnaturally bright. "Come now. You seem to be a bright girl. There's a war going on in Europe. What would a lawyer want in Washington?"

It didn't take a genius. Anybody who had enough intelligence to know how to turn on the radio could figure that one out. "I guess it would help your clients if you knew the government's plans. Like for instance, how much aid we're going to be giving to England. If it's a lot, they could make a lot of money." I should have said "profit." Rich people don't like the word "money."

But it didn't seem to bother Mr. Leland. "Very good," he said. "Any other ideas?"

I swallowed hard. My throat hurt. He was playing a game. No, he was giving me a test, and for the life of me, I didn't know whether it would be better to pass or to fail. But I gave it the old college (or, in my case, high school) try. "You could be, well, a person who feels we shouldn't get mixed up over there and you're trying to make sure we don't." In other words, an America Firster, an isolationist bastard. If he kept asking questions, sooner or later (sooner) he'd figure out my politics; they would not put a song in the heart of a Republican. But how could I stop his examination? Bash him with my steno pad? Run?

"I'm an isolationist? An intriguing theory, but I'm quite open about my interventionist leanings. But I find this interesting. I like to know what people are thinking and sometimes"—he picked up a gold and black fountain pen and rotated it between his palms—"I get rather out of touch. Tell me more." My throat closed tighter. I hated his cold, upperclass, "rahther." He put down the pen. "Go on, Miss Voss."

It burst out: "Maybe you're doing some kind of spy stuff for the government." I tried to laugh at my crazy imagination (and prayed he would join me), but I couldn't even begin to push my face muscles into a laugh. You know why? I believed it was true. Sure, I just tossed off the remark, but I must have been thinking it, deep down, for a long time. This guy across the desk from me who's always taking trips could be doing *anything*. And something dangerous seemed more like Edward Leland than something just clever.

Then suddenly I thought: This isn't fair, calling me in here, pressuring me, forcing me to talk. He could ask me anything he wanted, and if he didn't like my answer, or didn't like me, there went my twenty-five bucks a week. There went my life.

"This isn't fair," he said. "I've been cross-examining you and haven't given a clue to why I asked you to drop in."

How do you figure someone like him? I saw a man who could almost read minds, who made trips to Washington the way I made trips to the five-and-dime. But I also saw something more than a powerhouse New York lawyer. I'd seen a few of those. He was different.

It showed in Edward Leland's fascinating face. For some reason, it was a face every big shot in the country was drawn to look into. And every little shot: I had to force myself not to stare at him.

Although Edward Leland's voice was tough—gravelly, low—and although the word around the office was that he'd grown up poor, on a Vermont farm, talking to cows, the way he sounded seemed strictly champagne-at-the-Ritz. "You're quite perceptive. I am doing a bit of work for the government." A bit of work. "Although certainly not your 'spy stuff.' "

Certainly not, my behind, I thought. "Yes, sir," I said.

"The thing of it is, what with the situation in Europe, I need someone who can do some secretarial work—in German. Not a great deal. Nowhere near the sort of thing I'd want to hire someone for."

"If there's anything I can do, Mr. Leland . . ." That was the best I could come up with. No secretarial course at Grover Cleveland High School had offered Good Manners in Potential Espionage Situations.

"I've taken the liberty of checking your personnel file and making a few inquiries," Mr. Leland went on. "Do you know why?"

God, if the law business ever went bust, this guy could make a fortune playing Twenty Questions. Then I started talking fast, because I didn't want him to read *that* thought. "If you're doing stuff for the government, then you probably don't want someone taking dictation who has a secret crush on some German general."

"Who's your favorite German general?" he asked suddenly. For that second he seemed playful, almost young. I guess he was relieved I hadn't gotten up and goose-stepped yet; so far, I was okay.

"You mean who do I hate most?" He nodded. "Right now, I guess Kaupitsch."

Wow, he stopped being lighthearted real fast; I'd pushed the magic button. But it was weird; it didn't take a Yale lawyer to know about Kaupitsch, the Nazi bum running the invasion of Denmark; his name was plastered on page one of every newspaper in the city. "I see you're up-to-date on the invasion," Mr. Leland said, not sounding too thrilled about it.

Not up-to-date like I bet you're up-to-date. Would I love to have said that. "I read the *Daily News*, Mr. Leland," was what I said instead.

And then, boom! My mind went straight to that sweater in his valise, that heavy snowflake sweater on a warm April day. I bet it wasn't so warm in Denmark. But then I thought: Nah. How could he be going anyplace near an invasion? He could go down to Washington and read spy reports, but—

"This is how it stands, Miss Voss. Your file looks fine. The next stop, because this does involve the government—in the most peripheral way—is to have one of the agencies check into your background."

"You mean like the FBI?"

He just kept going. "I have some papers for you to fill out. The usual information: name, school, previous employers. But before you do, I think we should make certain"—I got another smile from him, a little smaller this time, not real; a smooth lawyer smile, like the ones John gave out—"that you don't mind having your life under, shall we say, scrutiny. Do you understand?"

"You want to make sure my favorite uncle isn't in the SS."

"Exactly. I'd like to know a bit about your family."

"Well, my mother's side is all English, I think. But not English English: American." He picked up a pencil and jotted something down. I could have saved him the trouble, taken it in shorthand and given it back, word for word. "My father's family is one-hundred-percent German, but dead. And even when they weren't—dead, I mean—they weren't Nazis or anything." I could have said, Hey, listen, there's nothing to worry about: they're Jews, and cleared up the whole thing. Cleared it up so much I might lose my job. So I just went on. "My father worked in a sausage plant. He was foreman. But you know, the Depression . . ." There was something about Edward Leland that made you keep talking. If I didn't watch myself I would give him my life story, from my first spoonful of Pablum to my father's religion to my being madly in love with his (for another couple of weeks) son-in-law. "My grandfather died when my dad was little—back in the 1890s, I guess. And my grandmother worked in a button factory until my dad got his first job."

"She's the one you spoke of so fondly, the one who taught you German?"

"Yes." So that's why he'd been so interested back in February.

"Any other family, friends?"

"My mother has four sisters, but the only one we keep in touch with lives in Seattle now. And we have some cousins in Brooklyn—Oh, you mean my father's side. Just a couple of old relatives in Germany—Berlin—that my grandma used to write to."

"Do you know their names?"

What he was asking was, Are they Nazis? "I can't remember their names. But they're probably in their late seventies by now. They were two old ladies, sisters. I think one was called Liesl."

"What was her first name?"

"Liesl's a first name, Mr. Leland." These guys thought everything female should be Mary or Babs. "I don't know her last name. Anyway, they could be dead by now. I think they were around my grandmother's age, and she'd be seventy-nine."

"Do you have any friends, relatives or neighbors who've expressed sympathy with Hitler or his policies?"

"Mr. Leland, the only people who really like the Nazis are

some of the ones who came over in the last ten, twenty years. They're still German. But people in Ridgewood are loyal Americans."

"I'm sure they are." It was weird; for a second we just eyed each other, both of us knowing that his gentlemanly "I'm sure they are" was full of bull. And in the next second, both of us decided to forget it. We looked away.

"All right," Mr. Leland said. "I think that's all." He pushed the forms toward me. "Naturally, you understand that what we've discussed here goes no farther."

"Yes, Mr. Leland."

"*No one* sees these forms. Should there come a time when you do work for me, that work is to be completely confidential."

I folded the papers carefully and stuck them in my steno pad and wondered: Does this mean I won't be working for John anymore? I clutched the pad so tight the wire top cut into my hand. Does this mean that with Nan in Reno, John might be leaving the firm and they had to find something else for me, that—

"I'll only need you now and then. Naturally, you'll continue to work for Mr. Berringer," Mr. Leland said. "Do you find the arrangement satisfactory, Miss Voss?"

"Yes, sir."

He stared at me again. "Well, I look forward to working with you, Miss Voss."

"Thank you, Mr. Leland. Will that be all?"

"For now."

By eight o'clock that night, I was overtired the way a little kid gets: clumsy, and so irritable I felt on the verge of tears. My whole body was so weary, so limp, that if I didn't watch myself, I'd flop forward and crack my head on my type-writer; I could see the blood dripping onto the semicolon and the *L*. And what made working late even harder was thinking about my mother home alone, all made up, with no one to tell her how beautiful she looked before she went out into the night.

But I perked up fast, and it didn't take a gallon of coffee. John came out of his office, stood by my desk and picked up the letters I'd typed. He signed them fast. "I spoke with Mr. Leland late this afternoon," he said. I stopped what I was doing, which was licking an envelope, and remembered just in time to put it down, or I would have wound up with an envelope dangling from my tongue. All day I'd been worrying about what to do if Mr. Leland had work for me. Since I wasn't allowed to talk about it, I couldn't say, Pardon me, Mr. Berringer, I have to stop what I'm doing for you and go to Mr. Leland's office and take a spy letter. And I couldn't excuse myself to go to the ladies' room and saunter back an hour and a half later. "He mentioned he'd given you some forms," John added.

"Forms?" Mr. Leland had ordered me to stay mum. What could I say? Sure, I've got this mile-long FBI form to fill out. Want me to show it to you?

John smiled, nodded, and gave me one of his special winks. "You're right, of course. You have no idea whether my interest . . ." His hand rested on my typewriter: long-fingered, elegant—but not too elegant. "Good thinking, Miss Voss. I'll ask Mr. Leland to let you know I'm all right." I was mesmerized by his hand. "You'll find"—his voice dropped to almost a whisper, but a whisper full of pride— "that I'm working very closely with Mr. Leland"—he pulled back his hand, slipped it into his pocket—"on this matter."

I wanted to believe in John completely. I wanted to think there was nothing he did that wasn't absolutely perfect. But I couldn't. If some guy's daughter had turned my life upside down, I wouldn't be bragging about working very closely with him.

And as far as Mr. Leland went, if a son-in-law didn't have what it took to hold on to my daughter, I wouldn't be sipping brandy with him and saying, Well, old bean, how do we best contain the growing Fascist peril?

And look at Nan. Twenty-one years old, a genuine intellectual, a girl everyone said, if she'd been a man, would have gone as far as her husband, or even her father. A brain, but she runs into her father's office blabbing away about Quentin when even a chimpanzee would have had the sense to close the door.

I couldn't figure them. They didn't act like real people— or even movie people. They acted as if they had secret rules no one else was in on. Stick John and Mr. Leland in a closed room where normal guys would throttle each other, and what happened? They got cordial. They worked "very closely." Put Nan Leland Berringer in a public place, under pressure, where you'd think: Well, here it is, Stiff Upper Lip Time, and what do you get? A Smith College genius jabbering so loud about marrying number two—while she still has number one—that you could hear her in Hoboken.

I could sort of understand John: not his pride, but at least his unwillingness to tell a man like his father-in-law to go soak his head. The one I really didn't get was Edward Leland. For all his expensive suits and good grammar, he was a guy *nobody* would want to cross. And what does he say to his one child? "Close the door, Nan." Okay, no one knew what went on after, but everyone could see she got exactly what her little heart desired: a first-class compartment on the next train to Reno.

Sure, Nan was probably a handful, but couldn't her father—a real tough customer, who handled handfuls for a living—couldn't he say: Listen, sister, you were so crazy about this guy you couldn't wait till college let out in June to marry him, so what are you doing? Throwing him over in less than three years? Come on. Give him a chance. Go home, have a couple of kids. And if I hear one more word about this Quentin, you'll get a good, swift kick in the pants.

That's what my father would have said.

The worst thing about being a secretary is the little chairs. They're very low, so when your boss comes over to your desk, that first instant you turn to him—guess what you're staring at. Not that you could see anything, because in the entire history of the Association of the Bar of the City of

New York there has never been one single pair of revealing trousers.

John came out of his office again. He was so near, reaching across me to put down a bill of lading. "You'll see this gets to Mr. Withey first thing in the morning," he said.

"First thing," I said from my chair.

He was so close his arm brushed against my shoulder, and that second my guard must have been down, because all of a sudden, wham! Desire that started deep, low down, then exploded, destroying my sense. My face got feverish. I was dizzy. I tried to get control, to slow my breathing so it didn't give me away; I concentrated on a piece of carbon paper. I held it up to the light, pretending to check if it was still any good. That let me turn away from him, because it wasn't just the heat of my own face I was feeling. He was close enough that I could tell some of that heat was coming from him.

But it wasn't me who was heating John up. I felt it anyway, the rising temperature of a man in desperate need of a woman, a man dying to rush out of the office, leave the day behind him. He shifted from one foot to the other, ready— more than ready—to break out into the night.

"Is there anything else, Mr. Berringer?"

"Excuse me?" He was distracted. It wasn't fatigue.

"Anything else tonight?"

"No. I'll be going now."

Where to? Back to his apartment? To eat dinner alone? To get into bed, to lie on sheets he hadn't changed since she'd left a month before, to breathe deep, trying to pick up the dying scent of her perfume?

Or to go with someone else? A lady, another Nan, who would ease him, massage his neck with cool, smart fingers? Or to some tramp, as hot and ready as he was?

"See you in the morning, Mr. Berringer. Have a good—"

But he was halfway down the hall. He didn't even take his briefcase.

Whoever made the modern furniture in John's office was a great craftsman. In the darkened room, lit only by the hall light, his black desk had such a gorgeous, deep glow it looked alive. I sat in his chair and swiveled back and forth. No one was left in the whole law firm, not even the cleaning lady. In the silence, I pushed aside all the other women I'd imagined John with and thought about him alone in his apartment. I pictured him throwing aside his jacket, loosening his tie, unbuttoning his shirt, feeling the soft night air on his chest. Standing there, in a foyer or living room as dark as his office. Alone, in the quiet, aching to be touched. Just like me.

I stroked the desk's silky wood, ran my fingers over the smooth corners. Beautifully made.

Strong too. There was no way you could get the locked lower-right-hand drawer open without a key. Not that I would have done anything funny with a hairpin, but with most drawers, you don't need burglary tools: one good fingernail and a sharp yank would do the trick.

I sat up straighter; I would never jimmy open a drawer. Then I felt under the blotter and the base of the desk lamp. Nuts. Nothing. Not in the unlocked drawers, either. But in the end I found it, inside a flap of his leather calendar: his desk key.

Talk about good craftsmanship: The key opened the lock without even the tiniest click, and the drawer slid out as if I'd whistled and it couldn't wait to come to me. I felt around. Just one thick manila envelope.

I got up and locked his door. If you know you're doing something you should be ashamed of, you should either stop or do it thoroughly; there's no such thing as a semi-sin.

Then I came back and switched on John's desk lamp. The envelope was one of Blair, VanderGraff and Wadley's. It had nothing written on it. I eased open the metal clasp, spilled everything out onto the desk, memorized the mess, then arranged it all into a perfect pile. I may have been a sneak, but no one could say I wasn't a great secretary.

Then I looked through it. It was all hers. John had collected enough mementos to open a Nan Leland Berringer museum. Except it would have been a pretty pathetic museum: love tokens of a wife in love with someone else.

I started with the two letters. The first must have been written right when they began:

*Dear John,*

*On Sunday, I told you I am congenitally incapable of being coy. Therefore, I will not try to subvert you with feminine wiles, nor will I have some mutual acquaintance drop my name before you at frequent intervals. I will merely say I want very much to see you when I get back to New York, right after my exams.*

*Yes, I realize this is awkward for you, that you did not intend an afternoon's conversation, a mild flirtation, to be taken so seriously. Your womanly ideal is not an eighteen-year-old college freshman. And yet . . . And yet, I know you were drawn to me as I was to you.*

*You see, John, I told you I could not be coy.*

*You said I must be getting the rush from the Amherst boys. I don't know if it is a rush. I do know I have no interest in boys. I want a man, a man of brilliance and sensitivity. A man like you.*

*I cannot begin to tell you how much our conversation in the gazebo meant to me, to have someone who not only cares deeply for the things I care about, but who can express himself with such insight and profundity. I want very much to talk again. I feel we have a great deal to say to each other.*

*I told you I was not coy. What I did not tell you was that I am relentless. If you don't call me, I will call you.*

*My best,*

She signed it "N." I thought: That's how they get rich, saving money on ink. And then I thought: I can't believe an eighteen-year-old girl would have the guts to write that kind of letter. And even more, I can't believe she had John Berringer alone in a gazebo and walked out in a tizzy over his profundity. Profundity? But there it was, in black and white.

The second letter was signed "N" too:

*Darling,*

*I can't tell you how sorry I am. It was my fault. I should never have gone to the hotel with you and let things get that far. I know you're not some adolescent, that you are used to having anything you want from a woman and that your needs are a man's needs.*

I put the letter down on the desk. This was the worst thing I'd ever done. It was like being the lowest—a Peeping Tom.

*But, John, when it happens, it has to be right. It has to be done (please, oh, please, don't think I'm being pretentious) in a state of grace. I love you. I adore you. And if you insist, I will do anything you want to prove I am indeed yours. But I beg you, don't insist until, well, until it is truly the time.*

*Forever,*

I held the envelope up to the light. The postmark was February 19, eleven days before they got married.

I put it down and thought of what I'd done with George Armbruster. If I hadn't come so cheap, if I'd played my cards right and said, Uh-uh, nothing doing without a state of grace, Georgie—who knows? He could have introduced me to his bachelor brother the next day, saying, This here is a fine, upright girl. I could have had a house, two kids, a dinette set.

The life before me was more interesting than my own. I went back to the pile on the desk. Ticket stubs. A book by Goethe, *Divan of East and West,* which I'd heard was pretty hot stuff. It was from her; in it she'd written, "To mein Liebe, From N." To my love. She may have been a genius, but N could have used a couple of German lessons; if she was going to use "love" like that, it should have been *Für meine einzige Liebe* or maybe *mein Geliebter*. John would know that, but what could he say? My darling, "mein Liebe" is stinko German. Your usage definitely isn't anything to write home about. But he couldn't say anything to Nan anymore. So he kept the book, the letters—all of it—because it was the closest he could get to her. In the late afternoons, when he said, No calls, Miss Voss, he was probably sitting there fingering the ticket stubs or rereading the Goethe.

There was a concert program from Carnegie Hall. The orchestra must have been rotten, because all over the page that told about Bach's B Minor Mass there were scribbles. "Putrid!" "The tempo!" and "Will it ever end?" in Nan's handwriting. "I love you" in his. There were a couple of clippings from the society page: their engagement and wedding announcements. I got a few new pieces of information: a list of bridesmaids with expensive names—"The Misses Floria Wyatt, Honore Delafield, Dorothea and Alice Brinton, Eleanor Randel and Victoria Courtney." I thought: I bet me and Honore Delafield could be great buddies. Hi, Honore. Linda, sweetie! Hi! I found out Nan's real name was Anne and that the late Mrs. Edward Leland's maiden name was Caroline Bell and that she was President Theodore Roosevelt's cousin. I learned that John was the son of the late Mr. and Mrs. Charles Berringer of Port Washington, New York.

I was so taken up with these new Berringers, wondering who they were and when they'd died, that I didn't notice the picture until my elbow rested on something slick. It was a small, glossy snapshot of Nan and John. They were lying together on a hammock, their arms and legs so tangled up they looked like one person. She wore shorts and a pullover. He wore cotton slacks. No shirt. Nan's head rested on his shoulder and her hand, with its wedding ring, seemed to have been caught by the camera as it caressed his bare chest. They weren't talking profundity in that hammock. What they had was what I would have died for.

God, was John beautiful! Nothing I'd imagined being under his suit was as good as what was in that little picture. His body was so perfect it almost didn't seem real. It looked as sleek and as hard as the modern furniture Nan loved. No wonder she hadn't been able to keep her hand to herself.

I took a deep breath. I put everything back into the envelope. Well, I thought, and let out a high half laugh, that was a good night's work.

Then I turned off the lamp, sat in the black room and started to cry.

# 5

The sun sparkled, and the surface of the dark water of Sheepshead Bay glittered as if someone had tossed in a handful of diamonds. Gladys Slade, wearing a middy blouse that would have looked great on a kid in third-grade assembly, stood with her hand shielding her eyes. But she did it so dramatically she could have been Admiral of the Fleet, saluting all the ships at sea. "Mr. Leland used to have a summer house right on the water. In Connecticut." She spoke a little too loud, as if to be heard over the crash of the waves, except there weren't any waves—only the relaxed slapping of water against the wooden piles of the pier. "He sold it when Nan went off to boarding school, right before the Crash. I hear he made a pret-ty penny." Gladys could take any subject—water, *The Private Lives of Elizabeth and Essex*, pickled watermelon rinds—and tie it up to the law firm.

I sighed. My best friend. But to tell the truth, Gladys was one of the unspoken minuses of being an old maid. Forget about your face shriveling into a prune, about not having children, about having to support yourself; the real bad news was that you got stuck with other old maids for friends. I know that sounds hard-hearted, but frankly, 99.99999 percent of them were walking around ringless not because of a receding chin or a polka-dot complexion but because of some tragic flaw in the personality department—no humor, or too much, or they were whiny or pathetically eager to please. All my friends from high school, bright, lively girls, had gotten grabbed up, and right from the start they were too busy keeping their husbands captivated to have any spare nights for girls like me: the Unfortunate Unmarried. And so, sure, maybe I did spend most of my time longing for John, but part of that yearning was pure: a prayer for someone to talk to who had something to say.

Gladys continued to squint out at the bay. A slight breeze ruffled her bangs, and she clapped them tight against her forehead as if her head had been hit by a hurricane. "So anyway, he had this house on the water," she went on. "And then his wife dies. Well! Linda, there were *days* at a time when he didn't show up at work. He didn't even call in or anything. You know what he did? He'd leave little Nan with her nanny—isn't that funny? Nan, nanny—and drive up to Connecticut and take out his sailboat and just sail for four or five days, *all alone*. Not that anyone ever said anything." She looked away from the bay, right at me. "They wouldn't have dared. I mean, even way back then, Mr. Leland had that way about him, and being a war hero and all that, he could pretty much do what he wanted. But you know what the most fascinating thing is? He chose classiness. It was what he automatically wanted, even in grief. I mean, sailing is *very* stylish."

"Why does going out in a sailboat make him classy? Is puking on a starboard or whatever it's called an upper-class mourning practice?"

"You just talk like that to get attention," Gladys said. " 'Puking.' And sex things."

"Never in the same sentence."

"I'm serious, Linda. And if you don't mind, while I'm on the subject of your talking: You kept forcing everybody at lunch Friday to listen while you went on about the war, like you were a man or a college professor and it was really interesting. You've got to stop it. I mean, name me one single person in the law firm—not counting lawyers—who wants to hear about troop movements. I'll bet you anything the lawyers don't even care."

I looked across the dazzling sunlit water. "Listen to me,

Gladys. Don't you understand that it's not just Europe—or Asia? It's the whole world. It's *you*."

"Stop it."

"I'm telling you, France will be next."

"Here it comes: Miss Linda Voss with her ever-popular 'The Big, Bad Nazis' song and dance."

"Gladys, don't you get what people are letting Hitler do to them? They're giving up because they're terrified—of a bully. What do they think he's going to do next? Send them roses? No, he's going to hit them again, harder and harder."

Unlike Gladys, the part of the world that read beyond the society news and the comics was actually surprised. That was what was so hard for me to believe: that all the military geniuses and hotshot politicians couldn't have figured out what was going to happen.

In Brooklyn it was a beautiful spring Sunday. People were smiling as if they didn't have a care in the world. But the Germans were on the march again. Holland was gone, Belgium was going.

"You always expect the worst from them," Gladys said.

"They always do the worst."

"But you're German, Linda."

"I am not."

"I don't mean you go around drinking beer from those funny glasses. It's just that . . . you are *very* interested in whatever they do."

"Aren't you?"

"Not the way you are. I mean, grabbing everybody's newspaper, reading *battle* reports." She looked at me accusingly. "Anita was talking about her bridesmaids' gifts, and you started going on about the Maginot Line."

The Sunday crowds filled the sidewalks. Teenage boys spilled onto the piers. They'd taken off their shirts, ignoring the slight spring chill, and rolled them into pillows and stretched out on the wood boards. Their chests, white from winter, rose and fell with each relaxed breath. But before long, a dark, leather-skinned boat captain yelled, "Hey, get outta here!" And the kids got up, put on their shirts and shuffled off, mumbling, "In your hat and over your ears, bud." But they were a good-natured bunch.

"Gladys, listen to me. If those boys lived in the countries their families came from, they'd be carrying rifles." Then I added: "Or they'd be dead."

Gladys started to stroll again. I gave up and went along. Everyone in the city wanted to be outside on a day like this. They all seemed to have grabbed a trolley and come to Sheepshead Bay to stare at the water and inhale the sharp salt air. For a nickel, it was like traveling to another country. Gladys and I weaved in and out of the crowd. Finally, we found an empty bench. I sat and put my head way back and let the sun warm my cheeks.

Gladys and I spent every Sunday together; I wasn't sure whether to feel grateful or doomed. It had started a couple of months after my Grandma Olga died. Suddenly, I had a long day with no company; Saturday was Binge Night for my mother, so Sundays she could barely manage to stagger to the bathroom, much less walk around the block. I'd said to Gladys one Friday in the office, Maybe if you're free Sunday, if you want to go to a movie or something . . . I was nervous she'd think I was overstepping the bounds of what was a nice office friendship, but she said, Well, I have nothing special this Sunday, as if every other Sunday for the next two years was booked up.

So we went to a movie and then out for a club sandwich, and while I was trying to decide whether to wait three or six months before asking again, Gladys said, Do you want to go for a ride on the Staten Island ferry next Sunday?

After all those years with the whole world married, I had someone to do things with. A friend. We went all over the city, mainly to movies, but sometimes to the zoo, the botanical gardens, a couple of times even to a museum.

She was my best friend, my only one, but all we ever had on those Sundays was more lunch conversation—although with hideously elaborate detail. Did you know Mr. Nugent was Phi Beta Kappa? You never saw his key? Or: Helen Rogers says Margaret on the switchboard says the widow Mr. Leland is keeping company with is a Mrs. Carter. Or Mrs. Carver. Last year he was seeing Mrs. Lambert Jones. The divorcée, but it wasn't her fault. Did I tell you about her? See, her husband fell in love with her son's cello teacher. Anyway, Mrs. Jones—the first one; she's not supposed to be musical and the husband *loved* music—she has practically a mansion on Fifth Avenue and . . .

Gladys was ecstatic to have all Sunday—an entire day uninterrupted by work—to talk about the office. Blair, VanderGraff and Wadley: that was the extent of her life. And I never asked for anything deeper from her, because I'd poked around and discovered her passion for the law firm was her sole passion. She liked the movies only to the degree that Gary Cooper in *Sergeant York* reminded her of Mr. Leland.

"If you're so American," Gladys suddenly said to me, "why did you bring German magazines to the office? And how come you know more about what's happening over there than Roosevelt?"

"If I know more than Roosevelt, then we're all going to be goose-stepping a year from now." I turned and looked at her. "Listen, don't you understand what's going on over there?"

"I read the *Mirror* and the *Journal-American*."

"So?"

"So I still can't see why you get so . . ." She paused to find a word. "Upset."

"Upset? Did the *Mirror* or the *Journal* happen to mention what those Nazi shit-heads did to Holland?"

"Linda!"

We both sat back and stared out at the bay; she wouldn't look at me. The boats at the piers right in front of us—*Little Muriel* and *Star of Brooklyn*—bobbed on the gentle, lapping water. The Nazis were bombing Belgium, mopping up in Holland—murdering the few good men they hadn't already slaughtered—and Gladys was reeling from shock because I'd called them shit-heads.

I couldn't understand people. Gladys, the other girls at work, my neighbors. Why weren't they angrier? I got hot under the collar just thinking about the excuses people had been making since the year before: Oh, Hitler had some good reasons for going into Czechoslovakia.

Come on. If you're a German dictator with a problem, you throw a few chancellors together in a room and you figure something out. You don't go rolling in with panzer divisions.

If you have a beef with someone, do you send in the Luftwaffe with a couple of tons of bombs, the way he did to Rotterdam, that son of a bitch?

"Do you really think he'll go into France?" Gladys finally asked. Her voice was a little softer; maybe I was too hard on her. She was no dope, but she didn't want any part of what was happening over there, so she'd simply put it out of her mind. Now, though, Americans were beginning to get troubled. Frightened, even. I could hear it—that tremor of fear, that Oh, no, I could get *hurt*—in Gladys's voice. But why wasn't she—why weren't all of them—angry, like me?

"Of course he'll go into France," I said. "And all we can hope is that the French are tougher and smarter than I think they are."

"What if he beats them?"

"Gladys, what do you think?"

"I don't know."

"England."

"No. Come *on*."

Gladys got up and walked over to an ice cream cart. It was an old white icebox on two bicycle wheels, covered with decals of ice cream pops, cones, and sundaes in every gorgeous color possible. Usually, though, all the carts ever had was vanilla, so soft that by the time it got scooped into the cone and handed over to you, it was mush that flowed over your hand and down your arm.

What if I could *really* talk to John. I'd say, You know, tw years ago, right around this time of year, I was sitting on a park bench in Ridgewood with my Grandma Olga. Such a smart lady, but she was still saying, "Hitler and his people. Trash."

John would believe me. He'd know that when Hitler came into power, most of the German-speaking people in America, like Olga, viewed him as if he was some slobby fifth cousin who shows up at Christmas dinner, shoots off his mouth, and then drools into the *Berliner Schlosspunsch*; he wouldn't be around long. But he was, and none of those smart German-speakers could explain it or understand it. So they said, Oh, well, what's the real harm in it? When I'd explained the harm to Olga in 1935 she didn't believe me. That day in 1938 in the park she'd said, "You'll see, he'll calm down, now that everyone takes him seriously." I answered sharply: "No he won't. And you-know-who he especially won't calm down about."

Olga didn't say anything, dismissing my reminder; she may have been a Jew, but she wasn't a *Jew*. Finally she said: "But even if you're right, Linda, what can we do?"

What can we do? That kind of thinking would make John as crazy as it made me. We'd agree that what got us more than anything else was the effect of that maniac on *everyone*, not just on an old German lady. On big, strong, smart men. Listen to any of his speeches—not the few sentences before the radio switched over to the commentator and the Jell-O commercial—and just *hear* the German under the voice of the translator. I would turn to John and say, Listen, you know he is out of his mind with his rantings about Siegfried and a whole bunch of stupid Germanic gods—what's he talking about? And his carrying on about inferior races. What was *he?* John would answer: The lowest of the low. He'd understand.

All you had to do was look at Hitler and you saw it—a flat, mean peasant face. But right from the beginning, all these big, strong, smart men fell apart the minute he challenged them. Old von Hindenburg, the cream of the crop, the best Germany had to offer: What does he do? He says, Here, Herr Hitler, take Germany. It's yours. Take whatever you want.

And before Hindenburg bellied up, all you had to do was read the paper to realize what Hitler and his group were: garbage. The worst kind of garbage, because they weren't just out-of-control animals or petty criminals. They were twisted, and so filled with hate that one or two nights' rampage wasn't enough to wear them out. *Nothing* would ever be enough for them, and I knew it and anyone with half a brain knew it, and what I wanted to know was *why*, damn it. Look at all the best men in Germany, the best men all over the world, and tell me why their guts turned to calf's-foot jelly over the Nazis—over garbage.

If men can't be men, who do they expect to be brave? Women?

John would say, Don't worry. There are men like me. . . . We'll take care of it.

Gladys came back empty-handed from the ice cream wagon. "They were out of strawberry," she said.

"Too bad." Maybe I'd sounded too sarcastic. Why should I be mad at Gladys because she wasn't mad at Hitler? Neither one of us had a life so full of wonderful moments that we could afford to throw away a perfect Sunday where passersby might smile at us, where a strange man might tip his hat. We needed whatever pleasure we could find—including strawberry. "You want to look for a candy store or something?"

"No." She sat down beside me. "I don't want to give up the bench." She waited for a second and asked her inevitable next question: "Anything new with Mr. B?"

"Nothing."

"He hasn't said *anything?*"

"Not a peep."

"No"—she gave me a significant stare—"signs?"

"Not even a twitch. But you know beneath all those Charlie Charming smiles he's not the most emotional guy in the world."

"Linda, do you honestly think he *cares* she's gone?"

"He's got to care. I mean, forget the marriage stuff—you know, man and wife. Who does he have to talk to?"

Gladys nodded. And then I thought, Who do *I* have to talk to? Not about Mr. Leland's dead wife or Mr. Avenel's unfortunately live one, but about the world. If I could actually talk to John, not just imagine conversations . . . He knows so much. We could discuss—

"Oh, look! There's another cart down there, past the big boat," Gladys said. "You want anything?" I shook my head. "Let me see if they have strawberry. I'll be right back."

Gladys hurried off to the right. From the left, a group of day fishermen in mashed-down sports hats clomped by, carrying their catch on strings; the flounders, still wet, dribbled along the sidewalk. Then one of the men opened his mouth wide and held up his string of fish over it and—while the others gave off loud, manly ho-ho-hos—let the fish water drip down his throat.

I wanted so much to *talk*, to be able to ask John why—forgetting Germany for a minute—why all the little countries and England and France could say, Okay, Adolf, old buddy, it's all yours. What was wrong with them? Were they terrified by a couple of torchlight parades? By rifles? Did Franklin Delano Roosevelt go belly-up to the Ku Klux Klan? No! So why did they just give in to the Nazis?

Gladys was coming back with a broad smile and a strawberry ice cream cone. Her Sunday was a success. We'd talk about John and Nan and the mysterious Quentin. We'd look out at the water some more, then close our eyes and once again put back our heads for a few minutes. When we'd open our eyes, the sky would be a gorgeous blue.

Whenever I thought of Europe, I imagined its skies clouded and dismal, like just before a storm. But it had to be spring there too.

Then I thought about Gladys and her ice cream cone, the fishermen, and all the people strolling along Sheepshead Bay in their flowered dresses and seersucker slacks. And what I was really dying to ask John—because he would know, he would care—was, Are we any different? Would we have the guts? Or will it turn dark here too?

But talking to him, kissing him . . . Forget it. It still was all a dream.

# 6

The file room had Blair, VanderGraff and Wadley's records starting from 1916, and the air was sour, as if some major case—the 1927 General Motors litigation—had sprouted mold years before. But although it smelled, at least it was private—at the end of a long, narrow tiled hallway, so you could hear the tap of footsteps ten yards off. And you had the absolute peace of mind of knowing the footsteps were made by a secretary. Guaranteed: Since the signing of the Magna Carta, no lawyer has ever retrieved his own files.

I waited, alone, peering up at the shelves sagging under the weight of old cartons of dead cases. Then Gladys slipped in and, three seconds later, Lenny Stevenson. Lenny came in on an angle; she really wasn't that huge, but her mental picture of her own bigness ruled her whole life. And while it was true that no one would ever slip and call her dainty, she wasn't King Kong. Still, she maneuvered as if anticipating the doorway would not be wide enough to hold her. "Hiya," she said quickly. She wasn't much for elaborate greetings. Then she gave Gladys an am-I-supposed-to-talk look.

"I'll tell her," Gladys said. Lenny sighed with relief at getting off the social-chitchat hook, a sound that in the funnies is written "Whew!" Meanwhile, Gladys patted her hair and blotted her lips together, as if cameras were about to roll and capture this earth-shaking announcement. "Linda, we found out who Quentin is!"

"Oh, come on!"

Gladys made a big dramatic deal of cleaning the clip-onto-the-nose glasses she wore for close work; they hung from a rust-colored ribbon around her neck. "We did some detecting," she said finally. She tapped Lenny gently on the arm. "Go ahead, Lenore. Tell her."

"Uh," Lenny began. She paused. She swallowed. "Um . . . you know Dahlmaier Brothers?" Lenny asked. "The investment banking firm?"

"We represent them," Gladys informed me.

"I know."

"Anyway," Lenny went on, "they had a question about our billing. I was looking at their letter and saying, Those financiers can't even add; no wonder there was a Depression—when all of a sudden something catches my eye. Guess what?"

"What?" I asked.

"On the top of the stationery, on the left-hand side, there were all these names. Nicholas Dahlmaier, Reynolds Dahlmaier—"

"Quentin Dahlmaier," I said.

"You knew!" Lenny exclaimed. She wasn't really dumb; she just didn't understand people. I think her size as well as her lack of any quality that might be called feminine had made her pull away from the world of women and men; she wasn't fish and wasn't fowl, so she hid in her ledgers, so much so that she couldn't even join in the easy give-and-take of everyday talk. When you said, Hi, Lenny, how are you? you could actually see her think before she answered.

"Go on, Lenny," Gladys urged.

"Wait a second," I interrupted. "Quentin's not the most common name in the world, but there's got to be more than one in the entire borough of Manhattan. It's probably—"

"Linda, would you please?" Gladys demanded grandly, like she was Bette Davis in a very-great-lady role. Then she nodded—graciously—at Lenny, a do-go-on nod.

So Lenny went on. "Anyway, I saw this name, Quentin, and I figured what do I got to lose? So I called up the bookkeeper over there to explain the billing—and I got chatty with her."

"I told her to," Gladys explained to me.

You'd think Lenny would have been insulted, with Gladys coming right out and saying she was running the show. But Lenny wasn't. She was gazing down at Gladys's plain, big-nostriled, I-know-everything face with so much respect it was almost adoration. Lenny could have been a nun (a king-sized nun) staring at a little statue of the Virgin Mary.

"Right," Lenny agreed. "I said everything that Gladys told me. I said to the bookkeeper, Gee, the name Quentin Dahlmaier is *so* familiar. Where do I know it from? Was he in the paper or something? And she says to me, Well, there was a story about him in the *Times* or the *Trib* when he gave all that money to the Philharmonic. So I told her, Yeah, that must be it, the Philharmonic. And then *she* says to *me*, What did I think about his picture, wasn't he distinguished-looking? And so I said, You know, it's hard to tell from a newspaper picture."

"Good work, Len," I said.

Lenny grinned. She had too much of everything; her smile was so vast it looked as if she had sixty-four teeth.

"She said he's very good-looking for an older man, so I asked her how old he was, and she said she thinks about forty—"

"Then that can't be him," I interrupted, "because Nan's just twenty-one and—"

This time I was interrupted, by Gladys. "Mr. Berringer's what? Thirty-four, thirty-five?"

"Thirty-five," I said.

"So? What's five more years to a girl like that? Go ahead, Lenny."

"Anyway, she said he's filthy rich—all the Dahlmaiers are filthy rich—and that he had a winter house in Palm Beach and a summer house in Southampton on Long Island, but—"

"Listen to this 'but,' " Gladys said breathlessly.

"He's planning on going away the *whole* summer. The bookkeeper said usually he just goes to Europe for one month—to Monte Carlo for two weeks and then either Ire-land or Scotland, but now with the war—"

"Terrible how it louses up people's vacations," I said. Gladys actually nodded, so I went on: "But listen, just because he's taking an extra month off doesn't mean he's going on a honeymoon. I bet you it turns out he's married."

"Well, you bet wrong, because he's *divorced*," Gladys said.

Lenny added, "She told me, Mr. Quentin's divorced, you know, so I said, Oh, yeah, I'd heard about it."

"Just because he's divorced . . ." I protested. This all fit my dream world so well, it was so perfect—from the debonair name Quentin all the way to the Palm Beach house, which I just knew had to be cream with a red tile roof—I couldn't believe it. "Rich people's marriages break up all the time. They have nothing else to do and they're bored, so a divorce is like going to the most emotional movie in the world—except it's starring them."

Gladys rolled her eyes the way the comedians used to do in vaudeville skits when they got stuck with a real dumb hopeless case. "Tell her what else, Len."

"See, I was kidding around with this bookkeeper about this Quentin Dahlmaier being a catch—"

"And guess what?" Gladys interrupted.

"The bookkeeper said, Not anymore he's not. At least she doesn't think so. There's all sorts of talk around Dahlmaier Brothers that Mr. Quentin is getting married, and his secretary told her—the bookkeeper—that he's on the phone two or three hours a day with a lady in Reno, but even his secretary doesn't know her name because Mr. Quentin told her, 'Just get me connected and I'll take care of the rest.' Like he didn't want anyone, even his private secretary, to know the lady's name. So anyway, I said, Gee, did the secretary happen to say where the lady's staying in Reno? I got a cousin in Reno."

"Good work, Len!" I said. "Did she know where?"

Lenny grinned. "The Bar None Ranch!"

"Now do you want to hear what *I* found out?" Gladys demanded.

I smiled. The two of them weren't exactly Mata Hari, but they weren't bad. "Sure."

"I went over to Marian Mulligan's desk to borrow her staple remover and said, Oh, by the way, when you sent all the papers to Mrs. Berringer in Reno, do you happen to remember the address? My cousin's boss has a sister who's going to get a divorce. And believe me, Marian didn't have to look it up."

"The Bar None Ranch," I said.

"How many almost-divorced ladies establishing residency in Nevada at the Bar None Ranch in Reno are going to marry men named Quentin?"

"What do you think, Linda?" Lenny asked.

"*Great* detective work!" I rested my elbow on a dusty carton. "God, Quentin Dahlmaier."

"And *Mrs*. Quentin Dahlmaier," Gladys added.

I smiled again, an even bigger one. If Nan was going to change her mind, she had a week and a half. And with good old filthy-rich, Philharmonic-loving Quentin on the phone with her two or three hours a day, she probably wouldn't want to.

It finally happened about two weeks later, in, of all places, the Blue Elephant, the bar all the secretaries went to. Any decent place with that name would have had lots of pudgy blue elephants pasted up on the wall, or girl and boy elephants on the ladies' and men's rooms, or blue swizzle sticks. But all the Blue Elephant had was an elephant painted on the mirror over the bar, and a pretty crummy painting too; most of the elephant's rear end had flaked off—probably into the bourbon.

Not that it bothered the drinkers at the bar. Though it was a Tuesday night, all the stools were filled. Despite the dark, I could get a pretty good idea of them from my table. Sad silhouettes: middle-aged associates never tapped for partner, brokers so down on their luck they couldn't even find a potential customer to buy a drink for.

The rest of the Blue Elephant, the cocktail lounge, was where the law firm secretaries went to sit in peace and quiet. The drinks weren't too expensive, and you didn't have to put up with who-do-you-think-you-are-coming-here stares, like in the fancier places. Also, the guys at the Blue Elephant bar were serious drinkers, almost always too far gone to think about girls, much less make a pass.

"Another?" the waiter asked.

I still had three quarters of my sloe gin fizz. I'd ordered it because what the heck, it was June, and I couldn't think of any other summery drink, but it was so sweet, like a lime rickey, that it coated your whole mouth and made you want to run out screaming for a toothbrush. "No, thanks. I'll wait for my friend to get here." He gave me a look, as if he had a mile-long line of parched boozers begging for my table, even though over half the tables were empty, but I didn't give in, so he walked away.

It was twenty after six, and it looked like Gladys was a lost cause. After lunch she'd said, Remember Pat Keyes with the club-foot, who used to work for Mr. VanderGraff, Jr.? I just found out her sister Marie is a keypunch operator at Dahlmaier Brothers. I'll give her a call and see what else I can learn about Mr. Quentin. Meet me for a drink after work, okay? Gladys's eyebrows had gone up and down. I think she was trying to look sophisticated, but she looked more like Groucho Marx.

But when I went to pick her up, Gladys was sitting at her desk, tapping her foot, waiting for Mr. Avenel to reword a clause. She said, He's *still* on the phone with Madame, so if I'm not at the Elephant by six, don't hang around.

I gave up and paid the bill. Whatever goods Gladys had gotten on Quentin would have to wait for tomorrow, because she didn't have a phone in the room she rented, and the owners of the house she lived in wouldn't take calls for her.

Still, I could be patient. If the information I'd pried out of Marian Mulligan that morning was right, Nan had left Reno and was probably with Mr. Quentin Dahlmaier—three days into their honeymoon. I tried to picture old Quentin, but all I could come up with was the standard rich guy: gray at the temples, tan from Palm Beach and Southampton, thin—like Basil Rathbone—with a smoking jacket. He and Nan would be taking glasses of champagne from a silver tray the butler was holding. It was like a hundred movies—all second features—I'd seen. Sublime honeymoon, Nan, darling. And we'll have the entire summer together too. Gad, how we shall frolic!

I passed the bar. Out of the corner of my eye, I noticed one of the men swing around and get up. I felt, more than I saw, that he was heading toward me, and not too steady, either. No big deal, I figured: This one's so pie-eyed he'll probably be using his nose for a pillow by the time I'm out the door. So I just kept going.

Not fast enough. Just as I reached the door, a hand tightened around my arm. Before I could say anything, the man pushed me against the wall of the tiny vestibule. His Scotch breath was humid on my face as he said, "Hello." Not letting me go. But what could happen to me in a public place? Still my heart started pounding as if it was trying to bang its way out of my chest. The man wouldn't loosen his grip, and it was tight. I pulled, trying to free my arm and get away. But he moved in closer, using his entire body to pin me to the wall.

"Listen, you creep . . ." I began, and real loud too. Nothing happened for a second, but then he backed off, tripping a little over his own feet, and mine. But he still held on to my arm. I tried to tear it out of his grasp. "Let *go*." I put a you-watch-it-Buster glint in my eye. It faded fast.

"I just wanted to say hello," John Berringer said softly. "I'm all alone. I have no one to talk to." Even in the near dark, I could see his eyes mist over. "Do you know what happened to me?" Even though his voice was soft, his question was for the whole world.

He was drunk. Not falling-down, but his words were a sad slur: Know wha' 'appena me? "I'm sorry," I said, and eased my arm out of his grasp. That very second, my heart started up again. Boom! He'd actually been touching me!

Then he started to sway so slowly that only someone who'd lived with a drunk would realize that any second he'd be crashing onto the floor.

"Hey," I said, grabbing his shoulders, bracing him.

We were so close then. In the red light from the exit sign over the doorway, his face was flushed, steamy. Strands of hair lay wet on his forehead. "Are you okay, Mr. Berringer?" He didn't answer. "Mr. Berringer?" Oh, this was going to be great the next morning, when I had to look him straight in the eye. "Would you like me to get you a cab?" I asked him.

I didn't wait for an answer. I started to slip past him. But then he moved fast, for a drunk. He blocked my path and gave me the beginnings of a smile—as if he wasn't quite in control of his gorgeousness and wasn't sure what effect the smile would have. I tried to smile back. But there wasn't time. Suddenly, he slammed me against the wall.

"Please, Mr. Berringer."

He pressed himself so hard against me I could feel something I never thought I'd feel in my whole life. "I'm all alone," he whispered, and started rubbing against me. "Don't push me away."

This has to stop, I thought, but when I opened my mouth I didn't say it. All I could think of was the feel of him, of his legs touching mine. If anyone walked by . . . I wanted to warn him, but there were no words. I tried. I looked up.

His mouth came down and right away I was kissing him back. And suddenly that kiss became all there was in the world. It went on and on.

We couldn't stop; we could go on forever. Both of us began to let out noises that weren't even words. And I lost all awareness of time, of reason, certainly of common sense. All I wanted was more of John.

I swear to God I would have done it right there, in that public vestibule, standing up. He grabbed my hair, yanked my head back so it hurt, and kissed me even harder. He was so drunk. He pushed against me so hard I could hardly breathe anymore. That's when I started to fight him, just to get some air.

"Don't leave me," he said. But then he backed off a fraction of an inch. "Come on, you want it as much as I do."

Oh, I did. "Yes." I put my arms around him and drew his face near. I rubbed my cheek up and down against his, then slowly brought my mouth back to his again.

But this time his kiss was gentle, brushing, barely touching—teasing. I tried to pull him back into the embrace we'd been in before, but he wouldn't be pulled. I thrust out my bottom to get his attention again, but he stepped back. "All right," he said. Still drunk, but I knew him enough to know his mind had started working again. Dear God, I thought, don't end it yet. Just a little more. He reached behind him, unfastened i. y arms from around his neck and placed them at my sides.

"I ought to be getting home," I whispered. It was hard to talk. My mouth was raw from kissing. But also, I did not want to cry.

"No," he said. "You'll come with me." Then he got behind me and pushed me out the door.

The electric chair probably hurts a lot, and so must being flogged, but for plain, ordinary agony, you can't beat embarrassed silence.

In the taxi, John gave the driver his address, then settled back into the seat like he was alone, with a lot to think about. His head tilted back, his eyes were half closed. It was a perfect profile, and each time we drove past a streetlight, his hair shone.

He didn't touch me. By the second red light, I wanted to jump out; I didn't want to see the expression of horror—Oh, no!—on his face when he sobered up and realized what he'd done.

I did try to relax, sit back. At least I could enjoy the ride. I'd only been in a cab once: to go to the hospital to identify what was left of my father. People from Ridgewood who took taxis sat in the driver's seat. I tried very hard; I looked out the window as we drove up Fifth Avenue, attempting to look rich and bored with being in a cab, but I couldn't concentrate. I kept turning around to get another look at John. I couldn't get enough of him.

A couple of times I almost spoke up: It sure is muggy out, and then, It's getting late and you look tired, so why don't I . . . You know how they say words get stuck in your throat? Mine never got that far. I was mesmerized by John's upstretched neck, still glossy with sweat, the fullness of his mouth. There was nothing I could say. Silence filled the cab like smoke.

The driver must have sniffed something, because he kept sneaking looks in his rearview mirror. At the same time, I could see his bald head and his reflected pale eyes. At one point, he seemed about to turn around and open his mouth—maybe with a breezy: Hey, by any chance you Dodger fans?—but he must have sensed something, because he quickly shifted gears and sped on.

"Do you know about my wife?" John boomed out so suddenly the driver and I both almost jumped out of our skins. "Do you know she's gone? Do you?"

I nodded.

"Do you know why she left?" His voice wasn't just loud, it was out of control, almost shouting. "I asked you a question. Do you know why she left?" I shook my head. "She said she needed something more." He looked at me suddenly, straight in the eye. I couldn't meet his glance. I turned away. The cabdriver was watching everything in the rearview mirror. A great show, and the tickets were free.

"Shhh," I said to John. I didn't say it as much as breathe it: to soothe him without angering him. He didn't hear me.

"What she meant was, she needed *someone* more."

"The driver," I mumbled.

"What?"

"The driver," I repeated, this time in German.

Drunk, but not that drunk. He switched languages. "She found a man who could give her more. Whatever more is. Do you know what more is?"

"No."

The driver was so beside himself he hardly had his eyes on the street anymore. "I don't know what it is, either," John went on. I met the driver's eyes in the mirror. He turned his away fast, but still, the suspicion was there; here was a guy who probably watched as many British movies as I did. Nazi swine! his eyes said. Secret agents! In his cab! "All I know," John continued, his voice softer in his educated German, "is that three days ago my wife got married. That's illogical, isn't it? If she's my wife, how could she have gotten married? Therefore, either she is not married or not my wife." His eyes filled up, and he wiped them with the back of his hand. "My wife," he whispered.

At a light, the driver turned around and very slowly, as if he wanted to make himself understood to foreigners (and foreigners up to no good), asked, "Sev-en-ty-fifth be-tween what and what?"

John was about to continue; I really don't think he heard. "Um," I said, "the driver. He wants to know what streets you live between."

"Park and Lex," he said, back in English.

The driver gave us one last once-over before he turned back. I knew what he was thinking. I could hear the lines from the movie of his life story, *The Isidore Pincus Story*, playing in his head: "Their English was exceptionally good, Mr. President, and that aroused my suspicions as much as . . ."

Silence filled the cab again, but this time John's eyes were open. On me. Not looking into my face for understanding. Looking south.

"That's a nice dress," he said softly.

"Thank you."

He lifted the hem and rubbed the material between his thumb and index finger. "Very nice." A rayon dress for $6.95 isn't very nice.

But by the time I got out another thank you, his hand had slipped beneath the dress. I watched it slide up under the fabric, snaking along my leg. The driver stretched his neck. I lifted my hand to push John's away, but he spoke again in German. "Kiss me." I kissed him lightly on the cheek. "Not like that." I kissed him on the mouth. When I glanced over, the cabdriver was watching the Nazi spies pretending to be lovers. Then I turned away and forgot him as I kissed John again.

His hand inched higher. His fingers slipped under the top of my stocking and started massaging the inside of my thigh. How did he know how good that felt? His other hand circled me and pulled me close. "Don't stop kissing me," he murmured. "Please." I didn't. I couldn't.

The taxi screeched to a standstill. My head banged against the window. And as we started to straighten up, we heard the driver. In a voice even louder than John's had been, he announced: "Achtung! Ve haff arrived!"

John hurried me through the apartment, so even though he flipped on a couple of lights, the only room I really saw was the bedroom. He was going so fast I got scared. I tried to calm myself by saying, Okay, you're thirty-one years old, and even though you're no Jezebel, you're no tender flower of innocence, either. What did you expect, a guided tour? On your right, Miss Voss, is an ultramodern couch. And over here on the piano is my wedding picture. Please, come into the kitchen so I can show you where I keep the can opener.

He pulled off his jacket and tossed it onto a chair. I waited for him to hang it up; he was so neat in the office he never even left a fingerprint. But no, he pulled off his tie. By the time it landed on top of the jacket, he was already unbuttoning his shirt. Oh, God, I thought, he's going to take off all his clothes!

I looked around the room. Nan's work. A double bed that looked like a mattress floating on air. A couple of expensive boxes—night tables—and a chair made of the same shiny wood as his desk in the office. A big, ugly painting above the bed, modern art—thick green smears, like someone had gone nuts with a can of peas. Not a dresser in sight, but a wall of doors, so maybe they kept their underwear and hankies and . . . Out of the corner of my eye, I saw his shirt drifting down onto the pile of clothes on the chair.

I started to study my shoes, but a second later, I knew his undershirt was off. I was about to look up, but that second I heard the sound of a zipper. I turned around and faced the door.

What was I going to do? Run into the closet? My heart raced.

"Aren't you going to turn around?" he asked me.

I shook my head. The hall outside the bedroom was a dark rectangle framed by the door. He came up behind me, put his arms around me and drew me against him. I could feel his nakedness along my whole back. For a minute I stiffened, but then my eyes started to close. I leaned back against him, almost drowsy. Then I opened my eyes and looked down. His arms were bare, strong, beautiful. The veins in his hands ran up his forearms. One arm hooked around my waist. The other held my shoulder, and his thumb moved back and forth in a slow massage. I took his hand from my waist and cupped it over my breast.

He didn't need much more, and neither did I. He spun me around, and the instant before he kissed me, I saw him. I whispered, "Oh, my." It was as if he'd been carved instead of born.

"Do you like me?" he asked, and he wasn't asking if I thought he was a nice guy.

"Yes."

"Let me see you, then."

"I can't."

"Come on, Linda."

I almost fainted, him calling me Linda for the first time ever, and so handsome he was beyond handsome; he was beautiful. And while I was concentrating on not getting the shakes, he put his arms around me.

I raised my head for another kiss, and he gave me one, but

his real business was unbuttoning the back of my dress. I kept kissing him, though, concentrating on him, on his smell of Scotch and sweat, the manliest smell, letting myself get so intoxicated from it that I hardly felt my dress dropping to the floor, my slip being pulled over my head. Suddenly it seemed the most natural thing, getting rid of all those tight clothes.

He took off my brassiere and touched me till I was dizzy. Then he dropped to his knees and unhooked my garters. My fingers played with his hair. He put his arms around me, pressing his cheek to my midriff before he stood up again and kissed me.

"Take off the rest," he ordered.

I pulled off my girdle, my underpants, my stockings. He watched. When I was as naked as he was, he pulled me to him again. I was thirty-one years old, and this was the first time I was alive.

Then he led me to the bed. He yanked away the covers and pushed me down.

"Do you know how beautiful you are?" he asked as he lay down beside me. Tell me how beautiful, I thought.

Then I remembered something I'd heard: When men were drunk, something happened to them in the bedroom. But I was too shaky to remember. It took longer? Shorter? They couldn't do it at all? They could, and better?

John could. Better. He ran his fingers from my neck down to my stomach, and below. Then he kissed me, his lips following the same path as his hand. "So beautiful." He wasn't talking about my face. He worked his way up again, "Linda." I was so beside myself that when we started to kiss again I had tears in my eyes. "I always thought you must be something," he said, "but not like this."

He'd thought of me before! I wanted to think about that, savor it, but when two bodies are that close and that hot, brains stop. There were no more words.

Magic. That's what happened between John and me. From his first kiss I knew all my imaginings were right. And I knew he'd brought me home because, in that ugly little bar, drunk, lonely, tired, his defenses down, he'd somehow understood there was magic too.

But neither of us realized how powerful the magic was until it happened. It was as if everything else we had done in our lives wasn't worth a thing. *This* was what each of us had been created for, to be half of something greater than any other two people in the world.

In that messed-up, sweaty bed, John Berringer and Linda Voss became a miracle.

# 7

They never touched this one in business etiquette. Not one teacher at Grover Cleveland ever told us: After you do everything in the book with your employer, including some things you'd heard about but didn't believe people really did, the correct behavior is to—how best to put it, girls?— get up, put on your girdle and say, Will that be all, sir?

So I was at a loss, and it's terrible to be at a loss and naked. Just minutes before, the two of us had been the perfect pair. And now, the perfect mistake. Lying beside John, no longer touching, but still close enough to feel the heat rising from his skin, I agonized, trying to think of something to say that wouldn't make him groan to himself, How the hell am I going to get out of this nightmare?

But as it turned out, all my agonizing was wasted; John's breathing grew slow, low, slower, and then very loud. He hadn't been going crazy over how to ditch me; he'd fallen into a drunken sleep.

At least I knew all about that. What he was to international commercial law, I was to boozers. And John was a doozy: stretched out flat on his back, one arm hanging limp over the edge of the mattress while the other gently cradled his pillow, his hand now and then moving as if he was still doing it, stroking the pillow or cupping a feather-filled corner.

Slowly, I slid off the bed and tippytoed over to my clothes. But no, I didn't have to be careful. I could have belted out "The Star-Spangled Banner"; it would have taken a ton of TNT to blow John out of bed.

I got dressed slowly, as if he was watching me—arching my foot like a ballerina when I put on my stockings, then lifting my leg up real high. When I hooked my brassiere, I turned my back to him, but then I peeked back over my shoulder: so coy. I said to myself, You must look like a soon-to-be has-been starlet in the back pages of *Photoplay*. But then I realized I was just copying any sexy gesture I could, because I'd never really felt that the part of me from the neck down was so . . . so useful. I touched—caressed, really—the skin on my shoulder and then turned around to look straight at John.

But then I couldn't stand to leave. What was there in Ridgewood—in all the rest of the world—that could beat this? I sat on the edge of the mattress, right beside him, like a wife. When I combed back his hair with my fingers, he didn't stir.

He was so wonderful to watch. Everything. The curlicues of hair on his stomach made little *c*'s and *o*'s. Finally he rolled away from me, over onto his side. His back was graceful, wide-shouldered, narrow-waisted and strong, as if he spent his days on parallel bars instead of practicing law. At last I stood, covered him with the sheet and left the room.

But when it came to leaving the apartment . . . Well, I couldn't. Not only did I want to know more about him; I wanted a detailed map of his life. I wanted every question answered. I moved around, poking into drawers and closets. I went through every room like a sleazy detective. Down on my knees to see if there was anything interesting under the pale living room couch. (Just beige carpet.) I opened the linen closet, to check the color of the towels: beige again, with Nan's monogram in white. I even examined the dishes in the sink: white.

If John and Nan's apartment meant anything, it meant good taste was the opposite of what I liked. *Nothing* there had any color, not even the food; all that was in the refrigerator was a bottle of milk that smelled as if Nan had bought it right before she caught the 8:02 to Reno (to prevent John, starving to death a day or two later, from committing some atrocious crime, like bringing orange juice or red meat or green beans into the apartment).

Only the few paintings she'd left had color. There were four or five empty picture hooks. But you'd have to be a big smear fan to appreciate the art she'd left. Yellow globs and black brush strokes in the hall. In the living room, one with skinny blue lines, like a close-up of varicose veins.

Suddenly, I felt so tired. I turned my back on the blue lines and walked over to the window. I opened it a crack, leaned my forehead against the cool glass and looked down at the street. Silent, except for one "Come on, stupid!" of a man walking his wife's toy poodle. Even from six stories up, you could see the rhinestone collar on the dog's neck. What kind of a man would let a woman make him walk a dog with a rhinestone collar?

My eyes closed. Oh, how I wanted to sleep. But one thing I knew: Either I got out right away and made the long subway trip back to Queens, or I'd be drawn back into the bedroom.

What got me going was the picture of John's horrified face as he woke in the morning—to me.

I left, and fast.

I invented whooping cough, imagined the mumps. I even created old Grossvater Oskar, who had a fatal attack, and— Listen, um, Mr. Berringer, I'm real sorry—the funeral arrangements had been left to me. But in the end, I was at my desk the next morning. I waited. Nine, nine-fifteen, ten, ten forty-five. John hadn't called. He hadn't come in.

I'd once read in an article in the *Brooklyn Eagle* that when you're afraid, you're supposed to force yourself to think of the most awful thing. Then, whatever finally happens will be a breeze. But that turned out to be crummy advice. I thought of all the worst things—how could I help it?—and by eleven o'clock my stomach was killing me. It wasn't a normal bellyache, like after an iffy piece of Boston cream pie. This was agony, so that every breath, every involuntary movement, was like being ripped open by a knife.

One fourth of a sloe gin fizz was no excuse for what I'd

done the night before. At least John was drunk. I hadn't considered the consequences for even two seconds and the consequences were frightening. I could get fired.

The pain was so bad. Just losing my job would be a picnic. I could get tossed out on my ear without a recommendation. Up and down the street, every employment agency saying, Sorry, Miss Voss, but without a letter from your former employer . . . Going home to concoct some story for my mother, having to take charity handouts.

John could call me into his office, call me names. A guy's drunk and you don't even have the decency to push him off. Slut. (Or whatever happens could be better. Ha-ha. He could burst into the office with one of those long white boxes they put roses in and announce—real loud—Linda, I love you. Talk about daydreams. But at least my stomach felt soothed for that minute.)

He finally came in, a few minutes after eleven. He nodded but didn't look at me, walked straight into his office and closed the door. I couldn't look at him, either, but out of the corner of my eye I caught the shadow of his dark suit.

It was keep busy or go nuts. I said to myself, No matter how terrible the pain is, you've got to move. I made myself squat down and spent a half hour straightening out file folders in the bottom drawer that were already as straight as a company in Rommel's Seventh. That was the German in me: neat, precise. Like my Grandma Olga's icebox, where the cheese had marched behind the milk, where the carrots almost stood at attention and the chicken wings practically saluted.

But I hadn't been so German the night before. I don't know what I'd been, but the scratch marks I'd seen on his back were not made by a controlled person. But then, neither of us had been exactly under control. I had the marks his teeth made along the soft underpart of my arm. When I thought about them, they throbbed, like a pulse.

"Miss Voss."

I hadn't heard the door open, but there he was, standing, waiting for me. I got up slowly. I walked into his office and closed the door, but then my heel caught on one of the tiny gray-brown nubs in the rug. It was a miracle I didn't fall splat on my face, although it took some fancy footwork— step, jump, step—not to go sprawling across his desk; for a second I must have looked like I was doing some dopey dance, trying to be cute. So when I sat down, I made my expression doubly serious, to show him this secretary was no silly, dancing fool. This was the ever-efficient Miss Voss.

He sat at his desk, hands clasped, looking at me, serious, lawyerly. Just let it be quick, I began to bargain silently. No "I'm sure you comprehend what an awkward situation this is, Miss Voss, and much as I wish we might avoid . . ." Oh, God, my stomach.

"Do you have your pad?" he asked.

"What?"

"Your pad," he said. "I have a few letters, and then I have some calls to make."

Nothing showed in his deep blue eyes. He wore the face of a man who had spent the night before at a Bar Association meeting instead of rolling around in his bed, naked, drunk, crazy.

"Is this a good time for you, Miss Voss?" A slight smile, about what he would give the guy at the newsstand, or a men's room attendant.

"Yes, Mr. Berringer."

I left to get my pad. So this was how he wanted it: It never happened. I could get all worked up and think about standing on a breadline, but in the real world, how many bilingual legal secretaries were there who took shorthand at one hundred twenty words a minute? In the real world, real men need real stenographers, so they pretend real things never happened.

But then I thought: Is it possible he could have forgotten? Could he have blacked out, blanked out, and not remembered what had gone on between us? I returned to his office, and even as I sat down he was saying, "To Gunther Hoffmann. Do you have his address in the files?"

"Yes, Mr. Berringer."

He wanted to forget. Or he couldn't remember. I would never know which.

I turned a corner in the hall and ran smack into Edward Leland. "Whoops!" It just slipped out, and when I said, "I'm sorry," I sounded too loud, too emotional. I lowered my head in embarrassment, but since he didn't move, I looked up again. He looked different, and for a second I couldn't figure out why. "Excuse me, Mr. Leland." That sounded better, although he just stood there, looking through me with those black, spooky eyes. But then, before I had time to become a basket case, I did a silent Aha! Mr. Leland *was* different: darker, healthier-looking. If he was in a movie, he'd adjust his tie in a mirror and say, I *do* feel fit.

But what he actually said was: "I'm glad I ran into you. Could you spare some time for me tomorrow, Miss Voss?"

"Yes, Mr. Leland."

He'd definitely been in the sun. His nose was peeling. It was easy to see his nose because he wasn't very tall. I realized I'd never seen him standing before and had assumed a giant was behind that desk. But he was only a few inches taller than I was. Big, though, with too-broad shoulders, as if his mother had snuck out on his father and had a fast one with a prizefighter.

The tops of his cheeks were peeling too. But when you looked harder, it wasn't the tan rich lawyers get sitting on one of their rich beaches. His skin was red beneath the brown—the kind of burn you get from wind as well as sun. That time I'd been in his office, looked in his valise at his heavy snowflake sweater and—crazily—imagined him on some spy mission in Scandinavia. Could it actually have happened? Could Edward Leland have—

He interrupted my thoughts. "I'll need you for at least an—"

But then all of a sudden he just walked away. Like I hadn't been there, like he hadn't stopped to talk. He just strode down the hall toward his office, taking confident, there's-only-me-in-the-world, senior-partner steps. I turned around; then I saw what Mr. Leland had heard. It was Mr. Conklin, an associate who would never make partner because he wore bow ties. It was spooky that Mr. Leland had *known* Mr. Conklin was there; even when he'd been talking to me, acting as if he hadn't a care in the world, he'd been listening, not trusting.

Mr. Conklin looked at me a little strangely: Why was a secretary standing alone in the middle of a corridor? And then I realized that was exactly what Mr. Leland had wanted him to see: a secretary. A secretary. Big deal.

Late in the afternoon, John came back from a meeting in the conference room. As he walked past my desk, his jacket sleeve touched my shoulder. Naturally, I was as cool as a cucumber; I jumped so that I nearly ripped out the *Kapital* to *Kartoffel* page of my German-English dictionary. He murmured, "In my office, please."

This time I was all set with my pad. But John just put a small piece of paper, the kind torn out of a pocket diary, on the far edge of his desk near where I stood. I waited for some clue—a nod, a wink—but I got nothing. I didn't exactly rush to reach for the paper, but since he didn't yell, Hey, what do you think you're doing? I picked it up. It said: Hebel's, 325 East 87th Street.

When I looked up, he said, "Seven-thirty." And when I looked back down at the paper, he added, "That's all for now. Thanks."

Unless you were a sauerkraut tycoon, there was no reason to like Hebel's. It was one of those phony gemütlichkeit places in Yorkville where waiters from Saxony ran around in Bavarian lederhosen. Their pale, fat thighs looked like bratwurst. Beside the cardboard Wiener schnitzel on the plates they were toting were balls of potato mixed with sauerkraut, sprinkled with caraway seeds; they looked like bombs made to Luftwaffe specifications.

Hebel's was a German restaurant strictly for Americans. It was always advertised in the papers, a place where some tourist from Indiana would say, Gee, Mary Lou, let's do something crazy and try this here Nazi food so we can tell the folks back home.

I sat alone at the table, ignoring the beer stein collection on the high shelf that ran around the restaurant. I made eyes, noses and mouths on the frosty outside of my water glass. John wasn't there, even though it was ten to eight. So that's when I started feeling sorry for myself again; if I'd had a hankie, I would have dabbed my eyes. I saw myself starring in a silent movie—the country girl led down the garden path by the city slicker: seduced, abandoned. There'd be a close-up, I'd blink a couple of times, my mouth would form a big, sad "O" and then the words would flash on the screen: Oh, the shame of it all!

That was so corny even I couldn't stand it. Anyway, if I still needed to be pathetic, I could feel sorry for myself all the way home. It was time to go. John—who in all the years I worked for him had never been more than forty seconds late for anything—wasn't going to show. So naturally, just as I pushed back my chair and stood up, my head crashed into his chin.

"God, oh, I'm sorry," I said. "Are you okay?"

"Yes," he said, with much too much heartiness for someone who's just been clipped. "Fine."

Slowly, we both lowered ourselves into our chairs. "Would you like a drink?" he asked.

I wasn't really ready to trust my voice, so I just shook my head. He moved his finger a tenth of an inch and a waiter leapt to the table, responding to John's handsomeness, his authority—his rightness—with menus and a wide lackey's smile.

The two of us got very busy for a few minutes examining the menus. You would have thought John was going over the toughest contract of his career, the way he was reading every word. I kept sneaking little looks at him. Hey, I wanted to ask, how come you were twenty minutes late? You left the office a half hour before I did. Where were you? He wasn't giving out anything, except, suddenly, a stare—right into my eyes. It made me nervous, but I could learn to live with it. His eyes, locked on mine, were something! Funny, but I never realized what beautiful eyelashes he had. They were light, but long, and they made thick shadows on his cheeks.

I tried to take in everything: the comb marks in his hair, the bulge of his knuckles. But then the waiter came, and John looked up.

"What would you like?" he asked me.

"Gee, well . . . I'm not . . . uh . . . Whatever you're having." My shining hour.

I was so nervous I didn't even hear John order, but two minutes later the waiter brought out two plates of stew; it had probably been simmering since the day of von Hindenburg's funeral. The way it was heaped on the plate, this was the cook's last chance to get rid of it. They must have been shouting with glee in the kitchen.

The waiter opened a bottle of wine. I couldn't believe it! *Wine*.

I sipped (I once read in *Look*: "Ann Harding delicately sips champagne by her swimming pool"), which was a plus, because so did he, because that was obviously what you were supposed to do. Both of us studied the mound of food in our plates with passionate concentration.

Don't think I didn't try to start a conversation. "Have you been here before?" I asked.

"No," he answered. He did give me one of his better smiles, but he wasn't talking.

That's when I remembered the advice the sob sisters give to girls. Never ask a question that has yes or no for an answer. Instead, ask him about his interests. I already knew two of his favorites. The law. And the interest he'd shown me the night before. Both of them were great icebreakers. What's your favorite international trade agreement? And how about: That thing with your tongue—did you ever try it on Nan?

John poured himself more wine.

Part of me wanted to stay with him forever. Another part was so sure it belonged in Queens, it was all I could do not to bolt and run like hell for the subway.

The awful thing at a time like that is you actually *feel* your eyes, your cheeks, the little valleys between your fingers. You're so miserable with your own wrongness, everything about you feels homely, clumsy. You're afraid to eat—not because of the lousy food, but because you know you'll dribble gravy down your chin. And the *worst* thing is to know it's more than just a matter of not being able to make light conversation. You have real questions you can never, ever ask:

Are you embarrassed? Are you ashamed?

Are you going to fire me? Or wait a few months—so I won't think it's because of what I did with you—and then fire me?

Now that you're not drunk . . . did you like it?

Did you really mean it when you said I was beautiful?

Are we going to do it again?

If we do, you don't want me to call you Mr. Berringer. Do you? And I can't call you John. Should I just not call you anything?

Is this your way of saying thanks and goodbye? (My mother would say, No, Linda, dollface. A man of his caliber would give you at least perfume—and I *don't* mean just eau de cologne.)

But if this is the big kiss-off, I thought in that silence, then what about me? I know—as you often dictate—it is not germane to the matter at hand, but if these are our final moments, if I have nothing more to hope for, then how can I bear the rest of my life? If this gloppy stew now and, later, memoranda of law at some other firm and watching Hitler consume the world are my present and my future, then why—

It was weird, but just then, at my saddest, I began to feel lighter. Better. And of all reasons, because I remembered I was also working for the tan, scary Mr. Leland. Spy stuff. It made me a little excited. I started wondering how Mr. Leland would explain his new color to his friends. Mountain climbing, Chip. Bit of a windburn, Dick. Deep-sea fishing. Golf. Polo. Tennis, Bob. The rich have a million opportunities to change color.

"Linda." I jumped, even though John's voice was so soft it barely made a sound. My imagination had been sneaking around, following Mr. Leland to Denmark.

"Yes?"

"It's getting late. Let's move on."

"Move on?" I repeated, not quite daring to get what he meant.

He didn't explain. One hand signaled the waiter for a check. The other hand moved under the table. Hidden by the cloth, it showed me specifically what he had in mind.

# 8

All those nights I had been working—legitimately working—I had never really given a second thought to my mother. Sure, we weren't having dinner together anymore, but all dinner was for her was pushing a hamburger around her plate, giving it exercise; I ate, we talked.

So when my nights with John began, when I began coming home at what my Grandma Olga would have called a disgraceful hour, I didn't think it could make any difference. Work didn't end until eight or nine at night, and then we went to his apartment, and then . . . so what if I was getting home in the hour before dawn? My mother wouldn't know. She never toddled in before daylight. How could she possibly miss me? Ten o'clock, midnight or four-thirty: it was all the same to her.

And even if she had known, I wouldn't hear any motherly shrieks of dismay. She'd squeeze my hand, kiss me, encourage me: Linda, sweetie, stay overnight! Buy yourself a black brassiere and it'll pay off—in spades! He'll be taking you to a furrier by August!

But then one Saturday afternoon, I glanced at my mother and actually felt that shiver of recognition they write about in serious *Saturday Evening Post* short stories. My mother had become a sick old lady.

Not that she acted it. "Baby doll," she cooed, as we walked past the German bakery on Metropolitan Avenue, with its basket of shellacked pumpernickels. We were walking arm-in-arm, like fifteen-year-old best friends. "I can't

110

*stand* the suspense anymore. So he gave you dinner, right?"
I nodded, and then—fast—managed to grab her around the
waist, just in time to keep her from falling. There hadn't
been a curb or a stray pebble; for the third time that day,
she'd stumbled over nothing. "Okay, dinner, which is very
nice, *especially* with the wine. I mean, it's a real gent who
orders wine. The small fries with a couple of bucks in their
pocket are always shoutin', 'Waiter, champagne.' Not
Johnny . . . What's his last name?" A car backfired.

"Berringer."

"Oh, yeah, right. You know, I *like* B names. Anyway,
Linda, lamb, what I want to ask you is this. . . ."

She looked me right in the eye. The whites around her
huge, gentle brown eyes were a dull yellow and shot through
with red veins.

Despite her white summer dress, scoop-necked, sleeveless, splotched with its pattern of pink and purple daisies,
there was nothing even remotely young about my mother
anymore. Her skin had turned from luminous to waxy; it
was sickness, not just a drunk's pallor. It was such an awful
shock.

Of course, she didn't notice how I felt. She just babbled
on. "Did Johnny give you anything else?"

"Like a present?"

"Li*nda*, you know what I mean, and I do *not* mean a box
of chocolate creams. Did he . . . did you do it?"

My mother's voice was not exactly well-modulated, and
we were just passing Hugo's Dry Cleaners, where there was
actually a line outside; half the neighborhood were bringing
in their wool coats and blankets. "Shhh!" I hissed. Ridgewood was mainly German, plus a little Irish, a little Polish.
It liked a few steins at the beer garden, potluck suppers at
church, and well-swept front stoops. It did not like public
discussions about doing it.

"Don't 'shhh' me. I wasn't talking *that* loud," she whispered. Some whisper: more like foghorn on an empty ocean.

Just then, a middle-aged couple with matching gray hair,
carrying their itchy winter coats, passed by on their way to

Hugo's. My mother ignored the woman, but wiggled her fingers—a cute little "hi" gesture—and then winked at the man. Some wink. It was like she was an act at the Palace and wanted to make sure some guy in the last row, balcony, didn't miss it. Well, no one missed it. The man went absolutely white but kept walking. His wife whined through her nose, "Walter, who is that? *Walter*."

I pulled her along. "Walter?" I demanded.

"Gee, I thought his name was Arthur," my mother said vaguely.

"Who is he?"

"He hangs out at Fritz's."

"What does he do?"

"He could drink you and me under the table. Now listen, sweetie, you and Johnny. Are you and him making beautiful music together? Oh, don't give me a sour puss. It's not such a terrible question."

"I know, Mom."

"That's not an answer." She wasn't *that* dumb a blonde.

It wasn't an answer, and why not give her one? She wouldn't be shocked by anything I could admit to. A woman who could not remember the name of a man she'd had sex with but could probably describe the color and texture of the upholstery of his Chevrolet—that was not a woman who would gasp at the thought of her thirty-one-year-old daughter lying on top of clean sheets underneath a lawyer between Park and Lexington avenues.

"We're getting along fine, Mom."

"Tell me *exactly* what he looks like."

All her attention was a little overwhelming. In my whole life, she had never shown so much interest before; but then, I'd never done anything so interesting. But here we were, a thirty-one-year-old legal secretary with pinned-back hair and sensible shoes, and a forty-seven-year-old drunk with brown age spots dotting her temples, gossiping about guys.

"He has blond hair, light, like ours, but not as full. You know, it's the kind that flops when he walks fast. And he has dark blue eyes. His nose is regular, but—"

"You already told me about his face. Come on, move south." I was blushing, not believing we were having this conversation walking past Steiner's Hardware with its window full of drill bits. "Tell me what he's like downtown."

"Well . . ." I paused for a second. "Mom, he's wonderful."

"No kidding! Oh, Lin, baby, that's terrific!" She reached out to put her arm around me and, with her left foot, stepped on the edge of the insole of her right sandal and tripped herself. I caught her as her knees buckled; we both pretended it hadn't happened. "Is Johnny"—she gave me a girl-to-girl smile, happy, delighted for me—"fun?"

"Well, you know, he's quiet. We don't talk all that much."

"The quiet ones surprise you." She raised her voice over the honks of cars and the rattle of trucks. "All those words they don't say go straight you-know-where, if you get my drift. Am I right or am I right?" she demanded.

"You're right."

"So?" she said, as the light turned green and we crossed the street. "What do I gotta do? Get down on my hands and knees and beg you to talk?"

"After work, I've been going to his place."

"And? Come on! Be fun!" I didn't know what to tell her: Hey, it's just great, Mom. We're having a swell time. Or the truth: Mom, you wouldn't believe what it's like with us. We can't wait for it, working all day, acting normal, being polite, and then finally, when we get to his apartment, almost tearing at each other. But all those in-between times, between the desk and the bed—good manners, a polite smile or two and . . . nothing.

"And," I finally answered, "I can't believe it's actually happening to me."

"You're in love, sweetpea?"

"Yes."

"And him?" Just then, she stumbled again, but before I could reach for her, she recovered on her own. "It's nothing. Damn ankle straps."

I tried to be gentle with her. "You know, you're looking a tiny bit pale—"

"Lay off! I ran outta rouge." She shut me up in a voice I hardly ever heard—hard, hoarse: the voice of a tough old broad.

I wasn't going to be shut up. "Mom, *please*. Have you been feeling okay?"

She changed back to her cutesy voice. "It depends on who's doing the feelin'."

"Have you been eating?"

"Sure. The olive in the martini. My green vegetable." Her oldest joke. "Now stop changing the subject. How does Big John feel about Little Linda? Huh?"

"I think . . ." It wasn't just that she'd aged. Every trace of her beauty was gone. You looked at her sallow, sunken face and scrawny arms and legs, and if you hadn't known, you would never have realized Betty Voss had once been the ultimately desirable female, a soft-mouthed, hazy beauty with a halo of white-blond hair and huge, liquid eyes. You'd think she'd been a sad little wallflower who'd grown up into a pathetic, drab drunk.

"Don't be shy about telling me about Johnny, lovie. I know the score when it comes to guys and gals." She smiled. "He's nuts for you, isn't he?"

"Yeah, Mom." I said. "He is. Absolutely nuts. He can't do enough for me."

"Linda, it's about time you're getting what you deserve!"

Almost every girl in the office had some sort of outside interest. Gladys's, naturally, was Lives of Important Lawyers; her eyes took in the society page with such intensity it was a miracle the paper did not ignite. Lenny Stevenson was such a Giants fan that she actually lived in a rooming house eight blocks from the Polo Grounds. Wilma Gerhardt loved clothes (*expensive* clothes), and Marian Mulligan probably had every color nail polish ever produced during the entire history of Hazel Bishop—including Ripe Plum, a red so close to purple that her boss, Mr. Wilson, asked her please not to wear it to the office anymore. (She took that as a compliment, deciding that her nail polish was too wildly exciting for a place of business; she claimed that when she wore it on weekends, she was besieged by passionate glances and had even had a couple of offers.)

So my particular outside interest, the war, was probably considered eccentric, but it was accepted. I bought the *News* each morning, but as the situation in Europe got hotter, so did my desire to know. By the end of the afternoon there would be a pile of *Suns, Journal-Americans, Posts, Tribunes, Mirrors, World-Telegrams,* and *Timeses,* all donated by the girls themselves or recovered from the bosses' wastebaskets.

The girls could no more understand my need to read every version, every interpretation of what was going on than I could comprehend why anyone with half a brain could work herself up over Ripe Plum or the Giants, but they were willing enough to help me with my hobby, as long as I didn't bore them by talking about it. Oh, sure, they'd join in a fast discussion of the Dunkirk evacuation, like, Gee, all those little boats were really something. But if I did anything like ask, Was Dunkirk inevitable? all I'd get would be a couple of shrugs, a sigh, and then Gladys pointedly clearing her throat and demanding if anyone had heard that Mr. Nugent was keeping company with a girl in New Jersey whose family raised something—either cranberries or chihuahuas.

One afternoon, after John and I had been together (I don't know what else to call it) for nearly three weeks, he glanced down at the stack of newspapers on my desk and asked, "How come you save all those papers?"

"I read them," I said.

"Oh," he said. "Good." Then he smiled in his most automatic way and wandered back into his office. I wondered whether he realized how interested I was in what was happening in the world or whether he just assumed I liked to clip recipes for Ground Lamb Supreme.

By that time he'd learned I could cook. After our first endless, awful restaurant dinner, we'd given up on going out to eat. But because we worked so late, we had to come up with something; it's hard to sit in a taxicab gazing hungrily at each other while your stomachs make grumbling noises.

So the fourth or fifth time, John asked, "Can you cook?"

"Well, nothing fancy, but I'm pretty good, especially with German dishes. My grandmother taught me to cook, and she was terrific. Did you ever try *Gefüllter Krautkopf*?" He shook his head, and it was pretty obvious he could live a rich, full life without ever trying my *Gefüllter Krautkopf*.

But the following Monday when we arrived at his apartment, I opened the refrigerator and instead of finding the slab of cheese and bottle of milk that we'd been grabbing, there were four lamb chops (four! lamb chops!), some potatoes and carrots.

"If you feel like cooking . . ." John said.

I practically leapt into the refrigerator at the chance to try something else to please him. I clattered about while he wandered into the living room to go through the briefcase he'd brought home with him.

I sliced perfect, tiny carrot circles. I boiled the potatoes and mashed them till they were absolutely lumpless. (I had to do it with a fork. Either Nan wasn't much in the potato department, or she had gotten the masher as part of her divorce settlement.) And the meat! I hadn't had a lamb chop since 1929, before the Depression. I broiled them. They were perfect.

And so every night when we got to his apartment, I cooked, he worked. We ate. And then . . . Dinner itself was the only real problem. When it came to the bedroom, real life with John was far better than my dreams. But the long conversations I'd imagined—with John guiding me into a deeper and richer understanding of the world, of Europe at war—still remained dreams. Give it time, I told myself. When it stops being so . . . wild, out of control, he'll give you a chance. And in fairness to John, he had twenty partners—worldly men—he could have stimulating conversations with. He wasn't starved for someone to talk to, the way I was.

One night in early June, right after Dunkirk, we sat over broiled chicken and rice with absolutely nothing to say, after he'd given me a congenial "Nice rice." It was late, after eleven, one of those nights when we'd been unable to keep away from the bedroom. After almost two hours there, I'd come out and cooked. But once off the wrinkled, sweaty sheets, he was tired and had nothing to offer me, not even an "It certainly is getting muggy," or an "I love the way you looked in there a minute ago, standing and cooking."

We sat at a table—dark wood, plain white linen place mats with Nan's white monogram, plain white dishes—in the dining room. I couldn't stand the silence, broken only by a clock ticking. It just burst out of me: "What did you think of Churchill's speech?"

"What?"

I put my voice down real low and took on an English accent. " '... The New World, with all its power and might, steps forth to the rescue and the liberation of the Old.' Did you like what he said?"

John looked a little taken aback, as if his chicken breast had spoken. "Churchill's quite articulate," he finally said. He smoothed the lapel of his beige bathrobe. It was the softest cotton, with light brown piping, so fine—and so neutral—I knew it had been a gift from Nan.

"I know he's articulate, but what I was talking about was, you know, the *meaning* of what he said."

His eyebrows went up a little. "The meaning?"

"Yeah, the meaning. Don't you think what he's saying is that it's inevitable that France is going to be beaten to a pulp and that all that's going to be left is England? Well, England and America."

"It seems that way." He gave me a warm smile and combed back the front of his hair with his fingers.

"I'm not saying that it's not a brilliant speech," I went on: " 'We shall fight on the beaches ... We shall never surrender.' Nobody, not even FDR, speaks like him."

John didn't say anything. For a minute I assumed he was being thoughtful. And then I realized: I was wearing his undershirt. The strap had fallen off my shoulder and he was staring at that. His mind, the mind everyone swore was so astute, so brilliant, so original, was not on Winston Churchill.

But I tried again. "Come on. Listen to me for a second. What I'm wondering is, for all the good this speech is doing for English morale—and I bet it's doing a lot of good— don't you think it's a terrible message to be sending the French right now? Look, no one's saying there's any real hope, but don't you think—"

John stood, walked over, pulled me out of the chair. He eased the strap off the other shoulder. The undershirt slid down to the floor. "Who wants to talk about politics?"

"I do." I looked at his beautiful intelligent face. "Hey! I have an idea. Why don't you do something crazy, something you've never tried before? Talk to me for five minutes."

"Come on, Linda. You know I think you're very intelligent."

"Then talk to me, damn it. Listen to me."

He started to kiss me—my eyes, my cheeks, my mouth. "You listen to me," he whispered. "We'll talk about politics some other time. I promise. But right now . . . you're driving me out of my mind. You know that, don't you?" He pulled me down to the bare wood floor of the dining room. "Let's do it again. Right here." And I was ready. More than ready. I tore at the sash of his bathrobe, wildly eager.

Maybe my mother was right. Maybe what I was getting was what I deserved.

# 9

Snoring, my mother sounded like a huge, slow, rusty machine. That would have been half bad. What made it worse was that she talked—yelled, actually—in her sleep. "SWEETIE!" she roared, exploding the soft silence of the Sunday morning. *"Sweetie!"* Sometimes I thought she was dreaming about my father, but she could have been calling one of her barroom guys, whose names she could never remember.

"Sweetie!" reverberated throughout the neighborhood. It was too hot to close the window; if I did, my mother would wake up soaked with sweat, retching. I knew that from experience. "Sweetie!" Whoever she was hollering at in her dream wasn't giving her the time of day.

I stretched my neck to look out the living room window from where I was sitting. Just my luck. Across the street, Buddy Knauer and his pregnant wife, Sally, who had gone to high school with me, were standing on the stoop of their two-family house, shaking their heads at my mother's howling. They were on their way to church. Their three dimply little girls came skipping out the door in their candy pink, daffodil and powder blue dresses, looking like Easter eggs. So Buddy and Sally just tsk-tsked at another "Sweetie!" with Christian forbearance.

If it had been a Saturday, Buddy, a telephone company installer, would have yelled across the street, Shut up, you goddamn bitch! and Sally would have tried to hush him up and then, later, tiptoed over and asked, in a voice like liquid sugar, Can't you do anything about your mother, Linda? I always wanted to ask her a question back: Can't you do anything about your idiot hairdo, Sally? Thirty-one years old—like me—and still pinned back the sides of her hair with bows. Teeny orange bows that Sunday, like dead goldfish glued to the sides of her head.

You really got to know your neighbors in the summer, and it wasn't only from sitting on the stoop. Summer meant wide-open windows, and I could hear them all, just like they could hear my mother. Mrs. Schwarz next door talked to her cat, Peaches, like they were best friends: What do you think, Peaches? Too low-cut? Think it'll cause a riot? On the other side, Jerry Morrissey practiced the "Toreador Song" endlessly on his accordion, even after his mother begged him to stop. And the Herrmanns, who lived above their candy store on the corner, kept their radio tuned to a shortwave band that broadcast Hitler's speeches. They were a fat couple who obviously ate too many of their own Baby Ruths. Their mouths were usually stuffed; they hardly said anything, except *Danke* when you paid for your paper, although now and then a little chocolate dribbled out between their lips. But certainly no political opinions. So I never knew if the Herrmanns sat on their couch listening to Hitler with nougaty smiles or expressions of horror on their faces.

"Sweetie," my mother called, quieter this time, but more hopeful. It was eleven in the morning, the second Sunday in July, but already it was a scorcher. I got off the couch, lay down on the living room rug and spread out the *Times*. I always splurged for it on Sundays. The carpet sweeper, unused, stood straight, soldierlike, prepared, against the wall a few feet away. I ignored it—and the dusty furniture—as I studied maps and charts like a general about to wage his ultimate battle.

Over a month ago, in May, Germany had gone and done what I knew was inevitable: invaded France. The Nazi bastards had done it so easily, so quickly, that even I was stunned; the French military genius General Huntziger had probably been yawning in front of his mirror, pomading his hair or aligning his medals, when the German high command stuck the armistice papers under his nose to sign.

Soon after that, in June, Churchill proclaimed that the Battle of France was over. The Battle of Britain was about to begin. "Let us . . . so bear ourselves," he intoned over millions of radios, "that, if the British Empire and its Commonwealth last for a thousand years, men will still say: 'This was their finest hour.' " Boy, could that guy talk!

In her bedroom, my mother had had it with dreamy patience. She yelled, "Sweetie, get over here!"

I thought: A thousand years. You've got to hand it to the Europeans. I mean, Roosevelt *maybe* is thinking beyond November, beyond his third term, all the way to the 1944 election. But a thousand years? That's for Reichs and Empires. In America, nobody really thinks much beyond next Tuesday.

The *Times* that morning was full of news about the Free French. General de Gaulle was already picking a fight with the British—although you wouldn't think he was in a position to be picky. But de Gaulle probably had his own thousand-year *Etat* on his mind and so wasn't about to worry about everyday niceties like politeness and gratitude to allies.

They all seemed so different from us. And that's what I was dying to ask John about: Why do Europeans have this sense—not just of history but of the future too? Are we missing something? Or are we the smart ones? John had gone to school in Germany for three years and was brilliant. He'd know.

I realized then that if I started mooning over John I'd go off into a fog. I didn't have time; I had to meet Gladys. I slid over a few inches and peered through the door, to the kitchen clock; it was five after eleven, and I was supposed to meet her at twelve. I was so late I couldn't believe it!

Gladys and I were going to walk on the Brighton Beach boardwalk, so she wouldn't actually have to descend to the beach. She hated sand, and the bathing-suited crowd, so near to naked, seemed to make her nervous. We'd sit on a bench.

She'd say something like what she said the week before: Mr. B. must be coming out of his funk. He's not working till midnight anymore. Her voice would fall to a whisper, as if there were spies all around us: Helen Rogers saw him waiting for the elevator Wednesday night and it wouldn't come and he kept pushing the button. *Very* impatient—Gladys would do her eyebrow lift—like he had someplace to go, if you get my drift. Linda, has he gotten any calls from people of the female persuasion? No, I'd say. Then *why*, she'd demand, is he acting like he has someone? She sensed I was holding something back. Linda, swear to God, no crush? No, Gladys. Well, Marian says she sees a gleam in your eye whenever—No!

How could I explain to Gladys, who didn't like to see bare arms and legs, what was making Mr. B crazy to get on that elevator? And so, just like the week before, she would finally give up, and we'd go for a hot dog, corn and a beer at Nathan's in Coney Island.

I did a fast top-dusting and raced the carpet sweeper around the room, banging it into couch legs; it was a good thing Olga was already dead, because if she'd seen what a sloppy housekeeper I'd become, she'd have wanted to die.

In the bathroom, I turned on the faucets. The plumbing belched, then water gushed into the tub. I was in a mad rush, but too sticky and dusty from housework not to bathe. I stepped in; the water was so cold around my ankles, it took a second to work up the courage to lower my body into it.

And just as the icy water shocked me, the phone did too. I vaulted out of the tub, grabbed a towel and ran. The only calls we usually got were about my mother's family—another dead Johnston—or wrong numbers. But Gladys had my number, and if she hadn't been feeling well, maybe she'd dragged herself to a phone booth. . . . Not that I wished it on her, but I wasn't overjoyed at the thought of a stroll along the boardwalk, knowing that at three forty-five I was doomed to eat a hot dog and corn even if I was positively drooling for an ice cream sundae, and then to watch Gladys salting her corn with tiny little sprinkles and to hear her saying, with each shake, When (shake) do you (shake) think (shake) Mr. Berringer (shake) will find himself (shake) some (shake) feminine (shake) consolation?

I answered, a little breathless, on the third ring. "Hello."

"Linda?"

I nodded, then managed to come up with a word to say into the phone. "Yes."

"John Berringer."

"Oh. Hi. How are you?"

"Fine, thank you." What did I expect: Read any good newspapers lately?

"Are you in the city?" I managed to ask.

"Yes."

"I guess I just assumed you spent your weekends in the country or . . ." I'd pictured him as he looked in that picture locked in his desk drawer, in a hammock strung between two leafy old trees—but with no Nan curling around him.

"I'd like to see you," he said at last.

I could tell by the deepness, the slowness of his voice that he was still in bed, lazy, sexy, probably stroking himself— and had just decided I could do it better. He was right.

"I'd like to see you too," I said softly.

"Then why don't you come over?"

"When?"

"Now."

John didn't say "You look so pretty" or "What a great idea, spending Sunday together." What he did was grab my wrist and pull me into the apartment. "I've been waiting," he said.

"Oh, my God!" I whispered. Riding in on the subway, I'd pictured him in his Sunday best: tan slacks, a shirt—maybe striped—opened two buttons' worth, sleeves rolled up. Instead, he gave me his real Sunday best; he was naked. In the dim light of the foyer, his chest and shoulders gleamed like a Greek statue in the Brooklyn Museum.

He pivoted slowly, not showing off—more like a fashion model displaying a priceless dress. "You love looking at me,

don't you?" he demanded. This was a new John, full of himself, his beauty. Away from the office, he could do what
well-bred men do not: preen, strut, display. "Don't you?"

"Yes."

"I know. Tell me about it."

"You're . . . you have a beautiful physique."

"What do you like best?" I couldn't help it; my eyes
shifted downward. "I know that, Linda. What else?"

"All of you."

He leaned against the wall, standing right in the narrow
column of light thrown by the small ceiling fixture, and
observed me impatiently. "Be specific," he insisted. "Come
on. My shoulders, my legs." He did a complete—and
astoundingly graceful—turn. "My ass. Pick something and
*talk*. You're always complaining we don't talk. Now I want
to."

"Your legs are wonderful."

"*Tell* me about them." He stepped close, reached around
me and started to unzip my dress. He did it not like a man
undressing a woman but in a neutral way, like a Gimbel's
salesgirl. I put my arms around him, but he withdrew.
"Later. Talk now."

What does a girl say when a guy wants to hear about his
legs? It wasn't a topic I was naturally eloquent on. And
worse, I sensed from his impatience that this game of Naked
was one he'd played before, with someone else, someone
with a bigger vocabulary—and a Smith College accent. "I
love the muscles in your thighs," I said at last.

"Keep going," he said.

But I couldn't. He pulled my dress over my head. I raised
my arms so it wouldn't tear, praying there were no sweat circles after the sweltering subway ride into Manhattan.

It was my favorite dress, a cotton, the softest pink, the
pink I'd always thought of when I heard "peaches and
cream." Such a lovely, gentle color, but—as Gladys might
say when she was in one of her utterly Margaret Dumont
moods—a dress utterly inappropriate for the office. Its skirt
was all right, full, but it fit much too tight on top. It had been

on sale, and that had been my excuse for getting such an eye-popping dress. It had looked so sexy in the dressing room mirror, with its wide, deep V-neck and I even remembered standing there and daydreaming about John staring at my bust. Then, after I'd bought it, I'd been too embarrassed to wear it anyplace. It was a she's-asking-for-it dress. But John hadn't even noticed it; he just pulled it off and dropped it onto the floor.

"I like . . . I love . . ." I couldn't be specific the way he wanted me to be specific.

"Don't be self-conscious." He drew my slip over my head, then started to work on my girdle. "You shouldn't wear these. You're so beautiful, so female. I hate seeing you constricted." He let me step out of the girdle and pull off my stockings. "Keep talking," he urged. "Say anything that comes to mind."

"The hair on your legs is like red gold."

"A simile!"

"Don't talk down to me."

He moved in close, unhooked my bra and threw it on top of my dress. "You have beautiful tits."

"Stop."

He put his hands under my breasts and pushed them up as high as they would go. "I'm sorry. Beautiful breasts."

"Please."

"Please what? Do? Don't?"

"Don't say things like that."

"But it's the truth. You have ravishing breasts. Impeccable breasts. The Platonic ideal of breasts." He paused, smiled, then put his mouth to my ear; his words came out hot and damp. "Someday if you're a very good girl, I'll explain what 'Platonic ideal' means."

I stepped away from him. "I know what it means."

"You do? What?"

"Something to do with Plato."

"*What* to do with Plato?"

I swallowed. "I don't know."

He pulled off my underpants. "Of course you don't.

That's your charm. Come on, don't give me that hurt look. You're too sensitive. I'm not talking down to you." He smiled. "I'm just grateful that when I'm with you I can relax, be myself. I don't have to parade my intellect." He took my hand and put it on him. "I just have to parade this."

"But there's more to life than—"

"I know," he said, as he pulled me to him. "Oh, baby, I know."

Later that afternoon he was talkative. Well, talkative for John. He went into the kitchen and brought back two glasses with ice, and an open can of orange juice. He put the can on the shiny black night table, then quickly lifted it off, as if someone had snapped, Don't! It will leave a ring.

Then, defiantly, he banged the can back onto the night table. Juice splashed out and made two puddles on the black surface. He put down the glasses and poured the orange juice. "You're right, you know. There's more to life than . . . I haven't been giving you the attention you deserve."

"Five minutes on the strength of the RAF would take care of it."

"You're entitled to much more than five minutes—but you're too distracting."

He smiled again, but it was just the mechanical movement of his mouth; his attention was on the night table. He rested the freezing glass on my stomach. I managed to grab it before it spilled. "What are you thinking about?" I asked.

He stared at the glass of orange juice. At last, when the long silence became too heavy for him to bear, he murmured. "There's a name for gin and orange juice. Everyone in Bucks County was drinking it last summer." Just like that. He was giving me genuine chitchat. "It's not a mimosa. That's champagne and orange juice." He looked away from the glass on my stomach and out the open window. "Nan loves mimosas." I stared at him. Since the first night we were together in the taxicab, he had not mentioned her name.

"You still miss her?" But although it came out as a question, John knew I already knew the answer. He just shrugged and kept staring straight outside, as if watching Nan in a window in the building across the street.

He finally answered me. "Yes. Of course I still miss her." His cheeks and lips moved slowly, almost stiffly, as if talking like this was so against his nature he had to force the words. "I'm not going to pretend—"

"I know."

"I can't give you what you want, Linda. I wish I could. You're a fine, decent girl. You deserve—"

"I'm happy with what I have." But I was sure there could be more. All he needed was time. I mean, here we were having a conversation that a couple of days before I would have thought was impossible. I asked him, "Have you spoken to her since she remarried?" John shook his head, but he didn't seem as if he wanted to break off the discussion. In fact, he poured himself an orange juice and sat on the edge of the bed beside me, waiting for the interview to continue. "Were you surprised when she told you about"—I almost slipped and said Quentin—"the other man?"

"Yes. No. I don't know." He pushed me toward the middle of the bed and stretched out on his side in the space where I had been lying. He propped his head up on his hand. After he drained about two thirds of the glass, he said, "Our separation . . . it was inevitable. If I'd been the least bit objective, I would have seen it. You see, you can't look at Nan from a conventional perspective." He paused. "I mean . . ." he began to explain.

And I thought: To hell with it. I've had it. "You don't have to tell me what you mean. I can figure out the big words. Tell me."

For a minute he looked as if he didn't want to, but the subject was irresistible. "Nan is a law unto herself. It's not just that she's different from other women. It's that she's above them, beyond them." He looked at me for the first time since Nan's name had been dropped into the conversation; his

eyes were so bright, so alive, you could almost see the picture of her he had in his mind. "Do you understand what I'm
talking about?"

"You know, you never ask that question in the office. You
assume I understand everything: words—ideas, even. Why
would I suddenly turn into a moron when I leave Wall
Street?" Exhaling slowly, he made a big deal of showing me
how patient he was being. "I happen to know exactly what
you're talking about, and you want to know something? I
think you're dead wrong. She's not above *anyone.*"

"Then I'm sorry, but you don't understand." He turned
over, away from me, so I got to look at his back. It was a
magnificent back.

"Okay," I said to it. "She went to fancy schools, so in that
way she's certainly above and beyond anyone you'd find
punching a cash register at Woolworth's. But she's not God,
not even close. Okay, so she's brilliant. Terrific. I'm a big
fan of brilliance. And she's pretty—"

The back stiffened. "Beautiful," he muttered.

"Fine. But there have to be other brilliant, beautiful girls
walking around. Who else goes to Smith College? Are they
*all* above and beyond?"

"How do you know Nan went to Smith?"

"Does it take a Ph.D. to figure out why you're sending a
check to the Smith Alumnae Fund? I answer your mail. I
balance your checkbook. I'm your jewel of a secretary.
Remember?" He turned, reached over and poured more
juice. "Is she really different? Was she born that way?" I
honestly wanted to know. "Or is it just how she's been
brought up?"

"She's different," He turned onto his back. I couldn't help
glancing down. I knew it; he was ready for me (or someone)
again, but he was too involved with Nan to realize it. "She
has an extraordinary, analytical mind, almost a man's
mind—even though she's the most feminine person I ever
met." Talking about her, John's voice was almost reverent, as
if he was in church. "But Nan's restless, terribly restless. All

that brilliance, all that beauty . . . She was too much for Smith. Smith couldn't hold her. She had to have more."

Oh, God! It sounded like an advertisement for a bad Mae West movie: *She had to have more!* But I just nodded.

"It was the same when we were married. There's something larger than life about her, even though she looks so incredibly delicate."

"She had to have more?" I asked. John looked annoyed.

"Not in *that* way. Everything was fine."

"As fine as with us?" I actually asked.

"No," he said. "Does that make you happy? Is that what you want to hear?" Then his voice got all misty again. "She was my wife. But not a typical wife. There was nothing typical about her." He paused, then abruptly announced: "Fidelity is a middle-class virtue."

"So every upper-class person commits adultery?"

"Conventional rules don't apply to Nan," he said sharply.

I took a couple of sips of the juice. It was bitter, like drinking liquid tin. No wonder little Nannie preferred mimosas. I said, "Conventional rules don't apply to Adolf, either."

John gave me his first real smile. "That's really not an apt comparison."

"Why not? Everybody has to obey the rules."

"That's too simplistic."

"I don't think so. Because if you say Edward Leland's daughter or Edward Leland or Adolf Hitler has special rules, then why not Henry Morgenthau and Clark Gable? And who decides who gets special treatment? The person who wants special treatment? Me? You?"

"I admire your . . . sense of fair play, your democratic spirit. Really I do, Linda. But you have to understand, Nan is genuinely extraordinary: intellectually, emotionally—even socially." He exhaled slowly. "I could only satisfy her"—he got tongue-tied for a second—"that way. And intellectually. Socially . . . Her mother was related to a President, and her father, well, Edward is one of the most powerful men in the country. Nan spent her entire life in superior company. She went to the best schools, traveled abroad, had every possible cultural advantage."

"What does culture have to do with it?"

"With what?"

"With cheating on your husband?"

"Please stop it."

"Okay. I'm sorry."

"Try to understand: Faithfulness is for people who don't have the money or the imagination for pleasure."

"So how come you were faithful? What were you missing? Money? Or imagination?"

John pushed himself up and sat on the edge of the mattress. His back was toward me again. He put his glass down on the table. "You really can't comprehend the situation."

"Try me. In English or German. I'm versatile."

"But you can't grasp the subtleties. You see, just because someone was graduated from an Ivy League college does not make him upper class."

"What makes someone upper class? Money? Ancestors?"

"It's extremely complex."

"So what are you saying—in the whole history of the world there's never been an upper-class wife who's behaved honorably? You know that's baloney."

"I wasn't fun enough for her."

"Fun? The new husband is fun? What does he do—Jack Benny imitations?"

"Look," John said, "I'm not witty, I'm not particularly urbane. What can I say to make you understand? I'm not one of them. I can't get drunk at the Plaza and take off my shoes and wade in the fountain and scream with laughter over Louisa Buchanan's tasteless wedding invitations."

I sat up beside him. I took his hand, and he didn't pull it away. "Is that what you do for fun when you're so brilliant you're beyond rules? Get drunk in fountains and laugh screamingly about wedding invitations?"

John lowered his head. When he spoke, his voice was unnaturally slow, as if his throat had been numbed by the ice in the juice. He could barely form the words. "I told you that you wouldn't get it."

Did it bother me that I'd left Gladys Slade to broil on a hot boardwalk? I hardly gave it a thought. We'd once agreed, since she had no phone, that if I ever didn't show up, she'd wait one hour and then assume I'd had some emergency and wouldn't be able to make it.

I sat in the subway as it hurtled back into Queens, and I tried to think up a good excuse for Gladys. But I couldn't concentrate. I looked up at an ad for Prince Albert Crimp Cut Pipe Tobacco, with its picture of a boringly handsome middle-aged man who looked the way lawyers were supposed to but never did (except John, who looked better), and worked on feeling bad that I was behaving so rottenly to a friend. But the only thought that came to mind was that an hour in the sun would do Gladys good. Her skin was so white: not Scarlett O'Hara, southern magnolia white, but bloodless, like typing paper. Drenched in the dirty, humid night heat of the subway, I tried to feel guilty for not feeling guilty, but all I could think about was John.

Okay, even if we would never have a heart-to-heart about Rommel's strategy, weren't men supposed to sweet-talk their . . . ? I couldn't figure out what I was to him. Definitely not his girlfriend. And not his mistress; as far as I could see, letting John foot the bill for my lamb chop didn't constitute being a kept woman. Not his lover, either, because neither of us was a Greenwich Village bohemian type who had lovers, and also because I knew he didn't love me; worse, I wasn't even sure if he liked me. Was sex with me *that* good that he would put up with someone he didn't care about just to get more?

Yes. It was that good. It was perfect.

But what about me? How long could I love a man who might never love me back? What kind of love is it that basically says, Sure, fine, I understand that you can't be seen walking down the street with someone like me.

On that stifling summer night, as the subway screeched

under the East River, I said to myself, It doesn't matter. You
will love John Berringer forever. And he may learn to love
you someday. Search, look for small signs, anything is possible. But even if he never learns, your love for him—and
nothing else—is the central fact of the rest of your life.

I ran into Gladys at the newsstand in the lobby of the
office building the next morning when I bought my weekly
roll of Life Savers. She was handing over a dime for a tin of
violet breath mints.

I hadn't rehearsed my excuse, but I gave it everything I
had. "*Gladys*, am I glad to see you! I'm so sorry about yesterday." Then I noticed her tomato face. She looked
absolutely awful. "I feel *terrible*. I was all set to leave, but
all of a sudden my mother got so dizzy. . . ." Gladys's eyes,
puffy from sunburn, narrowed, so I knew I had to shovel it
on. "She actually *fainted*! If I hadn't been there to catch
her—"

Gladys simply did an about-face and marched toward the
elevator.

"Look," I said, rushing to her. "I can't tell you how bad I
feel, but that's why we made those emergency plans."

"For an emergency!" she spit out.

"But I told you, my mother actually fainted."

We reached the bank of elevators. There was one ready;
the elevator attendant waved us in, and a moment later, half
of Wall Street followed, pressing in, almost flattening us
against the wall. Gladys stared straight ahead.

"What's wrong with you?" I said softly.

Her eyes remained focused on the brass-grille door; she
spoke between clenched teeth. "It so happens I called your
house yesterday, after I'd waited for *two hours* in the burning-
hot sun. I spoke to your mother. And do you know what she
said?" *Oh, no*, I thought. I kept quiet, hoping, I suppose, that
silence was contagious. It wasn't. " 'Lin's not here, honey,' "
Gladys mimicked. "And so I said, 'Well, Mrs. Voss, we had
an appointment, and I'm a little concerned about her, not
that I want to worry you.' And do you know what she said?

'Listen, don't *you* worry, sweetie. Linda's probably kicking up her heels with her boyfriend. The one she's with every night. John Whatsisname. You know.' " Gladys turned and glared at me. " 'Her *boss*.' "

Someone in the conference room had eaten a sardine sandwich, and even though a thick, hot breeze came through the opened window and ruffled the paper napkins, you felt you were trapped inside an airless sardine can. Everyone sat around the table going through the motions of eating her lunch, but this day there was no fun, no gossip. In fact, the room had gotten so quiet you could hear the squish of pits plopping from Marian Mulligan's watermelon chunks as she coaxed them out with her pointy Mango Orange fingernails.

Everybody knew something was up. Why else would Gladys Slade have pointedly taken her seat at the head of the conference table and then said—tittered, actually—to Verna Glover, a human slug with a personality one inch from dead, "Verna, come sit next to me." Then Gladys graciously offered Verna the seat that had been mine for the last seven or eight years.

Helen Rogers sat beside me, but then was afraid to look my way because then she'd have to either talk to, smile at or snub me. Instead, she picked nervously at the caraway seeds from the rye bread that dotted the white polka dots on her blue blouse. The chair on my other side was empty; the girls had caught on fast that something was wrong.

Gladys sat straight, like a school poster for good posture. She'd tucked a napkin over the front of her dress to protect it from the drippy peach she was eating; the white of the napkin against her sunburn made her face look maroon. For at least the tenth time I tried to catch her eye, and, for the tenth time, I got looked through; it was as if I was invisible and she was examining the light switch on the wall behind my head.

What was she *doing*? In all my life, I'd never felt such anger. What I'd done to Gladys was wrong, but we'd had all those years, all those Sundays. I didn't deserve being cast out like this, like I'd committed some horrifying crime. No one would look at me.

The room was completely stiff and still, like an old photograph, except for the tiny dust twinkles that danced in the lines of sunlight coming through the wooden slats of the venetian blinds. Breathing was hard.

Suddenly, Gladys turned to Anita Beane and said, in her most regal, pearly Queen of Lunch tones: "You haven't spoken about your wedding plans in *days*. Tell me, have you chosen your tablecloth color yet?"

You could hear the great sigh of relief at the return to normalness: a chorus of ten or twelve voices exhaling together. And then, on and on, Gladys, Anita and the girls debated the pluses and minuses of daffodil versus goldenrod. But every once in a while, I'd get a look, a flash of wonder or curiosity—or downright antagonism.

And that's when I knew that if I didn't stop Gladys, I was finished. One by one, all afternoon, they'd float through the halls, slip over to her desk, ask, What's with Linda? and finally she'd say, I wish you hadn't asked, but you know me. I have to tell the truth. I called Linda's house Sunday and her mother said . . .

So right after lunch, when Gladys bolted for the door, I bolted too—and faster.

"Gladys," I called loud enough for all the girls strolling back to their desks to hear, "I know we talked about not sitting together all the time, but you know something? I kind of missed you." I clutched her elbow as though I wanted a quick arm-in-arm promenade with my best friend, and hurried her down the hall. From the relaxed murmur that rose behind us, I knew I'd subdued at least a couple of doubts.

"Let go of me!" Gladys tried to jerk away, squeezing her arms tight against her body as I rushed her along. Her elbow had red fingerprints where I'd grabbed it. "I want nothing to do with you," she spit out. "Is that understood? You played me for a *fool*."

"Please, let me explain—"

"You let me go on and on, all these months. Carrying on

with him, pretending you didn't even *like* him, even when I said, 'Oh, Linda, you *must* have a crush on him.' And you said, 'Oh, *no*, Gladys. I'd tell you. We're *such* good friends. But Mr. Berringer is so boring, with his big blue eyes. He's *too* good-looking. Like a third-rate movie star.' *That's* what you said. Oh, you must have felt so superior, you smug—"

"Please, let's sit down after work. I want to explain—"

*"Explain?"*

"Gladys, what else could I have done? I know you won't believe me, but I feel terrible. I've done you a great wrong, and I'm so sorry. I shouldn't have—"

"What does 'shouldn't' mean to someone like you? You've been *doing* it with him!"

I couldn't help it. "Oh, stuff it up your nose!" I blurted out. Was she ever the wrong person to say that to! "Look, Gladys, standing you up yesterday *was* a rotten thing to do, okay? And not confiding in you was ... maybe ... was worse. But let me tell you, what I did doesn't compare to how you almost ruined me in there. Everyone was treating me like a leper. They're going to think—"

She cut me off. "You must be so proud of how you deceived me. 'I can't meet you for a drink, Gladys. Mr. Berringer's rushing off.' He was rushing off to you! 'I'm sorry, but I have to work late.' *Work*." She rubbed out a fingerprint from the patent leather on her handbag. "What kind of 'work' do you do for him? Does he pay you overtime?"

"Is that what you want, Gladys? The details? Fine. You want me to give you a blow-by-blow description?"

"You are utterly revolting!"

"Listen!" My voice sounded far off, and strangely tough. "I don't want to hear one more damn word from you. And if you ever pull anything like what you tried at lunch today—"

Gladys simply walked away. Well, why not? She was positive she had me. She could be mysteriously cold to me for a week or two, savor the attention and then ... One word to Helen or Marian, and in ten minutes all the secretaries would be whispering. By three o'clock, enough hints would be dropped to enough bosses that the lawyers would start finding excuses to go past John's office, past my desk, to look me over, and then go laugh in the men's room. By four o'clock I'd be called in, maybe by John with a "You stupid . . ." or even by one of the senior partners. Oh, my God, by Mr. Leland: Under the circumstances, Miss Voss . . .

"Gladys!" I barked.

She stopped only because she hadn't expected to hear anything more from me. I caught up with her and walked along beside her. I smiled as Mr. Ervine from Real Estate passed. We made way for him and he said, "Hello, girls," and kept walking.

"Gladys, listen to me, because if you don't you'll be sorry."

"Don't you threaten me, you tramp."

"You say one word, just one word to anybody—the secretaries, Lenny Stevenson, the janitor—and you're finished."

"No," she said. "*You're* the one who will be finished." A nasty look, pretty close to a malicious smile, passed over her face. "I really wasn't going to say anything in there, you know. But now you're threatening me, and I *do not* like threats."

"I don't care what you like, Gladys. Just shut up and listen. I know that one word from you, and the whole office will know. And I guess that will give you satisfaction."

"I'm not that small-minded."

"It'll give you satisfaction," I repeated, "but it'll also get you fired."

"Oh, come on!"

"John is ready, willing and very able to do *anything* I ask him," I said. "I have him in the palm of my hand." She blinked, then did it again and again, until it became a nervous tic. Blink, blink, blink. She couldn't stop. "Don't test me, Gladys. No more cold shoulder at lunch, or you'll find yourself out on the street. Do we understand each other?"

She blinked again.

"John loves me. Whatever makes me happy makes him happy."

"All right," Gladys said at last.
"So if you like your job . . ."
"I never had any intention of saying anything."
And then she rushed away.

# 10

September 7, 1940. The Battle of Britain was in its second month. On that afternoon, a Saturday, the German *Dreckenschweine* sent three hundred bombers and six hundred fighters to attack the London docks. And later that night, they sent in more bombers; dark orange fires burned along the banks of the Thames, lighting the night fliers' path toward their targets. But that was over there.

Here, between daylight and dark of that day, I sat on a green plaid couch finishing an article in an overthumbed *Good Housekeeping* from January. "Hollywood has little trouble finding new and lovely girls to photograph—witness Dorothy Lamour, Rosemary Lane, Sigrid Gurie and the lush Hedy Lamarr, to mention only a few of today's raw recruits—but able actresses are not come by so easily."

*Good Housekeeping* knew. "You're a lousy actress, Linda." Dr. Guber shook his head wearily a few minutes later in his office.

*"Me?"* I asked, opening my eyes wide so I'd look honest and innocent, unlike lush Hedy Lamarr.

"Come off it, kiddo." His desk chair creaked as he leaned forward. "I've known you all your life."

Dr. Guber was so tall and thin you could see the stringy muscles where his arms dangled out of his short-sleeved white doctor coat. He was built like a cowboy but talked with a thick New York accent.

"I got a cancer and a rheumatic fever out there," he went on. "You think I'm gonna play *Let's Pretend* that it's your mother's specimen that killed the rabbit? Your mother drinks so much her uterus probably looks like a pickled corned beef." Dr. Guber pushed back his chair and stood up. He must have looked at me then, at the moment the smile I'd worked so hard on collapsed, because he came over to my chair and squeezed my shoulder. "Come on. You're a big girl." He paused. "You must've had a clue."

I must've. Even a supreme moron could add up what sex seven days a week plus two missed periods equals. It took high intelligence to have found new ways to keep avoiding reality the way I did. Every morning I woke up and ran to the bathroom, and when I didn't find my period, I'd think: Oh, God, oh, no, please! But then I'd think: No. Calm down. It's nerves. You're getting yourself in such a stew you'll never get another period again. Relax!

But then, oh, I knew. Every afternoon the last month, I'd felt sick. Like I was going to give back my lunch when I leaned over a drawer in the filing cabinet. And smells. Mum deodorant: sickeningly sweet, like decaying corpses in detective stories. The roll of Life Savers in my purse stank, especially the purple ones. And I couldn't help it, but I kept thinking of food, maybe because I wasn't able to eat all that much, but I'd imagine a hamburger patty or split-pea soup, and a wave of nausea would rise up in me.

I couldn't pretend anymore.

"Come on, Linda, let's go in the examining room," Dr. Guber said, in the too-calm voice people use with people about to get hysterical. "Five, ten percent of the time, it's something else that kills the rabbit—a heart attack, or who the hell knows. Anyway, their little pink noses stop twitching and people get nutsy for nothing. You could be fine."

His long legs took Texas-length strides, and I had to do double time down the narrow corridor. He opened the door to his examining room and stood back to let me go in first. The room had a black leatherette table in the center. He handed me a sheet and said, "Just take off your bottom stuff and your shoes and get up on the table." He turned away and whistled "Daisy, Daisy, give me your answer true," while I pulled off my pants and girdle and he pulled on a rubber glove. "You ever have an internal?" he called out.

"No," I said, and took off my shoes and stockings and stretched out on the cold paper that covered the table.

"Listen, it's nothing. Easy, just so long as you relax." He turned back and started to pull the sheet first down and then up, as if he was a fussy housewife, so it covered even more than the vast areas I'd already covered with it. Then he began the examination, staring straight into my eyes. "So how's your mother lately?" He pushed up with the gloved hand and, with the other, pressed down hard on my stomach.

"Fine," I gasped.

"Fine, I don't want to talk about her, or Fine, she's quit boozing and is studying ancient Greek?"

He was pressing so hard. If I really was pregnant, he could squash the baby. "She's still drinking."

He switched on a floor lamp, then pulled over a stool and sat at the foot of the table. "Too bad. She looked like hell last time she was in here." He lifted the sheet and bent over. "Such a beauty-ful girl. I remember when she first came in, years ago, pregnant with you." All I could see were the tops of his ears.

"Am I?" I asked. In London, the air raid sirens were screaming. In Dr. Guber's office in Ridgewood, it was still.

He looked up. "Yeah, Linda. You're about two, two and a half months into it, I'd say." Dr. Guber swallowed his discomfort; his Adam's apple bobbled nervously in his long, scrawny neck. "Sorry, honey." His hands appeared from under the sheet. He stood up and pulled off the rubber glove. It made a squeaky sound; I shivered. Before I could think of a thing to say, he lowered his head and stared at my toes. "Don't . . ." he began. "Uh . . . I can't help you with this." Five or ten possible sentences came into my mind, but they couldn't get from there to my mouth. The doctor moved his eyes and stared at his own feet. "And don't go anywhere else, either. Don't listen to your girlfriends." Did he think we sat in the Blair, VanderGraff and Wadley conference room chatting about getting rid of babies over our cheese sandwiches? "These guys are dirty, filthy. You could die."

"Oh," I said. Neither of us knew what to say next.

"The fella . . ." he said at last. "Is he married?" I shook my head, and Dr. Guber broke out into a smile. "Then you got nothing to worry about! Listen to me. He'll be surprised, yeah, sure. Maybe a little upset. You know bachelors. But then . . . he'll be thrilled." He pronounced it *trilled*. "You mark my words, honey. Absolutely thrilled."

The Monday after I went to Dr. Guber, I was sitting at my desk, in the middle of a tidal wave of nausea that came from some wandering secretary's eau de cologne—and from my almost continual state of pure terror—when the phone rang. It was Mr. Leland's secretary. "Mr. Leland has a bit of dictation for you. Would this be a convenient time?" Yes, especially if he'd like to see me throw up.

Lucky for me, Mr. Leland wasn't wearing any deodorant or hair oil or talcum powder—anyway, none with a smell. I sat across from his desk and started to take down another one of his strange letters.

"Dear Felix," he began. He was wearing a navy blue suit. A thick gold watch chain dangled from his vest, as if he was off to make a speech somewhere or attend a dressy funeral. "I hope you had a grand summer. It's so refreshing, being close to the sea. I am enjoying the breezes, and the sight of birds diving into the water."

He cleared his throat. I looked up from my pad. "Is there a word in German for seagull?" he asked.

"Probably," I said. "Canary is *Kanarienvogel*." God knows why, but I added, "We had a canary when I was a little girl."

"What happened to it?"

"The usual canary things. It sang a lot, ate a little birdseed, and died."

The half of his mouth that seemed to work right smiled at me. We weren't exactly what you'd call great buddies, but at least I was a lot less terrified of him. Gradually, I'd noticed—from the way he treated his own secretary to the way he talked on the phone during calls he'd take while I was sitting in his office—that Edward Leland was, for all his importance, all right. Sure, if you crossed him he probably would do something very, very horrible back to you. But as long as you did your job, you were okay. More than okay, because he had a sense of humor: joking to secretaries, witty to lawyers, hysterically funny to clients. Well, why not? He was so high up in the world he could afford to laugh. He was far beyond having to worry about being taken seriously.

"No canaries in this letter. When you get back to your desk, find a seagull or a tern or some sort of ocean-type bird in your dictionary." He paused and then added, "If you can't find it, check with Mr. Berringer."

A new wave of sickness came over me at the mention of John's name. And to make it worse, not only did Mr. Leland realize something was wrong; he had been waiting for it. He may even have tossed John's name out for curiosity, or a test, to see what it would do. It did a lot. For the first time in those five weeks of acute afternoon nausea, I felt I really was going to throw up. I lowered my head; it would be terrific, a bright addition to the dark colors in Mr. Leland's Oriental rug.

"Are you all right, Miss Voss?" I could hear in his voice that he felt bad.

"I'm fine, thank you." I raised my pencil—and then my head—so he could see I was ready to get going again.

But I must have looked pretty crummy, because he asked, "Would you like a glass of water?"

"No, thanks. I'm okay." He looked like he didn't agree. "Really I am."

So he began to dictate again. My dizziness didn't go away, but my stomach calmed down enough so that I felt assured Mr. Leland wouldn't have to witness the reappearance of my ham and tomato sandwich.

"I spent the month of August sailing with my three sons,"

he said. Of course, I knew he didn't have three sons (just one beaut of a daughter). But this letter was no crazier than any of the others I'd taken in the past couple of months. "Please send my fondest regards to Maria and the two little ones. I remain, Yours, Vincenzo. V-i-n-c-e-n-z-o."

I couldn't help asking, "Vincenzo?"

"That's Vincent in Italian."

"I see," I said.

"You do? Well, Miss Voss, tell me what you see." It was always questions with Mr. Leland, but working with him three or four hours a week, I'd learned that whether or not he liked my answers, he never held them against me personally. I was convinced the questions were completely impersonal, asked to get information or a reaction, not to test me—Linda Voss—in any way.

"My guess is the letters are some sort of code to someone in Germany." No reaction. "And maybe someone will be mailing this letter from Italy . . ." Annoyance. "Because of the Vincenzo business."

I typed the letters at an old Royal he kept in a closet in his office. I never typed envelopes for them. I never made carbons. When I gave Mr. Leland the typed letter, I had to give him the steno pad I'd used. Each time I went to his office, I needed a brand-new pad. I never knew who mailed the letters or where they went.

"Any other deductions, Miss Voss?"

"I hope I'm not . . . I don't want to overstep my bounds."

"Go on."

"If this has anything to do with harbors or ships or aircraft carriers or E-boats or U-boats . . ." My stomach did a flop, but I clutched my pencil tight, as if grabbing on to a subway pole, and I got through that bump. "What I'm saying is, the Germans aren't dopes. If this is a code, I hope it's about something . . ." I paused. "Something not watery." No reaction.

But I was starting to be able to read him a little. My father had always said I was really smart about people, and that if I didn't wear my heart on my sleeve about everything, I'd have made a good poker player because I could see past the faces people put on. And I think he'd been right. I bet most people wouldn't have noticed Mr. Leland getting annoyed about a comment that the letter was going to be mailed from Italy. The change in his face was so small it wasn't really a change at all. And I also knew that whatever the code was, it was okay; it had nothing to do with anything watery.

What I was curious to ask him, and naturally I couldn't, was how come he used me as a measure of how good his secrets were. I guessed I was his Miss Everybody, his Jane Doe, his Average American.

What I was also dying to ask him was what I should do about my whole life. He was so smart. He advised senators, judges. Everyone said he even got calls from the White House. I need some advice, I could say—just like FDR would. See, I'm two months down, seven months to go, and how can I possibly tell John Berringer that I'm going to have his baby?

I told him by just telling him. I went straight from Edward Leland's leathery, lawyery office into John's immaculate modern one and said, "I have to talk to you."

He smiled and said, "Later," but did not look up from the letter of agreement he was marking with a red pencil. I didn't move. My reflection in his shiny desk must have annoyed him, because when he glanced up, he took a fast, deep breath and then quickly forced his face into its I'm-not-only-handsome-I'm-a-nice-guy expression: His head tilted a little to the right; the corners of his mouth turned up just enough to show that despite the chilly blond superiority of his looks, he was truly good-natured. But I knew him well enough to know that at this moment he wasn't—at least not toward me. Still, I was under the influence of Edward Leland's world, where men with damaged faces made terrible, secret decisions, a world where a fringe of thick lashes over sapphire eyes didn't count for a damn. It gave me courage.

So I spoke. "I have to talk to you *now*." Whatever was in my voice made him put down his pencil.

"This can't wait for tonight?"

"No."

"Linda, I'm really under enormous pressure."

"So am I."

He cut me off. "I'm sure you are." He glanced down at the letter he was editing. "I hate to be rude, but the longer you stand here, the longer it will take me to get this back to you to be retyped. Are you in the mood to be stuck here until ten, eleven o'clock? Because I'm not. I'd like to get home and . . ." He gave me a little smile. It meant goodbye.

I sat myself down in the small, ugly modern chair by the side of his desk; it looked like a tilted soup plate.

"Please, have a seat," he said, really irritated now. "Make yourself comfortable."

"I'm pregnant."

*"What?"* But he'd heard me, because it was as if he switched gears. Now you could almost hear his mind whirring, as if he was starting up the most intricate argument against the toughest opponent of his career. "Are you sure?" he demanded.

"Yes."

"What makes you so certain?"

"I've missed two—"

"That doesn't necessarily mean anything," he interrupted. He was talking fast. "There could be any number of reasons for a skipped period."

"Two periods," I managed to say. To this day I can't figure out how I was able to keep such control. I sounded so composed I could almost have been a match for him. "I missed two periods—please let me finish—so I had a rabbit test. It came out positive." John's fair skin went from pale to white. "And I went to the doctor to double-check. And I am."

"Didn't you use anything?" he finally asked.

"Use anything?"

"Use anything! A diaphragm." I shook my head. "Jesus Christ!"

"I wouldn't know where to get one."

"From the same damned doctor who confirmed your pregnancy!"

"But he's been our family doctor for years."

"So?"

"I couldn't go to him. I didn't want him to think I was . . ." My hands were in my lap, clasped so tight my fingers began to throb.

His hand turned into a fist, and he crashed it down on the desk. "You did this purposely, didn't you? *Didn't you*, damn it!" He banged again, harder. "The minute Nan left, you started planning—"

Then came one of those moments that kill drama. John's eyes turned dark with anger, I tried to shrivel up to invisibility in that disgusting chair . . . and the phone rang. Softly at his desk, but through the closed door I could hear it shrilling at mine. Automatically, I reached over, picked up the receiver and very calmly said, "Mr. Berringer's office."

"Mr. Waring calling for Mr. Berringer," a secretary at some other, more chaste law firm said. She sounded so efficient, so calm. No two missed periods for her.

"I'm sorry, Mr. Berringer is out of the office at the moment." John's eyes moved back and forth, as if he couldn't decide whether to be grateful or grab the phone from me. "May I have him return Mr. Waring's call tomorrow morning?" She said I could, and I hung up with a courteous "Thank you."

And then I turned to John. My voice was still secretary sweet. "Let me just tell you one thing. I didn't lay any traps for you. If you happen to remember that first night, it was you, not me, who insisted on being friendly. I'm not a sneak, and I would *never*—"

"Fine. Wonderful. You're far beyond opportunistic intrigues. But somehow it never occurred to you in all these weeks that you might take precautions."

"I guess not," I answered. "You're the smart one. Did it ever occur to you?"

There was silence that went on too long to be a moment of

silence. At last he said, "Please go now. I have work to finish. We can continue this discussion later."

And then he picked up his red pencil, changed a colon to a semicolon. I returned to my desk.

When you're writing things down, no matter how detailed you try to be you always wind up leaving things out. So let me put in what I've left out. (You know what Dr. Freud says, that you don't leave anything out by mistake? It had always sounded like a lot of Viennese *Schlag* to me, but who was I to say? I was the girl who left out a diaphragm.) Anyway, the details.

After our first time together, I'd stopped saying Mr. Berringer, but I have never called him John.

He never asked me anything about my family, or even if I had a family. Once I mentioned something about going home to Queens, and he said, "Oh, I thought you lived in Brooklyn."

He'd grown up on Long Island, in Port Washington. He told me his father had been in business out there. I asked what kind of business, and he'd said, "Financial." He didn't like to talk about his parents. They'd died in a car crash in 1929, when he was in his second year of law school, and I couldn't tell whether or not it still hurt him to even think about them or whether maybe there was something about them he didn't want to talk about.

I'd asked him, "What church did your parents go to?"

"What?" he'd asked.

"What church did your parents go to?"

"Episcopal." He was staring at me like I was nuts, because we had just finished—we were still breathing hard, still sweating, actually—and most people wouldn't dream of discussing church before they took a shower.

"Both of them?" I inquired.

"Yes."

Another thing: He had been an only child.

Another: John was in demand. Two weeks after Nan left, the phone started ringing. It was this or that partner's wife,

wanting him to meet this or that girl. How did I know? How
do you think? Once, after John picked up in his office, I
clicked the button fast, covered the mouthpiece, then eaves-
dropped. "John, my dear, I have an absolute dream of a girl
you must meet. Laura Steele. Of the Steeles." John said he'd
love to. Not yet, but very soon. "You're not being naughty
and seeing anyone else, are you, John?" the voice
demanded. "No," he'd told her. "No one."

He called me back into his office about seven o'clock that
same night. It wasn't dark yet, but the moon was out, full,
risen so it was almost as high as John's head, and it had the
soft, slightly yellowish shine of a giant ball of taffy. His
office lamp wasn't on, so the room was illuminated by
moonlight; it made the hard furniture—and John—seem
more gentle.

His posture, though, was so straight, businesslike, that for
a second I thought he was going to give me the letter of
agreement to retype. But when I glanced down at his desk, I
saw he hadn't gotten any farther than the semicolon he'd
been working on three hours before.

"Sit down," he said. With the moonlight pouring through
the open window, his hair glowed, as if he had a halo. "Let
me be blunt, Linda. Are you willing to get rid of it?"

"The baby?" I whispered.

"Yes. I've learned of someone, a reputable physician. It
can be done in a hospital in Puerto Rico. Very clean. And all
on the up-and-up."

Here was this shining man, and all I wanted to do was
make him happy. But as I started to nod, to think the words
"Whatever you want," I thought about my being pregnant in
a way I hadn't before. Maybe not in a goo-gooish maternal-
instinct way, imagining something soft and pink and
smelling of Johnson's Baby Powder. But for the first time I
comprehended that my awful afternoon sickness and the
tight waistbands of my skirts were due to something more
than a medical condition that was lousing up my life.

I can't say I wanted a baby. I didn't picture myself buying

tiny, fluffy sweaters. It was only later that I thought it would have fair hair, like me and John, and wondered whether it would have his deep blue eyes or my brown.

"Please listen to me carefully," he said. "This is probably the most important decision you'll ever make in your life. I hope you'll make it . . ." His voice faded away, as if it wasn't worth the energy to go on.

"What?" I asked. "Finish what you were going to say."

"I hope your decision will be rational."

"Do I look like a raving lunatic?"

"Linda, must you be so argumentative?"

"If I'm capable of being argumentative," I said, "then I'm obviously capable of being rational, so you can relax." He never expected that from me; he stared, almost as if he was waiting for the ventriloquist who'd said that line to pop up behind my chair. "And being so rational, I'd appreciate it if you were a little clearer." I pulled my chair closer to his desk. "What do *you* want me to do?"

"You know what I want."

"Tell me."

"I would like you to get rid of it. I want you not to use the fact of your getting pregnant as leverage."

"Leverage?" I asked, but I knew exactly what he meant.

"To get me to"—he could hardly bring himself to spit out the words—"marry you."

"I don't expect you to do that."

"What am I supposed to do if you decide not to get rid of it?"

"I don't know. It's not anything I've thought about." I paused then, and I thought. It didn't take much time. "You could give me some money so I could have it," I said.

"So you don't want to . . . you won't consider even speaking with that doctor?"

"No. Please, now I'd like you to listen to me. No matter what you think, I'm not some cheap floozy trying to trap you."

"I never meant to imply that, Linda."

"And I'm not some dope who can't understand the pickle

she's in . . . and you're in. So just hear me out." I hated this, thinking on my feet or, more accurately, on my behind. But since I hadn't prepared myself, I had no choice. "I guess I'll have to get out of here pretty soon, before I start getting noticeable, or it'll be bad for you. I'll need some money to live. No more than I'm getting now, twenty-five dollars a week. Well, money for a doctor too.

"I can't go away anywhere, because I have to take care of my mother. But since no one you know would ever put even his little toe in Ridgewood, there's nothing to worry about." For him. For me, oh, God, it was going to be something going to the grocery with a belly the size of a watermelon. "And I'm not going to do anything to embarrass you after I have it. You don't have to concern yourself. I'm not going to come in with some little bundle in a blanket and stand weeping by the elevator bank."

John went absolutely green around the gills. "You'd *keep* it?"

"I don't know." I wanted to cry. "It's a baby."

He leaned toward me and rested his arms on his desk. "I could arrange for someone to take care of your mother, so you could get away. And then, later, for a nice, quiet adoption."

"As opposed to the usual noisy ones?"

He closed his eyes, as if he was silently counting up to ten for patience, but he only got to about four when he opened them. "If we can agree to a certain sum," he said calmly, "a very generous sum, would you be willing to sign a document absolving me of any—"

"How could you be such a bastard?"

It wasn't exactly a knife to his heart. He just went on. "Would you sign such a document?"

"Only if there was no generous sum involved."

"Don't be foolhardy."

"I can be anything I want to be. You're absolved." And I stood up and walked out.

But before I got to the door, he was behind me. He put his

hands on my shoulders, turned me around and kissed me. "Linda," he murmured.

I put my hands against his chest and pushed him away, hard. "Go find yourself some debutante with a diaphragm," I said. I clutched the doorknob, pulled, but he slammed the door and then stood against it, holding it shut.

"I'll marry you," he said.

"No."

"I'll marry you."

"*No*. You don't love me. I don't even know if you like me. If I disappeared off the face of the earth tomorrow, you'd only notice when it came time to take off your pants. And that wouldn't be any big deal. You know that. All you'd have to do is smile at somebody, and in five minutes you'd be having your needs taken care of." Slowly I lifted my head and looked into his eyes. "But there's no one who can take care of you like I can."

That night, for the first time, John asked me to sleep over at his apartment. Around midnight, when he went to the bathroom, I got up and smoothed out the sheet we had rumpled, then fluffed the pillows, shook out the quilted cotton comforter and turned it over, making sure Nan's [NLB] monogram was facing down. A few seconds later, when he returned smelling from tooth-powder, I was under the comforter, my eyes closed.

"Linda," he said. I breathed deeply. "Come on. You didn't have time to fall asleep." I opened my eyes. He slid under the cover and came up beside me. "Listen to me. There is really no alternative, since you insist on . . . having it. We'll get married."

"We have nothing in common," I answered. "Except sex, and we can't do that if we're invited out on one of the partners' boats for an afternoon." He stared at me. I think it hadn't occurred to him until that instant that if I was going to be his wife, he might, occasionally, have to trot me out of the bedroom. "Look, let's be honest with each other for once,

because now we have to be. I know how thrilled you are
every time I open my mouth to try and make conversation.
How do you think your friends will feel? I would be an
embarrassment to you."

"Is that what you believe?"

"I don't know. But you believe it."

"You don't know what I believe."

"So tell me."

Instead, he stared up at the ceiling. So I told him my
mother was a sick drunk, and I had to take care of her. He
didn't seem either surprised or interested. But he said, "I'll
give you money for her, if that's what you want."

"Look, a few hours ago you were ready to dump me—"

"That's not true. I was ready to be responsible—"

"Responsibility's one thing. Marriage is another. Am I
what you want to come home to every night for the rest of
your life?"

Instead of answering, he said, "Shhh," turned, and pried
apart my legs with his knee. We did it again.

At three in the morning, after we'd slept for a couple of
hours as far apart as the double bed would allow, we acci-
dentally knocked together and woke up, startled to find each
other. Quickly, we turned and pretended to go back to sleep,
but it didn't work. I could hear his shallow, nervous breathing, his swallows that were almost gulps. I sat up and
touched the silky hair on the back of his head. "Tell me
why . . . why you're willing. Is it to get back at Nan, to show
her how she destroyed your life, that you buried your troubles in your secretary—and knocked her up?"

"Stop it."

"Is it to give her a slap in the face, to show her that what it
*really* takes to satisfy you is a hot little item from Queens?"

"This conversation is completely inappropriate, so let's
end it." It was hard to hear, because he wasn't facing me; his
words were muffled in the pillow.

"Is it that it's so good with me you can't give it up, even if
you have to marry me and let me have your child?"

"Go back to sleep. You're upset. Worn out." He sounded weary, not tired.

I tried to act lighthearted, the way classy people are supposed to in nasty situations. "Think about your practice. Do you think marrying me is going to do wonders for your reputation for sound judgment? What are your foreign clients going to think, when they meet your pregnant dumpling with the *berlinerisch* accent?"

"Stop it!" he snapped. He took a minute to compose himself. "Linda, I'm responsible for this situation. I got you pregnant. And I want to do what's honorable."

"*Why?* Because that's what gentlemen are supposed to do?"

"Yes."

"But there is no love."

"You love me." He was so kind and so cold. "Do you want to leave me, Linda? Or do you want me to marry you?"

Maybe when he feels it kicking, I thought. He'll put his hand on my stomach and he'll look at me and all of a sudden . . . "I want you to marry me."

"All right, then."

I put my arms around him and rested my head on his shoulder. He grabbed me tight, climbed on top of me, and so we did it again.

# 11

The high-ceilinged room in City Hall smelled of cigarettes ground out on the already dirty brown and tan tile floor. Couples pressed against a wood railing, waiting their turn to enter into matrimony. Not holy matrimony; this was the Municipal Building of the City of New York, and in the interest of peace in the Melting Pot—to say nothing of keeping the line moving—the clerks were not supposed to utter You-Know-Who's name.

It was only then that I realized how much I wanted to hear it; I imagined a deep, velvety voice intoning, *Dearly beloved, We are gathered here in the sight of Gawd* ... If I'd had to put a face on that voice, I guess it would be the minister who was always burying Johnstons in Brooklyn. I didn't know his name or his denomination, but he looked like someone born to perform religious rites: white hair, a hawkish nose and ice blue eyes that appeared to look down at whoever was getting buried. But now and then he broke into a kind smile, which showed a couple of teeth missing on the side. The parsonage roof probably leaked too, poor guy.

Since I'd fallen for John, my daydreams had been detailed, but they'd almost always been about sex, not ceremonies. Still, my secret night dreams must have been traditional: being married by the Reverend Smith/Jones/Williams in a Christmas card church, a simple, pure-white building with a nice steeple. Out of respect to my Grandma Olga's memory, the reverend would just say "God" whenever he came to His name, and not make a big deal about details like the Father, Son and Holy Spirit.

A little runt of a groom-to-be next to me was puffing like a titan of industry on a giant cigar, and his about-to-be bride was chomping on a wad of spearmint gum. To keep my stomach from flipping over, I turned my head toward John and inhaled the aroma of clean wool from the sleeve of his suit. I realized that I'd not only pictured the minister; I'd even imagined my dress. An old-fashioned shirtwaist style, white, but instead of cotton, it would be handmade lace—a rosebud and rose design. Olga had brought a square of lace like that with her from Berlin: a handkerchief some rich cousin had given Olga's mother for her trousseau.

In the wedding dream I hadn't known I'd been daydreaming, I'd be wearing a strand of pearls from somewhere and carrying a bouquet of white roses and the tiny white dot flowers whose name I didn't know, all tied up with long white ribbons. I'd have on a white leghorn hat with a white velvet band. I wouldn't wear a veil because it would be a day wedding.

And it was a day wedding: no moon. And no June. It was September 16, a Monday, and I was wearing a blue dress that had seen its best days in 1937, when I'd bought it at Ohrbach's End of Summer Sale, which they held in July. (Some tight-mouthed red-headed lady had tried to grab it from me as I took it off the rack, but I'd held on to it and marched majestically to the fitting room. It had been a little baggy, but the redhead was giving me the eye when I came out, so I'd bought it.) It wasn't baggy anymore.

I didn't look pregnant, but my waist was rapidly vanishing. Each night, in front of the full-length mirror in the small, square dressing alcove just outside John's bathroom, I saw my curves disappearing—except in the bosom department, where I was getting like Hedy Lamarr: lush.

So there I was in City Hall in a plain blue dress and black patent-leather heels, my hair pulled up, pinned tight in place. A working girl's outfit, but who knew that morning when I came to work that I'd be a bride by lunch?

John called me into his office a little after ten. "I have a ten-thirty conference over at Two Wall Street. I'll meet you at eleven forty-five at the Municipal Building, second floor, by the elevators. Put some papers in an envelope and say I called and asked you to bring them to me. Also, you have no idea when you'll be back, because one of the lawyers is from Germany and he may have some memoranda he wants to dictate." My expression must have confirmed his estimate of my intelligence. "Don't forget, the Municipal Building," he said again. "On Centre Street. I've arranged to have matters expedited. We can get the license and get married right away, without a waiting period. We can be finished by twelve-thirty."

"You have a conference at one?"

"I thought we could go out to lunch afterwards, to celebrate."

He gave me a small smile. I gave him one back, but halfway through it I realized John's smile was a brave, public one: chin up, noblesse whatever, courage under fire.

He'd probably offer a gracious toast at lunch.

The little man with a little toothbrush mustache came up beside John and, tiptoeing, led us past a line of clerks, who sat in cages like monkeys on high stools, and into his little glassed-in cubicle, so we wouldn't have to wait on line. That's where we filled out the application for a marriage license.

"Listen," I said, "I didn't know we'd be here today. I don't have my birth certificate or—"

"Shhh!" John said.

"But—"

"I will see to everything, miss," the little man said. "Just write down your vital statistics—" His face reddened, his mustache twitched, and he glanced nervously at John, afraid he'd made some blot on my honor. "Parents' names, date of birth, borough of birth," he said quickly. "You *were* born in New York City?" he asked, a little suspiciously, I thought, like maybe I'd snuck in from Minnesota and was trying to pull a fast one.

"In Queens," I said.

He sighed, relieved. Then he turned to John. His manner turned too—embarrassingly eager to please. "*Delighted* to have been of help, Mr. Berringer," the man said. "Any friend of Commissioner Tuttle . . ."

But whoever Commissioner Tuttle, puller of strings for Wall Street lawyers, was, he cut no ice in the room where you got married. We had to wait our turn along with about fifteen other couples. Only two of them looked really happy. Most of the others seemed like sad stories. There were several young girls—very young—with their slit-eyed parents and miserable-looking grooms-to-be; the grooms ranged in age from about sixteen to sixty-five; all those girls had bellies. A couple of couples looked as if they'd been keeping company since Calvin Coolidge was elected; they seemed tired of everything, especially each other. An elderly lady with a corsage and marcelled hair was less tired, but she was holding the hand of a too-pretty young man of no more than twenty-five.

But all these couples—the happy and the sad—stared at John. It was so obvious he didn't belong. It wasn't just that he was wearing a suit—a few of the other men were—but it was the way the suit fit. And the way the shoulders under the suit were broad. Not broad like one of the men, a construction worker who'd rolled the sleeves of his blue shirt so high you could see his tattooed biceps. John's muscles didn't come from work; they came from playing sports in white uniforms.

His shining hair brightened that room. One of the other guys, an Irishman who had gotten a dark Jewish girl pregnant, had hair as fair as John's, but it just didn't gleam.

So in the end, John wasn't stared at because of his clothes, or even his looks. He was simply apart from them, as though some fairy of Good Fortune had waved her wand over his baby carriage. Or, if he hadn't been born different, maybe he'd been initiated into some Ivy League secret society that transforms boys into privileged men.

Just as everybody there knew he was different, John knew

it too. And he didn't want to be with . . . well, with people like me. He wanted out of that gritty, noisy, overlit, everyone-is-equal place in the worst way.

"Brenninger!" a clerk yelled out.

We walked through an opening in the railing to a small area where another clerk, a primly dressed man who looked like he sold caskets, checked our papers. He took a long time, so I pulled out my hairpins and shook my hair loose.

"Ready? John Wilson Berringer, do you take Linda Rose Voss to be your lawful wedded wife?"

No "to love, honor and cherish"? I wondered.

"I do," John said.

Apparently not.

"Do you, Linda Rose Voss, take John Wilson Berringer to be your lawful wedded husband?"

"I do," I said. My voice sounded so normal.

"Ring?" the clerk said.

And just as I was thinking: He forgot, John took out a box. I stared as he opened it. Brown velvet, and inside, on white satin, there was a gold wedding band. Nice. Not insultingly thin.

"Thank you," I whispered, as he slipped it on my finger. It fit. Well, maybe just a little loose.

"I now pronounce you man and wife." The man waited, then he cleared his throat with a very fake "Ahem!" We kissed so it would be over and the next couple could start their life together.

Then I looked into John's eyes. They were filled with tears.

"Mom." I shook my mother gently. It was five in the afternoon of my wedding day. The air coming through the open windows had a crisp, almost sharp, bite. It was that short, false New York autumn that comes in September and blows away the heat of the summer for a few days. I was chilly in my blue dress. My mother's shoulder was cold, which was not surprising, since her blanket had fallen to the floor.

"Five more minutes," she mumbled, and curled herself up into a shrimp shape.

"Mom, I have to talk to you." I switched on the lamp on her night table. She'd bought a pair of these lamps when she and my father were first married; the base of the lamp was an extremely fat cherub—even as cherubs go—standing on grapes he somehow didn't crush; he wore a lampshade on his head. "Mom, please wake up."

She put the crook of her arm over her eyes and said, "C'mon, Lin, baby. Don't be a pain." She'd gotten so thin that in the lamplight I could see the faint outline of the two bones in her forearm. "Two more minutes."

I sat on the edge of the bed. The pillowcase was soiled with her hair cream and, I guess, her droolings; it hadn't been changed since I'd changed it, the week before.

"Mom, I have to talk with you," I said. I was trying not to get angry. I'd heard her come in around five-thirty that morning, and now I could see she'd slept in her dress. From the streaks of dirt at the bottom of the sheet, she hadn't even bothered to take off her shoes, although they'd fallen off during her sleep. One had dropped to the floor and another lay on what had been my father's side of the bed.

On the way down to the Municipal Building, I'd had a yen to splurge and take a cab to Queens, pick up my mother and bring her with me. Mom, put on your good navy dress with the white ruffle collar and come watch me get married! I'd say, and she'd leap out of bed, splash some water on her face and say, Oh, Linda, sweetie, you've made me so happy you wouldn't believe it!

"Go 'way," she mumbled. "I got a lousy hangover."

"It's five o'clock, Mom. In the afternoon." This didn't seem to make a big impression on her. "I have some wonderful news for you." Slowly, she lifted her arm away from her eyes and squinted at me. "John and I got married today."

She couldn't stop squinting, but she broke out into a huge smile. "Oh, Lin! A lawyer!" She reached out, squeezed my hand and wriggled around as if to sit up, but didn't make much progress. Her hand was freezing. I picked up the blanket from the floor and put it around her, tucking it under her feet. Her big toe poked through a rip in her stocking. "When did you do it?"

"Today." I started to apologize: "We decided at the last minute," but since she didn't seem to notice she hadn't been invited, I stopped.

"Tell me *everything*. Did he get down on his knee and propose? That's what Herm did. It was my sixteenth birthday, and he got down on his knee and said, 'Will you be my birthday girl for ever and ever?' Was your John romantic?"

What could I tell her? That at our wedding lunch, right after the waiter poured champagne and we lifted our glasses but didn't clink them because either John didn't want everybody in the restaurant to know we were celebrating or because clinking glasses was simply not done, or naive or something, he'd told me to take off my ring before I got back to the office, since he hadn't decided how to "present the situation." Naturally, I'd be leaving in a week or two. "No, make that closer to three. It's not going to be easy replacing you." He smiled, for the waiter, returning with menus, as well as for me. After the waiter walked off, John added, "You're a good secretary, Linda."

"A great secretary."

"And very modest."

"That too."

"It will take a few weeks to come up with someone even remotely suitable."

"And you'll have to pay her more."

"Probably."

"So am I better at the typewriter or in bed?"

He put down his champagne glass. "Come on," he whispered, "let's forget lunch. We can go back to the apartment and celebrate." Not a chance. In fact, I told him, I had to take the rest of the afternoon off and get things set up for my mother. "Your mother?" he murmured. He couldn't seem to remember I'd come from parents, not an employment agency.

So after lunch I'd gone home to Ridgewood and stopped in to talk to Dr. Guber. He'd hugged me and said, "Hey, I knew the guy would marry you! Now relax, be a wife. I know a nice old maid, a practical nurse, over in Bushwick. She'll live in and cook, clean, take care of your mother. Don't worry," he'd soothed me. "This girl's got the constitution of an ox. For fifteen bucks a week, she'll do everything. More than you could do, working all day."

I put my hand on my mother's icy shoulder. "Mom, listen to me. I gave a key to Dr. Guber—"

"That old fart?"

"Mom, he's going to give it to a girl from Bushwick, who'll be coming in to clean and cook whatever you want and look after you. I'll pay her, and I'm going to give you money every week. But you can't spend it all in one day."

"Who, *me?*" my mother asked, and tried to wink, although it didn't work. Her cheek just twitched. "So tell me, honeybunch, what's your name now?"

"Berringer," I said.

"Write it down for me," she said, "so I can tell all my friends."

I took a piece of paper and a pencil from my pocket and wrote "Linda Berringer" for the first time, and added John's home phone number.

"Here's my phone number, Mom. And I'll call you every day. But if you need anything, you call me."

"Listen, dollface, you did good."

"Thanks, Mom."

"You pregnant?" She gave me an inquisitive smile.

"Yes."

"That's what I figured. Linda, lovie, you're one smart girl, hooking him before he could wiggle away to another rich one. I'm *so* proud of you."

Then, before she went back to sleep, she gave me a big hug and a kiss.

It wasn't until a few minutes after six, fighting the end of the crowd rushing down, that I pushed my way up the subway stairs on my way back to the office. I was wondering if, being a lawyer's wife, I could have taken a taxi to see my mother. In John's neighborhood, I'd seen rich ladies in suits and alligator shoes who stood on the corner of Park Avenue and raised one finger, and cabs pulled over and screeched on their brakes and drivers smiled.

I was preoccupied, coming up and out of the subway, wondering how John would give me house money, whether I'd just find it under a pillow or if he'd hand me two or three or four twenties—whatever lawyers' wives get—every other Friday, the day he got his check. And how was I supposed to know what it was for? I figured, okay, groceries, newspapers, a lipstick. Do lawyers' wives say, Darling, I need an extra forty for a sweet little peau de soie at Tailored Woman? What if he forgot to give me anything? Was I supposed to remind him?

Anyway, I was almost at the top of the steps, slipping my wedding ring off and putting it in my pocketbook, thinking that it was going to be pretty embarrassing, but I was going to have to ask John for a new winter coat because the old one not only was embarrassingly ratty, with an unsewable rip under the left arm, but wouldn't button over my belly when the time came, when—not more than two seconds after I'd gotten up to the street—I slammed into Gladys Slade.

"Excuse me," she said. She was so busy being polite, she hadn't seen me.

Those were really her first words to me since we'd come to the understanding that she'd keep quiet. Of course, she included me in a "How are you?" if I was coming through the door with a group of the girls. To do anything else would be to call attention to the fact that I'd done something terrible that called for a boycott, and she was nervous enough about my "power" over John that she kept herself under tight control. Any "Hello" or "What's new?" was just in self-defense.

To tell the truth, the only reason I missed my friendship with Gladys was that on a lot of Sundays we went to the movies together; since I'd started seeing John seven days a week, I hadn't been to a single movie. I'd missed Fred Astaire and Eleanor Powell in *Broadway Melody of 1940*, and I was dying to see Laurence Olivier in *Rebecca*, even though Joan Fontaine was so whiny I always wished her leading man would smack her across the face and say, Shut up, you pain in the ass!

Gladys was huddled in her office sweater, which she'd worn home because of the chill. It was a too-loose cardigan, the color of Wheatena. Suddenly, I felt cold and massaged my empty ring finger with my thumb. "How've you been, Gladys?"

She nodded, and I guess only because I didn't move out of the way, she said, "You weren't at lunch today."

"Mr. Berringer"—I blushed—"had a conference over at Two Wall. He wanted me there."

"Well, I'm sure he was delighted to have you."

"Look, Gladys, I'm not going to say anything corny, like 'Let's be friends,' but at least we could be civil to each other. We've known each other so long and . . . Why don't we go out for a drink, maybe early next week?"

"I can't see any point to it."

"There is no point, really. Just to talk." What I wanted to do, after John "presented the situation" of our marriage, was to sit down and tell Gladys before she heard it from the office grapevine. I felt I owed her that. Or maybe deep down I just wanted someone to talk to. Funny, I had nobody now.

Gladys opened her pocketbook and made herself busy searching through her change purse to find a nickel for the subway. "What you're obviously dying to talk about"—she spoke into her pocketbook—"I don't want to know about."

I should have felt angry, but all I could think of was how embarrassed . . . no, embarrassment was nothing compared to what Gladys was going to feel when she heard about me and John. Look, I wanted to reassure her, I'm never going to tell him how you talk about all the partners, especially not how you talked about him, how you went on and on about how gorgeous he was and said, "Can you *imagine* what he must look like in tennis clothes?"

She found her nickel. I stepped aside. "I'll let you go, then," I said.

But she wasn't quite ready. "I think I ought to warn you," Gladys said, "that your little interlude may be coming to an end." She stopped. She waited for me to beg her to go on. I didn't. "Mrs. Avenel is having a dinner party Saturday for all the partners. She's hired a butler to pass around the hors d'oeuvres. Mr. Berringer had been invited, and Mrs. Avenel had arranged for a *very* eligible girl to be his dinner partner, but . . ."

Her long, dramatic pause was so overly long and dramatic that I finally lost patience. I knew she was out to hurt me again, and I couldn't be hurt. Well, not by her, anyway. "But what, Gladys?"

"He called Mrs. Avenel this morning and told her"—she gave a long, supercilious sniff—"he'd met someone and was *getting married!*"

I asked softly, "Did he say if he was still going to the party?"

"Didn't you hear me?"

"I heard you. Is he going?"

"*Yes*, he's going." Her tone turned into a sneer. "With his fiancée."

No, I was dying to say. With his wife.

Right after we'd finally turned out the lights, I'd asked John when I could wear my ring to the office. "Oh," he'd murmured. I waited. "Whenever," he finally said. "When you went to your mother's, I spoke to Ed about our . . . and your leaving."

"Did you tell him I was—"

"*No.*" He turned his pillow over and, before he went off to sleep, added, "Stop worrying. He said it was fine with him."

Well, it was the day after my wedding and it wasn't fine. I was standing in front of Mr. Leland's desk because he hadn't asked me to sit down, and I was being yelled at by a man who was able to yell without raising his voice.

"Did it occur to you at any point, Mrs. Berringer, that you

had responsibilities to someone other than yourself?" Edward Leland was furious. "Did you ever consider that apart from the damned nuisance of engaging another bilingual secretary, it usually takes a minimum of ten weeks to get someone security clearance for the sort of work you've been doing? You're cleared for secret work. Do you think we can pick some German-speaking stenographer off the streets of Yorkville and dictate our codes to her? It could take weeks, *months* even, to find someone whom we can even approach for an FBI check.

"You know how things are heating up here. You know that the volume of this . . . this sort of work has increased a hundredfold. What am I supposed to do if I have a message to send tomorrow? Or three or four weeks from now?" I couldn't get an answer past the lump in my throat. "Send it down to Washington for fifty idiot bureaucrats to pass from hand to hand before they translate?" His face darkened. "Ask your husband to type it up?"

"Please, I'll be glad to—"

"To what, Mrs. Berringer?"

"To do whatever I can."

"You're a married woman."

"No matter what your wedding night is like, you don't forget shorthand." I couldn't believe I'd said that.

Neither could Mr. Leland. "I don't need clever retorts. I need a secretary with security clearance."

"I'm sorry."

"I assumed—obviously wrongheadedly—that you realized that despite the seeming simplicity of the letters I've been dictating, they serve a purpose."

"Mr. Leland," I began. But then I started crying. Not just a few cute tears. Real, true weeping. I covered my face with my hands, and as I did, my pad and pencil dropped.

"For God's sake!" he said. And then he added, "Oh, sit down." I sat. "Here." He leaned forward and put his handkerchief right in front of me on the desk. I hated using it, because I thought: How am I going to get this back to him? but I used it anyway; my nose was running. Except for my sobbing, it was absolutely quiet, and I think I finally spoke only because I didn't want him to fill the silence by telling me to get a grip on myself or, worse, that he was sorry he'd upset me.

I took one last sniffle and looked up at him. "Mr. Leland, I'm sorry to be carrying on like this." Nothing resembling an emotion showed on his face. "I'd like to explain things."

"That is not necessary, Mrs. Berringer."

"I think it is."

"All right. Go on."

"I know you think I'm inconsiderate, and you're right. I didn't consider that I was working for you too. I didn't consider it for a minute. You know why? I was carrying on with Mr. Berringer—"

"This really isn't necessary."

"I know, but please listen, anyway. I got pregnant, Mr. Leland." His black eyes widened, not because he was surprised; I'm sure he wasn't. He was surprised I was talking about it. "I know it's something people don't discuss in polite company—but I'm not such polite company. Anyway, I'm sure you've already figured out Mr. . . . that John didn't marry me for my money or my great mind. He married me because he had to.

"So you're right," I went on. "I was a wreck and I didn't think about anyone beyond myself. Well, I thought about my mother. She's a drunk and she's not in the best of health and I support her. But maybe you already know that from the FBI or whoever checked me."

"Yes, I know about it," he said softly.

"So all I can do is apologize and say this conversation is probably as uncomfortable for you as it is for me, but I want to set the record straight. Like you guys say, there were extenuating circumstances."

"I understand."

"But just because I got myself in trouble . . ."

"Go on."

"It doesn't mean I can't work. Okay, maybe I can't come to the office during the day, but I could come in real early or real late. I don't want to louse you up. I know . . . well, I don't *know*, but I figure what you're doing is very important, so until you find someone else, I'd like to do whatever I can."

"Thank you," he said. "I'm sure I'll be able to manage without you."

That was it. Like the sergeants say in all the army movies: *Dismissed!* I picked up my pad and pencil from the floor and took that long, familiar walk across his office rug again. When I was halfway to the door, Edward Leland called out: "Mrs. Berringer." I turned and faced him. His soft handkerchief was balled up in my fist.

"Yes, Mr. Leland?"

"Whatever happens . . ." For the first time since I'd known him, he hesitated. "You're all right. Don't ever sell yourself short."

# 12

Henry and Florence Avenel lived somewhere in West-chester, in an important-looking white house with pillars that would have been perfect for Thomas Jefferson or Scarlett O'Hara but seemed a little much for a bulgy-eyed corporate lawyer who looked like a toad in a striped tie. So the house was grand, although a couple of steps down from palatial, but whoever the Avenels had bought it from had obviously gone bust—probably in '29—and, before giving up the last of their mint julep dreams, had sold off most of the ole plantation. Just as you drove up and were about to go Ooh! you saw another, newer, smaller, semi-Tara on the left and an English Tudor squeezing in on the right. If someone in the Tudor had sneezed, it was so close—separated just by a border of trees shaped like lollipops—Florence Avenel might have said Gesundheit!

Mrs. Avenel was not only polite; she was wildly enthusiastic. "John!" she gushed, as we came through the door. "This must be Linda! John, she's lovely! Beyond lovely! Like Jean Harlow brought back to life!" I bore as much resemblance to the movie star as she bore to Minnie Mouse: barely any, but enough to comment on if you were truly desperate for something to say. "But she's *so* much finer-looking than Harlow, of course." She had to say that, naturally. She wasn't going to risk telling her husband's partner that his new wife was a ringer for a world-famous platinum-blond slut. "Congratulations, John!"

Then she beamed at me, not failing to take in my midsection, which, I'd made sure, was covered by the long, boxy jacket of the black faille dinner suit I'd bought. (I'd known purple and low-cut were wrong, but was less sure what was right. So I'd come out of the kitchen after finishing the dinner dishes and asked John if I could have some money for a dress for the Avenels'. He'd gone to his wallet and handed me two fifty-dollar bills and said, Is this enough? The hundred dollars had made me mute, but I'd nodded yes, it was enough. The next day, I marched into Saks Fifth Avenue and looked around until I found the perfect salesgirl; she looked like one of the executive secretaries: a Vassar type with a tight mouth and a tighter behind. I told her: I'm going to a Saturday night dinner party with a bunch of Wall Street lawyers. What've you got? She'd raised both eyebrows but picked out the suit and a soft gray silk blouse to go with it, and told me, Wear pearl earrings. Ha, but I'd worn my hair down to cover my ears. When I walked out of the bedroom, all dressed and ready to go, John looked flabbergasted. Like Mrs. Avenel, he'd probably been expecting red sequins and chewing gum. He was caught so off guard by my lack of bad taste that he mumbled, Oh. You look beautiful.)

Mrs. Avenel at last spoke to me. "My dear, Henry and I are so very, very happy for you."

All those years, Gladys had actually been managing to mimic Mrs. Avenel pretty well. "My dee-ahr." From the imitation, I'd always imagined an overpowering woman with a bust so commanding it could easily lead a battleship across the Atlantic. But Mrs. Avenel was tiny, barely five feet tall, and so thin the bones on her chest stuck out, like a chicken's. She was wearing a floor-length bottle-green dress with a deep V neck and a sash, which looked more like an overdone bathrobe than a hostess gown.

She took my arm and led me across a hallway with a marble checkerboard floor, toward the living room. "Now tell me, my dear, how long have the two of you been married?"

"Five days."

"Ah! Five days! You must call me Florence." She smiled up at me. I smiled back; it felt unnaturally broad—the smile you make standing in front of a bathroom mirror looking for food stuck between your back teeth.

But after a second, I realized she was no longer appraising me. Her eyes finally fixed on John, and now that she'd done what was proper with me, she could concentrate. Concentrate was putting it mildly. Little Flo was beaming at my husband with the intensity of a radio signal on top of the Empire State Building. Her gaze broadcast a powerful message: Wow! Wow! Wow!

And he, of course, was smiling back. Hey, I could have told her, that's the smile he gives to hatcheck girls and the building superintendent's wife. And to secretaries. Obviously to every female. That smile is his routine you-are-bewitching-and-you've-captivated-me-completely smile. It's pure reflex, like a jerking knee, and he does it to reduce you—and all of us—to jelly, so just in case he wants something from you, you're ready, available, thirsting to do whatever it is he wants. Come on, Florence, you're fifty years old, not very bright, eagle-beaked and chicken-breasted. Do you think he wants you?

She did. And so did they all. Florence led us into her living room, with its high ceiling, tall windows and long sofas, and every woman in the room fell into silence and gaped at my husband. Then John smiled, a general nice-to-see-you smile, but the women, obviously remembering previous, more personal smiles, like the one bestowed upon lucky Florence, all broke into joyous grins of gladness.

"Everyone!" Florence Avenel trilled. "*This* is Linda."

It was only then that the women's eyes turned to me. And their husbands' too. Seven or eight partners of Blair, Vander-Graff and Wadley opened up the tight knot they'd been standing in by the fireplace, glanced over and smiled at me. Not the way John smiled, of course, but courteously enough. A couple of them waved. After all, I'd become a wife. Their faces were a blur, but then Mr. Wilson lifted his cocktail glass in a toast. "To the newlyweds!" he said, and suddenly glasses were raised and ten or fifteen cultivated voices were repeating: "Nyoo-lyweds!"

And then there was silence as all those well-bred people, the toasting out of the way, just stared. For the men, seeing me in black faille, with makeup on and hair loose, was discomforting. It upset the normal balance of things, as if their barber had all of a sudden showed up at a partners' meeting in a three-piece suit and plunked himself down at the conference table and said, Hiya, guys.

The women gazed in cool assessment . . . well, maybe not so cool. A couple of fast looks were flashed between two older women in print dresses, and a stunner of about forty, with ivory skin, gray-blond hair pulled tight into a chic chignon, and brilliant red lipstick, lowered her glance from my suit (which I guess was okay) to my shoes (which, from her quickly sucked-in cheeks, obviously weren't).

"Well," boomed Mr. Avenel as he came over. He pushed a martini into my hand with so much heartiness I nearly spilled it. "How's the new bride?"

"Fine," I said, and then everybody, relieved, began to talk again, lots of tight, buzzing conversations.

"Well, let me introduce you to the ladies." He grabbed my free hand and pulled me across what I think was a Chinese rug—anyway, it was blue, with flowers—to the women. "Claudia Boland, Mimi O'Connell, Sarah Weedcock, Lorraine Wilson . . ." He spoke so fast I had no way of knowing who was who, although I guessed Lorraine Wilson was the freckled one with a big jaw, because she was such a good match for Mr. Wilson, who also had freckles and resembled a ventriloquist's dummy. "Mary Shawcross, who's here with Ed Leland . . ." I hadn't seen him. I made myself not turn around to the pack of partners by the fireplace. Mary Shawcross smiled just enough to show teeth like perfect tiny white tiles. She was the elegant one, with the pale, pulled-back hair and red lipstick. More than elegant. Almost beautiful, with high cheekbones and sleepy, heavy-lidded eyes.

I took a gulp of the martini. "Carrie Post," Henry Avenel continued, and I came face-to-face with the woman whose husband was spending all his evenings with Wilma Gerhardt and paid for Wilma's manicures—to say nothing of her fox jacket and an endless supply of silk stockings. The pudgy, cheated-on Mrs. Post summoned up her good manners and managed a "Glad to meet you." It took some summoning; this quiet, double-chinned woman had to work at being cordial because she *knew*—I just knew she knew—and the sight of a former secretary with a lawyer's wedding band on was, to say the least, painful.

"Oh," Mr. Avenel boomed on, "let me not forget our Ginger Norris!" I turned, expecting a pug-nosed tennis player. Instead, I saw a woman in her mid-fifties, who was a real pill; while all the others had managed a decent "So pleased," or even a plain "Hello," Ginger just inclined her head, as if she was doing a Queen Mary imitation.

And then, right after the introductions, things went back to normal. Mimi spoke to Sarah, Lorraine spoke to Mary, and everyone spoke to everyone—except to me. All of a sudden, I was alone with my martini. And I realized then that all that momentary graciousness had been exactly that: a warmth that lasted about sixty seconds.

So I just stood there, the only one not being talked to, and the only one being watched. I sensed it. Quick, sideways glances. And if I'd wandered over to inspect the Avenels' framed flower pictures or toddled off to the bathroom, they would have known how I'd felt: frightened and alone—heart pounding—in enemy territory.

I took another long sip of my martini. I hated gin, and vermouth and an olive didn't help the situation. I glanced across the room and watched the men murmuring to each other. They stood around the fireplace, which was filled with a giant urn of yellow chrysanthemums. A deep, manly hum arose from them, an uninterrupted hum, as if they were having an endlessly fascinating conversation. John was sandwiched between Mr. Norris and Mr. O'Connell, and all three were nodding in absolute agreement. I took a step to the right and saw they were nodding at who I thought they'd be nodding at: Edward Leland. Mr. Leland looked content, content with whatever he was saying, content with the way his high-powered partners hung on to his every syllable, and probably most content that after dinner was over he'd be taking Mary Shawcross, her chignon, her exquisite cheekbones and her bright red lips home.

There was one good thing about the dinner itself—the hot rolls.

There was more than one bad thing. First, watching the crazily elaborate ceremony of carving the roast beef. A maid carried the roast into the dining room and slowed down as she passed Mrs. Avenel, who gazed at it with so much pride you'd have thought it was her firstborn. Then the maid, with the heavy silver platter resting on both palms, continued down the length of the table, all the way over to Mr. Avenel, and lowered it before him. He pushed back his chair and lifted up the fork and carving knife laid out before him, cut a slice and held it up on the fork. Some blood dribbled back into the platter, and he said, "Voilà!" I looked away for a second; the martini—and maybe the pregnancy—had made me dizzy, and queasy.

As Mr. Avenel began to carve in earnest, he breathed hard. His eyes bugged out even more than usual, and his face got all flushed and damp. He was nervous, anxious to do it just right, as if he was the high priest of some religion, finishing up a sacrifice to a bad-tempered god. As he labored, the maid ran up and down the table, handing out the meat. I couldn't stand the smell.

The next bad thing was watching John at the far end of the table, seated between Florence Avenel and Carrie Post, being charming, laughing at Florence's clever remark, which I knew couldn't be clever, admiring Carrie Post's locket and listening seriously as she told him about something like her gall bladder or her son in boarding school. It wasn't that I was jealous. It was that I realized, observing John from a distance, how he gave himself equally to everybody—or, more accurately, to nobody.

He didn't look down the table at me even once. Why should he? I only had one reason for being; all I could do for him at the Avenels' would be to embarrass him, and since I hadn't, he could forget me until we got home—or partway home, when he'd take his hand from the steering wheel, reach over and grab mine, and press it between his legs.

Another bad thing was sitting back and having to listen to a roomful of Republicans talk about the presidential campaign. Okay, Wendell Willkie wasn't the worst person in the world; he'd even started out a Democrat. But to hear these so-called smart lawyers go on and on about him, you'd think he was Jesus Christ.

They called him Wendell, as if he was one of theirs, and I suppose he was. Edward Leland, of all people, sitting on Florence Avenel's other side, who I'd thought had more brains than the rest of the table combined, referred to FDR with sarcasm, calling him "our esteemed leader" and saying, "The average American cannot comprehend that it's a tacit New Deal policy to encourage unemployment. Their bureaucrats have nothing to gain from a healthy private sector. What they want is a perpetual Depression, so they can keep their jobs." I couldn't believe he was saying things like that. Of course, he was better than Henry Avenel, who called Roosevelt "the cripple" and said Willkie would "kill him" on election day. I felt like taking his wife's potato soufflé or whatever it was and dumping it on his fat head.

And the last bad thing was that after the soggy apple pie, the men went someplace to have brandies and smoke cigars, and I was left in the living room on a club chair, while the other women gathered in tight twos and threes and admired each other's outfits and hairdos. Occasionally one of them would allow a glance to pass over me. There'd be a whisper and then a soft "Shhh!" They didn't try very hard to hide their elbow nudgings; they barely muffled their giggles. And that was how I knew these ladies weren't ladies.

I wasn't going to fall apart. When the men came back, I made myself stay in that stupid chair; I'd be damned if those rich bitches would see me leap up and run to John.

So I sat there, staring out the night-blackened window, deliberately not watching John, although out of the corner of my eye I saw him swirl his brandy and nod at whatever Russell Weedcock was spouting off about. And just then, a man sat on the arm of my chair and said, "Well, how are you enjoying yourself?" I didn't have to look up, although I did. I knew Edward Leland's voice.

"It's a very nice party."

"You seem to be having a fine time," he said coolly.

"Very fine."

"Good!" he said in his deep voice, and everyone turned and stared. "I noticed how enthralled you were with the political discussion at dinner. No doubt you're a great fan of our Mr. Willkie."

"He has wonderful hair."

"Oh, come on. You can give him more than that."

"Okay. Other than FDR, he's the strongest supporter of the Democratic Party platform we have around."

"Please," he said, looking annoyed and disappointed, as if he'd overestimated my intelligence by five hundred percent.

"Look, Mr. Leland—"

"Please, call me Ed."

Oh, God, I thought. As if this night wasn't hard enough. "Willkie's a me-too candidate. He's for everything Roosevelt's for: the draft, aid to England—"

"Nonsense!" He shifted on the chair arm so he could look me right in the eye. I sensed, more than saw, the whole room watching us, trying to hear what we were saying. "He made it quite clear he feels Roosevelt is courting a war—a war we're completely unprepared for."

"Yeah? Well, it's a war we could have been prepared for if your isolationist Republican buddies, your big hero Lindbergh and Senator Vandenberg, hadn't been holding us back—and sending Hitler kissy-kissy, do-whatever-you-want signals."

"You must know better than that. Wendell Willkie has always been a friend of European democracies." I looked up and noticed a thin white scar running down the side of Edward Leland's face, from his temple all the way down to his jaw. "He's not that sort of Republican."

"There are a lot of dead Dutchmen and Poles and Czechs and Belgians saying, 'You made us what we are today, O Party of Lincoln.' "

He shook his head and began to smile. "You certainly fight the fair fight, Mrs. Berringer."

"Why not fight the way I want to? What can you do?" I smiled. "Fire me?" Then I looked straight into his eyes. "Oh, and please, call me Linda."

He let go and started to laugh. Really laugh. And everyone in that room turned and watched Edward Leland being amused, and suddenly, all of them, including my husband, were moving in, smiling at me.

John was pretty detached later that night. God forbid, he could have said, Well, that must have been a real strain for you, but you did just fine. Or even a casual, husbandly, What the hell was that potato glop? Instead, he whistled to himself on the way home, and not something nice, Rodgers-and-Harty, but a slow, creepy classical thing that sounded German, probably some Wagner stuff, a lament for Wotan or Kriemhild or one of those types.

"What did you think of tonight?" I finally asked, when he was sitting on the edge of the bed, pushing a shoe tree into his shoe.

"It was all right."

"Did you have fun?"

"No." He started on the other shoe. "But these things aren't fun."

"So why do you go?"

He stood, walked to his closet and slipped the shoes into their place in the lineup, between another pair of black ones, exactly like the ones he'd just taken off, and some cordovans. "I go," he said, as he took off his pants and folded them over the hanger, "because it's part of my job. It's a professional obligation. Just like a Bar Association meeting or sending out Christmas cards to clients." He took off his jacket. "Did you order the Christmas cards?"

"Yes."

"From Tiffany's?" He put the jacket on the hanger, buttoned it, and shook out the suit before returning it to its place among eight other dark, dark pinstripes.

"Yes."

"Did you pick out the one I showed you, the one I sent"—the one *they* sent—"last year? White with—"

"No. I picked out something with chartreuse polka dots and naked elves."

He smiled. "Sometimes you're very quick."

"You could say smart."

He moved close to me. I took off his tie. "I'll consider it," he said, and kissed me.

"I have some smart things to say about the party," I managed to say between kisses. "Want to hear them? Like about Roger Post. You know about him and—"

"Let's forget tonight," he said, as he took off my suit jacket and then my blouse. And so we did forget.

But the next morning, a warm, hazy Sunday, as he sat in the living room, surrounded by newspapers, it was clear he remembered. "What were you talking to Ed Leland about?"

"Willkie."

"Oh, Jesus! Did you say anything?" he demanded, his voice filled with something close to dread. "Ed's a personal friend of Willkie's."

"I didn't call him a creep or anything."

John let the *Tribune* financial pages drop to the floor. "What *did* you call him?"

"Hey, what are you so upset about? I didn't start anything. He . . ."—I made my voice very low—" 'Please call me Ed' . . . he asked *me* what I thought about the candidates."

John made a small circle with his lips and exhaled very slowly. "And so you told him. Leaving nothing out, I'm sure."

"Well, if I call him up on election day and say, 'Hey, Ed, I voted for FDR,' I don't think he'll clutch his chest and fall down with a major heart attack from shock."

I picked up the *Times*—the *London* one! After sex, and knowing that for the rest of my life I could look across the dinner table and see this extraordinary man, and (I hate to make myself look grasping, but I was, a little) being able to walk into Saks Fifth Avenue with a hundred bucks, the best thing about being Mrs. John Berringer was that I could buy every single newspaper and magazine I wanted—even English and German ones—because he wanted them too. Still, I was like a kid given a giant spoon and absolute freedom in an ice cream parlor.

I started to read again. Even though you had to take everything in the British papers with a grain of salt because of wartime censorship and their need to keep up morale, it was pretty clear that the Battle of Britain wasn't going to be the fast triumph the Germans had thought it would be: a few bombs, then invasion. That Wednesday, the Royal Air Force had lost twelve planes. Not good, but the Luftwaffe had lost nineteen.

"John, do you think if the German losses—"

He cut me off. "Tell me what you said to Ed about Willkie."

"For God's sake!"

"Linda, this is important."

"Why?" He just crossed his arms. "Okay. What I basically said was the best thing about Willkie was his hair, and he was a me-too candidate, and that his program was pretty much lifted from the Democrats' platform." John's mouth tightened. He was across the room, so I couldn't tell if it was with annoyance or anger. "Listen: Mr. Leland—Ed's seen my FBI papers. He must know I'm a Democrat."

"Christ."

"It's not like I'm a Nazi or a prostitute. For God's sake, my father was a sausagemaker who lost his job in the Depression. What am I supposed to do—be a cheerleader for Herbert Hoover?"

"You're supposed to have the sense not to alienate one of the most important men in the country."

"Alienate him? He was having a good time talking to me."

"He was being courteous."

"No! He was being amused. Listen: He doesn't need

another person to bend over backward not to offend him. The line's probably ten miles long."

"I'm not suggesting you be a sycophant . . . someone given to false flattery. But there's absolutely no need to be so damned direct."

"Why not? My pal Ed thinks I'm a breath of fresh air."

John leaned forward. His hair fell into his eyes, and he shook his head to get it off his forehead. "Can't you begin to understand the awkwardness of the situation?"

"Yes." He sat back. So I leaned forward. "He's your former father-in-law."

"That's right."

"And he's probably heard an earful about you from Nan, and you, being a gentleman, of course, can't defend yourself. You can't tell him that his daughter's an immature, spoiled—"

"Enough! We're not talking about Nan."

"Sure we are! When we're talking about Ed, we're talking about Nan. For God's sake, let's clear the air, John. Take an objective look at her. Forget her morals. Think about her character. She doesn't have any. She's a two-bit little sneak."

He stood up and roared at me: "Don't you *dare* talk about her!"

I found myself roaring back. "I am sick and tired of tippy-toeing around every damn time the name of one of the Lelands comes up. She was an *adultress*. Don't you get it? And for all her class, she didn't have the guts to come to you and say, 'Listen: I've made a mistake marrying you.' She betrayed you instead, and you talk about her like she was a saint!" John turned and stalked off toward the bedroom. I rushed after him, almost running to keep up. "And Edward Leland . . ." I was breathing hard. "You carry on like he's God himself. He's not. He's a *man*."

John turned to me in the corridor just outside the bedroom. "Edward Leland is everything I could ever hope to be."

"Like honorable."

"Yes."

"And brave."

"Yes."

"How about scary-looking? Do you think if you took a land mine in the face he'd finally have respect for you? Why is this man so important to you?"

It took a long time before he was able to answer. "It's not the sort of thing you'd understand."

"Try me."

"I care about excellence. Do you understand that? I care about decency, fair play."

"So do I." He shook his head, like saying, You don't get it. "Listen: I have a great idea. If you're so crazy about decency, why not practice it on me?"

"Did it ever occur to you, Linda, that despite all the self-effacing noises you make, you are monumentally self-centered? We cannot have one discussion without your saying, 'I want more! I *demand* more!' "

"John," I began, "all I want is to be treated like—"

"Like Nan. I'm truly sorry, but I can't accommodate you. You aren't Nan. But I believe I am treating you decently and fairly. I'm trying, Linda. I'm doing the best I can."

"But I want better. I know you're capable of so much more. If you'd only—"

"Please don't hold on to those kinds of hopes. This is not . . . this is not a love match. It has nothing to do with you. It's me. I'm the one who can't . . . Linda, you can't get blood from a stone."

# 13

During the bleakest days of the Depression, in 1931, the sausage plant closed down for nearly a year, and my father had no job. My salary, fifteen dollars a week, was all we had, and so we'd alternate: one week food, coal, doctor bills; one week mortgage money. But by March it was clear we couldn't keep up the payments, and sure enough, a foreclosure notice came in the mail.

My father sat on the couch, his face in his hands, his shoulders heaving, the letter on the cushion beside him. I stood in the hallway, not knowing what to say, when my mother slipped past me, brushed the notice off the couch and sat down beside him.

"Bad news, Herm?"

"They're going to foreclose on the house, Betty."

I don't think she understood what he meant, but she understood how he felt. She put her arms around him, spoke to him so gently I couldn't hear what she was saying, and then kissed him until he finally stopped crying.

She took his hand. "Everything'll be fine, Herm."

"Betty, honey—"

She turned his hand over and examined his palm. "Ooh! I see *lots* of good things. Lookit here, how the line kinda turns right. You know what that means? Money!" My father laughed. "No kidding. Money. A long trip. And a beaver coat. Ha-ha, go ahead and laugh. You'll see!"

My father kissed the top of her head, then her forehead, and when he took her in his arms, I'd walked away.

My mother had been quite a fortuneteller, though. Okay, no beaver coat, no trip. But money: The plant reopened and my father went back to work.

I bet anything he never forgot how much she believed in him and in the luck of their marriage. And I never forgot what it was like to look at an ordinary, down-on-their-luck middle-aged couple and be able to feel, across the room, the depth and power of true love.

So I knew what the real thing was, and I knew I didn't have it. But at least I had a lot: a handsome, educated husband, a spacious apartment not more than thirty-five steps from Park Avenue, all the newspapers I could read and all the sex I could desire. My husband didn't drink, gamble, beat me or womanize; he just didn't love me.

But by a little more than a month after we'd been married, in late October 1940, I'd come to understand that John couldn't really love anyone. Well, except for the Lelands, and maybe he didn't even love them. He idolized or idealized them. This may not have been an electrifying news flash to anyone else, but one chilly Thursday night, it came to me like a shock.

It was about ten-thirty. I'd snuck up into the office at seven. John's new secretary, Anna—an older woman with a thick German accent, a gray, chopped-up Dutchboy haircut and glowing, slightly demented blue eyes, so she looked as if she was suffering from a mild case of whatever Hitler had—was not a bad secretary.

"But she's so *slow*," John said, almost an apology. He sat on the edge of what once had been my desk.

"I don't mind. Honest." I put my fingers back on the home line of the typewriter and peered at the steno pad. I'd begun transcribing the ton of letters he'd been dictating to me for the last three and a half hours. "It gives me something to do."

"Would you rather be doing this than . . ." He paused and shifted so he almost sat on Anna's pencil cup; I pulled it out from under him in time. ". . . than being a housewife?" Not counting the Are you, Do you, Can I questions he asked during sex, this was the most personal question he'd ever asked me.

"I'd rather be married to you." He didn't look thrilled, but he didn't look unthrilled, either: just neutral, as if I'd stated the obvious and he was waiting for more. "But it's sometimes a little—you know—boring. There's not much to do." I went on, "at least not till the baby comes. Especially if you've got my streak of German efficiency, you can get through the housework in—oh—an hour. Except on Tuesdays, when I iron your shirts—and what's that, an extra thirty minutes? And how long does it take to make a pork chop presentable? I've got a *lot* of free time."

"You don't like all that leisure?"

"No. I know it sounds ungrateful, but I'm becoming *too* well-informed. I mean, I know the exact route of the invasion of Rumania and what the German army ate for lunch on October 7. I practically know the color of Antonescu's socks." (I also knew that on that same day, the Germans ordered all the Jews in occupied France to register with the authorities. For what? I'd asked myself. But I knew it wasn't a census to satisfy curiosity. The German military mind was purposeful; it didn't make casual inquiries.)

"Look, Linda," John began. But then he stopped.

"What? Oh, come on. I know something's on your mind."

"It's not a particularly good idea for you to be seen here."

"I'm your wife. Make believe I came by to say hello, or to drop off a pot roast sandwich so you wouldn't be hungry."

"I don't mean in the office itself. I mean here." He patted the desk.

"You mean it would be bad for morale if someone saw me doing your secretary's work?" He nodded. "But Anna's bad for *your* morale. She can't do it all." He nodded again. "Oh! Okay, I get it. You want me to say, 'Poor John, you're under so much pressure. Why don't you bring a typewriter with a German keyboard *home*, so I can help you in all my free time?"

"Yes." He smiled a little. "That's what I want you to say."

"Okay. I've said it. But you know, it would have been easier if you'd just come out and asked me."

John sighed and gazed up at the ceiling for a second, looking for patience. He found it. "All right. Let's leave now. Take the pad, and then you can arrange for a typewriter tomorrow." He seemed so pleased at having handed over the details of his life to a more efficient secretary that, as he was helping me on with my coat, he said, "Let's go out for dinner. I know a little French place that stays open late."

Everyone at the little French place knew John, although they clearly had not been expecting me. The headwaiter bowed, though, did the merest twiddle of his mustache and said, *"Bon soir, mademoiselle."* To my real surprise, John corrected him: "Madame Berringer." Give the French credit: They fall apart in battle, but they're imperturbable when it comes to affairs of the heart—or lower down. "Ah, Madame Berringer!" he said as he started to lead us to a table, and went into something fancy in French, which I assumed meant: Welcome to my humble abode, although, for all I knew, it could have meant: I see Monsieur Berringer knocked you up and had to marry you. He held out a chair for me. I prayed he wouldn't kiss my hand. He didn't.

He and John had a complicated French discussion then, and John turned to me. Apparently, it all boiled down to: Does Madame want chicken: I said, Sure, fine, and the man wriggled his mustache for a second and then left.

"I didn't know you could speak French," I said.

"Not as well as German, but I can manage."

"Anything else I don't know about you?" I watched him put his napkin on his lap and straighten out his silverware. "I mean, anything you want to tell me."

"Well, no other languages. I'd like to learn Italian someday."

"Tell me about your parents."

He peered around the restaurant. There was only one other couple, older. The woman was wearing a corsage. Then he studied a mural on the wall to his left. It was Paris,

I guess, because it had the Eiffel Tower right smack in the middle. The whole thing was kind of murky, so it was either Paris at dusk or the mural needed a good cleaning. "What about my parents?" he finally said.

"For starters, what were their names, what did your father do, did you have a happy childhood?"

"My father's name was Charles. My mother's was Julia."

"So what were they like?" He shrugged. "What does"—I imitated his shrug—"mean? You don't know, or you're not talking?"

"I guess . . . it means I don't really know. Honestly, I'm not trying to keep anything from you. It's just that my parents were very quiet."

"Did they ever say hi to you, or tell you to wear your galoshes?"

"Yes. Of course."

"What did your father do?"

"He worked in a bank on Long Island. He was a vice-president, but not . . . it was just a title. If you sat in that particular chair for twenty-five years, they called you a vice-president, but he was essentially a glorified transfer clerk."

"And your mother?"

"She stayed at home."

"And did what? Scrubbed floors? Gave fancy tea parties?"

"Neither." Another waiter came, opened a bottle of wine and poured some for John to taste. John nodded. The waiter finished pouring and then bowed, as if he was taking leave of Louis the Something. "My mother's family was one of the first families in Port Washington," John said. "They settled there in the early seventeen hundreds." I waited. "They didn't have money, but they had a lot of . . . pride." He took several too-eager sips of wine.

"It doesn't look like you think pride's a plus."

"Well, in my mother's case . . . it's as if her pride, her snobbery about her background, was her one and only character trait. I remember once—I was nine or ten—I broke my wrist in gym. We were climbing ropes, and I fell. They called her from school and she took me to the doctor's. We were sitting there a *long* time. My wrist was getting more and more swollen."

"It must have hurt like hell."

"It did. And so finally I said, 'Mother, could you ask how much longer it's going to be?' I mean, she was just sitting there, her hands clasped in her lap, looking straight ahead—not at me, not at my wrist, not even at a magazine. So she got up, and I heard her talking to the nurse or receptionist or whatever. I couldn't hear what she was saying, but all of a sudden she lost control. She raised her voice. Really raised it. 'My family was living in this town while Dr. Russo's family were still apes in Italy.' "

"Oh, God."

"I just kept staring at my wrist. My fingers were starting to swell too. And I kept thinking she didn't even flinch when she saw my wrist. She'd just spent an entire hour sitting next to me when I was in so much pain—and the only thing she could get worked up about was her lineage. A family tree, but so what? It was a tree that was completely undistinguished; the only thing to be said for it was that it was tenacious. It held on through the years—didn't die out."

This was not the moment to clue him in that he didn't have to explain "tenacious." "Did her tree cut any ice with your father?"

"I think so, when they first got married. He was from New Jersey somewhere, and came to Long Island to work in the bank. I got the impression he'd believed he was marrying into this great American family, a kind of Port Washington Adams clan. So they wound up being disappointed in each other. He never became a great financier; he stayed a bank clerk. The most interesting thing that ever happened to him was he got bald; I remember he used to touch the top of his head all the time, as if he couldn't believe his hair had gone. So he was a disappointment to her. And she wasn't the Junior League charmer he'd thought he was marrying. For

all her airs, she wasn't invited *anywhere*. She had no personality to speak of, no . . ." His voice faded as he looked
straight at me.

"No what?" He couldn't seem to come up with the word.
"No class?" I asked.

"I suppose that's it."

"So she played gracious lady to an audience of none, and
he pushed papers around." He nodded. "How did you turn
out so good?" I saw his expression. "Oh, come on! You
know what I mean. So *well*. They must have been smart,
terrific-looking."

"Well, my father was handsome . . . in a bland, clerkish
way."

"Which one had the brains?"

"Neither one of them, really." He turned back to his wine.

"So what did you do for laughs as a kid?"

"Nothing special. I had friends to play ball with, but I
never was, um, one of the boys. I was too serious for that.
You see, I really liked school. More than liked it. I loved it.
My mind came alive in high school."

"Came *alive?*" Oh, come off it, I thought.

"You sound so contemptuous of education . . . like everyone I went to high school with."

"And where are they now? you're going to say. Mopping
floors. Punching tickets on the Long Island Rail Road.
Right?"

He smiled and said, "Right." Then the waiter came with
chicken pieces hanging around in a sauce with a lot of mushrooms and tiny onions. I tasted it.

"Hey," I said, "this is great! I thought all that stuff about
French food was a lot of bull, but—"

"I'm glad you like it." I could have been chewing on the
tablecloth, for all he noticed; he was staring at the mural of
Paris again and chewing his bottom lip. His parents obviously weren't his favorite subject.

"Your parents died in a car crash?"

"In '29. A couple of weeks after Black Tuesday."

"How did their death hit you?" He shrugged. "I know you didn't say 'Whoopee!' But were you . . . shattered? stunned?"

"Well, obviously I hadn't expected it, but really, I was in law school, and I'd hardly seen them since I started Columbia. I used to spend Thanksgiving, Christmas with friends' families."

"Your parents never said, 'Hey, John, join us for candied yams'?"

"No."

"Weren't they hurt that you didn't come home?"

"Hurt?" He looked so startled. I realized then that Mom and Pop Berringer weren't the type to pick up the phone and croon a chorus of "Sonny Boy." John refilled his wineglass, held it up to the light of the candle on the table and stared into its depths. That was obviously it for the Berringers.

So I moved on. "Did you use to come here with Nan?"

"What?"

"Nan," I repeated. "Here."

"Oh. Sometimes. We had five or six places we liked to go."

"Did she ever cook?"

"Not usually. Well, she cooked selected things. She could make cheese toast and roast a duck and prepare a good salad dressing. Oh, and make a salad."

"But you didn't have duck and salad every night. Or cheese toast."

"No. But we liked to get out."

"Don't get mad at me if I ask one question." John's shoulders hunched up, as if he already was. "Relax. It's not such an awful question."

"Go ahead."

"Did you have fun with her?"

"I . . . valued her beyond anything I can express." He looked at me; his eyes began to take on the Nan Leland Berringer shine. "I loved her."

"Why?"

"Why did I love her? For her intellect—"

"Come on. You don't love someone for their *intellect*."

"You do if they have one."

I put down my fork. "What's that supposed to be? A knife in my heart?" It was.

"I'm sorry. Really I am. It was a cruel, unnecessary remark."

"So what else did you love about her?"

"Her beauty. Her elegance. Her taste. Her verbal facility. Her aesthetic sense. Do you know what 'aesthetic' means?"

"Does it mean having a rich society mother who was Teddy Roosevelt's cousin?"

He actually laughed. Then he asked, "How did you know about her mother?"

I wasn't going to tell him from spying in his drawer, rifling through his secret papers and finding his wedding announcement. "Office gossip." I took a piece of bread and buttered it. "So her mother had a *real* tree. And her father? How was Big Ed's tree?"

"He came from Vermont. His father owned a farm, but he died when Edward was young. They were very poor."

"But that's good, starting out in poverty, on a farm. It's pretty close to a manger. And look what he became! Edward the Noble: War hero. Adviser to Presidents. Legal genius."

"Edward's not a legal genius, if you want to know." John buttered a piece of bread. I would have given him mine. "Believe it or not, I'm the better lawyer."

"Then what makes him what he is? What makes all these smart men—you, everyone—think he's better? The best?"

"They recognize his special brilliance. Ed is a genius with people. And a genius at sizing things up, at manipulating *any* situation to his advantage."

"And?" I asked.

"And . . ." He hesitated, then tried again. "I don't know. He's just . . . never at a loss. And unlike . . . the rest of us, he always seems to do what's right."

*   *   *

Ha! I had it. I finally understood why John was so fascinated by Nan and Edward. What the Lelands had—and what John, what most people, didn't have—was fearlessness.

Fearlessness. Not that I thought Nan didn't ever get scared. Even if she wasn't frightened by thunderstorms or the idea of hell or vampire movies, she had to have let out a screech the first time she saw the cockroaches that were living in the cabinet under her ex-kitchen sink. But that was minor stuff; in the major leagues, the social world, Nan was so sure of her brains, her looks and her place that she didn't fear anyone. And being unafraid gave her the freedom to do whatever she wanted. She never worried that people wouldn't want to sit next to her at lunch. She knew her own worth, how high it was, so she was free—to chase after John, drop out of college, buy ugly modern art, walk out on her marriage, take on a new husband twice her age. I remembered her stride down the office corridor to her father's office; it had been so absolutely lacking in indecision. I'd never seen a woman like that, ever.

But my pal Ed's fearlessness was different from his daughter's—and far beyond hers. It had nothing at all to do with being confident that no matter what you did, any dinner party invitation you desired was, ipso facto, yours. What Edward Leland possessed was true courage.

Obviously physical courage: Crawling through a forest you know is mined, moving *toward* German fire because you calculate you have maybe a thirty percent chance of knocking out their cannon and saving your men . . . well, that's courage. It's a willingness to take risks and to accept consequences. And Edward Leland wasn't just some foolhardy kid. He'd been thirty years old—a volunteer, not a draftee—when he'd assessed the risk, taken it and had his face blown up.

But my guess was that as soon as Edward came to and understood what had happened to him, he'd taken charge. He'd said, Get me the best doctor, one of those plastic surgeons, the guy who takes the neatest stitches, and let him do what he can with this mess.

So while the results weren't exactly ravishing, while he looked as if half his face was the distorted reflection in a fun-house mirror, he'd been courageous enough to say, Okay, I've got to spend the rest of my life not looking like Douglas Fairbanks. And he'd gone out and wooed a society beauty—and won her.

His courage lasted beyond the Great War. Here he was, in his early fifties, in 1940, going on mysterious missions that *had* to be dangerous. He was still willing to take risks, accept consequences. I wondered whether it was harder now, because his life was so soft and safe and successful: he had so much to lose. And I wondered whether it was harder because he *knew* how vulnerable he was. He knew it every morning, when he shaved his lifeless half face.

But it wasn't just Edward Leland's physical courage that made John so in awe of him. It was his ordinary, day-to-day courage. I'd seen enough of Edward Leland to understand he couldn't be cowed by anyone: not clients, Presidents, Nazis, or even elegant blondes with tight chignons.

He really interested me, and I'd tried to figure him out. I was dying to ask him, How could you not be scared? And I decided that knowing you're tougher and shrewder than most other guys is a definite plus. And the other plus was Edward's comprehension (a comprehension John lacked) that Edward Leland wasn't God. He could get hurt, and he knew it. So he'd look his opponent—a German soldier, a Ford Motor Company lawyer—right in the eye and say, Go ahead, you son of a bitch. I understand what you can do to me and I'm willing to take it—but you'd better be good and ready to take what I'm going to dish out to you.

I bet almost all of them backed off, because Edward Leland could dish out plenty.

Trick or treat. It was Wednesday, the night before Halloween. The stew was simmering, the table was set, and a little before seven I plopped down on the bed and turned on the radio. No treat. War as usual: the Italians and the Greeks at each other's throats in Albania, U-boats and British ships sinking each other in the Atlantic, the blitz continuing over England, Hitler trying to dazzle General Franco in the south of France, while farther north, the Vichy government passed laws prohibiting Jews from public service and from anything much beyond menial jobs in industry, radio, newspapers and magazines.

The Vichy regime smelled like a rose compared to the German scum. In Germany, Jews were outlawed from going to public parks or to restaurants; they couldn't use public telephones, stay in railway or bus station waiting rooms or buy newspapers. Oh, and they couldn't go to "Aryan" hairdressers. All these prohibitions were a little something extra, in case you missed being stomped to death by the Gestapo in the street, or deported to God knows where. I shook my head, remembering my Grandma Olga, how she'd despised America and pined for her beloved Berlin.

The news went off and an announcer was going on about razors. His voice was thick, rich, as if the inside of his throat was coated with melted marshmallows: "Schick Injectors will make you like better the face that you like best."

I reached over and turned off the radio, and all of a sudden I remembered the two cousins in Berlin Olga used to write to: Liesl and someone else. Oh, God, what had happened to them? I didn't have a single doubt that not being able to go to a beauty parlor wasn't the worst thing in the lives of those two old ladies. My cousins.

I stared at the closed venetian blind. If the Germans came over here, and won, what could happen to me? When the Reich Citizenship Law had come out, in November 1935, an amendment of "the Law for the Protection of German Blood and German Honor," I'd read it over and over in the *Trib*. A person with three Jewish grandparents was a Jew. I'd be what's called a *Mischling*—a mongrel—because two of my grandparents were Jews. From what I read then, there was a chance I wouldn't be considered a Jew because my father didn't belong to a temple, didn't do anything Jewish. I remembered wondering whether Grossvater Otto Voss had

ever snuck off and hung out with rabbis. But now most of
them were saying, Make it simple. Anyone with Jewish
blood is a Jew. If I were in Germany, I'd be God-knows-
where. All my Aryan Johnstonness wasn't worth a pfennig.

I switched on the lamp on the night table and wondered
about John. I remembered all those warmhearted sermon-
ettes on Sunday morning radio church shows about Chris-
tians shielding Jews from the Nazis. You got the picture of
thousands of teeny-nosed people throwing their fair-skinned
bodies over the big-nosed and saying, No! Never as long as
I live! John would probably say, *I* didn't know she was Jewish. Oh, by the way, she's in the bedroom.

And then I got a terrible pain in my stomach. It was so
sudden and violent that I could hardly make it out of bed. In
the bathroom, I found myself staggering and tried to hold
myself up by bracing my elbows on the sink. But I couldn't
take the pain. I slid down onto the cold floor. And then I saw
it, on the tiny octagonal tiles and out on the carpet in the
bedroom: drops of blood.

Another pain, like the most excruciating period cramp,
came over me, as if some horrible fist inside my stomach
was squeezing my . . .

I knew then what was happening, of course. The cramp
subsided. I clutched a towel underneath me, so I would
bleed all over Nan's monogrammed terry cloth, not on the
floor, and made it to the phone. Another cramp. That was the
worst of it. Just when you might recover, the next pain
grabbed you so hard it knocked the breath out of you again.
No. That wasn't the worst of it. I picked up the phone and
dialed John's office. The worst of it was I was going to lose
the baby.

"Why do I feel this way?" I asked John. He sat on the edge
of the hospital bed, tie dangling, unknotted, vest unbuttoned.

"They gave you something." His suit was like a black hole
in the spotless white room. "For the pain. It makes you
drowsy."

The pillows were plump and smelled like fresh air. I turned my head away from him and closed my eyes. "It hurt so much."

"It was the womb. It contracted. The way it does during labor."

"It was labor," I said softly. He took my hand between his. "It's over, isn't it?"

"Yes." My whole body felt so heavy I couldn't roll my head back toward him; I was so drained I couldn't even manage that half-cough, half-whimper of heartache that starts up a good cry. "The doctor said it was what they call inevitable. There was nothing they could do."

"It was about four months old. Do they know if it was a girl or a boy?"

"Try to get some sleep," he said.

I must have, because when I woke up, John was in a chair at the foot of the bed. Outside, the sun was rising. The sky over the East River was pink and gold. "Where am I?"

"Lying-In Hospital."

"That's where babies are born," I said, and began to cry. My tears were quiet, not at all elaborate, but I drew up the starched sheet and used it as a handkerchief. "Why did it happen?"

John came over and sat on the edge of the bed. He tugged the sheet out of my hand and gave me his handkerchief. "They don't know. Probably because when things aren't right with the, um, the fetus, the body senses it and gets rid of it. It's better that way."

"Oh, it's terrific."

He smoothed the hair off my forehead. "I'm sorry," he whispered, and kissed the top of my head.

This tenderness was so awkward that for a minute neither of us could find anything to say. Finally I found something. "Did you want it?"

It took him a moment, but he said, "I don't know. . . . It would have complicated our lives."

"Babies aren't so complicated."

"We would have had to move." He'd picked up a lock of

my hair, and he twirled it around his finger again and again. "And you might have felt tied down." He paused. "Did you really want it?"

"I must have. I feel so empty now. Maybe it's just—I don't know—a physical thing."

"I'm sorry," he said again.

I looked past him, around the huge, square room. Mine was the only bed in that stretch of blinding hospital whiteness. I eased myself up and looked out the window. Across the river, Queens was flat and colorless, even in the bright dawn. A barge drifted along so slowly you could hardly see it make any progress, like the hands on a clock.

"What are we going to do?" I asked him.

To his credit, he didn't say, About what? He said, very composed, "Nothing."

"You married me so there wouldn't be a little Berringer bastard running up and down Wall Street calling, 'Daddy! Daddy!' "

"Don't talk that way." His voice was so comforting, as if he was singing a lullaby.

"You're being calm on purpose. You're afraid I'll lose control."

"I want you to get some rest."

"And then what?"

"You'll come home."

"Oh, come on, John."

"What do you think I'm going to do, Linda? Toss you aside?"

"Look, I don't mean to sound bitter. But you did what you did because there was a gun to your head. You had no choice. But the gun is gone now. You don't have to drag me around for the rest of your life. Come on. No one will think any less of you. They'll only think less of you if you *stay*. 'He's with her out of choice. How unspeakably odd!' "

"You don't give me credit for having any character at all, do you?"

"I think you're an ethical lawyer. And you were decent to marry me."

"And that's it?"

I started to cry again. "I love you," I said, and put my arms around him.

He held me tight against him and murmured, "I know."

# 14

December was a miserable month, bitter cold. And almost the whole world had fallen under Fascist control. Only England stood—alone. America was busy wrapping Christmas presents.

John reached up and pulled down a carton of Nan Leland Berringer's Christmas tree ornaments from the top shelf of his closet. "Wait until you see how *exquisite* these are!"

He knelt down, wiped the top of the carton off on the sleeve of the flannel shirt he was wearing, and then took out the decorations one by one and held them up so they caught the light. Well, I had to admit it; they were gorgeous. All glass. Big, small, clear, frosted, etched with angels, embellished with hair-thin silver designs. "I don't want them," I said.

"Linda, I appreciate how you feel, but you're being—"

"It's half my tree. If you want to put your ex-wife's stuff up on your half, that's fine with me."

"Don't you think you're being a little unreasonable?" He was being tolerant.

No, I didn't think so. The apartment wasn't big enough for three people, but I couldn't get rid of Nan. I slept on her pillowcases, ate from her soup bowls, looked at her paintings. Now I was supposed to ooh and aah over her glass balls. What I really felt like doing was to take a running jump, land smack in the middle of the carton and hear a loud, glorious, soul-satisfying crunch.

"What do you think I'm going to do? Go out and buy orange plaid reindeer?"

"Not at all. It's just that these ornaments happen to be very beautiful. It would be a shame not to use them."

"Maybe what I would buy would be beautiful too."

"I'm sure they would." I wanted to say, Oh, come off it! "But these were very expensive. Wouldn't it be foolish to go out and buy others?"

"I could learn to live with it."

He smiled and lifted the carton. "Come on. Let's get the tree up."

Sure, I could have another big confrontation: You still love her. You can't let her go. You won't give me money for new towels because you want *pieces* of her in the house. And so forth. But how many times can you accuse your husband of desiring another woman when—if pushed—he'll willingly plead guilty? Did I really want to hear: "Yes, I love Nan and I love her glass dingle-dangles that make crystal music"?

Next year, I said to myself, next August, I'm going to Tiffany's or Bergdorf Goodman or whatever is the ultimate glass-ball store and pick out—

The bell rang. "Damn," John said, and then added, "You get it."

I was wearing a yellow fleece bathrobe, and I hadn't combed my hair. "You get it."

"I have a carton," he said.

"Put it down."

"Damn it, Linda, just get the door."

The bell rang again. John carried Nan's carton into the living room. I stomped, barefoot, into the entrance hall and yanked open the door. And standing there, right before me, homburg in one hand, the other poised to ring the bell, was Edward Leland.

"Merry Christmas, Linda."

"Merry Christmas," I managed to say back. I stuck my hands in my pockets, so I wouldn't start patting down my messed-up hair.

"John!" Edward's deep voice was full of holiday warmth. I turned. John had come up behind me; the look on his face was astonished and overjoyed, as if Santa Claus had truly come down his chimney. "Sorry to drop in on you unannounced, but your doorman seems to have been enjoying his eggnog. Nodded off, so I slipped by."

"Please, come in," John said. I bet his jaw was hanging open. "We were just putting up the tree." He turned to me. "How about making us some coffee, dear?"

"Sure!" I said, like I couldn't wait to dash to the percolator. Actually, I needed a few seconds to get over the surprise of Edward's visit and the shock of my husband's calling me "dear." They moved off to the living room. I hung up Edward's coat, put away his hat and went into the kitchen.

Being two classy men, they spoke in what they'd call hushed tones, but I could hear almost all of it, except when I rattled the pot and banged a closet door to show how absorbed I was in being a hostess.

"Forgive me for the intrusion, John."

"Not at all."

"Obviously this is something best not discussed in the office." Maybe it was going to be about Nan; my hand must have shaken, because a scoop of coffee was suddenly all over the sink. "And I'd rather not use the phone."

There was a slight pause, probably John nodding.

"I'll be as direct as I can," Edward continued. "Lend-Lease is going to pass." In a press conference a few days before, FDR had put forth a plan that England could get all their war matériel from us now and pay for it later—in effect, a giveaway. I put the coffeepot on the stove and lit the gas. "And Donovan's done a complete turnabout. He's all for it now."

The Donovan Edward was talking about was William Donovan, a Wall Street lawyer from O'Brian, Hamlin, Donovan & Goodyear, who'd gone on to become head of the COI, the Office of Coordinator of Information, which was a typically overcomplicated, lawyery way of saying U.S. espionage headquarters. Unlike Edward, who clearly preferred private meetings and secret missions, Donovan was a much more public man, a diplomat—or politician. He was known for being outgoing, congenial and very, very clever.

"Have you spoken with him recently?"

"I spent most of the last week with him in London." There was the silence of John nodding again; I could almost see him, awestruck but managing to look merely respectful. I took out a fruitcake I'd baked, sliced it, and fanned out the pieces on one of Nan's white serving plates. "He's finally come around to seeing how vital Britain's survival is."

"If they're defeated," John agreed, "we're next on their list."

"Very likely," Edward replied. I opened a cabinet, took out a tray and arranged the cake, cups, and saucers, plates, milk and sugar, spoons and forks. "Don't forget, if Germany defeats England, they would have both the French *and* the English fleets at their command." I folded three napkins. (Unfortunately, all our napkins had you-know-who's monogram. I'd once said to John, All I want is to buy *plain* napkins. I don't want my initials or anything. And John had said, It's foolish to throw out money. And *you're* the one who keeps calling attention to them. I never even notice them.) "With a navy like that, Germany would strangle us in the Atlantic," Edward was saying, "and with Japan making nasty noises in the Pacific . . ."

What's the point of all this cordial, manly chitchat? I wondered. Why had Edward Leland dropped by? So far, the only semisecret thing he'd said was that he'd seen Donovan in London the week before. That information was slightly interesting, but I don't think it would make a Nazi spy jump up and down and clap his hands.

I took the coffee off the stove and poured it into the white china pot. Once I brought everything in, I'd have to leave and go into the bedroom, and I probably wouldn't be able to hear much from in there. Nuts, I thought, as *I* walked into the living room.

"England is the key, you see," Edward was saying. "In more ways than one. British intelligence has several first-rate sources within the German foreign office and the Abwehr." The Abwehr was the espionage and counterespionage service of the German General Staff. "The Vatican has a couple of sources too. And Donovan has one. But—" John cleared his throat as I came in. Edward fell silent. I put down the platter on the coffee table. I couldn't believe that Edward Leland, who could hear a fly climb up a wall in the Bronx, hadn't heard me walk into the room. And hadn't seen me. My bathrobe was not exactly the most subdued yellow ever invented.

Both men made a tremendous fuss over the fruitcake. I didn't know what to do next: Did I leave everything on the tray or was I supposed to do one of those sophisticated Mrs. Berringer-is-pouring routines? Neither of them leaned forward from his chair, so I quickly set everything out on the coffee table. Then I asked Edward: "How do you take your coffee?" I tried not to sound like Miriam Hopkins.

"Cream and one sugar, please," he said.

I lifted the top of the sugar bowl, but John put his hand over mine and said, "It's all right, dear. I'll take care of it. I know you have more presents to wrap."

I stood straight, but before I could go, Edward said, "John, really. Her security clearance is better than yours." He looked up at me. "You haven't developed Nazi sympathies since you filled out those forms, have you, Linda?" I shook my head. "Then please sit down and join us." I waited for him to add, If it's all right with your husband. He didn't.

I sat across from them, on the beige couch, and went ahead and fixed his coffee, and without being asked, John's. I served the fruitcake and tried not to stare at the men. The contrast was so powerful I had to force myself to turn away; I looked over at the naked Christmas tree.

Obviously, Edward was older than John, seventeen or eighteen years. But the age difference was just for starters: fair, dark; graceful, hulking; handsome, not; John's blue eyes glowed; Edward's black eyes glowered. I turned back to them. Edward held the cup and saucer in big, clumsy farmer hands; his fingers were too heavy to hold the cup

handle properly, but—I couldn't help this thought—they'd
be perfect for choking somebody on a dark night. John laid
aside his cake; the hand that did it was elegant, long-fingered,
pale and tantalizing.

Edward started talking again. "I was telling John that
Colonel Donovan of the COI"—he waited until I nodded
that I knew what that was—"has long had a source, a spy if
you will, high in the German government. This source has
provided us with some interesting information about the
internal politics of the Reich, some of it quite valuable. And
over the last year, both I and another associate of Bill's have
spent a good deal of time renewing old business friendships
and cementing relationships with individuals in high circles
in Germany." He smiled. "My sources, fortunately, are fluent in English." He leaned back. "Last week, Bill asked me
if I'd be willing to spend some time in Washington—a great
deal of time, actually—organizing a unit within the COI to
be called the Office of Commercial Analysis." John began
to nod, until Edward added, "A meaningless name, obviously."

"Then what kind of office is it?" I asked. "If I'm not out of
line."

"It will be my job, and the job of my men, to corroborate
what our sources are telling us, not only in Germany but
throughout Europe. Much of it will be the simple checking
of facts."

"Not so simple, I'd guess," John said.

"Not so simple is right," Edward answered. He took a bite
of fruitcake and smiled first at me, but then much more win-
ningly at John. In fact, his attitude toward John's observa-
tion was so flattering I figured he had to be up to something.
"How do we learn the unknowable?" Edward asked. Then he
answered himself: "By gathering facts—from radio trans-
missions we can manage to decipher, from recent refugees,
especially those from Germany, from resistance organiza-
tions within the occupied countries. Then we must put all
the pieces of this terribly intricate puzzle into a picture that
makes sense. It *has* to make sense. Not merely for the infor-

mation itself, although that is important; you and I, John, have long agreed that our entrance into this war is inescapable, and we must know all we can. But there's a further need for our brilliant puzzle-solvers."

This was too interesting. I couldn't *not* open my mouth. Anyway, Edward had invited me to join them. "You want to make sure if what your high German sources are saying is the truth," I said, "or if they're"—I knew my Nazi spy movies—"double agents."

"Yes," Edward murmured. "Precisely." Both of them looked surprised at my conclusion. John, of course, always looked astonished whenever I figured out anything more complicated than his checking account balance. But I was disappointed; somehow I'd expected better from Edward. "And it goes without saying, John—and that's why I asked Linda to join us—that I'd be very happy and relieved if you'd consider moving to Washington for a time . . . to be my foremost puzzle-solver."

The girl who took care of my mother had one of those Slavic names no one wants to bother to pronounce, Mrshk-lva or something, so she told everyone to call her Cookie. At about sixty, she wasn't a girl, and she wasn't such a cookie, either. She was short, with long, skinny arms and legs and a pudgy little body, and when she moved around fast—she was never slow—she looked like a monkey in a nurse's uniform.

Cookie hoisted my mother out of the taxi onto a Fifth Avenue sidewalk. It was a bright day, cold but without a hint of wind. "She's not too bad, Missus," she explained to me, as if my mother wasn't there, right beside her, but home in Queens. "Except she's hiding gin somewheres." My mother immediately became absorbed in getting a new slant to her hat. It was an old brown felt she'd had for years, with a wide brim and a crown that looked like a huge, upside-down soup pot. But when she moved it forward I realized she'd gone out (or had sent Cookie out) and bought a holiday pin: a sprig of artificial holly, with slightly limp fabric leaves and berries of red beads. She was so absorbed in her hat she didn't notice the seventy-foot Rockefeller Center Christmas tree straight in front of her nose. "I could smell the gin fumes when she came out of the bathroom this morning," Cookie went on, "fresh on her breath, and I searched high and low, even down the toilet, but it wasn't there."

"Cookie smells like toilet water," my mother announced loudly. "*Real* toilet water. Stinky!" In the cold air, her breath came out in a weak white puff. People on the street, walking toward the tree, pretended they had heard nothing more than distant carols.

"Shut up your mouth. It's Christmas," Cookie said, but it was obvious she thought my mother was funny, and she might have cackled and gotten into a whole toilet tête-à-tête if I—the person who paid her—wasn't there.

"You shut up *your* mouth, stinkpot Bohunk." My mother laughed, a very feeble laugh, because she didn't have the strength to do more. Her arm was draped around Cookie's shoulder; she could no longer stand by herself for any length of time. About a month after I'd gotten married, when I made one of my twice-a-week visits to Ridgewood, I'd been so frightened by how she looked—closer to a skeleton than to a woman—that I called Dr. Guber. He'd come to the house, checked my mother over and pulled me into the hallway, closing her door. He said, She's got cirrhosis of the liver. She's not just falling down because she's weak. In his gruff Brooklyn voice, he'd gone on: Linda, not good. She's got nervous system damage, jaundice, edema. She's a mess, kid. You gotta be able to see it yourself.

I could. And although I knew the answer, I finally asked him, Can you do anything? He'd answered, Not anything that would help. Is she going to die from it? I'd had to ask, and he'd said, "Yeah, kid. Six months, a year. What a waste. Such a beauty she was."

Cookie had been standing beside me the whole time, listening to the doctor. She shook her head and said, Most of them get mean sooner or later, but she's such a *cute* drunk.

"Where's Johnny?" my mother called out, her volume higher than ever.

"He's over at the restaurant, checking if we can still have our reservation. You know you're over an hour late, Mom." She gave me an innocent, Oh really? look and fluttered her eyelashes. I wondered if she'd be fluttering if she'd seen the look on John's face after sixty minutes of watching every taxi going up and down Fifth Avenue. I took her arm and, with Cookie on her other side, half led, half carried her toward the tree. She gawked at it, like all the tourists, but paid much more attention to the women's fur coats.

"Beautiful!" she said of a passing sheared raccoon. "I'm dying to meet Johnny," she went on. "He better be as gorgeous as you say or I'll tell him, 'Hey, my Linda's got taste up her—' "

"Cookie," I interrupted, "why don't you take a walk around the tree. I'll stay here with my mother."

The minute Cookie stepped away, my mother grabbed my collar. "A blue wool coat? You marry a filthy-rich guy and he gives you *cloth?*"

"Mom," I said, as softly and as gently as I could, "please be on your best behavior today. You know what I mean."

She patted my hand. "I know, honey. Gee, you look stunning. You look terrific in blue. And you're wearing mascara, finally?" I nodded. "So how're things?"

"Fine," I said.

"How's the baby coming along?"

"Mom, I had a miscarriage. Over two months ago. I told you."

"Oh, sweetie, I'm sorry. I swear to God, I forgot. You know, who wants to remember something like that?" She pushed back the sleeves of her coat—a too-vivid brown, purple and cream-color plaid I knew would make John's jaw go rigid—but the sleeves were too long and drooped over her hands again. I tried to make a cuff, but she pulled away. "Cuffs are for old ladies," she said. "I had one, you know. A mis. You weren't even a year old when it happened. But the

doctor did the mis on purpose. We asked him to. You know
what I mean?"

"Dr. Guber?"

"Nah! He was chicken. A guy on Queens Boulevard.
Twenty bucks he charged, but Herm said, 'It's well worth it.'
Listen, I was just seventeen, and I already had you." Her
eyes filled with tears. I thought she was thinking about her
lost baby. But then she said, "I loved your father." She swallowed, sniffled and then hollered: "Merry Christmas,
Herm!" A Negro family who'd been standing near us gave
each other this-one's-a-lunatic looks and edged away. My
mother reached out and put her cold hand in mine. "You
think he hears me?"

"I'm sure he does."

"He wasn't all that crazy about Christmas, to tell you the
truth. Him being a Jew."

"Mom," I said, "don't mention anything about that to
John."

"Why not?"

"I just never got a chance to tell him. Not that it would
matter."

"You ashamed of your father?"

"No!"

"Jews are smart!"

"Shhh!"

"Where do you think you got your brains from? Me?
Johnny wouldn't care. Anyway, you look more like me, even
though Herm didn't look like one, or I'll tell you, I wouldn't
have married him. Not with those dark beards and greasy
hair like they got."

"Well, just don't say anything, okay?"

"Okay."

"And—"

She cut me off. "You gonna give me a list?"

"Please don't talk about him being a rich lawyer."

She glanced at my coat again. "Maybe he has a nice
Christmas surprise when you get back home." Actually,
John had already given me my gift: a gold pin shaped like a

butterfly, with two tiny rubies for eyes and emerald chips down its body. It was a little too large and a little too fancy: in other words, what he thought I'd appreciate.

Just then, John arrived. He was wearing his good navy suit with a red tie. His gray topcoat was open. His darker gray cashmere scarf was tossed around his neck with the perfect degree of casualness.

"Merry Christmas, Mrs. Voss," he said. I could see he was shocked at how sick she looked, to say nothing of his reaction to her coat.

"Merry Christmas!" My mother was genuinely impressed. John started to button his coat, as if to cover himself. "Hey, relax." He took a small step back. "So you're my son-in-law. Well, my girl's *very* lucky." She turned to me. "He's some guy, Lin! You shouldn't let him go out for a walk by himself."

Cookie, realizing mother-daughter time had ended, rushed over. "Merry Christmas, sir!" she greeted John. Her voice was breathlessly girlish.

He seemed stunned to see this sudden servant who looked as if, any minute, like a chimpanzee, she might leap up and swing from branch to branch of the Rockefeller Center Christmas tree. "Merry Christmas," he mumbled. Then he looked at my mother, then at me. His eyes closed for an instant. When he opened them, he said, "I took care of the maître d'. Why don't we walk over to the restaurant?"

After everything I'd told him about my mother, John's idea of a perfect Christmas probably would have been giving her a year at a sanitarium as a present. But he knew I wouldn't go for that, so when I started talking about what to do Christmas Day, he immediately suggested we bring her to the apartment, give her her presents (fast), have a (quick) dinner and say good night. If he could have managed to have her slipped in the back door and brought up in the freight elevator, he would have. Not that I could blame him; unfortunately, I'd told him the truth about her, including her tendency to fall on her face, call out to strange men and to get my father's attention, shout to the heavens. I could see her making a megaphone of her hands and booming "Herm, lover!" in front of our building, in front of the neighbors.

But I'd told him no dice, I wanted to treat my mother to Manhattan, take her to see the tree and then out for a dinner fancier than she'd ever had. I said, John, it's probably her last Christmas. He picked a large, well-known restaurant that catered to blue-haired ladies whose idea of Christmas dinner was three martinis and a stuffed tomato: a respectable, even stuffy place, but no one he knew—no graceful people—would ever go near it.

"Isn't he something?" my mother asked Cookie. "Better than a lifeguard. High-class."

I took my mother's arm to help her walk. John moved reluctantly to the other side.

"Don't worry," my mother said to me, as she grabbed onto his arm. "I won't say nothing to embarrass you, sweetpea." She looked up at John. "You gonna buy me a cocktail, Johnny?"

"Hey—" Cookie called, from behind the three of us.

My mother didn't bother to look around. "Big fat deal. It's Christmas."

"Mom," I said, trying to sound calm, "you're not allowed to drink anymore. You know that."

"Why not?"

"Because it ain't good for you," Cookie blurted out. "You know that, Missus."

My mother stopped, so abruptly that Cookie banged into us. "And *you* know and *you* know," she blared out to me and Cookie, "that I got six months, a year, tops. You don't think I listened in when Dr. Creep came over?"

I couldn't move. I couldn't think how to answer her. Then I started to cry.

"Come on, Linny, your mascara'll run in front of Johnny, and you look so pretty." I tried to absorb my mother's calm, collected knowledge of her doom. I peered into her eyes—outlined with seven or eight times the amount of mascara I had on, coated with pistachio-green eye shadow—when she leaned toward John. It was a jerky movement, and he had to catch her so she wouldn't fall. "You'll take good care of my little girl?" she asked, still in his arms. "Promise?"

I think he was touched. At least his voice had a catch in it. "Yes," he said quietly, "I promise," and stood her upright. Somehow, we got her to the restaurant.

"Wow!" she said, looking at the wood-paneled walls and the eight-arm brass chandeliers. "Johnny, you sure can pick 'em!" She picked up a water glass and clinked her nails against it. "Nice stuff." Then she smiled at John. "Well, cocktail time!" It was two-thirty. "Come *on*. A big-money lawyer like you can afford a little gin. Order me a double, okay?" I made no move to stop him—I was too numb. How could my mother bear knowing? But I was also a little numb anticipating what her next move could be, once she'd had her double: making a pass at John; telling a few Jew jokes while winking at me broadly.

John called over the waiter, ordered us drinks and slipped away to the men's room. It could have been in Cleveland if you judged by how fast he took off. "Oops," my mother said, as soon as he was out of earshot. "Sorry about the rich business, Linda, lamb."

"That's okay, Mom."

"I know I got a big mouth." I didn't give her an argument. "But listen, while he's gone . . ." I could see her trying to come up with her version of maternal wisdom. And she did. "He's built like a dream! And he talks so cultured, Lin. He's really smart. You know, smart-smart. And so-o-o good-looking you could die." Suddenly, her chirpy, life's-a-party tone fizzled out. She touched my chin with her fingertips. "Baby, watch out for him."

"What do you mean?"

"You know what I mean. Deep down, he's a rat."

It took me a minute to find the words. "What makes you think that?"

"Oh, Lin, I know guys. He's not good, like your father. And I can see it in *your* eyes, how he feels about you. Don't tell me no." She took a deep, shaky breath. "Oh, Linda, I wish you could've found someone to love you."

# 15

North Africa, the Balkans, East Africa, Crete, Iraq, Yugoslavia. The black cloud grew bigger, more poisonous, but I remember waking from an afternoon nap in May 1941—a few months after we moved to Washington—and, still in bed, looking through the sheer curtains at the red geraniums in the window box and thinking: My life is nice. Okay, almost.

At first, the best part of moving to Washington was putting all the New York furniture in storage; the sight of the movers carting off Nan's couch was—up to that point—the greatest moment of my marriage. The next-best part was renting a pretty furnished house in a neighborhood not far from Washington Cathedral. John insisted the area was exclusive, but in spite of that, it felt comfortable to me; our block could have been plunked down in half a dozen spots in Brooklyn. The big difference was the rent (high) and the tranquillity (total). The streets were absolutely silent. No one in Washington hung out their windows and waved or whistled hello when you walked down the street on your way to the fruit man's or the candy store—if there'd been a candy store, which there wasn't. People sat back on their private porches, not on their it's-okay-to-be-nosy stoops.

Maybe they'd decided life in Washington was too predictable to bother. What was there to look at? The men worked for the government and looked like lawyers, even if they weren't. The wives all seemed to have been born in Alabama. They said "Ha" instead of "Hi," and they never sat down unless they were sewing something. They needle-pointed pictures and piano bench covers and eyeglass cases; they repaired their mama's old lace tablecloths; they made quilts for their beds and everybody else's beds; they took endless hems up and down.

"Ha, Linna," my across-the-street neighbor Lucy MacPharland said. She stood at my door with her sewing bag and a chocolate cake. At the beginning, I thought the cakes were welcome-to-the-block gifts, and they were, but later I realized that while it was okay to drop in unannounced, you never knocked on any door without at least a pound of baked goods.

"Hi," I said. "Come in."

"Sure you're not busy?" she asked, as she pushed past me and walked down the hall into the kitchen. She set her cake on the table, where there already was a pecan pie. "Katie-Lou was here?" The evidence was undeniable; Katie-Lou Wilcox edged her pie crust in overlapping scallops.

"This morning," I said. I opened a drawer, got out the roll of waxed paper, and covered the evidence of Katie-Lou's visit. I put it in the refrigerator, next to Bessie Campbell's sticky buns.

Lucy elbowed me aside and snatched the percolator out of the dish drainer. "Well, now," she said, and then murmured, "three, four," as she measured coffee. "Tell me every little thing that's occurred since I"—they all actually said "Ah" instead of "I"—"last saw you."

"Let's see. What's happened since yesterday?" I murmured. "Oh! I know! Cora Sue Young left"—I paused dramatically—"for a visit to her mother."

"No! She said she was visitin' her mama?"

"Rita Harwood saw her leave the house with a suitcase and get into a *car*."

"Mah word, Linna!" She wasn't just whistling "Dixie."

What all the fuss meant was that one of our neighbors, whose husband was third man at the Argentinian desk at the State Department, had discovered a driving school instructor who had no interest in Argentina but a lot of interest in her.

His parked Ford had caused comment long before Cora Sue confided in yet another neighbor, Rebecca Jean, that she was having an affair and was making plans to spend a weekend with her instructor—and not to practice shifting to second, either. She was using a visit to her mother in Opelika as an excuse, knowing (she disclosed to big-mouth Becky) that her husband was too involved in South American trade routes to even think about her, much less check up.

What all the fuss meant to me, personally, was that finally I was one of the girls. I was included. On the five blocks that made up Rosedale Avenue, the only person who cared that I hadn't gone to Mount Holyoke College, didn't play tennis and couldn't whistle *Das Lied van der Erde* by Gustav Mahler was my own husband.

Okay, so maybe it wasn't a social plus to be a Yankee. And I couldn't thread a needle. But I was a whiz in the kitchen; I could bake a cherry pie with the best of them, to say nothing of *Apfelkuchen* and *Schwarzwalder Kirschtorte*, and after all those years of lunches at the law firm, I could gossip like a champion.

The fact that I was a cultural minus didn't matter at all, since hardly any of the neighborhood wives had gone to college—and those who had didn't bring it up all the time, the way they did in New York. And while a lot of them seemed to come from wealthy families—Mama missed goin' to Paris in the spring for her clothes, what with the war on, and Daddah was always callin' on his brokah—my neighbors didn't act Wall Street Lawyers' Wives rich: clannish, heartless, indifferent to any hurt their coldness might cause anyone (me).

Strangely enough, for a person from Queens, I looked like my neighbors. I blended in with a group of pretty women who worked much harder at being pretty than I did; if we'd kept silent, you wouldn't have known I didn't come from where they had.

In Washington, I didn't feel *wrong*. In New York, all the other wives seemed to buy their shoes in a top-secret store; they put on their private-color-*you'll*-never-be-able-to-find-it lipstick in exactly the same way, as if they had a classified blueprint for thin lips in a drawer in their vanity table. In Washington, no one gave me a mean once-over; when Lucy, whose husband was an economist in the Treasury Department, said, "Ah *adore* that blouse, Linna," she wasn't being snide. It was the sort of blouse she'd buy, or Mama would run up on her Singer and send up from Tuscaloosa.

After three months, there wasn't any one of these women who I would have sworn would be my friend for life; it was still a little hard to distinguish them. Sure, I knew Lucy was vivacious and had a low, loud voice, and Katie-Lou was dreamy and always crocheting doilies, but I couldn't get far enough past the southern accents and hospitality to see which of them—if any—I really cared about.

But if they didn't matter so much individually, they mattered a lot as a group, because they were the only people in my life. I hardly ever saw John, although I often felt him, when at two or three in the morning he'd wake me, slipping underneath the cover, and come up beside me or on top of me. Unlike Bessie's husband, a colonel assigned to the War Department, John was not "limp as an ol' dishrag, an' I do mean *limp*" after his eighteen-hour day. John's interest in me thrived in darkness. In those late nights, he wasn't just hot; sometimes he was tender, stroking my hair, curling around me and cradling me in his arms as he fell asleep.

The only fly in this warm, loving ointment was my tendency to—now and then—open my mouth and say things like "How are you?" That blew it for him. "Fine," he'd answer, and get busy making the perfectly puffed pillow. "A little tired." And I'd say, "Well, you have a right to be," and he'd say, "Hmm-hmmm," in agreement as he'd shift away from me, just enough so we were no longer touching, and fall off to sleep.

One night, though, there was no chance for me to work up to being anonymous. John came home about eleven. I was in bed but still wide awake. It was an awful early-June night, hot and unbearably humid. The air was so thick it almost hurt to breathe. I'd thrown aside the thin patchwork blanket, but was half covered with the already read *Washington Times Herald* and *New York Times*. I held *Time* magazine against my chest and said, "You're so early! What did they do? Throw you out?"

John's white shirt clung to him and was sheer with his perspiration. "No. I just had to get out of there. The place is a hellhole."

The COI's main offices were bad enough, but John and a French professor from Yale shared what sounded like a room not much larger than a stall in a men's room, in a mysterious subbasement in the State Department.

I got out of bed, cleared up my reading matter and said, "I'll make you some lemonade." I was juicing the lemons when he came into the kitchen and practically flopped into a chair. He'd taken off his shirt and pants, but looked too drained from the heat to do anything about his underwear, which was drenched. "Are you sure you're okay, John?"

"I'm fine." He watched as I added water and sugar and slammed the ice cube tray around to get the ice unstuck. "I appreciate this," he said, and took the glass and held it against his forehead before he guzzled it down.

"Not so fast," I said in German. "If you drink something cold too fast it will give you a headache." I switched back to English. "That's what my grandma used to tell me. That and"—I spoke German again—" 'Potato soup is good for a chest cold' and 'If you sing at the table you'll get a crazy husband.' "

"Did you sing at the table?" he asked in his impeccable German.

"Probably. Before I knew what could come of it."

We always spoke English, so when he reached out, pulled me onto his lap and kissed the tip of my nose, I assumed it was the change in language that had loosened some screw and was making him so . . . I couldn't think of any word except affectionate. "I want some more lemonade," he said, "but I don't want to let go of you. How do we arrange that?"

"I'll come right back."

I made another glass of lemonade, and as I handed it to

him, he pulled me back into his lap. "Can you stand being so
close to me?" he asked. "I must smell like something that's
just come out of a jungle." That took me a second to figure
out, because I'd never heard or seen the word before:
*Dschungel.*

"Some wild jungle beast," I said, but then I sat back and
eyed him closely. "No, some exhausted, pathetic, half-dead
animal." I took a paper napkin out of the holder and wiped
his face.

"Thank you."

"You're welcome." I eased off his lap. Unfortunately, he
didn't try to stop me. I guessed that was it for affection, so I
shifted back to English. "Why don't I run you a cool bath?"

"That would be nice," he said.

I walked up the stairs, one of my favorite places in the
house. A steep, old-fashioned staircase, it had a carpet run-
ner of dark green, with big roses that were even darker
green, almost black.

Everything in the house was unstylish and very old, but it
didn't look down-at-the-heels. Thirty-eight Rosedale Avenue
had an all-American classy shabbiness that said: I was furnished with quality materials in 1903, and I expect they will
last for quite some time.

In the bathroom, the tiles were small black and white
squares; some of them were cracked, but they gave the floor
character. The big tub had claw feet, and its thick porcelain
was chipped. I put in the plug and turned on the water, sitting on the edge of the tub, occasionally holding my fingers
under the flow to make sure it wasn't too hot or too icy.

John came in, dropped his underwear and socks, and
eased into the water with a soft "Aaah."

"Is that what they call a sigh of relief?" I asked. He
smiled. I closed the lid of the toilet, sat down and watched
him. He threw back his head, scooped up some water and
poured it on his neck. It was the best sight in town—*much*
more beautiful than the Washington Monument. "Do you
want me to wash your back? Like those Japanese women."

"Geishas. No, thanks. Um, Linda . . ."

"What?"

"Ed Leland's back in Washington."

"I know. I read about him. He was at the White House last week, the night Roosevelt made the national emergency proclamation." The Germans had been sinking British boats much faster than the British—or we—could replace them, and FDR had issued a statement saying we had to strengthen our defenses "to the extreme limit of our national power and authority." What he was saying was: This is our next step toward war. I handed John a washcloth. "The paper said everybody was pretty tense after Roosevelt spoke, so they had music. 'Alexander's Ragtime Band.' Irving Berlin was there. And Donovan." I paused. "Have you ever seen Ed Leland tense?"

John put the washcloth over his face. "No."

"*Intense,*" I said. "That's what he is. Anyway, how is he? Has he been up to anything you're allowed to talk about?" I reached over and pulled away the washcloth.

"We went for a walk this afternoon," John said.

"A walk? It was ninety-seven degrees."

"I know, and it was a long walk."

He lowered his entire head into the water. When he brought it up, his hair dribbled water down onto his shoulders. He gazed, seemingly fascinated, at a little stream running down his arm. "Are you going to play Watch the Water? Or do you want to tell me about what Ed wants?"

"Why do you think he wants something?"

"Come on, John. What does he want?"

"He wants you," John said, very, very seriously.

"As what? A human sacrifice?"

"Be serious."

"Okay."

"Aren't you going to ask *why* he wants you?" he said at last.

"I know why he wants me."

John looked annoyed. "Why?"

"He needs a bilingual secretary who can get top-secret clearance, and he probably needs one fast. Hey, don't look so disappointed I guessed."

"I'm not." His chin had sunk down almost to his knees. But then it perked up. "Well, what's your inclination?" he asked.

I remembered being pulled into his lap downstairs, about how it felt to receive his affection, even though I now understood the reason for it. "What's yours?"

"It wouldn't be a bad idea. It would take some pressure off Ed." And make him indebted to John: Say, old boy, thanks for your wife. "And I know I'm no prize, working these hours. It would give you a chance to get out a little more." Into a ninety-eight-degree sub-subbasement in the Interior Department, or an elevator shaft in the Bureau of Mines. "Do something for your country."

"Oh, come off it!"

"Don't be so touchy."

"I'm not touchy."

"Come in the bathtub with me."

"Are you trying to seduce me so I'll do anything you want?"

"Is seduction necessary?"

"No," I said. "I'll do anything you want." And then I took off my nightgown and climbed in.

Two days later, at two-fifty in the afternoon, I stood inside the lobby of an office building on Massachusetts Avenue in one-hundred-and-two-degree heat, waiting for five minutes to pass so I could get in the elevator and arrive at Edward Leland's office precisely at three. The hundred and two degrees was the outside temperature, but there was nothing—not the smallest stirring of air—in that marble box of a lobby to convince me that inside was any cooler than the streets I'd just survived.

Still, the marble was so white it looked like the walls in some delicious, frosty waiting room just outside heaven. I leaned against it, but all I got was an icy jolt. I pulled away. My whole body felt disgusting: My skin was gummy and my slip clung to it like a revolting phantom in a horror movie.

I was watching my watch, trying to hypnotize it into moving faster so I could get upstairs, where I imagined Edward Leland sitting in an office with two fans: a small one he'd managed to requisition from the government and a huge one he'd gone out and bought himself. And suddenly there he was: Edward Leland.

"Hello," he said. "What are you doing down here?"

Like he didn't know. My bet was, this was a trick he pulled more than once, catching someone who had an appointment with him waiting, nervous, off guard. "I'm waiting."

"Why didn't you come upstairs?"

"Because I would have been early. I gave myself an extra ten minutes so I wouldn't be late, because if you're even part German, being late is a major felony, but being early isn't terrific, either. I spend half my life hanging out in lobbies or on street corners so I can be *precisely* on time. Does that answer your question?"

"Fully," he said. "Let's go for a walk."

"A walk?"

"You don't want to walk?"

"Do you?"

"That's not what I asked, Linda," he snapped.

I couldn't figure if he was grouchy from the weather or was giving me a hard time for fun. Or not for fun. For work. To see if I could take the heat. I didn't know if I wanted it. For the first time in my life, I was doing nothing except being female, and I was really liking it; I wasn't going to trade it in for a steno pad and a boss, scary enough to begin with, who was going to give me a hard time.

But why was he giving me such a rough time about going for a walk? Hah! It was another Edward Leland Test: How far would you go for him? How fearful of his power were you that you couldn't say, "Listen, in all this heat I'd rather not?" How many miles would you trudge by his side? Because one look at Edward, with his tough face and tougher, massive build, and you'd know that he could—and would—walk forever.

"Okay," I said. "The answer is, I don't want to go for a walk because it's over a hundred degrees and the sidewalk feels like it's starting to melt and I even have a little headache, but if you insist on it I'll go because I'm the secretary and you're the lawyer."

"Let's go upstairs," he said.

His workroom was not some government-issue cubicle but an office in someone's law firm, larger than he had in New York but with the same lawyery leather and wood and Oriental rug, except this version was all brown and yellow and gold, with brocade drapes that were so beautiful you figured the Washington lawyer had given his wife the green light and a blank check.

There was no fan, but it was cooler than the lobby. Edward offered me a chair in a couch-chair-coffee table setup across the room from his desk. "You're always two steps ahead of me, Linda," he began. "I suppose you know why I wanted to speak with you." He sat across from me, on the couch.

"You need a secretary."

"Yes."

He stopped talking and just stared at me. Not stared, but probed. Then his eyes moved downward, and I thought: He wants to see if I'm pregnant. "I'm not pregnant," I announced. This time he did stare. "Well, you were . . . you seemed to be looking . . ."

"I was *not*."

"Okay, so I have an overactive imagination," I said.

"I think you do."

There was a long, uneasy silence. I'd overstepped the invisible, unknowable bounds. Finally I stood up. "Listen: This isn't going to work." He crossed his arms and glared up at me. "I can't be a secretary anymore."

He stood up too, slowly. "I see." Boy, was he cold. "You've forgotten how to type."

"No. I've forgotten how to be a sweet, obedient girl. I can't be what I was. I can't—"

"Sit down!" he barked at me. I sat. Then he did too. "I really don't give a damn whether you're sweet or not. I'm not in the market for a subservient little creature who gets the vapors every time I raise my voice. I need someone efficient, someone with a brain, someone I can trust and someone who is fluent in German. Period. Do we understand each other?"

"Yes."

"Fine."

"Do you want to tell me about the job?"

"No."

"I'll just show up one day and you'll have a typewriter and confetti? Like a surprise party?"

"Sarcasm doesn't become you, Linda." Boy, did that remark make me feel lousy. And he knew it. "You need some additional security clearance. It will take another few days."

"They're already working on it?"

"I took the liberty of assuming you'd agree to help me."

"Can you tell me what the hours will be?"

"Long."

"Will I be working here?"

"Now and then."

"Will I be working for anyone besides you?"

"Perhaps."

I took a deep breath. "Are you always going to act like this, or are you going to get nicer?"

For a minute he didn't react at all, but then suddenly he started to smile. "I'm going to get nicer."

"When?" I asked.

"Tomorrow. Friday. I can't say with any certainty."

I stood up again. "Well, I'll look forward to it."

"To what? An improvement in my disposition or to working with me?"

"Both," I said.

"Good." He got up, reached across the table and shook my hand. "Welcome aboard, Linda."

# 16

I'd never thought my life could be so interesting, but working for Edward Leland, it was. To begin with, this wasn't any "Take a letter to Herr Teufel re issuance of convertible debentures"; a girl can get just so enthusiastic about convertible debentures.

This was war: ugly, but real. I took down every word of a meeting at COI headquarters between Edward and a Herr Kaufmann, who'd once been a rich industrialist in Düsseldorf and was now a poor old Jew with a pitiful cough and an incredible, near-total recall of the location and layout of every machine-tool factory in Germany—at least as they were until 1936, when the Reich had seized everything he owned and then imprisoned him for "crimes against the Fatherland." (Herr Kaufmann had been lucky to have a cousin in St. Louis who'd managed to move enough money into the pockets of enough German officials so that he'd been released and "deported" in 1939.)

He and Edward pored over maps, while a simultaneous translator rendered English into German and vice versa, so the men could have an easy exchange. I sat in the corner, a quiet, conscientious, invisible stenographer, taking down the English version. I only spoke once, when I said, Excuse me, Mr. Leland, could you repeat that, please.

When Herr Kaufmann and the translator left, Edward said, Poor old fellow. Still doesn't comprehend what hit him. Probably never will. And I changed the subject: The translator's no good. What do you mean? he demanded. So I told him: He's accurate when he's translating Kaufmann's information about factories in major cities. But listen, he'd have to be; anyone, even you, would have spotted it if he'd translated "north Stuttgart" as "west Frankfurt." Even I would have . . . I mean, he thought I was just another dopey American stenographer who could hardly speak English, much less German.

Then I explained how the translator, precise about city manufacturing, had been way off when it came to the countryside. He doubled, tripled or, once, halved the number of kilometers of a factory from a town, and did the same with the capacity of a factory. Edward demanded, Are you *sure* they're not just careless errors? *No.* Listen: I may not have the biggest vocabulary, but I know German well enough—and have been typing contracts for industrial deals long enough—to know that *Dieselkraftstoff* isn't a small truck, it's diesel oil, and Kaufmann's next three or four sentences—about underground oil tanks and their storage volume—the translator just ignored. See, in the beginning he was testing you—making sure you had no knowledge of German. If you'd known anything beyond *auf Wiedersehen*, he wouldn't have taken the risk. Edward said, But it was rather clear I'm abysmally ignorant. I smiled and said, Yeah. Abysmally.

Edward said, We'll have to take care of him. Make him disappear? I breathed. For God's sake, Linda, you've got to stop going to the movies. So I asked, What else do you guys do with someone like him? You know he's bad, probably SD. (That was the *Sicherheitsdienst*, the Nazi Party's intelligence service.) Edward said, Well, since, um, forced disappearance strikes me as something of an overreaction, how about we stop using him as a translator? I said, That's *it?* No, Linda, that's not it. We'll turn him over to the FBI. Of course, he said, looking disgusted, they're the ones who recommended him in the first place.

We'd gone down to the car by then, to drop Edward off at the State Department to meet with John and to take me to the office he used. We talked about the rivalry between COI and the FBI, and then, because I asked, he told me what he thought about J. Edgar Hoover (brilliant bureaucrat, monumental ego), and then he asked me if I still had such an inordinate fondness for Roosevelt, and I said yes, I was crazier about him than ever, and added that if Willkie had won, he'd have folded under isolationist pressure—that had been clear enough in the campaign—and instead of being in Washington, we'd all be at some lawyers' dinner party on Beekman Place, saying, Tsk-tsk, isn't it too bad about those nice little English schoolchildren being forced to say *Heil Hitler*. He told me I'd make a poor lawyer because I always overstated my case, and I told him I'd make a great one because I always picked the right side (like Roosevelt's), and what he called overstatement was actually a forceful presentation of the truth. The car stopped at State, and then, instead of saying goodbye, he smiled and said, See you in court, counselor.

Most of the time it was like that. Working for him was at least worthwhile and interesting, usually fascinating and sometimes fun. And always hard. He was the head of counterespionage for a country that believed that gentlemen do not open other people's mail; his responsibility was to seek out enemies pretending to be friends on behalf of a government that wasn't at war.

He was an honest man doing an underhanded job in a deceitful world. He had to be more flexible, more alert, had to move faster than the enemy: the Germans, of course, and the American officials who didn't want a new intelligence service.

The car became Edward's main office; he said he didn't want to build an empire—a central organization with easy-to-spot telephones, secretaries, bookshelves and staplers. Empires, he said, are apt to be infiltrated or overthrown. So he spread his people out, and we went from meeting to meeting, from his borrowed law office to government buildings to, now and then, the backs of stores, mansions in Virginia or, once, a shack in rural Maryland.

One day we were in the car, a big old Packard he had somehow managed to seize for himself from the government. But this time it wasn't interesting or fascinating or fun.

Edward's voice had an edge—a sharp one: "Don't tell me! There are actually limits to what Linda Voss—excuse me, Linda Berringer—can do?"

"Just one limit," I replied lightly, trying to convince myself the edge wasn't there. A cold November rain streaked the windshield. Everything looked distorted, like when you try on someone's too-strong eyeglasses. "One per secretary isn't so terrible." I'd finally gotten up the courage to tell him I couldn't take dictation in the back seat of his car. "I'm sorry, but it makes me carsick."

"I find it hard to believe that we've been driving all over Washington for the past few months with you feeling ill." He paused and leaned forward to his driver, a man named Pete with a deeply lined red neck, who always wore a Washington Senators baseball cap. I thought he'd say something like: Easy on the sharp turns and the brakes, Pete, with Mrs. Berringer here, but instead he told him, "While we're at COI, double back to my place. I forgot my evening clothes. They're in a black garment bag, probably still hanging on the door of the closet."

"Yes, sir," Pete said in a happy, snappy voice. He'd retired from the navy a few years before, and always seemed thrilled to be subjected to unreasonable demands. Edward would say, Pete, would you mind picking me up at 3 A.M. I have to meet with someone in a coal mine a hundred miles into West Virginia, and Pete would declare, Yes, sir! With other lawyers and government officials, Edward commanded respect—usually mingled with a little awe and sometimes fear. With Pete, he commanded unqualified obedience—and probably love.

He sat back and peered at me. "Why didn't you say anything sooner?" he demanded.

"I don't know," I murmured.

"It's not as if you're a shrinking violet."

"No. I mean, I'm not."

"And I'm not some sort of ogre." When I didn't respond instantly, he snapped, "Well, am I?"

"No. But . . ."

"But what?"

"Sometimes . . . you're kind of . . ."

"Kind of what?"

"Formidable."

Ninety-nine point nine percent of other formidable men would have said, Me? Formidable? Don't be ridiculous. Edward didn't go anywhere near the I'm-a-regular-guy routine. "I really don't see what my being"—he shook his head in annoyance—"formidable has to do with your unwillingness to tell me that the work I'm asking you to do is making you feel ill."

I turned from him and stared out the window. People were huddled in raincoats and taking small, cautious steps, as if the sidewalk was icy. Pete, of course, sped along. "I didn't want a . . . a minor problem of mine to interfere with you," I explained, still gazing out, not wanting to face him. "Anyway, it's not *that* bad." It was.

"Then why mention it?"

I swiveled around and probably glared at him. "I'll be damned if I know." I flipped my pad back open and added, "Go ahead. Dictate."

"So you're going to grin and bear it after all?"

"Right." He looked straight ahead, at the back of Pete's neck. "Come on," I said. "I know you want to get out that memorandum on Pharaoh." Pharaoh was the code name of the valet of the German ambassador to Spain. He'd approached a third secretary of the American Embassy in a café and offered to photograph documents. He didn't want any money; he claimed to be anti-Nazi, said that the Gestapo had arrested and then murdered his niece. No one, including Edward, had yet decided whether the valet was for real or a plant.

"The memorandum can wait," Edward snapped.

"I told you I really don't mind—"

"Enough!" He reached over, swatted shut the cover of my

steno pad and resumed staring at Pete's neck. The bad side
of his face was toward me, so there was no expression I
could read. But I could feel his anger.

I thought: If he only knew how miserable these fights—or
whatever they are—make me feel, maybe he wouldn't start.
They happened every few weeks, and I never knew precisely
what I'd done to trigger him. The same kind of remark he'd
normally be neutral about—or even amused by—would set
him off. His temper would flare up for a minute, but then,
even worse, he'd withdraw into cold, silent fury.

Once I'd gotten up my courage and touched his sleeve,
about to say, Is it really what I said or is it that they cut the
thirty thousand dollars from the cryptographic budget? but I
never got my words out. *Leave me the hell alone!* His teeth
were clenched, and if I hadn't heard his words I wouldn't
have believed he'd said them; they were so harsh, and his
rejection of me was complete, final.

I tried to tell myself at these times that he had terrible
pressures on him, decisions to make that were truly life-and-
death, and he had no one to blow up at. Was he going to call
Nan in New York and fume? Was he going to blow up at
John, at one of the other geniuses who were working for
him? At Donovan? At the President? Was he going to start
screaming at one of the society beauties he was always
squiring around to wherever men need women?

Maybe he picked on me, I thought, because I was almost
always available, and what the hell, for eighteen hundred
bucks a year, Linda Berringer could take a little temper. Or
maybe over time I was too great an irritant; I kept going a little too far, being too wise-guyish, too outspoken, too
relaxed—even happy in his presence. I'd forgotten who I
was.

For days after one of these blowups, I'd feel unbearably
low. Going to work, facing Edward, wasn't the only strug-
gle. Just getting out of bed was; I'd put my feet into my slippers and my throat would close up and I'd walk past John,
who was busy getting dressed, with my head lowered, so he

couldn't see that my eyes had filled up. And not breaking into tears during work was a monumental effort. We'd sit in the car a day or two later, everything seemingly friendly and jolly again. Edward would smile, say, Excuse me, and bury himself in a report. I'd gaze out the window and be overcome by sadness, which seemed stupid—even to me—because Edward, having blown off steam, seemed to have no recollection of the incident that still had the power to make me feel cold, alone, without hope.

Well, this definitely was one of those incidents. Pete drove around to the back entrance of COI headquarters—we never used the front—and Edward got out of the car. I slid across the seat to follow him upstairs, and he slammed the car door in my face. Then he hurried through the cold rain into the building.

Pete sat straight in the front seat, silent. He was Edward's man. I never knew what he listened to or what he thought.

"See you later, Pete," I made myself say.

"Okay."

So I took a deep breath, stuffed my pad and pencil into my pocketbook and got out of the car. The rain had turned to sleet, and it pelted my face and dripped down my neck. I stood there shivering. Then Pete pulled away, and the tires spun out a thick spray of dirty, icy water all over my stockings.

I had a choice then: to do what I wanted to do or what I ought to do. So I didn't stand there in the sleet and sob. I said, "Oh, shit!" and kicked a puddle of freezing water with one of my new suede shoes. Okay, maybe I had tears in my eyes when I did it. But then I went back to work.

The Japanese bombed Pearl Harbor on December 7, 1941, a Sunday, and everybody in Washington kept asking everybody else: Where were you when you heard the news?

"Where were you when you heard the news?" Edward Leland's latest lady asked John. Her name was Felice Benedict, and someone at the party at Edward's house had whispered that her father was Granville Publications and her former husband was Benedict Aluminum, who was now married to Pendleton Timber's widow.

"Where were you?" John asked, smiling back at her, thereby avoiding either a lie or the truth, which was that we were doing it on the floor in the living room, with the New York Philharmonic on the radio as background music, when an announcer broke in, proclaiming: "Ladies and gentlemen, the Japanese have bombed Pearl Harbor! I repeat . . ." For an instant we lay frozen in a position not appropriate for a momentous public event. Then, as we pulled apart, I said, Oh, my God, it's happening, and John said, I'd better get to the office and see what the cable traffic is. Where are my pants?

"I was at home—in Florida," Felice answered. She stood close enough to John to get a good view. She appreciated quality; you could tell from her expensive perfume and the emerald on her right hand, so big it looked like half a broken beer bottle. "I have a little place down in Palm Beach where I spend the winter. I was enjoying a peaceful Sunday . . . or so I thought." But although she stood close to John, she stood closer to Edward. Whatever Edward had seemed to be what she wanted. Felice withdrew a cigarette from a gold case, and before she could flick her gold lighter, five men's matches and lighters rushed forward to meet at the cigarette's tip. She chose Edward's. "I was listening to the Philharmonic broadcast—"

"So was I!" John cut in.

"Weren't you absolutely *jolted?*" she asked. He sure was, I thought.

"Stunned," he agreed. A waiter in a white jacket put a round silver tray right by his hand, and John picked up a cheese straw. It was December 12, the Friday night after Pearl Harbor, and we'd all been invited to Edward's house to celebrate going to war.

That sounds horrible, twisted even, but it wasn't. I think almost all of us there had felt that someday we'd have to fight to stop Hitler, stop the spread of his evil, and now, finally, we could. The day before, Germany and Italy had declared war on the United States, and Congress had responded with declarations of its own—and voted as well that American troops could be dispatched anywhere in the world.

The waiter swiveled toward me and I took a cheese straw. I'd been wondering what dinner at Edward's would be like, since I couldn't exactly imagine him basting a leg of lamb. We'd been working at a killing pace all that day, and if John hadn't told me about the invitation the night before, I wouldn't have had a clue that Edward—who was keeping me and two other secretaries, borrowed from the Justice Department, busy—was hours away from having company. I kept waiting for him to tell me, Call my housekeeper and remind her to wash off the watercress—*something* to show he was aware he was having a gang over for a meal.

But when we got to his house, a beautiful old brick place that had to be the ultimate example of some sort of Great American Architecture, in, naturally, Georgetown, I saw that there had been no need to worry; it had all been taken care of. Cooks, waiters and a butler were busy creating perfection, and all it had probably taken was one phone call to some Rich Persons' Whims Agency. Dinner for ten at eight-thirty on Friday, Edward would have said, and they'd have said, *Of course*, Mr. Leland. You can rely on us.

"And now the Italianos and the Nazis," Felice said. She pronounced Nazis the way Winston Churchill did: Nazzies. "All in one week! Did they declare war on us because they're friends of the Japs, Edward?"

"Yes, but I think there's probably more to it."

"Oh, there's always more to everything with you." She sent him a meaningful smile, then took a deep drag on her cigarette.

Felice Benedict sounded like all of Edward's women, with that slow, smoky upper-class voice. She looked like them too, in that she had a hairstyle that would remain unmoved in a hurricane, perfect, chiseled features and a posture that suggested a spine of steel. But she was older than the others—closer to fifty than forty—and flashier.

Not that Felice chomped on gum and had a skirt slit up to her thigh. But she had a big bust and a small waist and wore a figure-hugging bright green knit dress that flashed Go! She touched Edward as often as she could—smoothing back a supposed out-of-place hair, reaching into his vest pocket to look at his watch—and in case anyone didn't know what the score was, she'd said, My God, it's nippy! a half hour earlier and then added, I'll get my shawl. It's with my things, upstairs. Upstairs, of course, were probably a few guest rooms—and Edward's bedroom.

Well, no one really thought she'd come to Washington to stay at a hotel and visit the National Gallery, but Mrs. Something Weekes, whose husband, Norman Weekes, was, despite some ridiculously confusing title, one of COI's top spy coordinators, had pursed her thin lips in disapproval as she'd watched Felice's bright green backside disappear up the stairs.

I have to admit that for that instant even I had felt my face get hot with embarrassment, because Felice drew arrows and flashed blinding lights around her private life. Where I came from, people didn't do that. (For that matter, where she came from they didn't, either.)

All the other women John and I had seen Edward with were so classy and fashionable they'd looked like beautiful heads plopped on top of Parisian dresses, with no human body inside. But despite her aristocratic accent, her emerald, her ropes of pearls and her little place in Palm Beach, which probably had fifty-six rooms and was right on the ocean, Felice was more than just a well-dressed set of cheekbones; she let you know she was female—and doing female-male things with Edward.

John had once told me that Edward was quite a ladies' man. I'd said, You're kidding! No, John went on, he always has someone. He spoke carefully, analytically, as if he was dealing with a fascinating legal concept instead of Edward

Leland's sex life. You see, he explained, by the time, um, Ed's wife died (the "um" was because he was on the verge of saying "Nan's mother"), he'd established himself as, well, as quite important, both socially and professionally. He was therefore *extremely* eligible. And aside from his obvious credentials, he has a way with women. I must have made a face, because John added, Sophisticated women. So all along, he continued, Ed's been inundated—he's had more women than he knew what to do with. All wealthy, all intelligent, pleasant, pretty, chic. And because the supply was so abundant, his demand seemed to diminish. Do you understand? Someone perfectly suitable was always available for . . . whatever he was interested in at the moment. He had no particular need for anyone permanent.

But what about love? I asked. He must have been so lonely after his wife died. And he was young. Didn't he want someone?

He had the law, John declared. You have the law, I said. It never got in your way. John sighed: Ed had responsibilities to Nan. Come on, I interrupted again, don't tell me he couldn't find time to get married because he was so busy making chocolate pudding and tying Nan's little shoelaces. Great men, John humphed, don't concern themselves with conventional domestic matters.

But it looked to me as if Felice was looking for something nice and conventional, and I wished her well. She had a nicer nature than the others. For instance, she didn't ignore me. She'd actually talked to me. "Tell me, Linda, were you listening to the Philharmonic too?"

"Well, I was in the room, but I'm not the music lover John is. I was probably reading the paper or something."

"Your favorite boss"—she took Edward's hand—"was in New York, you know." I nodded. "Listening to the New York I-think-the-Giants playing football with people from Brooklyn. Can you imagine? But the announcement didn't come as a shock, because he'd already gotten a call from Donovan and Roosevelt over an hour earlier." Edward stood there, his hand in hers, looking amused and, I thought, a little charmed at her name-dropping. "He was on the telephone after that, but kept the football game on for God-knows-what reason. Probably to listen to all those masculine grunts of agony. So coarse, but that's what men like, don't you think?"

"Maybe I just wanted to hear the news when it came over the radio," Edward suggested.

Felice gave him an aren't-you-clever smile. Then she took my arm, said, "Girl talk," to Edward, and led me over to the couch. She sat right beside me and took a deep breath, as if getting ready to give a prepared speech. She delivered it fast: "Linda, dear, Edward has such respect for you. I *know* you're his right hand." I knew she wanted something, and it wasn't to give me a prize as Washington Secretary of the Year. I felt a little ill at ease, but it must have been harder for her; she rubbed her cigarette case between her palms as if it would warm her hands. "I hate to intrude on—oh, Linda, you know—the relationship between a private secretary and her employer." She was so nervous, swallowing too often, fiddling with her cigarette case, crossing and recrossing her legs, that for a minute I thought I'd gotten her wrong. Maybe what she was after was government secrets. But then, one look at her, chewing off her dark lipstick, and I knew she wasn't looking for Germany or Italy or Japan. Her long fingernails, the exact same color as her lips, tapped out a nervous rhythm on the gold case. "You know what they say," she murmured. "A man has no secrets from his valet. But we're so modern nowadays, it should be: no secrets from his secretary." She eyed my wedding ring. "Oh, not that you're just a secretary."

"Felice," I broke in, "I really don't—"

"I'm not going to ask you about the others. If there are others." Her voice had a tiny question mark at the end, but I pretended not to hear it. "I was just curious if he ever—oh, you know—ever mentioned me."

I shouldn't have looked up that second, because my sixth sense was poking me in the ribs, telling me that Edward was looking right at me. But naturally I did, and there he was, carrying on a deep and serious conversation with Norman

Weekes, getting a fresh drink from the waiter—and still managing to take in everything going on between Felice and me.

"I'm not asking *details*," Felice said softly. "That wouldn't be right."

Edward was giving us one of his unreadable stares, but I knew him well enough to read it anyway. He was something less than delighted at Felice's "girl talk" with me. If I could read between the lines, it said: Keep your mouth shut. But what was I going to tell her? That the most personal Edward ever got with me was when he'd climb into the car on a Monday and say: Did you have a nice weekend?

"Felice, I only know him in a business way. As his secretary—and as John's wife."

"But surely he *must* have said something. . . ."

I made a big deal of glancing over to Edward, but she was too intent on our conversation to pick up the hint. "I'm asking because—you see—I've grown quite attached to him." She put a beautifully manicured hand on mine; veins stood out, prominent and pale blue against the deep green of the emerald.

"I'm sure he's attached to you," I said. I wanted to give her something because, well, she loved him.

"He's mentioned something?" She was so overjoyed.

"No." Her face fell. "But you know Ed. He's . . . he plays things close to the vest." She smiled and nodded. "But he wouldn't have asked you here, with all this . . . this war fever, unless he wanted your company. I mean, it's a crazy, hectic time. He must feel so comfortable . . ."

I could hardly hear her. "I'm afraid I presented myself as something of a *fait accompli*, my dear. You see, I turned up on his doorstep Tuesday evening. I'd just thought, well, with all this tumult, it would be great fun to be at the center of things. I hoped he wouldn't be . . . irked. And he didn't seem to be."

Just then I glanced up, and there was Edward standing before us. Irked. His hands were jammed into the pockets of his trousers, and his dark eyebrows were drawn together, shading his eyes; even though I couldn't see them, I knew

they weren't twinkling. Still, as he held out his hand and
pulled Felice up from the couch, his expression eased. The
scowl passed. His eyes were warm. And I was willing to bet
that the smile he gave her erased the memory of his displeasure in Felice's mind. If she'd thought he was mad at
her, that outstretched hand and lit-up face made her think:
Oh, no, he *adores* me.

Edward led Felice over to a former judge from Albany
who'd joined the White House staff, an old political crony of
FDR's who Edward had suddenly become great pals with
when one of his budget requests got stomped on. The judge
had something to do with loosening up executive-branch
money, and although he was supposed to be an old shrewdie,
it was clear it didn't occur to the judge that he was being
used; Edward Leland was his true friend.

Both the judge and his wife were obviously thrilled to be
at Edward's house. It was more real than the White House.
An invitation to Edward Leland's wasn't a political courtesy; it all but said, You've arrived. Every time the wife
walked past another piece of furniture, she'd give a fast
stroke to the upholstery. When the waiter came over to ask
what she'd like to drink, her elbow nudged her husband's
side, as if to say, Wally, we're *here*.

I was just starting to get up, to walk over to John, who was
stuck with witchy Mrs. Weekes, when Norman Weekes sat
down beside me. Too close, naturally. "Linda," he said. I
waited, but that was all for a while. He said my name as if it
was a code with a very deep meaning.

"How are you?"

"Now I'm fine," he answered. His thigh wasn't touching
mine, but it was close.

I suddenly realized that it was his conversation with Norman Weekes that had made Edward cross the room with
such a glowering expression. I understood, as I edged away
from Norman's thigh, closer to the arm of the couch, that it
wasn't girl talk that had caused Edward's eyebrows to come
together in anger. Felice wasn't the problem. At most,
Edward might be irritated by the notion of the lady who

showed up on his doorstep (but whom he'd shown upstairs) pumping his secretary for secrets. Okay, and a little annoyed with me, because even from across the room, he'd spotted that I was reassuring her, and maybe he didn't want her to feel so comfortable, so free to just "show up."

So it wasn't the rich, eager and willing divorcée. It was Norman Weekes, a banker who had moved through Germany in the twenties and the thirties as smoothly as he moved through upper-class Boston, where he'd been born and raised. Norman, Edward's esteemed colleague at COI, obviously made Edward *furious*; he didn't make me exactly delighted, either.

"You look quite delicious tonight, my dear," Norman said. "Good enough to eat." John had told me Norman was related to all sorts of Boston names: Cabots, Lowells. I wondered if he'd inherited his yellow teeth from them—to say nothing of his tendency to dribble spit out of the side of his mouth. Norman leaned in closer and asked, "Can I take a bite out of you?" His breath smelled like a stale onion roll. "Just a little bite."

I laughed, pretending it was all a joke, that he wasn't a repulsive old lecher but a delightful predinner companion. He didn't join me, though, not even with a chuckle. But he did shift about a tenth of an inch away from me, so I sensed my laughter had succeeded in pulling his fuse. Good.

Norman Weekes was in his early sixties. He had thin white hair, except for wisps—like cotton cosmetic puffs— over his ears. Still, he seemed to see himself as irresistible, and the three or four times we'd met, he always made a beeline for me, on the theory, I guess, that if I was already married to a magnificent-looking man, I might have room in my life for another. Also, he was enough of a wise Washington operator to want to get as much as he could on a colleague, and a colleague's secretary was a first-rate source. That he got absolutely zero in either department didn't stop him.

"How are things over in your office?" I asked. He was staring at my legs. In my eagerness to pull away from him, the skirt of my dress had ridden up above my knees; I wanted to tug it down, but I wouldn't give him the satisfaction. "This must have been a hectic week."

"Ghastly," he said. "I wish I had a girl like you to help me out. Edward's a lucky man." I smiled. Across the room, Edward was charming the judge; his arm was around Felice's waist. But he turned and saw Norman Weekes drooling over my legs. "Of course, your husband's a luckier man, if you know what I mean. Tell me, is John happy, working for Ed?"

"Yes. Very happy."

"Not a bit awkward, all this incestuous business. Oh, come, my angel. Don't give me those big, innocent brown eyes of yours. Incest. Your John was married to Ed's girl . . . what's her name?"

"Nan."

"And now you're working day and night for your husband's former father-in-law. Tell me, isn't it a bit much? Don't you wish you could have your husband all to yourself . . . cut those old family ties? Hmmm, Linda?"

I didn't know why Edward detested Norman Weekes so much; I was just able to sense him seething whenever Norman called or his name was mentioned, or now, across the room, watching Norman breathe into my ear.

But I knew why I hated Norman Weekes. He was a snake. Not some dumb, slithery thing that bites, but a smart one. His genius was finding people's weaknesses and playing on them. I'd heard he'd recruited agents through flattery, appeals to patriotism, bribery and, when all else failed, blackmail. But all else rarely failed, because Norman was such a skillful serpent. "Linda, lovely Linda," he said, "you deserve a husband who's a hundred percent."

"I have one. Thank you."

"Counterespionage is dreadfully tedious. Isn't he bored with working for Ed?"

"You know John can't discuss what he does with me . . . or anyone."

"Of course not. But really, my love, you should encourage him to break his ties to Father Edward. He'd have much more independence—to say nothing of personal satisfaction—working with me. I need someone like him, and believe me, dear Linda, with me . . . how best to put it? John could be the man he will never be with Edward Leland."

"Mr. Weekes, I don't see any point in—"

"And furthermore," Norman went on, "it would be in *your* best interest to get your handsome husband away from the, um, House of Leland, shall we say. My dear, the word is seeping out that my dear old friend Quentin's pretty little wife is somewhat discontent. Yes, isn't that surprising? Young Nan is rumored to be on some quiet island in the Caribbean right now. 'Thinking things over,' as they say." Norman took my hand in his; his skin was horribly dry, like something dead for a long time. He spoke so softly his voice was hardly louder than a hiss. "Rumor has it the sweet thing may just decide to visit wise old Père Edward, to get some fatherly advice. Who knows, she may stay in Washington for some time. It's *so* exciting here." He squeezed my hand tight. "I know you're listening, my dear, even though you don't like what I'm saying. But do your best to persuade John. I promise you, if we have any . . . sweet young visitors to our beloved capital, I'll see to it that John has to make an urgent trip out of town. For as long as is necessary." He turned my hand over and scraped the nail of his index finger across my palm. "And when the cat's away," he said in his high-class Boston accent, "the mice can have a most stimulating time. Do consider that possibility, dear Linda. You look like a girl who can appreciate . . . stimulation."

So what was I supposed to do—say to John, Want to hear some terrific gossip about Nan Leland Berringer Dahlmaier? That was the last thing in the world I wanted him to hear.

My husband had never stopped loving his first wife. On good nights, when John didn't roll over and sleep right at the edge of the mattress, when he stayed in the middle of the bed with his arm slung over me in his sleep, his hand resting on my shoulder or, once, on my cheek, like a night-long caress, I'd think: Okay, so Nan will always be his ideal woman. Big deal. It's not her as a person John loves; it's the idea of her. When he talks about her, he talks about her mind: her passion for music and art; her misery at having to go through the debutante ritual (as if Edward held a carving knife to her throat and said, Have a tea dance or die). And he thinks she's beautiful, because she almost is, with her pale, flawless features and delicate, small-boned body.

On good nights I'd think that sure, maybe every day with me wasn't New Year's Eve, but he never really had fun with Nan. He never mentioned long walks or picnics—or grabbing her the minute he got home and doing it standing up.

As for Nan, my guess was that John's big attraction for her (besides whatever culture he had that made her intellect squeal with pleasure) was exactly what made me crazy about him: his beauty; his quiet seriousness, so you were always dying to know what he was thinking, because you were never sure of where you stood; his powerful appeal to all women, so by picking you he had somehow shown the world—and you—how special you were; and, finally, his real gift: his ability as a lover. But in that department, even though he would never go into it (Linda, this is *not* a subject for discussion), I knew Nan never set him on fire. He adored her, and it must have given him enormous reassurance to know he had such a hold over her, but . . . Okay, so maybe I was reading between the lines, but I was good at that, and I *knew* Nan wasn't woman enough for him. And I knew I was.

But on bad nights, I knew Nan was everything John wanted and loved in the world. He loved her nanny; her father's town house on Washington Square, where she grew up; her romantically-dead-at-an-early-age rich Theodore Roosevelt cousin of a mother; her dancing lessons, her harp lessons, her boarding school; her summers in Europe, her winter vacations skiing in Vermont; and her horse, Daisy, who died in a stable in Central Park when both Nan and the horse were fifteen. John loved how Nan's eyes would fill up whenever she spoke about Daisy. And he loved—worshiped—her father.

To have been taken up into that family was the acceptance

John had always dreamed of. He'd been allowed to be one of them; it was too bad wives take on husbands' names, because he would have loved nothing more than to be John Leland. But then Nan got rid of him. It must have been like an angel being tossed out of heaven, doomed to live in the workaday world after knowing paradise.

So I wouldn't talk to John about Nan. And I couldn't tell any of my forty-seven Alabama neighbors, who I hardly ever saw anymore with my crazy work hours and who anyway didn't know my husband had been married before and, besides, wouldn't say anything more than "Ah do declare!" and then run out and give the other forty-six the big news bulletin. And I couldn't tell my mother, because even though I wrote her every day, I doubt if she looked at or even listened to Cookie read my letters. I called her once a week, but her voice was so faded, so thin, that even if she had the strength to concentrate on what I was saying, I didn't have the heart to tell her: Mom, maybe you were right about John.

And I couldn't tell Edward. Listen, Ed, did you hear about my husband's ex-wife? The sweet petunia may be on the loose again. You got any of that famous Edward Leland wisdom for me? Any ideas about whether this little intellectual flower is going to come for a comforting visit to her daddy and screw up my life? Huh, Ed?

"Linda," Edward said to me. It was the Monday morning after his dinner, and Pete was driving up over a narrow, hilly, icy road somewhere in Virginia horse country at sixty miles an hour. "I need a breath of fresh air." I was about to crank down the window when he added, "Pete, pull over for a minute." The Packard skidded to a stop. Edward opened the door and said, "Come on."

I followed him, and we walked for a few minutes in silence. Then he turned right, onto a dirt road. After another few minutes, he stopped and leaned against a white fence. I buttoned the top of my coat and fished my gloves out of my pocket. I had no idea how long I'd be breathing fresh air.

God knows Edward needed some. Since Pearl Harbor, his

job had become a horror. Before December 7, he had been
head of counterespionage for all of Europe, to make sure
that the agents who were feeding us information were really
ours—and to make sure their information was accurate, that
someone, somewhere, in German intelligence hadn't discovered that a diplomat or a prostitute or a chauffeur was a spy
and was allowing him to pass us misleading information.

But now Donovan and the President wanted more.
Edward would continue to oversee Europe, but he'd also
have to take on the United States. That was the FBI's job, of
course, but the three men had agreed a little extra coverage
couldn't hurt.

Meanwhile, Norman Weekes and ten men just like him
signed up agents—lawyers, writers, college professors—
free-lance agents living in America and coming out of the
woodwork to offer us wonderful secrets, agents for desk
work, like John, and agents, spies, to be slipped into whatever dark cracks we could find in enemy territory. Edward
would have to make sure they were what they claimed: good
Americans, or dedicated anti-Fascists.

I blew on my hands and glanced up at him. He had deep
circles under his eyes. He'd nicked himself shaving in three
or four places on his bad side, where he had no feeling. I'd
never seen him look tired before.

"Tell me about Friday night." He spoke so suddenly I
jumped.

"Oh. It was . . ." I tried to think of one of those appropriate words, like grand, or divine, and I did, but they sounded
jerky, so I said, ". . . a terrific party. Your house is beautiful.
Felice was very nice." I couldn't believe I was standing
right near a horse field in December telling him what a great
host he'd been, but if that's what he wanted . . . "And the
dinner—"

"Oh, stop it!" he snapped. "Do you think I'm fishing for
compliments?"

"How am I supposed to know what you're fishing for? I
thought I'd give compliments a try." I turned up my collar.

"Are you cold?"

"I'm okay."

"Tell me what Norman Weekes said to you."

"Oh, God!" I said. "Please."

"I'm not talking about his . . . advances toward you. It's obvious he finds you . . . whatever."

"He makes me want to throw up!" I suddenly said. Edward examined the painted wood of the fence. "I apologize," I said. "That just slipped out."

"Understandable," he muttered. "He makes me want to throw up too." I stared at him. "Norman Weekes is a foul human being. Now that we have that established, please go on."

So I told him. I told him about Norman's saying how lucky he was to have me as a secretary. Naturally, Edward didn't say, Well, at least Norman's right about one thing. He just waited for me to continue. "Look," I said, "this isn't my favorite kind of conversation."

"I'm sorry, Linda. I have to know what he said." He waited. And he knew how to wait, until you became so uneasy with the silence that you'd do anything to stop it.

"He wants John to come and work for him."

"Goddamn it! All right. What precisely did he say about John's leaving me to work for him? Don't waste my time, Linda. I know when you're . . . when someone's holding back on me." I gazed out at the field. "As you know, I have a very full schedule today. Don't make it more difficult."

"You're being unfair," I blurted out. But I didn't take it back. "I told you what's important."

"It's all important."

"Some of it's personal stuff."

"I want to hear it."

"Why?"

"Because Norman Weekes would like nothing better than to destroy me." He glanced at me and said, "You look cold. Let's walk." He chose the direction: farther down the dirt road. "I suppose you'd like an explanation."

"Only if you want to give me one." I took a deep breath of cold air. "Don't you know I'd take anything you said on faith?"

"I appreciate that." He walked fast, and I had to hurry along the road to keep up with him. Finally he spoke. "For years, Norman's been doing business with a banker in Munich. A conservative, a Catholic and, according to Norman, a man contemptuous of the Nazis. And yet this man has been close to the government—through his contacts at Krupp, United Steel, I. G. Farben. In late '39, he met Norman in Switzerland with a briefcase full of documents— page after page of statistics on industrial production. He swore to Norman he was a good German, a good Catholic, and precisely because of this he was morally obliged to take a stand against Hitler's regime. He told Norman: I know you have friends in Washington. Please see that these fall into the right hands."

I stopped for a second to take off my shoe and shake out some gravel. "The statistics—were they important?"

"If they were accurate, they were an invaluable picture of German industry—and from that, we could derive quite a clear idea of their military strength. And so, throughout '39 and '40, we accepted these figures—and passed them on to the British. And Bill Donovan asked Norman to come to Washington and do more of the same."

"But he wants to *destroy* you. So you must have found out that his statistics . . . ?"

"I did my homework. To this day I don't know what made me do it. A hunch. And through the years I've come to trust my hunches. I had John and an economist compare this banker's information with data we'd gotten from different sources. Linda, none of it gibed. The figures were grossly understated. The Germans were far stronger than we had been led to believe."

"Did you go to Norman?"

"Not right away. I did some checking on this man from Munich—nothing terribly difficult; the sort of investigation someone in Norman's position ought to have done."

"But he hadn't."

"No. He was so damned sure of this friend of his, this honorable, refined, old-money banker. When I finally brought my findings to him, he told me, 'Ed, please. The fellow's wife's a von Schleicher, for Chrissake.' " He stopped and turned to me. "How was my accent on von Schleicher?"

"Terrible," I told him. "As usual." I paused. "What finally happened?"

"Ultimately, Norman did himself in with his own arrogance. He went to Donovan and issued an ultimatum: Either Ed Leland goes or I do. Well, the next day the three of us got together for a drink. Bill was being congenial, trying to minimize our differences; Norman was saying his honor was at stake, and that his source was a Catholic. He looked right at Bill when he said it."

"Real subtle."

"Yes. And then I did what I'd come prepared to do: I handed Bill my documentation and said, 'Forget the statistics. Look at the pictures.' "

"You got pictures?"

"Yes. Some photos of Norman's friend with *his* good friends: high Nazi officials—including Göring."

I tucked my hands under my armpits to keep them warm, but it wasn't just the weather. "Where did you get the pictures, Ed?"

"Linda, everyone remarks what a bright girl my secretary is. So you tell me: Where did I get the pictures?"

"You had someone go into the man's office or house—"

"Very good. His house."

"And they stole—"

"I prefer to say appropriate."

"How did Donovan react when he saw them?" I asked.

"Gracefully. The we-all-have-our-bad-days approach."

"But Weekes must have looked like something less than a bargain."

"Considerably less. Bill had relied on Norman, on his judgment, and it was faulty—in the extreme. And we simply cannot afford that. Look, you've seen how we've had to operate. Until last week, when we declared war, we were the most rudimentary operation. We had no great network of agents, no committees to assess intelligence. All we had was a few men. Norman Weekes was one of them. Still is. But no longer, shall we say, the force he once was."

"You're right," I said. "He does want to destroy you."

"Yes. But look on the bright side. If he succeeds, you'll have time to read or go to the dressmaker or whatever it is working for me keeps you from doing."

I didn't smile. "The scary thing about Norman Weekes is that he's very smart, but he's not intelligent. Do you know what I mean?"

"Yes. I'll tell you what it is. He sees small pieces with . . . well, amazingly acute vision. But he has no sense of the big picture—or even that there is one." He paused. "Now, Linda . . . will you tell me what he said about John?"

"I'll tell you because you have to know what this guy is doing, what knife he's going to stick in your back."

"Thank you."

"But I hate doing it. I want you to know that."

"I understand."

"He said counterespionage was boring, and that John would be better off with him. Not just because of the boring part. Because . . . he said . . . John can't be the man he could be if he's . . . working for you."

Edward's voice was much colder than the frigid air. "The implication being that I somehow . . . what?"

"Take away John's independence. He looks up to you too much to be his own man."

"And?"

"And . . . the family business. That maybe it's—you know—awkward for me because John was married to your daughter."

"What else?"

"That's it."

"No. There's more. You and he were talking a long time."

And that's where I decided to stop. I wouldn't tell him.

Hey, Norman tells me someone besides Santa Claus may be coming to town. "That's all."

He turned abruptly and we hurried back along the long dirt road to the main road, and the car. We didn't have anything else to say. But when we reached the car, Edward stood at the rear of the car and put his foot on the bumper. "You know, I used to close my eyes at night, and in two minutes I'd be sound asleep. Now . . . sometimes I'm up for hours. It's not just the business about Norman. The whole damned COI is filling up with men like him, men who are still playing Cowboys and Indians. Norman says, Trust my blood brother . . . and look what happens.

"Last August, he had a boy, fresh out of college in Maine. French-speaking parents. He sent him into occupied France, someplace outside Paris where a German official kept a mistress. He tells the boy—a good-looking youngster—to seduce the mistress and get all he can on the German. It was an idiot plan . . . created by Norman but approved with great enthusiasm by two of our top men. Well, the boy was caught the first day. Caught and killed. And Norman says, 'At least we tried. You can't make an omelet without breaking a few eggs.' "

I wished I could have taken his hand and held it. "I'm sorry."

"I meet with men like myself, men who should know better, and they're hatching half-baked schemes. Playing games. I like games. I'm good at them. Golf, bridge, chess . . . But these games they're playing use people as pawns. I sit at a conference table and hear things that make me sick, and when I object, I'm told, Ed, old man, you've lost your nerve." He looked at me and suddenly aimed his finger at my heart. "Bang! You're dead! Cowboys and Indians. That's how these lawyers and bankers and businessmen are going to win the war. With clever strategies. Games. Bang! But when the Germans and Japs go bang . . ."

"You really are dead," I murmured. He nodded. "But the

other men in COI . . . some of them are like you, aren't they?"

"Some of them are." He stared straight and motioned me to the car door. Before he opened it, he said, "I don't know if we'll ever make the omelet, but we're going to have dozens—hundreds of dozens—of broken eggs before this war is over. Linda, it's going to be a mess."

# 17

John had a new office, but that was only to be expected. He was now running the counterespionage operation in Germany and France—that part that could be run from behind a desk in Washington. Technically, of course, the entire world was still the Edward Leland Show, but Edward was busy flying around, not only looking for concealed enemies but also trying to calm down a close-to-berserk J. Edgar Hoover and his pet politicians, who were convinced that anytime anyone from COI breathed in the United States, he was stealing the oxygen, the life, out of the FBI.

The American flag behind John's desk, with its thick pole topped by a gold eagle, the long view of the Capitol dome from his window, and his executive secretary, who was fluent in French as well as German, showed just how far John had come. Okay, the office was only slightly larger than an orange crate, but it had a carpet. And while his secretary was a strange, bent-over woman with coarse, shoulder-length brown hair, who resembled a grizzly bear, she did have a Phi Beta Kappa key from Barnard College.

"Edith," John said to her, "this is my wife . . ." He paused for a fraction of a second. Normally, as wife, I'd be introduced to a secretary as "Mrs. Berringer." But since Edward had flown off for three weeks of mysterious meetings in secret places, I'd been sent over to work for John. ". . . Linda Berringer," John said, leaving it up to Edith what to call me.

"I am pleased to meet you, Mrs. Berringer." Actually, she said "Frau Berringer." John was going to spend the morning interviewing refugees from Germany, and we were warming up our German.

The refugees were key pieces of the puzzle Edward's unit was trying to put together. The more information we had— on everything from changes in train schedules to the extent of the flour shortage in eastern Germany—the better we were able to get a picture of how their war effort was going and, just as important, to check if our sources were giving us accurate accounts.

"I'm glad to meet you, Edith. And please, call me Linda." Her small, too-wide-spaced eyes fluttered a little when she heard my accent. She spoke the same educated *hoch Deutsch* John did.

"Edith," John said, "would you be good enough to take down the preliminary background information for Herr Doktor Schwerin? Also, you might want to offer him some coffee." Edith nodded, did an about-face and walked out the door, to the anteroom where John's visitors waited. Walked is maybe too normal a word for what Edith did. Her legs were heavy, short and strangely far apart, so her progress was more like an animal's lope. If she'd growled or scratched the scalp under her thick hair instead of saying "Yes, Mr. Berringer," it wouldn't have seemed out of character.

"Poor girl," I said, after she shut the door. "To look like that. I wonder if she's ever had a boyfriend. I mean, do you think some guy can see beyond her homeliness?" John shrugged. Edith's love life was obviously not an item on his agenda. "Is she a nice person?"

"I don't know. She's all right, I suppose."

"Is she madly in love with you, John?"

He let himself go enough to smile for a moment. "Probably." He was behind his battleship of a desk; it took up three quarters of the room. I left the straight-backed chair I'd been in and went to sit on the edge of his desk. He motioned me to come over further and pulled me onto his lap. I rested my head against his shoulder. He massaged the back of my neck, then slid his hand down the back of my blouse and stroked my skin. "Edward's let you sit in on all his meetings with Schwerin?" he asked.

"Yes, he needs me there. Schwerin doesn't speak a word of English. What could he do? Play charades? Can you see Edward pantomiming 'panzer divisions'?"

"Your hair smells nice. I wish you'd wear it loose."

"It doesn't look right at work."

"I guess not." John kissed me.

The more Edward trusted me, the more attentive—and affectionate—John became. "Schwerin's not one of these refugees you should get all teary-eyed about," I murmured into the woolly lapel of his navy chalk-stripe suit. "He's a two-bit Berlin lawyer who happened to be at the right place at the right time—and did the wrong thing. He got involved in some sleazy black market stuff—selling silk that was going to be used for parachutes to a company that made ladies' panties. He's lucky he got out."

John's deep-blue eyes blazed at me with such intensity they seemed to be lit from within; he was madly, passionately in love with my inside information. At first, John could barely believe that I was allowed to sit in while Edward made phone calls to Donovan. Or that, riding around in the Packard, Edward would analyze the differences between the French and Dutch resistance movements—or tell me about the love affair between Wendell Willkie and the book review editor of the *New York Herald Tribune*. John had gaped when I told him: The Democrats got hold of some of Willkie's letters to her! "Dolly notes," they were calling them, and they were actually going to release them, except the Republicans found out that Wallace, FDR's running mate, was tied in with some weird Russian mystic and had written some crazy religious-nut letters. John had asked, "He *tells* you all this? Or do you overhear it? He tells me, I'd answered. You know, when we're driving around, or sometimes when it's slow, like when we're waiting around for a transatlantic call.

For a while, John couldn't accept that Edward actually

talked to me. I think he tried to come up with excuses for these lapses: Maybe Edward was thinking out loud, or perhaps he was tired. But finally John's awe won out; Edward was so perfect, so sound in his judgment, that if he talked to me, I was—for whatever reason—obviously worth talking to.

What I never told John about were what I called the private talks. About a week after Edward told me of his concern over the COI boys in three-piece suits playing Cowboys and Indians, we'd slowly drifted into conversations I knew we never could have had with anyone else. In my case, the need for someone to talk to was obvious; no one, least of all my husband, showed any inclination to listen to all the things I wanted to say. And in Edward's case, I guessed it was that he had a lot on his mind—too much—and needed more than an ear; he had to have a mouth that would stay shut.

So what began on that dirt road in Virginia kept going. The next talk had taken place about nine o'clock one night in the middle of December. Edward, not looking up from a letter he was proofreading, told me he was going to have a late dinner and a brandy with Donovan in an hour; Pete would drive me home. I said fine. But a minute later, as I was collecting his day's mess of paper clips, which were scattered all over his desk and on the floor around his chair, I suddenly squeezed all the paper clips tight in my hand. Their metal edges made painful little pinholes in my palm; my mouth went dry. But I stood up from the rug and asked him, Why do you think all the wives in the law firm hate me so much?

Scared as I was, I somehow knew that he wouldn't think I was going too far in asking that question, or that I was a jerk for thinking such thoughts. And I was right. He got out of his chair, went over to the antique cabinet where he kept a couple of bottles of liquor for visitors (and a bottle of schnapps for hysterical refugees), took out two glasses and inquired: Scotch all right for you?

Yes, I said, and he poured me enough to anesthetize a patient for a twelve-hour operation. He poured himself a lot less.

They don't hate you, he told me.

Well, they give a pretty good imitation of it, I replied.

It's that you're not one of them. Then he said, Sit, and pointed to the wing chair where he usually sat when he talked to other lawyers. He sat on the couch, put his drink down on the coffee table and leaned toward me. Linda, they've created a nice, neat little world for themselves, where everyone speaks the same language, knows their place, where wives are wives and secretaries are—

Less than human.

I thought he'd disagree, but all he said was, Well, perhaps not quite as high on the evolutionary scale.

But why are they so rotten to me? You know what they do every single time? They say, "Oh, hello-o-o, Linda, dear," and then ignore me for the rest of whatever dinner party we're at, and let me tell you, lawyers have too many damn dinner parties. If they're so classy, why aren't they nice to me? You know, like they are to their cooks? "Dear old Martha. She's one of the family."

Are you going to drink that Scotch or look at it? he demanded. I took a sip. All right, he went on, the reason they can afford to be nice to dear old Martha is that she probably *is* old and rather plain, and even if she's not, she doesn't marry an attorney and want to join them for lunch and matinees.

I never wanted that!

I'm talking in generalities, Linda.

Maybe talk in specifics. I didn't go to Radcliffe.

Specifically, you frighten them. You lured one of the most eligible lawyers in Manhattan—

Oh, stop it! They all know what kind of a lure it was, and I'll bet anything they spent weeks gossiping about how noble he was to marry me. And I'll bet you double they all knew I had a miscarriage and he wound up stuck with me.

He said quietly, You're very hard on yourself.

I said, You know how everyone admires you, calls you tough-minded, a realist? He nodded. Okay, I'm a realist too. I understand my own situation.

He took a long drink. Do you want to know why they don't like you? Let me be direct. You have blond hair, a nice figure—and a bit of a Brooklyn accent.

Queens, I whispered.

You attract their men. You are precisely what they fear when their husbands call and say, "I'm working late tonight, dear." And there's more. Shall I go on?

Yes.

You're intelligent and you've got, well, let's call it guts. Deep down, they recognize you're as good as they are. This nice, pleasant world they've created is really a rather fragile one, dependent on the illusion of their superiority. And, Linda, you walked into the Avenels' living room that night and, very simply, they sensed their world starting to crack a little around the edges. So they did what they had to do to save themselves—and their illusions. They forced you to remain outside.

I must have drunk too much; all of a sudden I wanted to laugh. I asked, Will they ever accept me? Like in thirty-five years?

Edward's deep voice had been so soft I could hardly hear him: How hard are you willing to try to emulate them? Are you willing to bend? Break? How much do you want to become what they are?

I don't.

Then, Linda, when this war is over, and if we are all still here, free, alive . . .

Then what?

Then you'll live happily ever after with your husband and, I'm certain, your children . . . except for a series of obligatory dinner parties where you'll be ogled by doddering attorneys and snubbed by their wives. Does that answer your question?

So there I sat in my husband's lap, cradled in his arms—somewhat happily, although not in Cinderella post-glass-slipper ecstasy. Maybe it was because I'd learned that John was not affectionate by nature. Sex, sure. But as for cuddling, only for cause, as the lawyers say. What he wanted from me, at that moment as he kissed my forehead, was the inside scoop on the low-life Berlin lawyer Herr Doktor Schwerin.

John, of course, was no male Mata Hari, seducing state secrets out of me. He had as much right to know what I knew as I did. Of course, he was too much the gentleman to ask directly. But I'd discovered he liked to hear what was going on so he could test his theories, his conclusions: to see if they jibed with Edward's. "This Schwerin's not important for himself," John observed.

"No. Just for being able to corroborate Sunflower's information."

Sunflower was Edward's best source inside Germany. He was head of one of the country's biggest mining firms, a brilliant financial planner, a manager, and a man who, right from the beginning, had hated Hitler and all he stood for. He was one of the German industrialists who were great believers in boosting their economy through *amerikanisches Geschäft*, doing business with America, and he'd gotten to know Edward in the late 1920s. By 1933, when the Nazis came to power, he had started keeping Edward informed about the ties between business and Hitler's government.

Once the Germans went on the march across Europe, the relationship between these two men became less casual. They would meet every few months in Paris and, after Paris fell, in Switzerland. Through his family, Sunflower had ties to upper levels of the military. Through his business, he spoke with other industrialists. And finally, the treasurer of his company was a fanatical Nazi—and a boastful one. The man was proud of his stature in the Party, and he'd brag about his coffees with Himmler, his dinners with Göring and, most of all, his frequent lunches with his old school pal Karl Hanke, the Gauleiter of Silesia. Hanke was a powerful man in the Third Reich—a friend of Mrs. Goebbels, who was the patron of Albert Speer, Hitler's favorite architect. And because Sunflower was so charming, so interested, his treasurer gave him elaborate reports on the smallest details of Nazi high society. And these details eventually found their way back to Edward.

Sunflower's only liability was his honesty. He was discreet in his office, but for years, among friends, he'd made no bones about how much he hated the Nazis, about how they were duping not only the German man in the street but the upper classes, and how they would bring the country to ruin. Because he was so successful—and wellborn—most people ignored Sunflower's rumblings, or passed him off as an eccentric, foolish for speaking his mind, but harmless. Edward, though, was always afraid that someday, someone in government would catch on to Sunflower; at worst they would kill him, and at best, feed him false information to pass on.

"So far," John asked, "Edward seems satisfied? Schwerin's information dovetails with Sunflower's?"

"Yes," I said. "So far."

"Did Edward say anything else?"

"No, nothing else."

Not about Schwerin. Actually, he told me a lot else. And there were some things he didn't have to tell me. One was that he'd chosen John to run the counterespionage show in Germany and France not only because of John's proven ability but—since there were two other trilingual geniuses who could have fit the bill—to keep him out of Norman Weekes's clutches, and also to prove to Norman how well he could defend his own territory.

And without Edward's saying so, I knew this latest trip of his would somehow get extended, and that sooner or later I'd get a static-filled telephone call, and he'd say, Bad connection, and I'd know he wasn't where he was supposed to be, in Philadelphia or San Diego, but at an air base in the south of England, or an island off the coast of northern Africa. He'd say, Take down these messages for Matthew (Donovan's code name): Mr. Cannon has two dogs. And: The rose garden is in full bloom, especially the yellows. Repeat that, Linda. I would, and then I'd say, How's the weather in San

Diego, Ed? and he'd say, as the phone made loud, crackle-of-lightning noises, Very pleasant, thanks.

It's funny; whenever you read articles about diplomatic negotiations, you keep coming across the phrase "tacit agreement." Without saying a word, there's an understanding. And that's what Edward and I seemed to have—an unspoken understanding that some of the things we talked about were never to be talked about again: not to outsiders and not to each other. Talk about tacit: I don't know how I knew what subjects came under our agreement, because neither of us ever said, Please don't repeat this. Some discussions just seemed to have an invisible asterisk next to them.

Like the time, about eight-thirty one night, right before he went off on his trip, when I brought in a transcript of an interview he'd had that afternoon with a banker from Zurich who had sources—high sources—inside Germany. The banker, one of the fifty million people who had done business with Edward over the years and become his friend, had given him an earful: Hitler's whole Russian strategy was based on seizing the Soviet oil fields. He'd failed, and so had his whole Russian dream. The Germans, the banker reported, didn't have fuel enough to attempt to occupy Moscow. The only major German offensive would be on the southern front.

I walked across toward Edward's desk, still reading the transcript and going Wow! to myself. This was golden information—information that, incidentally, should have been unearthed by Norman's unit, so in Edward's eyes would be doubly golden. When I reached his desk I looked up, expecting him to have his hand out, ready to receive it. Instead, he seemed to be staring down at his desk blotter, in another world.

I wasn't going to do anything like say "Ahem," because he was so clearly taken up with that world that a rustle of paper or even a throat-clearing could set him off on one of his mean-rotten-icy binges. So I just stood there, sensing that even tiptoeing out the door would not be a plus.

But then I followed his eyes and saw that he hadn't been diving into the depths of his blotter. He'd been staring at the silver-framed picture of his wife.

He lifted up the picture and asked, Have you ever noticed this?

Yes.

But he handed it to me as though I'd said no. I put down the transcript and took the picture. She was young, as young as Nan or younger, so they looked like sisters. But pretty as Nan was, Edward's wife had been prettier. Her features weren't quite as fine, but they were sweeter. Her eyes had a slight Oriental slant to them, although they were very light, probably that blue-green shade that's so pale it's almost white; they were the sort of eyes you couldn't look away from.

I met her after the war, he said. The last war. I'd spent eight months in a hospital in England, having my face and my shoulder put back together.

I knew I couldn't just stand there like a totem pole, holding the photograph, so I sat down.

Her father was the judge I'd clerked for right after law school. When I came to New York, Judge Bell and his wife asked me to dinner. We were in the parlor, and Caroline walked in.

He paused, so I asked, Did you fall in love with her right away?

I think so. I'm not an expert in the fine gradations between infatuation and love at first sight, but I remember thinking: This is absurd. I'm thirty-one years old. I know a great deal about the world, perhaps more than I ever wanted to. And here I am, a man who earns his living by being, well, articulate. Calculating. Rational. And I was struck dumb by a seventeen-year-old girl. She wore a black velvet ribbon around her neck.

What was she like? I asked.

High-spirited. Good-natured. Edward smiled to himself. This was 1918, he said, and she appeared a very proper young lady, and she *was* proper, but . . . she had a great sense of fun. And enormous energy and determination. I got her permission to ask her father for her hand—we did that sort of thing in those days—and her parents were quite taken aback. Not that they didn't like me, but I came from a rather undistinguished background and I'd only known Caroline a week and a half when I proposed.

A week and a half? I repeated.

Well, I knew it was right. And so did she. But for all my persuasive abilities, it was she who convinced her parents to let us get married right away. She was very strong-willed.

She must have been very smart, I said.

He turned his inkwell around and around, as if he was thinking of his wife's intelligence for the first time and needed to concentrate. Finally he said, I honestly don't know how smart she was. Most of the time, we'd just talk about everyday things. Who I spoke to in the office. What I ate for lunch. Did I like potted palms . . .

That second, if Edward had been almost any other man in the world, he would not have had the self-control to keep his eyes from welling up; the potted palms had obviously reminded him of something terribly tender he hadn't thought about for years.

But he just went on. If she wasn't a great thinker, he said, at least she was bright enough, and lively. And very, very kind. He looked straight at me. She died three years later. Cancer of the liver.

That stinks, I said.

Yes, it does.

Do you think about her a lot?

Not so much anymore. But at first, all the time. Do you know the strange part? I think back to Caroline now and I really can't remember . . . the texture of our life together. What I have are very clear memories of certain events, the moments I recalled over and over right after she died. But after a while, the memories themselves—a hike we took in the Adirondacks, the night Nan was born, a pink hat with a plume she bought for Easter and I'd laughed at—the specific memories became the reality. That's when I knew that I'd truly lost her.

I said softly, I guess in a way you mourned her twice.

Yes. First her death and then . . . her spirit. I can say: Caroline was lively. But I say it more than feel it. I hate . . . Edward's voice got very quiet. I hate it.

You never found anyone else?

Caroline made me happy. That much I do recall—vividly. And no one else ever did.


I worked for John from January 1942, when Edward left, until April, when he came back to Washington. He might have stayed away longer, in "San Francisco," as the cables said but that I knew was London, or at a so-called army base, Camp Brady. The wires would read: "Farmer [that was Edward's code name] and Matthew in San Francisco Stop Farmer on to Camp Brady to check tractors Stop."

I went ice cold the day I read that wire, because what it really said was that Edward had gone into German-occupied Poland. No one, not John or any of the other men who worked for Edward, knew the entire code, so for all they knew, Camp Brady could have been some dirty, sweltering army facility in Mississippi or a swank officers' club in Los Angeles.

Of course, they sensed he was somewhere important. Dangerous. But all those lawyers and corporation men and Yale professors had modeled themselves on Edward. They were little Lelands, not only courageous but casual, so they didn't go cold with fear. They murmured, Wonder when Ed'll be back, or, Funny, you'd think Ed would've sent a postcard from Camp Brady: "Having a wonderful time. Wish you were here." Chuckle, chuckle. A couple of million Nazis couldn't scare the little Lelands.

I remember coming home very late one night in March with John, both of us taking tiny, cautious steps up the iced-over front stairs of our house. It was old snow, with specks of coal soot frozen solid since February, when René Villiard of the Free French had come to Washington, and John was so busy meeting with him (and I was so busy typing up transcripts of his meeting the day before with German refugees) that we didn't get home before midnight. But almost every day had been like that. By the weekend, by the time we bought a shovel, the ice was rock hard, too hard to make a dent in, and so it stayed.

John and I zigzagged our way up the steps, finding small patches of stair safely unfrozen. We skidded across the small wood porch with its snowed-on glider. As I opened my change purse to get to my key, John asked, "Do you know where Camp Brady is?"

"You mean where Edward is? Yes."

"I just wondered if you knew. Don't tell me."

I opened the front door, and a blast of dry, overheated air hit me. "Why can't I tell you?" I asked as I switched on the light and walked into the house.

He followed me, closed the door behind us and said, "Shhh!"

"What do you think, some Nazi secret agent has been hiding under the bed all winter, waiting to hear me whisper classified secrets to you?"

I opened the closet and reached for a hanger. John leaned against the wall, and in a voice too casual to be his, said, "Really, Linda, it's of absolutely no consequence. If Ed wanted me to know, he would have told me."

It was his little-Leland, fake-Edward voice that got me upset. Whenever any of the guys in counterespionage wanted to show how brave and noble they were, they put on that voice, and no matter where they came from—Long Island like John, or Ames, Iowa, or Charleston, South Carolina, they pitched their voices low and talked slo-o-ow, the way Edward did, even down to the trace of the Vermont accent, like when they talked about the Republican Pahty.

It didn't get me angry when all the Yale guys talked as though they'd spent their golden boyhoods pitching hay on some New England farm. Half of the COI (which had just changed its name to OSS, Office of Strategic Services, probably because someone's uncle had the contract for government stationery), maybe even three quarters, had graduated from Yale, including Edward Leland, and if he was their ideal of what a Yale man should sound like, it was okay with me. But it was another thing to hear my husband, whose only connection to Yale had probably been a football game they'd played against Columbia in 1925 and he'd gone to. What bothered me about John's fake nonchalance, his false I-can-go-face-to-face-with-Adolf attitude, was that it showed him—like all of them—to be exactly the opposite of what he was trying to be: brave.

Talk about Cowboys and Indians. It wasn't just that they were playing games with people's lives; it was that they saw themselves as heroes. They put on Edward's hat and became the marshal who moseys into a dangerous town with his trusty six-shooter and gets rid of the no-good varmints.

Edward *was* the sort of man who thrived on going eyeball to eyeball with no-good varmints. But John was a thinker, a legal scholar, a born puzzle-solver. Why couldn't he be happy being what he was? What he was was so impressive.

I put my coat away, gave John a hanger, and asked, "Is it okay if I just make eggs tonight?"

"With toast." His voice was muffled by the coats in the closet. "Not too dark."

What I wanted from my husband was not a lot of talk about honor and valor, but a display of it right where we were, at home in Washington, D.C. I wanted him to be what he was, to be *real*. Let him just say to me, Hey, I'm dying to know where Ed is. Tell me, and I swear to God I won't say a word to anyone.

And I didn't want to see him in a warm kitchen, eating scrambled eggs and buttered toast and pretending to be light-hearted after a grueling, eighteen-hour day. He and all the Yale men and even the guys from Ohio State and City College who had somehow managed to sneak in—they all acted easy, relaxed, as if nothing fazed them.

Listen, I wanted to tell my husband, you're an extraordinary man. You're doing important, exhausting work, work you should be proud of. *I'm* proud of you. Don't pretend to be someone else. I want you here, John. I want you safe. Do you think I could stand it if you disappeared for months, like Edward? Do you think I want you to have his crazy, rigid sense of honor, so that you won't endanger anyone else by sending them to meet what's left of the Polish underground, and you insist on going in yourself? And most of all, do you think I want a man who deep down cares so little about what happens to him that he has no fear?

"You look exhausted," I said to him, as he came into the kitchen.

He shut his eyes and shook his head, as if to deny his fatigue. "It's nothing I can't bear," he said. But he pronounced the word *bayah*, as if he'd spent his summers in northeastern Vermont. Come *on!* He'd been caddying at the Sands Point Golf Club. "Linda, you have to understand. I have to bear it. This is war."

No, *this* was war. At the end of June, Norman Weekes called a conference in his office. Six of his men and John and Edward sat at one end of an interminably long table with fat feet and a deep red-brown shine so rich it looked like it had been stolen from the White House dining room.

Norman's secretary, a man in his late forties wearing a light brown suit so crumpled it resembled a paper bag, sat next to me; our rickety, government-issue chairs were placed against the wall. We both took down every word that was said. I considered myself something of a shorthand whiz, but he was faster, and determined to prove it to me. He obviously knew I was there because my boss didn't trust his minutes of the meeting, but he was a prissy man, full of stenographic pride, and didn't get that I was there because of OSS politics; he viewed the meeting not as a critical discussion of our Berlin espionage network but as some fight-to-the-death shorthand contest.

Norman rested his elbows on the table, made a tepee with his hands, rested his chin on the tips of his fingers and contemplated Edward. "Shall I begin?" he asked.

"It's your meeting," Edward responded.

"Very well. We are here to discuss Alfred Eckert. A second-rate little dress designer in Berlin, although quite popular with the wives of high-ranking SS officials, women not generally revered for their chic." Norman's men looked amused. Once he saw they were—and my guess is that besides a Harvard degree (his unit was the big exception to the Yale rule), finding Norman Weekes amusing was part of the job—Norman glanced toward Edward.

But Edward's expression was absolutely blank, almost scarily empty, as though he'd vacated his own premises. I had never heard of Alfred Eckert, and I couldn't tell if Edward had or not. Norman waited, a little uneasily, for some expression to appear on Edward's deadpan face. When it didn't, he quickly turned away and looked to John, who was sitting with his back to me. Still, I didn't need to see John's face. I could read his back; he was edgy, anxious even.

"Well, whatever our Mr. Eckert's weaknesses in couture," Norman continued, "he was a first-rate agent."

John said, " 'Was'?"

"Yes. Unfortunately, he died." Norman turned to one of his men. "Martin, can you bring us up-to-date on the situation?"

Martin looked like the rest of Norman's gray-suited, striped-tied men, except he had rimless eyeglasses that kept sliding down his nose. "We're in a bit of a bind," he said, his Boston voice so nasal he sounded as if he had a clothespin on his nose. If there were little Lelands in counterespionage, there were miniature Weekeses in espionage, German division. "You see, whatever Alfred's motives were for working for us—they were always a bit unclear, and alas, now we shall never discern them—we do know he was fervently anti-Nazi. Since '38. Until then, he was just . . . what he appeared to be. With suspiciously thin, arched eyebrows, I might add."

"For Christ's sake!" Edward broke in. Martin jerked up in his chair, as if he'd gotten a violent shock. "Do you think I have time to listen to talk about eyebrow arches?" He turned to John. "What did this fellow do for us?"

"I believe he worked for *us*, Ed," Norman interrupted.

"I meant us, the United States of America, Norman." He looked back at John. "Do you know what his role was?"

"He began by passing gossip he picked up from the wives of Party officials. That was during '38 and the beginning of '39."

"Who was his contact?" Edward asked.

John was direct: "I don't know. I've only been following his work for the last eight months."

So Edward looked back to Martin, who was still upset after Edward's last words to him; he fidgeted around in his chair as if he had a sore behind. "How did he pass on his information to us?"

"A florist. A friend of his who did all the flowers for the American ambassador's wife. Very efficient. We'd often get it out the same day we received it, by diplomatic pouch."

The secretary sitting next to me was scrawling away at top speed, glancing over now and then to my pad, just to make sure I was behind him. I always was. Unlike him, though, I was consumed by what was being discussed. But he just wrote on; the nine men in the room could have been discussing a Securities and Exchange Commission regulation or comparing apple cobbler recipes.

"And what happened in '39 to change this fellow's status?" Edward demanded.

"I'd gotten wind of him," Norman said. "That he was quite an asset. So on my next trip to Berlin, I brought my wife along. She was a brick. Loathed his dresses, of course, but went through fitting after fitting at our hotel." Norman added, "Didn't want to arouse unnecessary suspicions, so I had him carry away a pile of pinned-up dresses. Actually bought the damned things. Priced like they came from Paris. My wife gave them to the maid. The ugliest colors and—"

"What did you talk to him about, Norman?" Edward asked impatiently. "Hemlines?"

Norman pretended Edward was joking and chuckled. Then all his men chuckled too. "Obviously I recruited him."

"As?"

"As an agent. You see, I saw war coming, saw we didn't have much time left in Berlin—wouldn't be able to rely on the florist and the old diplomatic pouch—and needed more than 'society' gossip. We needed specific intelligence, and we needed it fast. That's where our friend Alfred came in. He had friends in high, fashionable places. He had a car, all the gas ration coupons he could possibly desire, and was welcome everyplace, be it a villa near the Grunewald or a disreputable nightclub where what was left of the city's demimonde gathered. And most important of all, he had the wife of one of the most powerful foreign office officials as his confidante; she considered him her closest friend—her only friend—and he was always welcome in her quite splendid home . . . a home confiscated, I understand, from a wealthy Jewish mercantile family."

Edward nodded to Norman, then turned to John. "Alfred Eckert was reliable?"

"Yes," said John. "As good as they come. He was able to glean an enormous amount of information from this official's house."

"I see. And now we have lost our gleaner."

"Yes," Norman responded.

"Any candidates for the job?"

"None. You know what it's like there, Ed. You can't slip a refugee into the home of a foreign office official, a man who is a prominent Nazi to boot; the danger of his being recognized is, well, enormous. And you can't expect to pass off a Yale German major." No, I thought. Even someone like me, an ordinary person with a working-class accent; if I worked as this guy's file clerk or as one of his wife's maids, even, I probably couldn't pass. No matter how much a person knows—and I knew a lot about Berlin and its ways—it would still be a foreign city. To a German major from Yale, it would be another planet. "And who over there is going to take the chance? A clandestine meeting in a private house, perhaps. A word whispered in passing in a men's room. But who would risk going into this man's house, sneaking into his study, searching through his papers? No one is that brave."

"Your little dressmaker was," Edward said.

"Ah, yes," Norman agreed. "But he's dead now."

"Assassinated, I assume?"

"Yes." Norman lifted up his yellow legal pad and his pen from the table before him. All six of his men pushed back their chairs, ready to leap up the instant Norman rose. "Well, I thought it was important to pass this on to you and John, Ed. It puts us in somewhat of a pickle. We'll all have to give it some thought." He stood, and his six men sprung to their feet. His secretary closed his steno pad with an embarrassingly loud slap.

But Edward remained seated, and so did John. Edward said, "One moment, please, Norman." I took it down. The other secretary was in agony, not knowing whether taking down Edward's words would be viewed as his job or as an act of betrayal. He peered around, then finally, with one of those overdramatic silent movie gestures, clutched his pad passionately against his chest. "This recruit of yours worked for us in one capacity or another for four years. Is that correct?"

"Yes."

"He had powerful friends, people willing to vouch for him? Other fashionable women married to influential men. Perhaps a highly placed deviate or two." Norman said nothing. "Am I correct in that assumption?"

"Yes."

"No untoward incidents before this? No hairbreadth escapes?"

"None."

"And yet suddenly he is assassinated."

"Yes."

"Obviously not by our man, the one who replaced the florist, who passed Eckert's information on to us." He inclined his head toward John. "That is code name Cactus, correct?" John said it was. Cactus was a German citizen, a surgeon, whose mother had been American and who had a brother, also a surgeon, in Ohio. "And we've cleared Cactus?"

"We've checked him over and over. He does eye surgery in Berlin, and every month he flies to Switzerland, to a clinic he owns. He operates there for a day or two, buys medical supplies unavailable in Germany and returns. We know he's clean, and even better, they are convinced he is."

Edward turned back to Norman. "Let's move on, then, shall we? Was your man held incommunicado for a while? Tortured?"

"I don't believe so."

"That isn't the usual pattern, is it? They must have been afraid that he was a threat to them."

"Possibly."

"And—I'm just thinking out loud now, Norman—they weren't afraid of us. Once they had him in custody, he couldn't give us any more. But perhaps they were fearful that his friends in high places could help him get free, or just manage to speak to him. What information could he pass on to them that was so threatening?"

"I haven't the foggiest."

"Could it be, Norman, that he suspected—or suddenly discovered—that one of the people in his own secret circle, perhaps one of the few he trusted, a seemingly devoted anti-Nazi, is a traitor? And the traitor had to silence him? Could that be why he was killed?"

"It's your theory, Ed."

"But it is safe to assume that the manner of his murder was rather swift and brutal?"

"I gather it was," Norman said coldly.

"You talk about my theory. But tell me, have *you* given any thought at all to the possibility that your network may not be inviolate?"

"I resent your tone."

"And I resent your passing this off as just another nasty little wartime mess. You listen to me, Norman. Both of us have been around a long, long time. And both of us know there *has* to be a double agent operating in your network. And if I can hazard a guess, you realized it the moment you heard of Mr. Eckert's sudden death." Norman's six men looked away or cleared their throats. "Someone found out your dressmaker was onto them. And so they quickly passed the word and—no more messenger service." Edward paused. "Do you have any idea who the rotten apple is?"

"No," Norman said.

"Not even a guess?"

"Not even a guess."

I couldn't get Alfred Eckert out of my mind. All that afternoon, while John sat in Edward's office, I sat in the little vestibule right outside, trying not to hear them. "Calamity." "Disaster." "Catastrophe." "Terrible blow."

The strange thing was, normally my ears would have been positively throbbing in an attempt to absorb every syllable. This wasn't just an Ivy League war; it was Grover Cleveland High School's too. I was always right in there, having to know what was going on. Over the months working for Edward, I'd mastered homing in on the low pitch of his voice, so—nearly all the time—I could hear his end of telephone conversations even if I was busy typing away. And when his door was closed for a meeting, I'd file; I'd learned to save up my *S* through *Z* correspondence, and at those times, squatting to insert letters in the bottom-drawer folders, I could listen in on at least seventy-five percent of what was being said.

But that afternoon I just wanted silence, so I could reflect on Alfred. Because right away, I was on a first-name basis with him. And I could *see* him: tall, with too-thin eyebrows, probably plucked; blond, marcelled hair; and a fairyish, fuss-budgety walk—like Edward Everett Horton in *The Gay Divorcee*.

Sure, I knew it was all in my mind. For all I knew, he could have been short and fat and resembled a fire hydrant. But his picture came to me over the ocean, and even if it wasn't accurate, it was real. I could see him riding through Berlin in his dark green roadster, wasting gasoline. He kept an alligator or a crocodile—whichever was better—briefcase on the seat beside him, with some sketches of evening gowns and his pincushion.

God knows I'd heard enough about Berlin from Olga. And I'd stood before enough open maps of the city, seen enough photographs, while refugees pointed out this Gestapo house to Edward, that armory, that new pipeline. I knew the streets, the neighborhoods, and I could see Alfred being admitted to the villa of the important foreign office official, kissing the lady of the house on the cheek, standing by a window in her dressing room, letting out or taking in some darts under her bosom, then, later, sipping tea with her. Her husband would come in and be delighted to see Alfred: such a delightful, amusing fellow, always welcome. Then the official would go to his study, and then—somehow— Alfred would figure out a way to get in.

And I saw him parking his roadster, getting out for his twice-a-week walk in the Grunewald, the forest on the edge of Berlin, humming some tune about champagne. He'd pass a chestnut tree with a knothole in it, and he'd keep strolling along so casually that even someone spying on him would probably have missed seeing him slip the message inside the hole, to be picked up the following day by someone Alfred would never meet. Then, still humming, he'd return to his car and put the nosegay of wildflowers he'd picked on his walk on top of the dashboard.

Alfred wouldn't be as fascinated with me as I was with him. In fact, he probably wouldn't give a girl like me two minutes. I didn't hold it against him, though. I wasn't his type. I would never go Ooh! over a bolt of silk shantung— although he might be a little intrigued with me when he saw John, because that would make me special. If he met me, he'd probably say, Delighted, although he wouldn't be. I spoke with the accent he'd been trying to hide since he was fourteen.

Still, Alfred meant so much to me. It was as if I *knew* him.

Somehow, I felt for him in a way that I'd never felt for all the refugees we'd interviewed: all the Jews—shoe store owners, movie directors, bus drivers, labor union organizers, even a butcher, like my father and grandfather—and all the others who had to get out: Catholic priests, Communists, intellectuals, financiers, journalists.

All that day I'd put Alfred in different places, driving along Unter den Linden, walking along the beach, the Strandbad Wannsee. I'd dress him in different outfits and watch him puffing out sleeves and being a spy.

It wasn't until I was in bed late that night that I realized my newfound friend, the man who had become so alive to me so fast, who was doing the work I admired most in the world, was dead. Murdered.

# 18

The fourth of July fell on a Saturday, and for the first time since we'd been married, we actually took a vacation. It was just for the weekend, to the Eastern Shore of Maryland, but at least I got John to take me somewhere. I wasn't exactly subtle, either. I called him at his office on the third and said, "Hey, you owe me a honeymoon."

"Hmm?" he said. He was probably reading a report.

"John, can't we get out of town this weekend?"

He muttered, "I think Ed said he wanted to work straight through."

"But I don't. Please. Don't you think I'm entitled to two days?"

And he actually sounded guilty when he answered, "Yes. All right. I'll try to figure out something."

We stayed at a country inn that was decorated in Early Duck. There were carved ducks—decoys—on every mantel. There were duck doorstops, duck designs on curtains and wallpaper. The innkeeper, who must have been in his eighties, had ducks on his tie, to say nothing of duck designs on every plate, soup bowl, cup and saucer. From our room, we could see over the treetops, to Chesapeake Bay.

"I see a lot of fishing boats," I said Sunday evening, as we were getting dressed after a last time in a too-soft bed that was probably stuffed with duck feathers.

"Any ducks?" John asked.

"No. Not a single one."

"I haven't, either. But I think I heard some quacking in the middle of the night."

"It was probably me, talking in my sleep. The atmosphere gets to you after a while."

He smiled, then came over and put his arms around me. He was so sweet that weekend that at first I thought he might have me confused with someone else. But then I thought: Getting out of the office has done wonders for both of us. We took ferry rides, ate every form of oyster and crab known to man, went for long walks, and even talked. I told him all about Sheepshead Bay in Brooklyn, and he told me all about Long Island Sound, and how Port Washington, where he'd grown up, had once been called Cow Neck. Okay, so it wasn't "My darling Linda, I love you madly." But it was still time together. And it wasn't like weekends at home, when he was editing a brief or reading the paper or listening to Mozart with his eyes closed. I had his full attention, even with my clothes on, and on Saturday night, when we saw *The Pride of the Yankees*, with Gary Cooper and Teresa Wright, we held hands, and he gave me his handkerchief before I even thought to ask for it.

So that Monday afternoon, when John unexpectedly walked into the anteroom outside Edward's office, where I worked, I was still so full of honeymoonish happiness that it didn't occur to me to wonder why he was there. It was just a pleasure to see him. After two days in the sun, his skin had a bronze glow. His fair, silky hair was streaked with pale platinum. He came over, sat on the edge of my desk and took my hand between his. I mumbled something like, "Ed's over at the War Department," even though I sensed, with a sudden flush of joy, that he'd come to see me.

"Linda." His voice was gentle: not caressing, but compassionate. And that minute I understood he'd come to see me for a reason. Something was wrong. "I had a call from New York." He squeezed my hand. "Your mother's nurse . . ."

"My mother?" I asked. It was a real question. I'd spoken to her right before we'd gone off to Maryland. Her voice had been so feeble it shook. She wouldn't let go of the idea that I was still pregnant, but she'd joked about being too young to be a grandmother, and told me to get smart with John and have him buy me a mink stole in the summer, when furriers are desperate for customers and you can pick up a good buy.

John squeezed my hand harder. "I'm sorry."

"She died?"

"Yes. In her sleep. The nurse—"

"Cookie."

"Cookie thought it would be better if I broke the news to you."

I sat back in my chair; it squeaked. "I've got to get this thing oiled." I said to myself, My mother is dead. It made sense, but it didn't mean anything. "What do I do now?" I asked him.

"I'll take you home so you can pack."

"Where did they take . . . where is my mother?"

"The doctor arranged for her to be brought to a funeral home, Linda." John's voice was so sympathetic that for a second I wanted to say, Oh, come off it! It's not like someone died or anything. "Did she go to a church where she'd want the minister . . ." I nodded. "We ought to call before we leave, to give him some time."

"I forgot the guy's name. But all the Johnstons get buried in Brooklyn." I swiveled around in my chair, but it started squeaking again, so I sat still. "Did you know my mother's maiden name was Johnston? They all have brown eyes—and they're very good looking. A little short. I guess I never told you about them." I thought: You never asked. "The men work on the subways. Maintenance men, conductors, but one cousin was a motorman. They looked up to him like he'd gone to Harvard. 'Jim's a motorman!' "

Again he said, "I'm sorry, Linda."

"It's okay. They're not such a close family, and they're kind of dumb, but they always show up for funerals. I'll have to call one of them." That's when I started to shake. My whole body started to shiver as if I'd climbed out of a hot bath into a cold room. I hugged myself and rubbed my arms to try and control it, but it only got worse. "I can't remember any phone numbers," I said. My voice sounded screechy.

"Do you know where my address book is? The little one, with the alphabet tabs?"

He helped me up and led me toward the door, one hand around my waist, the other steering me by my elbow. "We'll find it when we get home." He was so soothing.

I jerked my elbow out of his grasp, went back to my desk and started piling up the folders I'd been working on. John came up beside me, as if to stop me, but I snapped, "Classified documents. I have to put them in the safe."

"Of course."

"You don't have to say 'Of course.' I'm not going to get hysterical!" I wasn't hysterical, but I was trembling so hard by then that I could barely stand, much less walk. I grabbed up the papers and tried to cross the room. I banged into the safe. "Oh, damn it, John."

"It's all right," he said, his voice patient, tolerant. "I'll take care of everything."

And he did. Well, for the next three days, because, as he explained, he couldn't stay away from Washington that long, but he got me home, packed, called Edward to explain I'd be gone, eased me into a cab to Union Station, where—despite the mobs of soldiers and sailors pushing to the ticket windows—he got us a private compartment on the next train to New York. He would even have been willing to talk to me the whole trip. How are you holding up? he'd asked, sitting back, obviously prepared for four hours of hearing the answer, but I'd said, "Okay, I guess," and then I fell asleep. When I woke up, the train was in Newark, New Jersey.

In New York, in a hotel that overlooked Central Park, he spoke to the minister again, arranged for a burial service Wednesday morning, and then asked me, very gently, if I wanted to see my mother. When I said yes, he didn't even blink; he took me in a taxi to Hannemann's Funeral Home in Ridgewood.

I gazed down at my mother. The heavy funeral parlor makeup job, with its crimson bow lips and bright rouged

cheeks, did nothing to disguise the fact that she had died a
sick, wasted woman. Other than the dress Cookie had picked
out for her—one of my mother's typical choices, a ridiculous pink gingham pinafore suitable for a fourteen-year-
old—there was no sign that this old woman had been a
beautiful, sweet-natured, not-too-bright goodtime girl. Her
blond hair had turned a dingy white.

She lay in a coffin that had obviously been her son-in-
law's choice: a dark, costly wood, but with simple brass han-
dles and plain white satin lining. A casket for a proper
citizen; she would have chosen something decorated with
gold cherubs and lined in lilac velveteen. And if it had been
up to my mother, the coffin would have been covered with a
blanket of flowers more appropriate for the winner of the
Kentucky Derby. John had chosen a perfect wreath of white
flowers that looked like it had been made up by the Leland
family florist and probably had been. I didn't ask.

John stood right beside me the entire time, waiting, I
guess, for a moan of despair or a shriek of anguish to break
out of me, so he could do something—hold me in his arms,
lead me away and say, There, there. Once he glanced down
at me and said, You're very pale; he may have been expecting a swoon or a faint. But I just stood straight and still, and
thought about my mother and father and Olga—and for
some reason about Alfred Eckert too. And I asked myself,
Who do I really have in the world who loves me?

At last I said, I'm ready, and John led me outside, but not
before Mr. Hannemann, Jr., came rushing out of his office to
hold the door open for us. His voice was thick with respect
and courtesy: *So* sorry for your loss, Mrs. Berringer. If we
can serve you in any other way, I *do* hope you'll call on us.
He made it so much worse for me, because his was the tone
people in Ridgewood took with important people, and all of
a sudden I felt even lonelier. I'd lost the last of my family. I'd
become a rich lawyer's wife in expensive shoes, an outsider.

The taxi was waiting outside, meter running, and I asked
John, Do you want to see our house? And he said, I really
would like to, but we have to get back to Manhattan. You

need a dress for the funeral, and I have to go over your mother's papers. I stared at him and he explained, I called Russ Weedcock at the firm and had him send over one of the secretaries to get your mother's papers together. I asked, Which secretary? and he shrugged, with a what-does-it-matter offhandedness. I looked down at my twenty-five-dollar black-and-white spectator pumps, which I now knew should only be worn between Decoration Day and Labor Day, and I thought: Where do I belong?

When we got back to the city, John said, I think you should rest. I'll have Saks send over a few things to the hotel so you don't have to deal with salespeople.

You're being so nice, I said. John, thank you. I appreciate everything you're doing. You're really a wonderful husband. He said, Please . . . Don't be embarrassed, I told him.

John put through a long-distance call to my Aunt Annabel in Seattle. The Johnstons were a little vague about family ties. Forget Christmas cards; my mother had completely lost touch with three of her four sisters. I got on the phone: Aunt Annabel, this is Linda. Betty's daughter. She started crying, and for a minute I thought she'd heard. Then she told me her husband, a navy man, had been killed in June, at Midway. She said, He was on the *Yorktown*, Linda. You hear about it? She cried some more and said her older boy was 4-F, but the younger one was a midshipman on the U.S.S. *Saratoga*. His name's Lester, she said, and then, without taking a breath, she asked, Did Betty die? Yes, I told her. She told me she was sorry and to send her love to everybody when I saw them at the funeral.

That night we had room service. Um, John said, your mother didn't leave a will. I answered, Estate planning was never her strong point. He went on: Her only assets were the house and a very small bank account. I looked up from my steak: You thought you were marrying an heiress? No, he said. I just wanted to keep you informed . . . as your attorney. Actually, I've asked Russ to handle whatever has to be handled. Is that all right with you? I told him, sure it was fine.

The bad part of being a working girl—and an old maid—is that you learn to do things for yourself, so when a husband finally comes along, you forget to be fluttery and helpless. This was the first time John had really done anything for me.

When we got into bed I said, You're so good at everything. He said, You don't have to if you don't want to, and then I realized he thought I was talking about sex. I pressed up against him. No, I want to, I said. But hold me for a while first. He put his arms around me, but since neither of us was wearing anything, it took much less than a while. He climbed on top of me and I ran my fingers down his back, over his behind and then lower. Oh, Jesus, he groaned. You do it to me every time. Linda, I can't take it. I moved my hand away and let my fingers drift down the backs of his thighs.

Want me to stop? I asked.

No. Oh, Christ, do it some more.

I love you.

Do it more.

Okay. "Do it more" wasn't French for "I love you." But that night I went to sleep with more hope than I'd ever had since my marriage. John had been so tender, so decent. Not just since my mother died; even the biggest crumb in the world can manage to act appropriately for a couple of days when there's a death in the family. But he'd been so wonderful during the weekend in Maryland.

As I fell asleep, I only wished the change in John had happened one week sooner, so I would have had time to call my mother and say, Hey, Mom. You were wrong about him. He's really a good man. And I think he's learning to love me.

" 'I am the resurrection and the life: he that believeth in me, yea, though he were dead, yet shall he live.' "

The Reverend Bradley Norris of Brooklyn, the burier of Johnstons, had a voice that sounded like Cecil B. De Mille's in a coming attraction for *The Sign of the Cross*: resounding, important, slightly British. But he was a very old man, probably close to eighty, and pretty frail. And poor. His black suit

was so worn it had a silver shine. He kept squinting in the
blinding July sunlight and losing his place in the prayerbook.

" 'The Lord giveth, and the Lord taketh away. Even as it
hath pleased the Lord, so cometh . . . so cometh . . . ' "

One of the cousins—I think her name was Etta—shouted
out, " ' . . . so cometh things to pass'!"

I flashed her an angry look, but the Reverend Norris was
either one of the genuinely meek or he was too old for out-
rage. He just brought the prayerbook up closer to his nose
and continued, " 'Blessed be the name of the Lord.' "

It was hot in that Brooklyn cemetery. The grass around
the tombstones had large, parched patches, and a lot of the
earth dug up around my mother's grave was dry. I couldn't
make myself look down into the grave, even though we were
standing pretty near the edge.

John had his arm around my shoulder, both for comfort
and for support, but I didn't feel I was going to lose control.
I looked out at the cousins—more than twenty had come—
and even though they were my family, I hardly knew half
their names. They were a group of strangers who knew "The
Order for the Burial of the Dead" the way I knew "The Star-
Spangled Banner." I felt like an outsider at a ceremony for a
member of a club I didn't belong to.

And yet the weird thing was, when I looked out over that
cluster of Johnstons, I knew I was in the club. I could see my
mother's features in so many faces—a couple of them as
beautiful as hers had once been. And I even saw variations of
myself there: my hair on Ralph, Agatha and a boy of about
seventeen; my exact eyes—the precise shade of brown and
even the straight lashes that I bet were also immune to an
eyelash curler—on a former Johnston who'd introduced herself as Lorna, although in her Brooklyn accent, a hundred
times thicker than mine, which John had to control himself
from shuddering from, it sounded more like Lawww-na.

The minister droned on: " 'Man that is born of a woman
hath but a short time to live. He cometh up and is cut down
like a flower . . . ' "

John whispered, "How are you doing?"

"Fine." But I pressed against him even more. The relatives
had obviously heard about John, and it was just as obvious
by the way they were gaping at everything from the part in
his hair to his perfectly polished shoes that they were awed,
except for one of them, whose name I didn't catch. She'd
taken him aside while we were waiting for the Reverend
Norris and asked him if he would sue her dry cleaner for her
because he'd ruined her husband's overcoat. John told her he
was sorry, but he was in Washington now and wasn't practicing law in New York. Don't worry, she said, I'll *pay* you,
and when he told her he couldn't, she looked disgusted.

" 'In the midst of life we be in death.' " I thought: Come
on. In Brooklyn? But then I thought: In Berlin. " 'Of whom
may we seek for succor but thee, Oh Lord, which for our sins
justly art displeased.' " Alfred, I said to myself, this funeral's
for you too. I bet you didn't have one. And so, as the minister went on, I translated a few sentences into German in my
head for Alfred. " ' . . . ashes to ashes, dust to dust, in sure
and certain hope of resurrection to eternal life . . . ' " I
thought, still in German: Alfred, I hope it's not only eternal;
I hope it's beautiful and elegant, the way you like it.
" 'Death, where is thy sting? Hell, where is thy victory?' "

The Reverend Norris intoned: " 'Lord have mercy on us.' "
I thought again about my mother and hoped that for her,
heaven would be a rose-covered honeymoon cottage where
my father would be waiting. And for my Grandma Olga—
But at that very instant the minister proclaimed, " 'Christ
have mercy on us.' " I said Whoops! to myself, put Olga off,
and instead said silently, 'Bye, Mom. At last, the Reverend
Norris said, " 'Lord have mercy upon us,' " again.

But I guess I'd already mourned Olga and my father
enough, because instead of giving them their turn, I thought
about the men and women and even little kids who'd been
shot and burned and bombed in the lousy, goddamn war.
Slaughtered. And that's when I wept. O Lord, I thought,
have mercy on us.

\* \* \*

John asked, Are you sure you'll be all right? The limousine he'd hired for the funeral pulled up in front of my mother's house. His eyes widened for a second, but then he composed his face into a bland expression, as if this was the sort of house he saw all the time. Through his eyes I suddenly saw the sagging roof and the tape on the windows where they'd cracked, and that's when I realized we had been poor.

I inched forward to the car door, but the damp black silk of my dress stuck to the back seat. He went on: Linda, I hate leaving you like this, but I have to get back to Washington. He kissed me softly on the eyes, and the driver slid out silently to get my suitcase from the trunk.

I tried to sound reassuring: Don't worry. I'll be fine. What I really wanted was for him to say, "Oh, the hell with the OSS!" and stay with me. John kissed my fingers. I'll call you every night, he said, and if it gets to be too much, let me know. I'll come back. But I just gave him a final kiss goodbye, got out of the car and watched it as it pulled away, like a big, black yacht, and eased down the street toward Manhattan and Penn Station.

I thought I'd just sit in the kitchen and stare out the window at the Knauers' elm tree that afternoon, but instead I took off my heels and went to work on my mother's room. After six hours, all I could salvage from the mess of her life was her wedding ring, a gold bracelet, a picture of her and my father on the boardwalk in Atlantic City, and the silliest of her dresses—a slinky purple thing with two giant roses of the same fabric sewed onto each bust.

In one of my mother's galoshes I found an empty pint of gin; there was lipstick around the neck of the bottle.

Her medicine cabinet was worse than her closet. Aspirin and Bromo Seltzer were hidden behind lipsticks, tins of rouge, boxes of powder and eye shadows. An open cake of mascara had dried and crumbled years before, so a fine layer of black powder covered everything.

John called around ten. He was in the office. Everything's all right, he reported. Just the usual catastrophes. Are you managing, Linda? I'm fine, I assured him, and he asked, Would you forgive me if I cut you short now? I have hours of work here. I said of course, and we kissed each other good night on the phone.

The next day, I worked and I waited. The real estate man came, looked over the house and said he thought I could get two thousand dollars for it. Try for three, I said. Look, Mrs. . . . he said dubiously. He was a slick man in a suit too dapper for Queens and an Errol Flynn mustache. I gave him Russell Weedcock's name and telephone number and said to him, My attorney. He'll be handling the negotiations and the closing for me.

After he left, I went into the living room. I realized that for all the years I'd lived in that house, my vision had conveniently blurred. Now I saw how bedraggled everything was. The brown wool on the couch and the chairs had worn away completely in spots. White upholstery stuffing sprouted in little bumps on the seats and arms. One of the lamps was cracked, another chipped, and the lampshades themselves were threadbare and had brown burn marks from too-strong light bulbs. The little end tables I'd remembered as being pretty weren't pretty at all; they were so flimsy that they shook if you put anything as heavy as a glass of water on their surfaces.

I turned away and went into the kitchen. It was in order— sparkling clean, in fact. Since my mother never ate, Cookie only had to cook for herself, but she'd cleaned, after a fashion; the faucets glittered like just-polished silver, although the corners of the floor were probably not meant to be noticed. Cookie had also bought: The pantry was crammed with row after row of canned candied yams, fruit cocktail, liver paste spread, and there were five large boxes of White Rose tea. I was fixing my lunch, cold candied yams and iced tea, when the doorbell rang.

"Coming!"

I wiped my hands on the white cotton butcher apron I was wearing, one my father had brought home from the plant, and hurried to the front door. It wasn't the gas meter reader. It was Gladys Slade.

"I . . . I hope you don't mind," she said. She held out a manila envelope. "Your mother's deed. Um, Mr. Weedcock says it's in order. He was going to send Mildred Treacher, a new girl, but I said . . . well, I said I'd come because—" She was overheated, nervous, her too-white face wet with perspiration, like a glistening hard-boiled egg; her dress, her best, a green faille with a white lace collar, was meant for a Christmas dinner, not an errand on a blistering July afternoon.

"Come in, Gladys." I held the door opened wide.

"Oh, no. I don't want to intrude—but I want to say—I am sorry for your loss." Her speech was so jerky that I knew she'd memorized it, but she was so fidgety it was obvious she'd forgotten two or three sentences.

I took her by the arm and pulled her inside. "Hey, stop talking to me like I'm Mrs. Berringer. I'm Linda. Sit down." Hesitantly, as if waiting for me to bark, What do you think you're doing? she inched into the living room. "How are you?" I asked.

"Fine."

"Want some iced tea?"

"No, thank you." She was inspecting the room: the tables, chairs, curtains. "It's a nice house. Very homey." I guess I had become accustomed to living in John's world, because for a second I thought she was being sarcastic. But then I remembered her single, rented room up two steep flights of stairs in a stranger's house. Gladys was gazing up, above the couch, at a picture of a field of red and pink tulips with a windmill in the background. It was framed, but without glass. In tiny letters on the lower right it said: Compliments of Roscoe & Schmidt Meat Packers 1908 Chicago. It had been a wedding gift from my father's boss. "That's a beautiful picture."

"Thanks." If John had seen it, he'd have smiled, a compassionate it's-so-pathetically-predictably-tasteless smile, full of pity and superiority. But Gladys was drawn to it as if it was the Garden of Eden. "Sit down, Gladys."

"I don't want to interrupt."

"Please. There's nothing to interrupt." She sat stiffly, as I figured she would, on the edge of the couch. She'd come to see what I'd become, and probably also to find out if I'd given up the secrets of lunch, if I'd sat at parties with lawyers, regaling them with tales of their star-struck (lawyer-struck) secretaries. But seeing me in my high-priced black dress under the butcher's apron, my silk stockings, my expensive haircut, my wedding ring, she couldn't ask. "How have you been, Gladys?"

"Fine." She clasped her hands tight over her patent-leather pocketbook.

"How are all the girls?"

"Fine."

"Lenny?"

"Fine." She looked away from me, up at the tulips.

"Marian?"

"Fine."

"Wilma?" She shrugged. "Oh, come on, Gladys. I've never said a word about anything. You can tell me what's going on." She glanced around, as if still expecting to be encircled by cops, ready to arrest her if she opened her mouth. "I can see it in your face. There's some news about Wilma! How can you possibly hold back on me?"

It took her a minute, but finally she breathed: "Fired!"

"She was fired? No! By Mr. Post?"

"None other than. Actually . . . I *knew* it was going to happen."

"How?" I sat down beside her. I was dying to hear everything, and she knew it.

"Well, all of a sudden he started going home at six on the dot."

"You think Mrs. Post gave him an ultimatum?"

"No."

"No?"

"Wilma did!"

"You're kidding!"

"No. After she saw what happened with you . . . You know. Getting married. At lunch one day, we were talking about you. . . ." She lowered her head.

"Listen, it's okay. If I was there, I'd talk about me too."

Gladys, unthinking, put her hand on mine. "So Wilma says, real sure of herself, 'Who says lightning don't strike twice in the same place? There could be other bosses who find certain other secretaries definite marriage material.' Anyway, two days later Mr. Post is rushing out at six, with his briefcase packed. And by the end of the next week . . . Well, at least he got her another job. At Dahlmaier Brothers, the investment—Oh! You know about them."

"I say a little prayer of thanks to Quentin Dahlmaier every night. Hey, remember when Lenny found out about him? God, that seems a hundred years ago."

"Linda?"

"What?"

"I'm sorry. I mean about how things wound up with us."

"I'm sorry too, Gladys." There was a silence that was comfortable for a couple of seconds, but it stretched out too long. I could feel her yearning to ask: What's it like? Being married. Being married to *him*. Going to lawyer parties. Being rich. Is it everything we always dreamed about? But I realized I didn't have any answers, not for her, not for me. So instead I asked, "What about Anita Beane? Did she and Herbie get married?"

Gladys sat up straight. "You mean you didn't hear?"

"No! What happened? Tell me."

And she did, for two hours.

When we finally said goodbye, we both had tears in our eyes. And she had the picture of the tulip field tucked under her arm.

Late that afternoon, I went into Olga's room. I'd gone through it soon after she died, but now, while I waited for the janitor from the Lutheran Home for the Aged on the other side of Ridgewood to come and pick up the furniture (the

Salvation Army had turned me down when I'd described
what I wanted to give them, but the Lutherans were clearly
having a bad year), I went into my grandmother's room
again.

There was nothing except her narrow, stripped-down bed,
an armchair and a nightstand. For some reason, I opened the
two small doors under the drawer of the stand. It looked
empty, but I felt around and discovered a pile of papers
neatly tied with string. They turned out to be about a hundred different recipes Olga had clipped from her favorite
German newspaper. *Salat von Geräuchertem Aal*, smoked
eel salad; *Zwetschgenknödel*, plum dumplings—she'd
taught me to make them. I groped some more and found
another pile. Letters, all yellowed, some so old they were
falling apart, all written in the thin, spidery penmanship that
was taught to girls in German schools. I realized they must
have been from Olga's cousins in Berlin. They'd probably
been corresponding since she left Germany with my grandfather, in the late 1880s. But then I looked closely. One of
the letters wasn't a letter but a folded piece of parchment. I
opened it up carefully and saw it was written in foreign letters that I was sure were Hebrew. I couldn't get a clue to
what it was, but I folded it back with the letters and put
everything in my suitcase.

It's so sad I can't even cry, I told John that night when he
called. There's nothing left of my old life. I'm sorry, he said.

Friday was a bad day. There was nothing to do but call
Con Edison and Brooklyn Union Gas and Russell Weedcock, and then wait for all of them to call me back. That
night John said, When do you think you'll be home? I'm not
used to being without you. I told him that I'd probably have
to stay through Monday or Tuesday, because Russell had
papers for me to sign and I had to have an extra key made to
give to the real estate man. I miss you so much, I told him.
Linda, he answered, I know it's not easy, but get all the ends
tied up, so you don't have to go back. Listen: I have an idea.
Call me when you're ready to leave, let me know what train
you'll be on, and I'll pick you up at the station. If you can

get in about six or seven, I could come right from the office . . . and then we'll go out to a restaurant. I don't want you having to cook on your first night back.

That night, in my old bed, I yearned for John. The desire was as strong and powerful as it had been two and a half years earlier, when I'd been his old-maid secretary. But the difference was that now I knew what I was missing.

So at six o'clock the next morning, I slipped my key and a note under the door of the real estate office, took a subway to Penn Station and then a train back to Washington. I got home in time for lunch, but I knew John would be at work. Still, I figured I'd have time for a nice long bath, and then I could go to his office. Surprise him. I did.

# 19

John wasn't at his office. As I came through the front door,
I heard classical music playing full blast. I put down my
suitcase, smiled and walked into the living room. There was
John stretched out on the couch. And in his arms was Nan
Leland Berringer Dahlmaier.

"Oh, God!" They pulled apart. John sat up straight, stared
at me for less than a second and then hung his head. I kept
staring at him, wanting him to meet my eyes again. I
couldn't make myself look at Nan, but I sensed her inching
across the couch, toward the safety of its big arm. But my
mind wasn't on her. More than anything, I wanted to see
John's face, but all I could see was his hair. "What can I
say?" he breathed.

"You're really a wonderful guy, John," I said. What a clear
voice! I felt cool then, or at least in control. But a moment
later, anger came upon me so suddenly and with such force
that it was as if I was being attacked by a gang of toughs,
kicked, punched. I could hardly breathe; I kept trying to
gasp for air, but every time I did, my throat made a high-
pitched squeal, like the cry of a helpless baby animal.

He'd abandoned me at the very moment when I needed a
friend. He'd betrayed me. Toyed with me that weekend in
Maryland. I had been stupid enough to believe that his tenderness, his kindness, had risen out of love. Well, I thought,
I guess it did. Love for Nan.

I turned to her then. She was scrunched up in a corner of
the couch, clutching the arm. Her head was lowered too, but

288

in terror, quivering, as if expecting that any second I'd pull a gun or rush over and start to pummel her. "Oh, stop it!" I said. She looked up. I thought to myself: All she inherited is good bones. Not her father's guts, not her mother's spirit. Her face was ashen—a close match to her perfectly cut beige linen dress. I couldn't think of anything else to do, so I jerked my thumb toward the door and said to her, "Out!"

John lifted up his head. "Please," he said. "Don't be angry with Nan. It's all my fault."

"No," Nan interrupted. "It's my fault." She had her father's eyes, and though they weren't as black or as brooding, they were compelling—bright and dark at the same time. "I know I can't ask your forgiveness, Linda . . . May I call you Linda?" I just glared. That shut her up for a minute, but then she said, "The last thing I want in this world—and I know I speak for John too—is to hurt you. This entire situation—"

"I want you to leave now," I told her. Somehow I was polite. Like in the movies, when you say: Madam, would you please remove your hat. *"Now."*

"Please. Hear me out. I know all three of us are in a state of shock, but personally, I feel a . . . a moral imperative—"

The politeness evaporated. I bellowed, "You're pushing your luck!" I took a step toward her, around the coffee table, which had their two cups and saucers and the morning papers spread on it. My shin smashed into the table, but I didn't feel a thing. The dishes rattled hysterically. Then I took another step.

And Nan Leland Etc. Etc. was out the front door in five seconds flat.

For me, there were no tears, no screaming, no enraged slamming of doors. As for John, he just sat there. I stared down at the cups; there was just enough left in them to reveal that she, too, took her coffee black.

"I'm sorry," he finally said.

"Sorry for what? Being caught? Or betraying me?"

"Both, I suppose," he said softly.

"Sorry that you didn't go chasing after her when she ran

out the door? You want to run down to the corner? She didn't
have a chance to call a taxi."

For a second, he shifted and glanced out the front window. But then he looked back to me. "Could you sit down?
We have to talk."

I sat in the rocking chair that was across from him. I
waited, but he just looked at the rug. "You asked me to sit
down. You said we have to talk." John didn't say a word.
"Look, you're trying to come up with a brilliant presentation
of the facts in your case. Forget it. You don't have a case.
You're a cheat and a liar and a first-class son of a bitch.
Those are the facts."

He looked up. "I won't argue with you."

"When did it start?"

"In May. She came to Washington the end of May. But it
wasn't what you think."

"Come on. I bet it was. She came to visit Daddy and cry
about Quentin, but maybe Daddy got a little impatient with
her. And so she called you because she needed a friend. A
sympathetic friend. Neither of you had any intention what-
soever of letting it go any further than that." All of a sudden,
I reached out and swept the cups and saucers off the table
and onto the rug. A cup hit the table leg and the handle broke
off. John pretended nothing had happened. "How am I
doing, John? Did I guess right?"

"I suppose . . ." He said, staring at the handle. "If you
want to look at it superficially."

"How am I supposed to look at adultery? Deeply?"

"What I mean is, it's not as simple as you make it out to
be."

"So tell me, what is it? Go ahead, be profound, if that
makes you happy. But I want you to try and understand one
thing—something you've never understood before."

"What?"

"I'm as smart as you are. Probably smarter. So don't try
handing me a line of bull about poor motherless Nan or
about two intellects that beat as one. I just want to know

what happened. Who, what, where and when." I kicked a saucer away from my shoe. "I don't care about why."

"We had drinks a couple of times." He rubbed his hands together as if he was warming them over a fire. "She just talked about her marriage."

"Which one?"

"Please, Linda. She was unhappy with Quentin right from the beginning. He treated her like . . . like some . . . some object he'd purchased for his collection."

"That must be some prize collection."

"You're not making it easy for me."

"I've made it very easy for you. Keep going. When did you start playing house?"

"Do you have to put it that way?"

"What would you rather have? A word starting with *f*?" My heart was racing, and once again, I couldn't get enough air.

"Ed went up to New York for a weekend the first week of June. I stayed with her. Is that what you want to hear?"

"But you came home every night."

"Yes."

"And you never stopped . . . You were having sex with her and with me?"

"Yes."

"Why?" He didn't answer. "Okay, I'm asking. *Why?*"

"Because I didn't want you to suspect."

"So you did it to me out of kindness?"

"No." He stopped rubbing his hands and began to wring them. "I didn't want to . . . to give up everything I had with you."

"Which is what?"

"Sex."

"Sex and what else?" He didn't answer. My heart, which had been pounding much too fast, suddenly skipped a beat. I thought: Wouldn't it be funny if I had a heart attack and died? But I made myself go on. "What else do you have with me besides sex that you don't want to give up?"

"Nothing." He swallowed. "I'm sorry, but you seem to want the truth."

"Yes." The truth, I'd been positive, as we held hands over a bowl of oyster stew in Maryland, and later that same evening, when he lit the hurricane lamp in our room so we could watch each other's pleasure by candlelight, the truth was that he was falling in love with me. I could have sworn I'd seen it even in that dim, flickering light.

If my heart hadn't been thudding against my chest and if I hadn't been breathing deeper and deeper until I was dizzy, fighting for air, I would have thought I was dead. Because I felt nothing. Absolute emptiness. I said, "So what happens now?"

"I don't know."

"Do you move out? Do I move out? You're the lawyer. What's the next step?" I couldn't believe part of me was still able to talk. "Do I hire a private detective? Or do I just go upstairs and find Nan's nightie on the bed and bring it into court?" He looked toward the stairs. I waved an imaginary frilly thing in the air. "Here's Exhibit A, Your Honor." I thought he was going to faint; I felt a little better. "Come on, John. How do we get divorced? You must have talked to her about"—I deepened my voice—"the Future. She must be waiting. She's not hanging around Washington all summer because she's crazy about humidity."

"She's waiting."

"For what?"

"For me to come to a decision."

I broke out into a loud laugh. Who could help it? "You've been stringing *her* along?"

"It's not a matter of stringing anyone along."

"Sure it is. You're playing with her. You're getting back at her for leaving you. 'Nan,' " I imitated him, " 'you left me. Did you truly believe your unmitigated insensitivity to be without consequences?' How's that?"

"Not bad."

"Tell me what to do, John. Do I go to a lawyer?"

"Only if you want to divorce me."

"And what do you want?"

"I don't know. I love Nan. I've never stopped loving her. I know how that must hurt—"

"It's wonderful how you're both so worried about hurting me. Look, just tell me what you want, for God's sake. Do you want to marry her again?"

"Part of me does."

"Which part? The top part?" He put his hands in his lap. "But the bottom part still's got the itch for me. Is that it?"

"I suppose so."

"It's that good with me?"

"I think . . . that's fairly obvious."

"Is it that bad with her?"

"Linda, I won't discuss that."

"That wouldn't be honorable."

"That's right."

"And you're a man of honor." He turned and peered out the window. "Now listen to me. I'm a fool for you. We both know that. But I'm not a complete fool. I won't wait around while you resolve the conflict between your top and your bottom halves. If you really love her, then marry her." I smiled. "She's what—twenty-three? And she'll be Nan Leland Berringer Dahlmaier Berringer. I can't wait to see her notepaper when she's thirty."

"Oh," John said. "Do you think she'd leave me again?"

"What do *you* think?"

"I don't know." He took a deep breath. "But I do know I'm not . . . quite ready to leave you."

"Why not? For twenty bucks, you can get someone to do whatever I do, and you won't have to take them to dinner parties."

"It's not just sex."

"Two minutes ago you said it was."

"I feel a moral obligation to you."

"It's canceled. And listen: I know half the reason you're even thinking of staying is that you're worried you'd look bad—a heel, or a patsy for Nan. But don't worry. Just tell them I was this grasping, conniving bitch who broke up your marriage and that when you didn't give me a mink and a diamond tiara I ran off with a cardsharp from Canarsie. You know what the beauty of it is? All your friends will believe it!"

"Linda, stop." He gave me one of the tender looks he'd given me on the shores of the Chesapeake, and in the cemetery in Brooklyn. "I know you love me."

"So? What does that mean? Did it stop you from going to bed with Nan? From telling her you loved her? Did my loving you ever once get you to look at me like I'm a human being who has meaning outside the bedroom . . . who has dignity, goddamn it!" I stood up. "You make love to her. You *talk* to her." I started to get a picture in my mind, John and Nan, afterward, draped with sheets, conversing, smiling, nodding at each other's astuteness. In my imagination, the bed was so vast it went on into infinity. "Where did you do it?" I demanded.

"I don't think it's an appropriate—"

"Here?"

"Just these past few days. Two or three times in a hotel. But usually in her father's house."

"Oh, that's terrific. I'm breaking my back working for her old man till nine, ten, every night so you can have plenty of time for hot stuff in Georgetown." Suddenly, I felt horribly sick, as if I was going to start to heave and heave and not be able to stop. "Was Ed in on this?" I managed to say. John didn't answer. "Damn it, was he keeping me there nights so you and his little girl—"

"No! Of course not. But he knew, naturally."

"Oh, naturally."

"Linda, he's a man of the world. He suspected early on—"

"He's known since when? Late May?"

"I don't know. Since early in June, anyway. He made it clear to Nan then that he disapproved. More than disapproved. And last week, he asked her to leave his house, practically ordered her to go back to her . . ."

"Her husband."

"Yes. The . . . situation has soured my relationship with

him. More than soured it. Destroyed it, I think." If John had looked uncomfortable and unhappy before, he looked miserable now. There was a catch in his voice when he talked about Edward, almost like tears in his throat. "Not that he's said anything about me. But it's obvious he thinks it's all . . . unseemly. He's very distant to me."

"Do you think she'll listen to her father, go back to Quentin?"

"Only if I . . ."

I finished his sentence. "If you don't want her back."

"Yes."

"Well, you have a week to decide."

"A week? It's my *life* you're talking about."

"Listen to me. If you walk out on me, do you know what you'll have? A wife—and you don't even have to buy new monogrammed pillowcases. A profession. Friends with country houses and sailboats. A roof over your head. A place in the world."

"Linda, there would be alimony."

"John, alimony is money. If you walk out on me, what else will I have?" He looked down, to his summer-white shoes. "So do you think I'm going to sit around for six weeks or six months watching for hopeful little signs? Praying that maybe you'll find something of value in me? And do you think I'm going to be able to stand having you touch me when you get home late, not knowing if what you're doing to me is the same thing you did to her a half hour before?"

"I wouldn't—"

"You would. You have. Okay, you're a stylish kind of guy. You probably took a shower in between. But there's not going to be any more in betweens. It's her or me. Choose."

He chose me. He chose me because two days later, Nan chartered a plane and went back to Quentin. I asked myself, did she do it because the whole episode was so tawdry and not to her taste, or because she'd had her fun playing off one husband against the other, or because she'd had enough passion for the time being and wanted to go back to a man with three houses, a dozen servants and a seat on the board of trustees of the New York Philharmonic?

It was pretty easy to figure she hadn't flown back to Southampton, Long Island, because she was afraid John would choose me. Even in her panic she hadn't lost her wits, and I guessed that huddling in that corner of the couch, she'd still been able to appraise me—and to determine there wasn't anything much beyond my face value.

Listen, I said to him the night she left. Even if she's gone for good, you're not stuck with me. It's like what they say in car advertisements: Now's the perfect time to trade me in for a new model. Or just unload me.

Linda, please don't talk like that. We're married.

We've been married for two years, I said. What if she changes her mind again? What if she wants you back?

It's over, he assured me. His voice was quiet, firm, sincere. Well, at least he had the sense not to swear on his honor.

I didn't go back to work until the following Monday. Officially, I was in mourning. Unofficially, I was sad about my mother and, even more, depressed that I was alone, with no more family. I didn't count the Johnstons, because they appeared so infrequently, and only in black. And when I read the letters I'd found in Olga's room and brought back to Washington with me, I knew I'd probably never see the writers. They were two sisters, Liesl and Hannah Weiss. They'd never married. They lived in the same apartment in Berlin and wrote interminably long, misspelled, ungrammatical letters about events like Cousin Manfred's wedding to one of the Geist girls, with unending descriptions of the bride's dress and how chewy the hen was.

The correspondence had probably lasted over thirty-five years, and in that time, Liesl complained about the weather a lot, and Hannah about her teeth—eventually, her dentures. But in none of the letters was there any clue that they were Jews, and no indication that Hitler's coming to power had any effect on their lives—except for one sentence. In Hannah's last letter, postmarked February 23, 1937, she wrote: "As you can imagine, our life is not so happy as it once was."

I knew it wasn't. On Sunday night, John glanced up from a report he was reading. Listen to this, he said. After the end of the year, Jews won't be permitted to own pets anymore; they'll have to turn them in to dog pounds, and they'll be destroyed because they're tainted by Jewish blood. I couldn't speak. John didn't notice. He just went on: There's no limit to this insanity. I mean, I can understand someone not wanting to live next door to them, but this . . . And to kill *dogs*. He shook his head. Then he went back to the report and asked me to make him a glass of iced tea.

And also unofficially, I didn't go back to work because I didn't want to face Edward. That whole week I kept waking up three or four times during the night. I'd relive walking in on John and Nan, and think about all the clever or brutal things I could have said. Eventually, I'd fall back asleep. But when I thought of Edward's knowing about the two of them practically from the beginning—and how all that time I'd been talking to him so privately, giving over my life—then I'd be up, shivering in the Washington heat, for the rest of the night.

I knew, unofficially, that he'd talked to me in a way he'd never talked to anyone else—about Caroline, and about other things: How he felt like such a hick when he first went to Yale and no one wanted to bother with him, and how he had to force himself to stay and not run away, back to the farm. And how when he was recuperating in the hospital after all the operations on his face and shoulder, he couldn't understand why he didn't hear from his kid sister; he wrote and wrote, but it wasn't until he got home that his mother told him she'd died from polio a year before. He said he'd felt deceived in the cruelest way; someone who hadn't wanted to hurt him had caused him the greatest pain.

Well, old buddy, I wanted to tell him now, I know just what you mean. Because in this whole world, you were the

closest I had to a friend—and you deceived me in the cruelest way.

"Linda," Edward said. He stood, walked around his desk
and came up beside me. He put his hand on my shoulder. "I
was so sorry to hear about your mother."

I pulled myself back, so his hand dropped off. "Thank
you." I thought: For a whole month you knew, and you
didn't give me a clue. You could have said, I've been pretty
busy lately, with Nan in town. Or if you're telling me the
whole damn story of your life, forget the economics professor who took you into the bosom of his family and gave you
warmth and sherry in New Haven, and instead drop me a
hint that your daughter and Husband II may have had a bit of
a tiff. That's all it would have taken, Ed, my friend.

"It must have been a double blow," he said. "She was the
last of your immediate family, wasn't she?"

"I really don't feel like talking about it."

"All right. I understand."

He did, a second later. All of a sudden, we had one of our
flashes of tacit understanding. We were looking at each other,
and just like that, he stiffened. He knew that I knew—not only
about John and Nan but about his knowledge of the whole
business. The whole affair. Then Edward did what I never
thought I'd see him do: He averted his eyes. Suddenly, a telephone message on the edge of his desk became overwhelm-
ingly important. He picked it up and studied it as if it was a
new cryptographic code he was just getting familiar with.

"Excuse me," I said. "I've got to get to work. That girl you
had sitting in for me left about three days' worth of dictation
to transcribe, and her shorthand's a mess."

He put the piece of paper back down. "Linda," he began.
Then his voice fell, and I had to strain to hear him. "I don't
know what to say, but I want to say something. I—"

"Thanks for your condolences." And then I walked out of
the room.

I became an efficient machine. For days I followed
Edward to meetings, took dictation, answered phones,

typed, translated. The line of refugees streaming in, offering up information, grew longer and longer. The anteroom where I worked was packed with people on folding chairs, chalky-faced people who never looked right into anyone's eyes—not mine, not each other's. They studied the floor, or their shoes.

When Edward was ready for the next one, I'd say, "Frau Schluter [or: Herr Abendroth], please follow me." And they'd shuffle inside, staring down at the floor like it was a treacherous path that might crack open, engulf them and then smash shut, crushing them so they couldn't even shriek for help before they were obliterated forever. For every one of them, I'd think: Poor lady, Poor guy, as I steered them over to the couch. Because Edward would never just question them, seeking out whatever intelligence he needed; he always wanted to know what had happened to them. So when I translated their unbearably sad stories, I'd think: Terrible. But it was the automatic pity of a machine. Tsk-tsk. Next. Tsk-tsk.

But then, a week after I went back to work, I led Werner Liedtke into Edward's office. He'd worked for the electric utility in Berlin, dispatching meter readers all over the city: an ordinary man, but one who might confirm or challenge the information we'd been getting on power-generating plants all over northern Germany.

"Would you like some coffee?" Edward asked him. Herr Liedtke, who had come into Philadelphia two days before on a boat full of refugees, didn't speak any English, so I translated as I took notes.

"No, thank you," he said. "No coffee." He gazed down at his shoes. New shoes, American, maybe a little too wide for him.

"The government of the United States appreciates your cooperation in coming here today. We know it must be difficult to talk about what you have just left, but we need all the details, all the facts, we can get."

"Thank you, sir," Herr Liedtke mumbled.

"And it is urgent that we get whatever information we can

on power generation as soon as possible, before conditions change."

"Yes, sir."

"Did you come here alone?"

"Yes. Alone."

"Do you have any family still in Germany?"

"My family . . . My brothers. A sister."

"Are you Jewish?"

"Oh, no. Not me." He pulled back his feet and hunched over, as if trying to make himself smaller, less of a target. "My wife. She was a Jew. They took her in 1940. May 18. Gestapo came to the apartment and said, 'Ruth Liedtke?' and she said 'Yes.' "

"And they took her then?" Edward asked softly.

"Yes."

"You never saw her again?"

"No."

I thought to myself: How many of these pathetic stories did Edward want to hear? "Did you have any children?" he asked.

"A boy."

"What is his name?" Herr Liedtke shook his head. "I'm sorry," Edward said. "I won't ask you any more—"

I was translating almost simultaneously, and so we were both interrupted when Herr Liedtke said, "Jurgen. His name was Jurgen," he said to his new American shoes.

"I see," Edward said.

"No. He was not taken when they took my wife. After that . . . nothing happened. I waited, but a long time passed and I knew . . . I thought: Jurgen is safe. He was allowed to go to school. No questions were asked. He was a good boy. Twelve, he was. He'd been a little fat, but he was growing, you know, so he grew more lean, except his face was round."

"He sounds very nice," Edward said. "A fine boy."

"Yes. A fine boy." The father shook his head. His hair was gray. He had a bald spot the size of a silver dollar. "There was a roundup of Jews the last week of June. I didn't fear very much. But suddenly they were at the door, banging on it, kicking with their boots, terrible noise, and they ask for Jurgen and I show them the boy and say, 'Look, he is no . . .' And I show them his papers. 'See?' I said. There were two of them. They each took an arm and dragged Jurgen out, down four flights of stairs. I ran after, and all the time he was screaming. 'Father!' And they dragged him over to a small bus and tried to put him on and I ran to him and he was screaming and they told him to shut up and get on, but still he was screaming. 'Father!' "

Herr Liedtke spoke in a monotone, and I tried to translate like that, but I called out "Father!" too loud.

Herr Liedtke said " 'Father!' " again, quietly, but his hands stretched out, involuntarily, reaching for his son. "A soldier came down off the bus. Not Gestapo. An ordinary soldier with a rifle. A rifle with a bayonet. And Jurgen struggled with the men holding him, trying to break away, and all the time screaming for me, and I ran toward him, but before I could get there . . ." He lifted up his head and looked into Edward's eyes. "The soldier—just a regular soldier—he drove the bayonet into Jurgen's throat. To silence him." Herr Liedtke touched his Adam's apple with his index finger. "There was blood, so much of it, and his mouth said 'Father,' but he could not speak. And he could not . . . he could not die yet. He was in agony. Oh, his eyes. My boy's eyes, crying for me to help him, then looking down . . . at the thing in his throat. He didn't believe . . . He kept waiting for me to help him." Herr Liedtke's eyes were dry.

I turned in my chair, so I could look out the window, hide my face. Edward said, "Linda?"

"I'm fine," I said. I could see that nice, fat-faced boy, howling in terror, making no sound. My shoulders jerked. A shudder. A convulsion. A machine breaking down.

"Try to keep going, if you can," Edward said to me.

"Yes," I said. "I can."

Herr Liedtke's voice remained flat. "The soldier pulled out his bayonet. The blood then. He was almost gone. I was nearly beside him as he started to fall. But they would not give me . . . my Jurgen. They hauled him onto the bus, had

the driver shut the door so he wouldn't tumble out. They
drove away." He shrugged. "And that was the end of it."

Two weeks later, at the beginning of August, on a day so
cool and pleasant and, therefore, so abnormal for Washington that it was almost suspect, part of some sinister Axis
plot, Norman Weekes came to Edward's office to discuss the
OSS's crisis in Berlin. He had not given up a single member
of his usual company of six; they trooped behind him in
twos, like obedient first graders.

The ill-will level was lower than it had been at the earlier
meeting. The two groups of men seemed to realize that since
Donovan did not have the time to fire Norman Weekes (and
perhaps also to realize that Norman's Boston bank gave its
New York business to Donovan's law firm), they were
doomed to work with each other. They were gathered in the
couch and chairs around the coffee table, which was covered
with legal pads, pens, coffee cups, water glasses and ash-
trays. Everyone was determinedly congenial.

Well, except for Edward and John. They sat beside each
other, but the relaxed give-and-take between colleagues had
been replaced by strain. Bad strain. John's head was drawn
down, his shoulders up, as if he half expected any minute to
be yelled at.

Maybe he thought he had it coming. Three nights before,
he'd slipped out of bed. It was two-thirty. I'd murmured—
fake-murmured, since I'd woken up startled and full of
dread—What's the matter? and he'd said, Shh, go back to
sleep. I'm just going downstairs for a glass of milk. When
he'd been gone for a minute, I'd tiptoed to the head of the
stairs. There were no sounds at all. But then I heard him
hang up the phone. I went back to bed and pretended to be
asleep. All of a sudden, I knew what the word "heartsick"
meant.

The next night, John called home a little before eleven.
We have a bad situation at one of the safe houses. I'll be late,
Linda. He came home at three. His hair was perfect, just

combed. I knew. I *knew*. It's Nan, isn't it? She's back. *No*, he said. I swear.

Whenever Edward spoke to John, he turned toward him but never quite looked at him.

"Norman," Edward said, "we've gone over your list of candidates for the, um, position vacated by Alfred Eckert. We've read your evaluations, had a look at their security clearance reports where they existed and done some preliminary investigating on our own. Shall we take them one at a time?"

"It's your meeting, Ed," Norman said. They both smiled, hiding their loathing of each other pretty well.

I sat about two feet away from Edward. We were both facing Norman, who'd obviously just been to the barber, and a bad one; his one claim to distinction, his white hair, had been cropped close to his head, so he looked less like a Boston big shot and more like some old man who'd somehow been captured and sent away for basic training. Throughout the meeting, his hand kept drifting up to where his tufted sideburns used to be. He felt vulnerable.

Edward opened the first of three folders on his lap. From where I sat, it looked as if John had a couple more. I couldn't stand to look at him. He was so beautiful. The night before, he'd called and said he had to conduct an interrogation. He'd called again around midnight. This is going very slowly, he said. I said, Why can't you be man enough to tell the truth? Would you stop your nagging! he'd snapped. Then I heard his deep intake of breath. All right, he said, I'm with Nan. Then he added quickly, But we're just talking. They must have had a lot to say. He didn't come home at all.

"Klaus-Dieter Fischer," Edward said. "Age, twenty-seven. Born in Leipzig. Moved to Berlin in 1925, at age ten. Father taught history at a *Gymnasium*—the German equivalent of a high school—and was also a Communist, something of a rabble-rouser. Father lost his job in '33, arrested in '34, presumed dead. Klaus-Dieter took up the cause, handed out pamphlets, escaped to Czechoslovakia in '35, just before he was about to be arrested. Escaped again to England in July '39, again by the skin of his teeth. Has worked at odd jobs—grocery clerk, waiter—but lives for the party. Made overtures to British intelligence, but they turned him down because of his political leanings." Edward closed the folder. "We should decline too. His loyalty is highly suspect."

"He's willing to go in wherever we want him," Norman said. "And I've spent time with him. He is a Communist, but a realist too. Not at all the raving ideologue."

"Is it likely he'd wave *Das Kapital* in your face?" Edward demanded. Everyone chuckled. "He wants the job, Norman. And from what we can gather, he wants it badly—so he can pass information back to the Russians."

"They *are* our ally, after all," Norman protested, although without much conviction. A moment later, he waved his hand and said, "Next."

"Hugo Dreyer. Age, fifty-two. Born, raised and currently living in Berlin. Secretary to an officer of I. G. Farben, has been passing information to us for years through Sunflower."

"He's really ideal," Norman said. "Right in place. And willing."

"Excuse me," John broke in. "He's out of the picture. He had a stroke three weeks ago. He's incapacitated."

"I see," Norman said. He flashed a look of such malice at one of his men that if I'd been that guy, I would have had a stroke myself. Then Norman turned back to John, gracious, amicable. "Any more surprises?"

John smiled. For a man who had been up all night, John still had unlimited energy to charm. The entire espionage unit smiled back. Even Norman bared his yellow teeth. "No surprises I know of, Norman. Unless Ed . . ."

Edward alone remained uncharmed. John's smile faded. Edward simply shook his head. "No surprises. Well, perhaps, in that for once I'm not going to give you an argument, Norman." He lifted the last folder on his pile. "Peter Fuhrmann. I don't have to go through his credentials. He's done some remarkable work for Special Operations in Ham-

burg. He appears clean as a whistle. I think he's your man,
Norman."

"Well, I have a surprise for you," Norman said. "Peter
wants out. Out of Hamburg. Out of intelligence entirely.
He's pleading exhaustion, and his contact seems to agree—
says he's on the edge of a nervous breakdown. Sorry to have
put you to all this work. We just received the message this
morning."

"Quite all right," Edward said. Norman nodded, and
everyone in the room muttered "Too damn bad" or something like it. "All right." Edward glanced at John, but it was
an icy glance, and he didn't say his name. "You checked on
the last two fellows. Please report."

"Hans Kuhn. Age, thirty-nine. A lawyer. Born in Cincin-
nati of German parents, moved back to Dresden when he
was eighteen." John adjusted and readjusted his tie in a nervous, almost desperate manner. Edward's coldness had
thrown him completely. "He's a single practitioner in Berlin,
and from time to time has passed information on to us
through Alfred Eckert. We've done what checking we could,
with refugees, lawyers who practiced in Berlin, and from
everything we can gather, he's no good."

"No good in what way?" Norman asked, almost off-
handedly.

"Rumors he's looted escrow accounts, stolen from wid-
ows and orphans. That sort of thing. Womanizer. One person
claimed to have seen him drunk and disorderly."

"Sounds like one of your partners, Ed," Norman chortled.

"Sounds like quite a few of them," Edward responded.

There was subdued male laughter. Everything was still
pleasant.

"The last name on the list is Erich Erdmann." Norman's
face brightened; I could see this was his man. "Forty years
old. Born in Munich. Professor of Romance languages at the
university in Munich until 1935. Jewish. Came to the U.S. in
'36. Taught at Tufts until this year, when he came to work
for the OSS . . . Foreign Nationalities unit."

"He wants to go back in," Norman said. "He's cultured,

good-looking. According to Rex"—Rex was Norman's highest-placed spy, a career man who had worked in the foreign office since before the First World War but had had little contact with Alfred's important Nazi official—"someone sophisticated like Erdmann would appeal to the foreign office fellow. And he's open to any suggestion we have."

"That's the drawback, as far as I'm concerned," Edward said. "All this Erdmann wants is to make trouble for the Germans. It's certainly a commendable goal, but he's too intent on revenge. I'd send him in with a demolition team in a minute—if we could slip in a team and they needed a professor of Romance languages with them. But he's seething with anger, Norman. You can't send someone like that on a mission that requires infinite patience and self-control."

"I think he could control himself if he's willing to keep his eye on the ultimate objective," Norman said. "And I know he's more than willing."

"But he'll be in there alone," Edward said. "He'll have no one to get him to shape up when he starts losing his sense of balance. Look, whoever takes Alfred Eckert's place is going to have to walk on an invisible tightrope. We know there's a traitor in the resistance movement. People will be suspicious. We'll have to ease him in with extraordinary canniness. And only one person—as yet to be determined—will know his true identity. Then, gradually, he'll have to make a place for himself. It's an operation that calls for great subtlety, and this Erich Erdmann, for all his academic attainments, is about as subtle as a bull in a china shop."

"But we're *desperate*," Norman interrupted. "Goddamn it, Ed, you keep shooting down almost every candidate we come up with."

"Then come up with better candidates," Edward replied. The congeniality was evaporating fast.

"Erich's a courageous man. I tell you, he would rise to the occasion."

"He'd fall flat on his face. He can't even sit through an interview with me without banging his fist on the table every thirty seconds for punctuation. The man has no command over his emotions. It's not that I blame him. Believe me, I understand his rage. I applaud it."

"He doesn't look Jewish," Norman said. "He'd fit right in."

"I don't care if he looks like the archbishop of Canterbury. He's an accident going someplace to happen, and I'm not going to let it happen in Berlin. I'm against him. I vote no."

"Ed—"

"I'll go to the mat with you on this one, Norman."

The veins in Norman's neck and temples started to bulge. His face got so red it was almost purple. He tried to yell, but he was so infuriated he choked on his words. "You're doing this deliberately!"

"Don't be ridiculous. This isn't a plot to foil you. But I won't allow any more suicide missions. I won't send a man to a meaningless, unnecessary death."

"I need an agent! You find one for me, then, goddamn it to hell! *You* find me a man we can slip in, someone with the brains and guts to knock on a Nazi's door and invite himself in."

There was silence. John, weary, closed his eyes. And all of a sudden, I found myself asking: "Hey, how about me?"

# 20

"This isn't foolish!" Edward's fist crashed down on a table. "This is insane! What's gotten into you?"

Two days after I'd suggested going into Germany, Edward had directed Pete, his driver, to forget his instructions to take us to a meeting at the Research and Analysis unit. Drop us at my place, he directed, and wait. I slid out of the car, not even bothering to take my pad and pencil, and strolled up the walk to his house.

I knew Edward; he was going to play gracious host, offer me a drink, and then, with great subtlety, try to talk me out of the idea. But the minute he closed the door, he'd yelled, "You idiot!" That's when I realized that the only reason he'd brought me to his peaceful Georgetown home was that he needed a place where he could scream his head off.

"If it's all so insane, then how come Norman's whole espionage unit's for it?"

"Are you some kind of imbecile?" I had no idea such a low voice could be so terrifyingly loud. "What the hell is wrong with you? Don't you know by now that all he wants is another player for his game?"

I was stunned—and frightened—by his outburst. But I knew if I started quaking in front of Edward, the closest I'd get to Berlin was a map. So I banged my fist, hard, against his living room wall. "You have no damn right to shout at me like this," I yelled back.

Besides, I'd had it with him. He'd sat in that meeting two days earlier letting Norman and his men and even John

308

debate my going into Berlin. Well, John had said, her *berlinerisch* is not flawless. Not an American accent, but it's not . . . quite on the mark. But close enough? one of Norman's men had queried. And John had admitted he couldn't be sure. Edward had sat rigid and wordless, and no one except me had noticed how spooky his silence was.

"The thing that's *really* getting you is that you know I can do it," I went on, "and you don't want me to because of your dumb feud with Norman Weekes. And because it would be too much trouble to find a new secretary."

"I have no patience for asinine remarks!"

"Would you please listen to me! I know the network, the codes, the whole operation. And I'm not some Tufts College professor with a crazy grudge. I'm an ordinary person. And give me three days with one of your refugees who speaks the *berlinerisch* dialect, and no one will ever know I'm not Frau Schmidt from around the corner."

Edward stalked away from me, across the room toward the mantel. Suddenly he spun around, took three fast steps and was beside me. Before I even realized what was happening, I saw he had a fireplace poker in his hand. He drew it up fast, like a fencer; it was an inch from my throat. "Are you crazy?" I breathed, staring down at it.

"Come on. This is Berlin," he said. "You can manage anything." I turned my back on him, walked away and sat down in a big blue club chair. "*Now* do you understand that you can't begin to manage something like this?"

I looked up at him. "I just managed it. You didn't poke out my jugular with that thing."

"For God's sake!" he said, and hurled the poker to the floor. It bounced from the fancy old rug and clanged onto the dark wood floor. Then Edward began to pace. His hands were stuffed deep in his pockets. He wouldn't look at me.

"I know what's going to come next," I said. "You're going to take your hands out of your pockets and come over here, sit down, and try to talk me out of it. You're going to be very understanding and patient."

Edward pulled his hands out of his pockets and took a seat

not far away, in a club chair that matched mine. "Linda," he said understandingly, patiently. "You haven't thought this through."

"I have."

"No, you haven't. Don't you realize that your life means nothing to a man like Norman Weekes? He's just using you for his own purposes."

"Let me clue you in on what I've learned in the last couple of years. People like Norman Weekes—people like you— *always* use people like me. Why else bother having lower classes? You use us to work for you, to clean up your messes, to fight your wars. You use us to listen to your secrets, so you can say: 'What? *Me* a tough, unfeeling bastard? No! I'm a deep, fine, compassionate human being. If you don't believe me, just ask my secretary.' "

He rubbed his watch chain between his thumb and index finger. "Is that what you think of me, Linda?"

"Pretty close."

"It's a shame you didn't say anything. I wouldn't have wasted your time. It would have been easier just giving you a five-dollar raise in exchange for your promise to vouch for my compassion."

We sat there, half facing each other, not speaking. It was a terrible, long time. Finally I said, "There's really no point in sitting around here." I started to get up, but then Edward stopped me.

His voice, subdued, almost hypnotic, was what got to me. "There's a beautiful simplicity in all this. What you're looking for is precisely what Norman is offering: a suicide mission." I sat back in the chair. "You feel your life is . . . is unrewarding." Edward paused. "You've lost your mother. And your husband . . ." His voice trailed off.

"My husband has been having a flaming affair with your daughter."

"Yes."

"So you think I want to go into Berlin, go undercover, because I really want to kill myself, but I'm too chicken to do it, so I'll get some pig in the Gestapo to do it for me?

Why when you do it is it heroic, and when I want to do the same thing it's suicidal?"

"You're distraught."

"You didn't answer my question." But all he did was give me one of his kindly looks, his hard eyes softening, his head tilted a little to the side: the kind of look he gave all the sad victims of the war. And the lousy part of it was, it wasn't a phony look. His pity for me was real. "I walked in on them," I told him. He stiffened. "No, not like that. It was when I got back from New York, from my mother's funeral. Oh, they were in each other's arms, but they were dressed to the nines and listening to classical music." He reached over and tried to take my hand, but I jerked it away, into my lap. "You really must be proud of her."

"You know I'm not."

"I don't know anything. All I know are the stories you decide to tell me." He drew his watch from his pocket and stared at the case, but didn't open it. "It's getting late," I said. "I really want to get out of here."

Edward spoke as if he hadn't heard me. "Nan's my child. I love her. That doesn't mean I approve of what she's doing. It doesn't mean I understand her." He slipped his watch back into its little pocket and looked at me. "That's a sad admission for a father to have to make, but even so, I have an obligation—"

"You know, you're all sensational at throwing around words like 'obligation,' 'honor,' 'moral imperative.' Go ahead, if it makes you happy. You can carry on about your integrity, your profound humanity, until you're blue in the face. I just don't want any part of it. I want *out* of your world." I got up and stood in front of his chair. "Send me to Berlin."

Edward rose. He wasn't all that much taller than I was, so we were almost eye to eye. His voice was very calm. "Don't throw away your life on John Berringer. He's not worth it. He has good looks and a good mind. But that's all he has. His character isn't worth two cents."

"You know what the problem is? I've seen you at work

too often. You're shocking me back to my senses with a brutal dose of honesty; you always have pretty good results
with that technique."

Edward broke away then and walked over to a cart that
had whiskey and glasses on it. "Would you like a drink?" I
shook my head, and he poured himself one. "I've been
drinking too damn much lately. I wake up nearly every
morning feeling . . . not right."

I thought: What does he want—another heart-to-heart?
"So don't drink so much," I said.

"Thank you. I'm touched by your concern."

"You want my concern? Maybe you should drop the brutal-
honesty business. John could wind up being your son-in-
law."

"I would hope not."

"You ought to thank me for taking him off your hands.
Well, temporarily. I don't have what it takes for a long run,
for chitchat in the drawing room. But for the short run, I'm
great upstairs."

"Don't denigrate yourself."

"Hey, I'm not. I'll give you my other credentials. I'm
smart. Imaginative. And you were the one who said I have
guts. If you'll just listen to me, I'll tell you *exactly* how I can
get into Berlin. I figured the whole thing out."

"You're not going. You're not going to destroy yourself—
and possibly put into jeopardy what few shreds of resistance
are left."

"I'm better than any name on that list, and you damn well
know it!"

"You're staying here."

"*Please*. Don't you understand? This is my war. I want to
fight it. I belong there."

Edward took a long drink. "You don't belong there."

"Why not?"

"For one thing, you're a Jew."

I stared at him. "What are you talking about?"

"Please. I saw your FBI report two years ago. Why do you
think you were cleared so damned fast?"

"I'm not a Jew," I said. He gave me one of those cool, neutral upper-class glances that still say, Yeah, sure. So I added, "My father was, but he never did anything Jewish in his life . . . whatever it is they do."

"If you were to go into Berlin, if they were to find you out—and believe me, they inevitably would—do you know what they would do to you?"

"Yes. And they'd do it to me, anyway—Jew, half Jew, no Jew at all."

"They'd do it worse to you."

"Come on! You think I'm going to walk into Germany with a big yellow star on an armband?"

"If they captured you, do you think it would take them more than ten minutes to find out everything they could possibly want to know?"

Without thinking, I reached out and took his drink. It was only after the whiskey radiated through me that I realized what I'd done. "Excuse me," I said, handing him back the glass. I took a minute to collect myself. "To answer your question, if I saw myself sitting under a naked light bulb in an interrogation cell, I wouldn't be making this pitch. Okay? And if you'd let me tell you what I have in mind—"

"Sit down, please." Edward motioned to the couch. We sat on opposite ends; his drink sat between us on the table. He cleared his throat. "If you read the editorials, listen to Buy Bonds speeches, it's very fashionable these days to call Hitler's regime hellish. 'The hell that is Nazi Germany,' and so forth."

"Yeah? So?"

"Listen to me, Linda. It *is* hell. More than you can comprehend. It is absolute evil." He held out the glass to me. I didn't take it, so he did. "I'm going to tell you something only about ten people in the government know. Some . . . shocking news has come out of Switzerland, through Sunflower; he learned it from that disgusting little Nazi who's treasurer of his company, Himmler's friend." He fell silent, as if he didn't want to continue.

"What? What's going on?"

"They're killing the Jews."

"I know they are."

"No. You don't know. They've started something new. Gas chambers. They expect to exterminate three to four million—did you hear that number?—three to four million European Jews in the next two years. More, if they can build fast enough and maintain their supply of prussic acid. Men, women, children. They want to annihilate the Jews completely." He hesitated, and then added quietly, "Your family, Linda. Your people."

How do you react to something like that? I sat on that sumptuous couch in that rich, civilized house in Georgetown and I was numb. Not feeling numb, but as if everything inside me had frozen. My only sensation was thousands . . . millions of tiny prickles of horror along my skin and scalp. "Why?"

"There is no answer."

I thought about the two old ladies, Liesl and Hannah. "I have to go there," I said.

"You can't stop them."

"But I can do *something*. I can help. I can be one bullet, maybe one bomb. I can make a difference."

"You can't. You'd be one more dead Jew."

"Don't talk to me like that!"

"Linda, my dear, I am going over to the telephone. I am calling Norman Weekes and telling him to scrap immediately any plans he has involving you. I am going to stop this preposterous scheme *now*. If you don't have the brains or the desire to stay alive, I'll have to see to it for you."

I don't know how I got through the rest of that day. Edward made his phone call, finished his drink in silence and poured another. I walked out and waited in the car, staring straight ahead, at the back of Pete's baseball cap. Edward came out a half hour later and acted as though nothing the least unusual had happened.

At five o'clock, he went off to a meeting at the White House, saying, "I should be back by seven-thirty or eight."

Just like that. At six, I put a flawlessly typed note on his desk.

*Dear Mr. Leland:*

*This is to inform you that I am hereby submitting my resignation from the position of your secretary; the resignation is effective as of the close of business today.*
*Thank you for your consideration and courtesy.*

*Very truly yours,*
*Linda V. Berringer*

Then I walked out of Edward Leland's office for good.

When I thought about it—and I now had plenty of time to think—the idea of my going underground and surfacing in Berlin seemed right.

Sure, when I thought: Hey, I want to be a *spy*, the actual word would make me feel all fluttery. Worse than that: agitated. I'd pace from room to room, grab a sponge and wipe around the faucets for the twenty-seventh time, open the refrigerator and check if the peaches were too soft since I'd last looked, fifteen minutes before. *Spy*. Inspecting the bathroom to make sure we hadn't run out of toilet paper. I could almost hear the creepy music they play in movies when the secret agent walks down a cobblestone street and fog swirls around his feet.

But when I'd said to Edward, This is my war, I'd meant it. Okay, it was just something I'd blurted out because I was so unhappy, so frustrated, but there's value in misery. It's a test. When you're so oppressed and depressed by your life, you can cave in and show the world you're the sucker they've always thought you were, or you can finally come out fighting and say: Listen, you bastards, this is unfair; I won't put up with it. I'm entitled to . . . And whammo! Out pops what you really want. Out pops the truth. And the truth was I wanted to fight just as much as every eighteen-year-old boy who'd up and enlisted the day after Pearl Harbor.

Why not? I was as American as apple pie. Okay, the way I talked, no one would say, Wow, you must be from Nebraska! But there's apple pie in New York too. A little more mushed up, a little spicier, but still apple pie.

There can be more than one truth, though. I was all-American, but not all American. I'd grown up in a house with two women, where English was the language of dopi-ness and German the tongue of whatever intelligent thought there was. It was my mother's "Linda, angel, what would *you* call this nail polish—coral or salmon?" versus Olga's "Do you think the Dawes Plan will really help the German economy?"

Okay, there was my father too. He was almost like me in that he spoke English and German with almost equal ease, but although he was smart, the fact that he was fluent in a foreign tongue meant zero to him. He could have been speaking Pig Latin for all he cared about Germany. He could talk about the Dodgers or Herbert Hoover or his chance of getting a raise down at the sausage plant in either language, but his life was purely American.

But maybe because my parents were so busy with each other, they didn't have a lot of time for me. So I'd listened a lot to my Grandma Olga, who'd reminisce when she was waxing the floor or stuffing cabbage leaves or cutting out a corn plaster. The old country was her life, and I guess in a way it became mine; I'd always been fascinated with Ger-many—and especially Berlin—because she made it sound like a fairy-tale place, the Enchanted Kingdom. The longer she stayed in America, the greener the German countryside became, the more graceful the boulevards of Berlin, the more glamorous and cultivated and merry its inhabitants. Maybe that's why when Hitler rose to power, she thought of him as a disagreeable quirk of history; he was a blot on her dream of perfection, and she figured it was only a matter of time before the neatest people in the world cleaned up their blot.

But as far back as 1923, when I first heard about him and his NSDAP party, I knew he was dangerous. I was a girl raised on fairy tales—not Cowboys and Indians—and so I'd learned there was more to life than good guys and bad guys. In every enchanted kingdom, there are monsters. When I heard Hitler's speeches, his combination of hysteria, hatred, pride and vengeance all tied up into a package with the gaudy ribbon of Germanic myth, I knew that here was one doozy of a monster.

And just as Cinderella and the fairy godmother had always struck a chord in me, I knew Hitler and his gods would strike a chord in the German people. Oh, they would snicker at his accent and maybe cringe at his rantings, but deep down they'd say, *Ach!* He know *just* what I feel!

I guess I was too true-blue American to ever really have confidence in the basic goodness of foreigners.

And so Hitler's rise didn't stun me. Actually, neither did Pearl Harbor. Did it surprise me? Sure. I never thought the Japanese could fool us *so* bad.

But although I followed the fighting in the Pacific conscientiously, it wasn't my war. My war wasn't the good guys against the bad guys. My war was against the monsters.

And damn it, I was finally ready to fight.

Edward left Washington the last week of August for, as usual, places unknown. I knew he'd been planning a trip, but just to make sure, I called his new secretary and made up a story about his promising to leave me a letter of recommendation before he went away. She said, Oh, dear, he must have forgotten. And I snuck in, And he won't be back for what—two, three weeks? More like four, I'm sorry to say, was her answer. Boy, did she have a big, dangerous mouth, giving out information like that. But I knew the coast was clear.

I hardly saw John. He'd called me late on the night after he hadn't come home, six hours after the meeting where I'd volunteered to go into Berlin. I waited for him to say, How

could you humiliate me in front of all those people by interrupting, by pushing yourself where you *know* you don't
belong? Or: How could you suggest anything so stupid?
What he actually said was, "I have to be honest with you.
Nan and I still haven't resolved matters. I don't know when
I'll be home." I didn't even feel like crying. I wrapped the
phone wire around my finger, tight, and said to him, "Do
you think it matters?"

I made up a bed for myself in the second bedroom. John
didn't notice, because he didn't come home for two days. I
was in the kitchen when he walked in. You here for a clean
shirt before you go back to talking? I asked. I was peeling a
carrot and didn't bother to look at him. Linda, he said, I
know how hard this has been on you. But it will be resolved.
Soon. I swear. He came up behind me and just rested himself
against me. But in a minute he was rubbing and pushing me
hard against the sink. His arms went around me. I need you,
he exhaled into my ear. How long do you have? I asked. I'm
going to stay the whole night, he replied. Oh, God, I have to
have you. I peeled a long curl of carrot peel into the sink. No
more, I said. Did you hear me? Get off me! Come on, he
insisted, you have to have it as much as I do.

But I didn't! I couldn't believe it. I turned around. He was
just another pretty face. It took me a second to catch my
breath. Was this another loss? There I was, right on the verge
of crying, but a second later, I found myself staring at the
sink drain, trying to fight off a giggle. He was trying his
Tragic Eyes routine, where dark blue eyes mist over, open
wide, gaze at me; he was going to break my heart with his
beautiful damp eyes, show me his infinite pain, his suffering.
Except now I realized he could do it at the drop of a hat. I realized I'd seen Tragic Eyes about four hundred and seventy-
two times. I glanced up. Well, I told him, if it's true—if I
have to have it—I'll have to get it someplace else.

At first I thought it would be smart to give Norman Weekes
just what he wanted—a throaty, promising voice and an even
more promising dress—so he'd give me what I wanted. But in

the end I put on brown oxfords, an old gabardine skirt and a white cotton blouse that showed nothing more than how well it was ironed. I wore no makeup. I pulled back my hair into a loosely pinned mess that could barely be called a bun.

"Oh," Norman said, as he lifted his behind from his desk chair when I walked in. I could see whatever his desire for me had been evaporating; it was a wonderful sight. "Please, sit down."

I came right to the point. "Look at me. Do you think anyone in the foreign office would look twice?"

His eyebrows did one of those Aha! movements. "Edward has said 'Absolutely not,' you know."

"I know."

"And your husband?"

"John has never said no."

Norman cocked his head; his mouth hung open a bit. He was obviously dying to hear more about me and John. All of a sudden, I felt queasy, thinking: Oh, God, people *know* about John and me . . . and Nan. The whole OSS may know, and when everyone came up to me after I got back after my mother's funeral, offering sympathy, they were really—

Norman demanded, "I really must know. How would he feel if you put—let me be perfectly forthright about this—if you put yourself in, well, a rather perilous situation?"

"How does a wife feel when her husband goes off to war? She doesn't want it, but she understands."

"I see." A bubble of saliva formed on the side of his mouth and then burst.

"And I'm sure you also see, because it's your job to see, well, everything, that things aren't so great right now between me and my husband. If I went off, it wouldn't be like you were tearing apart the perfect marriage. I think John could probably learn to adjust to my absence."

"I rather assumed . . . some distance . . . from his lack of . . . objections when we contemplated the possibility of your working for us at that meeting. But I didn't want to be presumptuous."

He was waiting for more, a dose of scandal he could mur-

mur about at his club. He'd light a cigar and say, Leland's
secretary, Berringer's wife, told me . . . But I just said, "Let
me be straight with you. I know I'm your best shot. Your
only shot."

He grinned. With all that money, you'd think he could
have afforded a decent toothbrush. "That may be true, but
we have that lit-tle problem with Mr. Leland."

I gave him a bigger, and whiter, grin. "But Mr. Leland is
out of town—probably out of the country—for four weeks."

"I can't." His office was bare in that old-money, New England way, but his desk was a mess. He tried to put down his
elbow so he could make a platform with his hand to rest his
chin on, but he had to shove over a stack of bound top-secret
reports to find the room. The reports looked unread. His
desk was like him: an important, repulsive mess. "Forgive
me for being profane, but if you went into Berlin, there
would be hell to pay when Ed returned."

I flashed a you're-so-damnably-attractive smile and managed not to gag. "What's a little hell to a man like you?
And . . . please, I want to be honest with you."

"Oh, do."

"I know you and Edward Leland are . . . well, at odds. I
want you to understand I feel a great loyalty to him. Not only
as my former employer but as the man who's really been my
husband's . . . patron." Wow, was that a great word. "But I
also know he's not right all the time. He's a human being. He
makes mistakes." Norman nodded. "Lots of mistakes."

"Yes," he said. His upper lip curled into something just
under a sneer. I'd been right. I'd sensed that puffing myself
up as Miss Espionage 1942 wouldn't get to Norman Weekes
the way a betrayal of Edward would. You've been right all
along: That would be my unwritten message, aimed directly
at Norman Weekes's limitless vanity. He's been wrong.
You're strong. He's soft, muddleheaded. Norman would
love the message and, hopefully, the messenger.

"Edward Leland is a very decent man, the way he cares
about people. But he's—" I stopped cold. "Please. No matter
what happens, I hope this conversation—"

He cut me off with an impassioned "Of course. Never to be repeated." He leaned forward, expectant, thrilled.

I made myself as comfortable as I could in that small, stiff wooden chair. "He's too cautious. Look, I know what I want to do is dangerous. I wouldn't be worthy of the job if I didn't have that much sense. But just because it's dangerous doesn't mean it's not worth doing."

"You're a smart girl. But Ed would go running to Donovan and . . ."

"You've, um, disagreed with Edward Leland and—let's be honest—has Colonel Donovan ever handed you your walking papers?" Norman gave a small, self-satisfied, yellow smile. "Please," I urged, "don't say no." I offered him a little bit of a husky voice so he'd pay attention, but not so much as to distract him. "Say maybe. Give me a week at Assessment School. You know they won't let me go if I'm not fit. But if I am, you'll have your man. . . ." We both smiled. "Your man in Berlin. And I promise you, it'll be worth it."

The next five weeks were the hardest I'd ever lived through, and the worst of it was that all along, everybody's expression said: You think *this* is bad? Wait.

My name was Lina Thiele. On Monday, the last day of August, 1942, I entered the OSS's Assessment School. The hunched-over man who let me in had a frighteningly flabby face with near-shoulder-length jowls. He looked like the door-keeper in a Dracula movie. For a second I thought he was part of the process of terrifying recruits, but he just called out, "Judy!" His jowls jiggled, and a girl about five years younger than me, with a lot of frothy Maureen O'Sullivan hair, came into the hall and said, "Follow me, please."

We walked down a steep flight of gray cement steps to the basement, and she led me into a curtained cubicle and said, "Please take off all of your clothing except your underwear." As I got undressed, she took my clothes and folded them.

Finally, when I was standing in my underpants and brassiere, she pulled a scissors out of the pocket of her shirt.

I forced myself not to flinch, and reasoned: The United States of America is not going to stab you. This girl is here to test you. And so, even though all the light in the room seemed to be shining on the silvery point of that scissors, I made myself stand motionless, all calm and collected. And Judy said, "I have to cut out any name tags or laundry marks on your underwear."

"Oh. There aren't any. But there may be labels from the department store. Do you want to . . ."

"No," Judy said. She really had very little interest in me. She kept squinting into a small, splintered triangle of mirror that was hung on the wall, obviously deeply involved with her eyebrows. "When . . . whenever . . . if you go, they'll give you stuff from . . . wherever." She licked her pinkie and wiped off the penciled end of her left eyebrow. She turned to me. "How does that look?"

"Better," I said. "Terrific." Oh, boy, I thought, the OSS in action.

"Good. Now, these are the rules. *Nobody* gets to know your real name. I'm going to take your clothes and your shoes and your pocketbook with me when I go out. You know, your whole identity."

"I'm supposed to walk around in my underwear?"

Judy rolled her eyes and said, "Oh, geez! I forgot. Wait here." And she slipped out from behind the curtain and a few minutes later came back with clothes. Some clothes! Men's army fatigues and a pair of boots so heavy I had to use both hands to lift them. They'd probably been designed for combat conditions in Antarctica.

Then Judy led me upstairs—which was some trick in itself with the two-ton boots—and out a back door. The next thing I knew, I was in the back of an army-green, canvas-covered truck, with four men dressed in the same outfit I was wearing. None of them spoke, and, like me, not a single one of them looked like an American GI.

My advantage was, having worked for Edward so long, I had a fair idea of how the OSS operated. In fact, once we bumped onto a hilly road ten minutes into Virginia, I knew exactly where we were headed. I'd been down that same road in the Packard; it led to an estate in Fairfax, with acres of open field surrounded by a thick forest, and, in the middle, an old white mansion dripping with honeysuckle charm. But if I remembered right, the interior smelled as though the mildew had been in flower inside the walls since the founding of the Confederacy.

I remembered right. We were herded in through the front door and stood under a giant brass chandelier. The hallway itself was so wide and high it seemed more like the main aisle of a giant church. It ran the length of the mansion; at the far end were two glass doors that opened up on a sloping green lawn.

We never got there. We heard a theatrical "Ahem" and glanced up. A man with a red face and a golf shirt was walking down the stairs very slowly. He would have looked like he was making believe he was a bride, except that instead of gazing straight ahead, he was looking down, scrutinizing us. This threw one of the four men I'd driven out with; he turned his eyes away from the red-faced man and started to smile nervously at all of us, as if we were his pals and would back him up. Then he wiped his palms—obviously sweating—on his fatigues.

When Red-Face reached us, he said, "I'm Mr. Jones." That seemed to be the limit of his conversational skills. He just stood there and eyed the five of us. Not a word was said for at least ten minutes, and when you're standing around in army boots in a southern mansion on a hot day with someone you know isn't really named Mr. Jones staring at you, that's a long time. The guy with the sweaty palms finally broke the silence by asking if there was a men's room. The sound of a voice was so unexpected that another one of the men flinched. "Down the hall, second left, first door on your right," Mr. Jones said. As the man headed off, I thought: He's not going to make it. And I probably wouldn't put my money on the flincher, either, I decided.

"Lady and gentlemen," Mr. Jones said, when the nervous guy finally got back. "Welcome. And now, down to business.

A few rules. You are never to deviate from your cover story. Never. You'll see a friendly face, and he'll say to you, 'Is that an Oklahoma accent I hear?' and just as you say, 'Why, it sure is!' you'll be out on your butt.

"Now, most of you have foreign covers. Stick to the story we've invented, but unless we direct you to do otherwise, speak English. Not all of us can speak Hungarian or Japanese or what have you, so you'll save that for later, for the specialists.

"Let me warn you that our purpose here is to get rid of you. You'll be under almost constant surveillance. We want to make you break your cover. We want to be there when you forget you're supposed to be a waiter and start talking like the truckdriver you really are. We're going to test you. We're looking for sweat. We're sniffing out weakness. *Your* weakness."

It wasn't that I didn't take it seriously. I did. But I also knew that it was a kind of game—a rough one, but with one basic rule for winning: Don't show you're scared.

By the end of the first hour, I knew the easiest way to hide your fear was to keep your mouth shut except when asked a direct question. And there were plenty. I had intelligence tests and psychological tests every day. "What does this inkblot look like to you?" they asked. I told the psychologist that it looked like a butterfly, and when he said, "Look again and tell me what else you see," I told him I saw a couple of big vases between the wings and the body. "Is that *all?*" he demanded. He was a small, mousy man, and he seemed unsatisfied. I told him, yeah, that was all.

There were physical tests, and not just someone with a tongue depressor and a stethoscope. After the first examination, I had to run for fifteen minutes. I thought I would drop dead, but I managed to do it. Then, after the doctor took my pulse, he told me to do ten push-ups. I stopped after three. "More!" he ordered. I told him I couldn't. "I said *more!*" I stood up, looked him straight in the eye and said, I can't. The next day, another doctor took me to a chinning bar and told me to do as many pull-ups as I could. I couldn't even do one. "Christ," he said, really disgusted, "just look at you. You sit behind a desk all day and you've got no muscle tone." I told him I didn't sit behind a desk. I was a house-wife. "What does your husband do?" I was a widow, I said. My husband had died the year before, in June, on the East-ern Front. "Your husband's a German soldier?" Yes. "Where was he killed?" Somewhere near Gorodishche. He waited, but I kept quiet. "What was his name?" Johannes. "Johannes what?" Thiele. "I thought that was *your* name?" It is. My married name. "What was your maiden name?" Fritsch.

Then he smiled at me. "Look, I don't like doing this. I'm really a nice guy." He put out his hand. "My name's Richard Peterson." He was Hollywood handsome. Maybe he was the in-house tempter for potential female agents, or maybe they'd brought him in special for me—my security clear-ance revealing a weakness for gorgeous guys. "But I want you to call me Dick, okay? By the way, I'm from Tampa. Before all this hullabaloo, I had a nice practice down there. Internal medicine." He shook my hand, holding it, naturally, a little too long. "Now I want to know everything about you." My name is Lina Thiele, I said. "Aw, come on, honey." I didn't respond. Someone should have told him that "Aw" and "honey" didn't necessarily work on New York girls. He smiled. I didn't. He gave me a nasty look. "Why the hell can't you do even one pull-up, Lina?" I don't know, I told him. "You're soft," he shouted. "I'll tell you right now, you're not going to make it. You're no good. You're too weak." I just stood there. "Get out of here," he said at last.

It was all a game. They'd said it would be hard, and it was, but not in the way they meant. I wasn't that scared by a bunch of Americans playing tough guys. Well, sometimes a little scared. But working for Edward, I'd seen the victims of the real thing, and I knew there was a world of difference. What made it so hard was, first of all, the fatigue. For a week, they kept you going day and night with tests, with jobs designed to frustrate you, exhaust you, make you sit down and cry.

One afternoon they led us to the bank of a stream and

gave three of us a bunch of boards, a pulley and a rope, then handed us a rock about the size of someone's head. "This is a very delicate communications device. You have to get it across the stream without jarring it or getting it wet."

The boards were too short to go across the stream. One of the men kept trying to lasso a tree on the far bank with the rope, so he could Tarzan his way across. The other guy and I tried to get him to help us, but he wouldn't, so the two of us worked on making a bridge by overlapping the boards. We had ten minutes. All the time, the three OSS men with us were hollering, "Come on!" "Time's running out!" "Hey, you lady. Don't you know what a pulley is?" I didn't. "Your time's almost up!" They started counting down: "Sixty seconds, fifty-nine . . ." At forty, I took the rock, lifted it over my head, told the guy who wasn't playing with the rope to try and stay right beside me, and walked into the stream. It was cold, but I made myself go slow, so I wouldn't slip. Soon though the water came up to my neck. You jerk! I thought. Why didn't you let the guy carry the damn rock? I hadn't realized it was so deep, and I called out to the guy, who was a little behind me, Hey, catch up! I can't swim, so get ready to grab this thing. Just then the OSS men on the bank called out, "Nine! Eight!" Talk about tripping up: The guy stumbled. I heard his splash, but I kept picking my way over the slick, moss-covered stones on the bottom of the stream. I didn't look back. On "Three!" I got to the other side. I was gasping, freezing and wanted to curse—shriek out filthy things to the OSS pigs, but since I couldn't catch my breath, I didn't have to practice any self-control. A minute later, one of them shouted, "Come back, Linda." I stood up and managed to call out, My name's Lina. Then I stepped back into the icy water.

They took us for a hike in the woods. My teeth were chattering, my arms were still shaking from the tension of holding the rock over my head. My boots were filled with cold water and made disgusting squishy sounds at every step. The hike went on for three hours; there was no time to change my clothes until right before dinner. I was too worn out to eat. After dinner, they sent me to a lady psychologist. "How are you bearing up? It must be hard." She had soft-looking, manicured hands and was wearing a beautiful gold cuff bracelet. Her voice was so sweet, so decent. "Are you chilled? Would you like to borrow a sweater?" I said, I'm fine.

But exhausted as I was each night, I could hardly fall asleep. I kept thinking too much. I'd called John at his office and told him I was going back to New York for a few weeks, to stay at my mother's and put pressure on the real estate agent. I added, I had the phone disconnected, so if you want to reach me . . . He said, with great seriousness, I'll talk to you when you get back. I said, If you want a divorce, you can tell me now. I won't drop dead from shock. Linda, he said, please don't make every conversation we have a confrontation. It's not helping, you know.

So I said, John, I'm not going to New York. They're sending me to Assessment School.

For Berlin? he breathed.

Yes.

How did you get Ed to go along?

I guess Norman must have convinced him, I lied.

Well, he said, I don't know what to say. So I waited. Sooner or later, he'd have to say something. And he did: Um, if you're planning on going in, maybe we should sit down first and, you know, talk things over.

You don't want me to go?

Linda, I can't make that kind of decision for you. It's your life that would be at stake.

And then I realized his talking things over meant: Hey, sweetie, if you're going to die in Berlin, let's be divorced so I don't have to wait seven years—or whatever it was—in legal limbo before I can marry Nan. If you're buried under forty tons of rubble or have a bullet in your head, I could be terribly inconvenienced.

I understand, I said.

Good, he said. We'll sit down and talk soon.

But what really kept me awake was the lie I'd told Norman Weekes. I'd said Edward was too cautious, but my unspoken words were: He's weak. You're brave, Norman. You're not some lily-livered lawyer who worries about the sanctity of life. You have the guts to send men out to their death.

I'd conned a weak man to get around a brave and strong one. I'd manipulated Norman to do what I'd wanted, and I'd turned my back on Edward Leland. Okay, he'd turned out to be a real crumb who'd sat back and let his daughter take over my husband and didn't have the decency—the decency that comes with friendship—to give me a clue that could save my marriage, save everything I had. But I'd betrayed him far worse. I'd denied all his advice, all his wisdom, and, even more, all the good things he stood for. I'd gone over to his enemy to join the game of Cowboys and Indians.

It was early September then, getting cold at night in the countryside, and they'd only given us a thin, and not very clean, army blanket. Probably another test to see if we were strong enough not to beg for a goose-down quilt. Maybe Edward was right, I thought, as I tucked the blanket under my feet. Maybe I am on some crazy suicide mission. Or maybe my heart is in the right place, but there'll be a bullet in it two days after I get to Berlin. If I get to Berlin at all.

I got one step closer. I passed the Stress Interview. I sat on a stool in a dark room with a spotlight glaring in my eyes. Three or four men screamed questions at me in German. Someone threw water in my face. Down the hallway, I heard a woman shrieking as if she was in agony.

I passed. Easily. The Stress Interview was so close to my nightmares that I'd already lived through it a dozen times. "You've failed this test," one of them taunted me at the end, his voice full of contempt. I sat still. I knew that had to be part of the test too. And I was right. The next day, they sent me to OSS Training School.

The training school they sent me to was a compound of drab cinder-block buildings in West Virginia, the sort of place that probably once housed exploited coal miners, or reform school girls. The whole area was bleak. The ground was mostly gray gravel, and even the small patches of grass looked scraggly and unhealthy. There were no trees, and by afternoon you felt weak. There was no Indian summer here; just dusty heat and a glare that made your eyes burn.

Everything was dry and half dead, except for inside the cinder-block buildings. Even after the hottest days, they were so damp at night that when I woke up from the few hours' sleep I managed to get, my knees and neck and shoulders would ache, like a stiff old arthritic lady's.

I hadn't planned on being the kind of spy who crawls around with a grenade between her teeth. I didn't need this place. But go tell that to the OSS. Whether your cover was going to be third kitchen assistant, grinding out spaghetti for Mussolini's mistress, or a dockworker in Le Havre, you had to take the Course.

They put me into a class in close combat and gutter fighting—a subject I'd never anticipated studying in my days at Grover Cleveland High School. The instructor was a huge Marine with a head shaped like a canned ham. I thought he'd hate me, because when it came to giving a knee in the groin or a sideswipe to the Adam's apple, I was his least able and least enthusiastic pupil. But at the end he took me aside and said, "Honey, you stink. So listen good. If you're ever in a hand-to-hand situation, you got one choice. Stick your thumb in the guy's eye. If you can't get your thumb, use another finger. Go *squoosh*." The best that could be said for the class was that it was the last physical effort I had to make.

If you couldn't crunch the skulls of four Gestapo guys with your bare hands, at least they expected you to be able to shoot them. "This veapon is the Walther P-38. It is the standard *Wehrmacht* pistol, *und* it replaced the Luger in 1938." From his posture to the way he clipped off his native Bavarian accent, it was clear that our gun teacher (although we weren't allowed to call the thing a gun) had spent most of his life in the German military. Four of us—me, an Italian guy from New York, and two college types with eyeglasses—

stood on the firing range, holding our guns—pistols—while the teacher said, "You vill note the signal pin in the rear of the slide, vich vill enable you to both see *und* feel that there is a cartridge in the chamber." He was all business. He didn't even bother with the usual false name: no "Call me Hans." And when I asked him a question about the safety catch in German, he gave me a dirty look, almost a hate-filled look, and answered me in English. When he taught us to dismantle the P-38, put it back together, and repair it by utilizing parts from other disabled weapons, there was no encouragement, no criticism, no nothing. Just *Ja* or No.

That was the worst of the Training School. There was no camaraderie, no sense that you were working together with people for a cause, no high-spirited feeling of We're gonna beat these bastards. No one had a name, not even a cover identity. It was a finger pointed, and someone said, "You."

"You," they'd say, and shove the camera into your hand as they were teaching you to photograph secret documents. "You," they'd bark, "who do you want to blow up—yourself or the Krauts?" when they taught us to handle explosives. I tried to explain to a man in a shirt and tie who seemed to be the administrator that no one had any plans for me to be blowing up bridges or derailing trains, that it was too funny to even think about; he just turned around and walked away.

What I hated about the place was that it was so un-American. Every once in a while at Assessment School there'd been a friendly "Come on, stop complaining. We've all been through it" from the OSS men, or at least a couple of minutes of kidding around with the other recruits. But West Virginia was cold and hard and dead; it felt like Germany. Some nights, especially at the beginning, when I was all black and blue and upset—shaken up—from the close-combat class, I tried to cheer myself by saying, Maybe they're really smart to make this place such a lousy, miserable hole. It'll get rid of the rah-rah types, the ones who see war as a giant Coney Island, with shooting ranges and rockets and parachute jumps as part of the fun.

But other nights . . . like after the Scare House, where I'd been sent up a dark flight of stairs with my pistol and heard footsteps behind me, and threatening German voices off so low I couldn't make out where they were or what they were saying, and then all of a sudden out popped a thing—a scarecrow in an SS uniform—and I had to turn fast and fire, and then, seconds later, at a door at the top of the stairs, I heard loud, guttural voices, and I had to reload, release the safety catch, kick open the door, then fire again . . . those nights I wondered what good all this was doing me. If I had to depend on my ability to reassemble a Walther P-38 or derail a train, I wasn't going to get out of Berlin alive. I was so cold and so scared and, I guess worst of all, so lonely in this school with no names that I started to think: What am I doing here? Am I crazy? All the brilliant and devious plans I'd made for Berlin, all the clever reasons I'd found for them to send me in, didn't make much sense after a day spent learning where to hide steel wool in a truck's engine.

But the wheel I'd put myself on was spinning too fast for me to stop it, and all I could do was hang on desperately to one of the spokes.

After Training School was over, they drove me up to Baltimore. And as we passed Washington, I thought: This is crazy. I'm just going to tell them, "Stop the car! Let me out!" I laughed to myself. But by that time we were almost out of Washington, and I realized that my silent laugh hadn't been high-spirited; it had been hysterical.

In Baltimore, I spent a week living with an old couple in the second floor of a white-stooped brownstone in a slum. They called me Lina and I was told to call them Mr. and Mrs. Pohl, which was pretty much like calling them Mr. and Mrs. Smith. The Pohls' only purpose was to drown me, smother me and choke me with *berlinerisch*. For fourteen to sixteen hours a day, the old bald man or his scrawny, washed-out wife carried on endless conversations with me and corrected my accent.

In the *berlinerisch* dialect, *g* is pronounced like the English *y* (or the German *j*), so that *ganz gut*, the phrase for "okay," sounds like *yanz yoot*. I managed "okay" okay, but after all those years of working for and living with John, sometimes I would slip and say something terrible like *gestern ist er gekommen*, "he came yesterday," using the correct (but forbidden) hard *g*'s. Or I'd use the High German *Ich*, with its guttural sound, instead of the *berlinerisch Ik*, for the word "I." Whenever I made a mistake, the old woman would put her hand to her forehead and make a grunting sound, as if my terribleness had given her a migraine attack. Mr. Pohl would just exhale and tell me to do it again.

I kept waiting for the good old Berlin sense of humor to break out of these two old people, but either they'd never had it or whatever drove them out of Germany had killed forever their ability to laugh. So for seven endless days I sat at the oilcloth-covered kitchen table in their ugly apartment, learning to speak *berlinerisch*, not as I had from my Grandma Olga, with a comfortable 1880s ease, but with a 1940s lower-class seriousness. I did learn some happy Berlin expressions: *dufte* for "nice" or "great"; *klamauk*, a word for loud fun or a juicy scandal. But they were drilled into me the way an unfeeling dentist would drill a tooth: without letup or a smile, and with no diverting chitchat.

Mrs. Pohl had apparently cooked the day before I arrived. It was a big stew, and we ate the grayish, stringy meat at one o'clock every single afternoon. At night, there would be cheese and some pickled cucumbers, and twice, an apple for dessert. And they would never let up: Is the meat good? Obviously, they weren't interested in the truth. What they wanted was a complete sentence, so I'd say, Yes, I am really enjoying the stew. How do you make it? Does it have a lot of onions? What seasonings do you use?

Neither of them ever smiled at me, and I couldn't figure out whether they were just two miserable people or whether the OSS, in one of its typical budget-cutting sprees, had gypped them out of half the money it had originally promised, and they were taking it out on me.

Then at last another car, a Packard, like the one Edward used, pulled up in front of the house. It drove me not back to

Washington, as I'd expected, hoped, but to a military airport outside Baltimore.

The driver said, "Inside those doors. Ladies' room on the second floor." When I went in, a woman with a Scandinavian accent was waiting for me; she was very tall, with brown hair down to her shoulders and long, thin arms dangling from her sleeveless dress.

She said, "Go into the stall and give me all your clothes, please," and handed me new ones over the top of the door. Old ones, actually, probably straight off the backs of German refugees: a German brassiere, which was about as graceful as a sling, German cotton stockings, German shoes that made my army boots look stylish, and a German dress. When I came out, she handed me a German valise, which contained a few more items like the ones I was now wearing. "Well," she said. "Good luck." Oh, God, I thought, I should get to a phone and make some calls. I'm leaving from *here*. I have to say goodbye.

But I just asked, "Where am I going?"

"To New York."

"And from there?" I figured the best I'd get from her was something like: I don't know, or: I'm not supposed to talk about that.

But she put her mouth to my ear and said, "Troop ship. England."

"And then?" I whispered.

"And then, to the place where you belong."

# 21

"$\mathbf{S}$ay as little as possible," Konrad Friedrichs muttered. We walked out of the small white building onto a runway in the Lisbon airport, toward the biggest plane I'd ever seen. "Your accent is not what it should be."

"Do I sound American?" I asked. I had to hustle to keep up with him. He was tall, over six feet, and took long, determined strides. Although he must have been at least sixty, he held himself as if someone had just yelled: *Achtung!*

"No. You sound odd, as if you had a rare type of speech impediment." I was about to chuckle, when I realized nothing Herr Friedrichs said was intended to be humorous. "That is why you have been sent in as a menial. If there are any questions about your pronunciation, people will assume you are slow-witted."

It's a measure of how dazed I was that I had even considered the possibility of chuckling. I'd been across the ocean on a troop ship where I had to lock myself in a tiny stateroom and have my meals left on trays outside my door so no one could see me. After that came three days in a metal hut with the rain beating down on it at an Army Air Forces base in England, where the head OSS guy, who looked like Al Capone, tried to convince me that no one they'd sent over had ever refused to go to parachute school and that, don't worry, when the time came no one would force me to jump if I didn't want to. I said no. I remembered Edward being angry once about the number of agents killed making blind jumps into enemy territory. It wasn't so much that they were

334

getting shot; it was that the partisans couldn't get their lights to where they were supposed to be half the time, so the OSS agents wound up impaled on trees, or drowned, or just plain pulverized.

After three days of being screamed at for being a coward, they sent me to a rooming house outside London, where I studied maps and memorized a safe address where I could go only in a life-or-death situation, although they admitted—after I asked them—that the Gestapo's track record being what it was, "safe" was maybe a slight exaggeration. Then I learned my peril code. If I was captured and forced to send a message, I was to use the word "simply" in it. Like if there was a noose around my neck and a gun in my mouth, I should write: Don't worry. I'm simply fine, or: The weather is simply lovely. Not that they would come and save me; they'd just know not to believe anything in the message.

They changed my name to Lina Albrecht. They told me I had to wear my hair in braids and pin them up; it was apparently the last word in Aryan elegance. They gave me my false identity papers and flew me from the air force base to beautiful, balmy, neutral Lisbon.

"What if someone asks me a direct question?" I asked Konrad as we hurried toward the plane. "Should I talk?"

"Obviously."

"But this is not the time for idle chatter," I observed. To put it mildly. About twenty feet ahead of us was the giant German plane, a Messerschmitt with six propellers—complete with an Iron Cross insignia on its side and a swastika on its tail. And talk about *Achtung*: a *Luftwaffe* officer, probably the pilot, whose posture made Herr Friedrichs look like a sloucher, stood at the bottom of the stairs, waiting for us.

There was a reason for this courtesy; Konrad Friedrichs was no slouch. He'd been working in the German foreign office since 1907, and was their ranking expert on Spain and Portugal. He was also a fervent anti-Nazi and Norman Weekes's most highly placed spy. Until he sat beside me in the waiting room in the airport, all I'd known was that code name Rex—Norman's famous Rex—would find me. In a voice just loud enough for the people nearest us to hear, he said, My dear Lina. I am pleased you have decided to return with me. Then he put his head close to mine and said, Konrad Friedrichs. Foreign office. You know you are coming back to Berlin as my cook? I nodded. Smile at me, he ordered. I smiled. He went on: It is possible that people will assume you are also my mistress. Do nothing to discourage this supposition.

We were almost at the plane. "Keep your eyes down," he whispered; they were. "No friendly glances. No hellos. You are a servant."

The pilot clicked his heels together and gave the stiff *Heil Hitler* salute as we reached the plane. A terrible chill went up my back. I'd seen that gesture so often in newsreels that it seemed like part of a movie: something unreal, accompanied by popcorn. But now it was happening. Herr Friedrichs saluted back and, I sensed, held his breath for a moment. But I had been trained. The salute was not meant for me. Like an obedient German, I did precisely what was expected of me: held back, let my employer precede me up the stairs and followed, head down, suitcase in hand.

And then we were in the air, flying over Portugal, Spain and France, on our way to Germany.

Konrad Friedrichs's house was pretty much what you'd expect of a high German official who'd been working in Berlin for thirty-five years and never married. But it took me two days to realize that. For the first forty-eight hours, I baked a cake, prepared his two favorite dinners, veal cutlets, *Naturschnitzel,* one night and codfish—the world's most disgusting food—the next. Somehow I managed to act in such a way that neither Herr Friedrichs nor his housekeeper noticed I was hysterical. But I was. As I grated a potato, I heard bombs dropping no more than a few miles away. All I wanted to do was crouch in a corner and cover my head with my arms and scream. Scream. Instead, I grated.

The house was a modest one of brick in the Wilmersdorf area, about ten minutes from the foreign office. It wasn't modest in an I'm-just-a-civil-servant way. It was on a pretty tree-shaded street with a lot of other small, well-kept houses. In a time of shortages and austerity—of wooden and cloth shoes instead of leather, when the bakers sold only day-old bread, to discourage demand for anything fresh and appealing—all the houses here had window boxes freshly planted with orange fall flowers. It was pretty obvious that this was a neighborhood for the privileged. Privileged but not prime; Goebbels didn't live around the corner.

My room was in the basement. To say it was small makes it sound wildly luxurious. The furnishings were a cotton rug (which back in Ridgewood would have been called a substandard bath mat) and a bed—a mattress on a wood frame. There was a strip of window, painted black, just under the low ceiling. It didn't open. It was a very poor room, but my room at home had been poor. Still, at least there'd been a lace doily on my night table, and a calendar with a picture of a girl with long hair on a windswept moor. This room, though, was so empty it was mean, as if someone had deliberately stripped it. The first night, I'd gone out of the room to see if maybe there was a chest of drawers outside that I'd missed, but all I found was the coal chute, when I banged my head on it.

If I'd gone out ten minutes later, I would have banged my head on Konrad Friedrichs. It must have been right around midnight. All of a sudden, the door to my room opened and there he was, in pajamas, slippers and a bathrobe. No one had even suggested that this would be part of the job.

In fact, it wasn't. I saw that right away, when I watched him reddening at my expression. He closed the door behind him. "This means nothing," he said. His voice was lower than a whisper; it was more like a whoosh of air. "My housekeeper is old, deaf, but I must maintain a fiction—in case. Therefore, to knock on your door would be inappropriate."

"I'm a domestic, so you can just walk right in?" I couldn't believe this guy.

"I am not interested in your egalitarian sensibilities. Now, shall we get on with it?"

I motioned for him to sit near the foot of the bed. I sat near the head, or what I'd decided was the head; there was no pillow. "Where does your housekeeper sleep?" I asked.

"On the other side of the furnace, the far side of the basement."

"She has no idea . . . what I am?"

"No!"

"Does anybody—"

"Please, you are not to interrupt. I will tell you all you need to know. If inadvertently I leave something out, you may ask a question before I leave." He blew what I guess was a speck of dust off the lapel of his bathrobe. "As you may know, I have permitted you to stay in my house only because Herr Forest"—Forest was Norman Weekes's code name—"put undue pressure on me." His thin lips drew so tight together that they became invisible; only the deep, resentful vertical lines that were etched into his upper lip remained. "A man in my position is entitled to better treatment. I am idealist *and* a good German. For years I have passed information to Herr Forest in the hope that his . . . your people would wake up to the danger. I have risked my life in doing so, and what does he do in return? He gives me you to take care of, someone so unschooled that she is not fit to enter a house through the front door. You, who are to replace a clever, sophisticated, native-born German."

"I was their only choice."

"That is painfully clear. And so what can happen? They send in an amateur, she gets caught, and I—who for years have been above suspicion—am suspect. It is wrong!"

What was I going to do? Argue with him? "You're right. It is wrong. Terrible. Outrageous."

He only seethed on. "The situation—seeing that you are placed in a certain official's household—compels me to associate with . . . with resistance types I would much prefer to shun entirely. Do I make myself clear?"

"Yes," I said. "You only pass information to Herr Forest. What goes on among . . . these people in Berlin is of no interest to you."

"That is correct. They plot over caviar. They care nothing about the Fatherland, only about their own circumstances. The degree to which they believe that that man will bring us to utter ruin is the degree to which they oppose him."

His bearing never relaxed, not even when he sat on that terrible mattress, with what had to be a spring poking his behind. Back home, I thought, only a person with a chest full of medals, a mahogany desk at the War Department and an office full of visitors would sit like that. I remembered walking through the War Department with Edward one day and glancing into an open office, with just that kind of officer: upright, his left side just slightly lower than his right from the weight of his medals. A real stiff, right? The guy suddenly noticed me and blew me a kiss. I'd kept going, and Edward had asked, What are you smiling about? Oh, nothing, I'd answered.

But then I caught myself. Forget back home. In Training School, they warned us: Think only of the present. The future, when it is of immediate concern. Never the past: The past will devastate you. And when you think, think in the language of the country you have been sent to. Speaking it is not enough. To survive, you must *be* Czech or French or Hungarian. Or German.

I sat there in that impoverished little room trying to be fair, to admire Konrad Friedrichs, not detest him. If someone spends his whole life agonizing about the fate of his fatherland instead of what movie to see over the weekend or if he'll ever fall in love or grow bald or get to visit Florida, he's not going to develop a rollicking sense of humor.

And he had to be frightened, doing what he was doing—living in this Nazi hell he hated, spying for the United States—all those years. And he had to be bitter too; I'd

clearly been shoved down his throat. Instead of being treated
as a treasure by Norman Weekes, Rex was being exploited.
The OSS was treating him the way they would routinely
treat some two-bit adventurer in an ascot who hangs around
the resistance for thrills, not like the paragon of virtues—
honor, bravery—that he was.

"You will continue to work in my kitchen as you have
been working for the next four days. On that day, Saturday, I
will suggest to my housekeeper that she deserves a vacation.
I will give what, to her, is a great deal of money and a train
ticket so that she can visit her family in Würzburg for three
or four weeks. She will think to herself that I am a foolish
old man to take up with someone like you, but of course, she
will not say anything. She will go."

The section of the mattress I was sitting on was incredibly
lumpy. I edged back and tucked one of my legs under me.
Herr Friedrichs's nostrils flared wide and then closed, and
you didn't have to be his best friend to figure out this was a
sign of intense displeasure.

"You will please," he ordered, "sit like a proper German
and not move about out of control as if . . . you are listening
to jazz music. Now, once my housekeeper is gone, your
training will begin. You are, as they claimed, a good
cook . . . for those with a taste for the cuisine of common
people. But where you are going . . . you must be taught to
cook and serve in a more elegant manner."

His house wasn't exactly the sort of place where you'd
find footmen slinging caviar at guests in white tie and tails.
But if Rex wanted elegance . . . I smiled and said, "I'll be
happy to try and learn whatever you like. I realize I'm not a
professional cook and—"

"Do not interrupt! In three to four weeks you must learn
to be an accomplished chef. That was the best cover they
could find, because it suits Herr Forest's purpose perfectly.
The plan is to get you into my colleague's household." Rex's
mouth turned down in disgust at the thought of the kind of
person who had risen to become his colleague in the foreign
office. "You are to be *in* the household but not *of* it. You

know our language, but you do not know our ways. So it is best that you be hidden away in the kitchen.

"Now, this colleague is a peacock who fancies himself a man of the world, a gourmet. His chef will have an accident in the next week or two." He saw I was going to interrupt again, and he cut me off. "I am assured it will not be a fatal—or even terribly serious—accident. Two weeks after that, a very respected person will mention what a glorious meal was served at my house and offer to help this official secure your services."

"What if the chef wants his job back after the accident?"

"Be assured we have considered that possibility. While he is recuperating, he will be offered another position, at a far greater salary."

"What's the name of the official I'll be working for?" I knew, naturally. Norman Weekes had given me his name. But I wanted to see how far Herr Friedrichs, Rex, would trust a fellow spy.

"Quiet!" Not very far. "You will know what you need to know at the proper time. It serves no purpose for you to possess this information now. So I will continue, and you will stop asking questions. This official for whom you will work has been chosen because he is known to bring papers—top-secret papers—from his office to his home to work on."

"I know. They told me—"

"Silence! This practice of his is, of course, forbidden. But those who know of his habit are in no position to suggest that he stop it.

"As far as I am concerned, there is only one redeeming aspect to this . . . this sanctuary *cum* cooking school I have been forced to run. The person they have chosen to teach you the fine points is someone I know, someone from the Abwehr. This individual comes from one of the oldest and finest families in Germany, and is the only member of the resistance . . . whom I consider a true patriot."

He stood up very slowly. At first I thought it was his age, but then I realized he was being careful that the bed didn't creak. "This individual will be risking everything to help you and your countrymen." His nostrils flared again, and you could see more than his anger as he spoke of Americans; you could see his contempt. "Your imprudent, arrogant 'freedom-lovers.'" He put his hand on the door handle. "Now listen to me! You must not compromise this individual. You are to keep quiet about your background, your destination, your mission. You must do nothing—*nothing*—to endanger . . ." He paused, took a deep breath and regained his composure. "You will be taught what is elegant, what is correct, by one who is . . . flawless. Be silent. Be obedient. And be grateful!"

The past will devastate you, they'd said. So what was I supposed to think about, those first few nights in that cell in Herr Friedrichs's basement? The graciousness of my host? The warmth of his housekeeper? When I heard him say "my housekeeper," I pictured a lovable, pudgy old family retainer with a white apron, someone who'd have tea with me before she went off on her vacation and tell me where she kept the towels. Or someone with a quiet smile, who would nod, listening to you, as she peeled an apple in one long strip—like my Grandma Olga.

But Frau Gerlach could have posed for the witch in *Hansel and Gretel*; she had claw hands, and the bottom of her face looked more like an elbow than a chin. She had so many warts that you couldn't help counting them. Her personality matched her looks. She hissed *"Hure"*—whore—at me a couple of times and wouldn't eat anything I cooked. She kept a crock of cheese in the refrigerator, and when she came in to eat, she shooed me out with insane waves of her hands, as if she was getting rid of a rodent.

When I turned out the lamp, my room with its painted window—cheaper than a blackout curtain—fell into complete darkness. But even if I'd wanted to, I couldn't have slept. Airplanes droned above the house, and my stomach squeezed into a hard knot. Then came the muffled blast of distant bombing and, closer, the demented siren of police cars. And, because my window was level with the street, the sound of feet. The second night, somebody stopped right outside, and I lay in the blackness in absolute panic, saying to myself, They're just lighting a cigarette or they have a pebble in their shoe or . . . I can't stand this. I can't take another second.

So I thought about America—and I thought about it in English. Like a sick baby who gets a warm bottle, I wasn't helped, but I was comforted. I thought about growing up in Ridgewood, where the Irish kids used to call the German kids "Heinies" and make fun of German last names: "Nudelfludel!" They'd howl with laughter. "Von Stupelpoop!" And we'd feel so superior that we never even called them dumb micks. Sure, it was prejudice, but from where I sat (lay) it seemed innocent. You got it out of your system, and sooner or later you got over the fear, the strangeness; the Irish and the German kids grew up and joined the same building-trades union, sometimes became friends or even got married.

I came up with all sorts of pictures I didn't even know I had filed away: How a horse-drawn truck came rattling up Fresh Pond Road in the summer with watermelons. Getting off the subway at Seneca Avenue after work on December nights, looking down from the el platform and seeing everybody's Christmas lights. Going to my graduation from Grover Cleveland, walking slow because my mother was wearing four-inch heels, and how Olga stopped three or four times to adjust my cap and the tassel. "A scholar!" she said to my father, and the funny thing was, even though I said, "Grandma, it's just high school," I knew she really meant it.

Naturally, I thought about John. I played "If it's 3 A.M. in Berlin, what time is it in Washington?" It didn't matter, because whatever hour it was, in my mind he was always with Nan. I envisioned him at his desk, on the phone with her, or at the house, listening to music with her in his arms, the way I'd found them, or up in the bedroom; she'd run her finger over her old monogram on the pillowcases and the top hem of the sheet, then run her finger over his lips and say, Oh John, being with you like this is so wholly, unequivocally right. And he'd probably do something like kiss her hand and quote some poem they both knew in French. And she'd say, *Mais oui, mon amour*. But then she'd hesitate: We're in limbo, my darling. I hope you realize that. I can't believe . . . She just disappeared?

In a manner of speaking, he'd say.

Do you know where she is?

I can't . . .

Oh, I know you can't tell me. You're right not to. But how long do we have to live like this, sneaking, pretending? Oh, John, this *has* to be resolved. When will she come back?

And he'd say, I don't know, my beloved. Maybe six months from now. Maybe never.

That Saturday, Frau Gerlach, warts and all, left for Würzburg. An hour later, my teacher, the individual from one of Germany's oldest and finest families, walked into the kitchen carrying a mesh shopping bag filled with groceries. She wore a burgundy skirt and a cashmere sweater set that was such a pale pink it was almost white. She held out her hand and said, "Margarete von Eberstein." I'd been up to my elbows in herring, so I quickly wiped my right hand on my apron, held it out and explained, "Herring." It was only when she started to laugh that I added, "Lina Albrecht."

She pulled off her cardigan, tossed it onto a chair, pushed up the sleeves of her pullover and demanded, "How is old Konrad treating you?" Margarete possessed two qualities that I hadn't seen in any of the hundreds of Germans I'd met in the past two years: vitality and humor. She wasn't beautiful, or even pretty. And despite the "von," her bones were no more aristocratic than mine were. But she had dazzling blue-gray eyes and a wonderful smile. "Is he as condescending as ever?"

"Pretty much," I admitted.

"I know he is a . . . special friend of yours, perhaps, so forgive me, but he is such a dreadful snob. He adores me without qualification. It's so tedious." Margarete's energy was a little overwhelming. As she spoke, she whirled around the kitchen, grabbing a crock of vinegar from the shelf, a paring knife from a drawer. She plunged her hand into the sack of flour, rubbed a bit of it between her fingers and made a face at the texture. "Nothing has been good since those bastards came in—in '33."

"Don't you think you should be a little more careful?"

"Why? Will you turn me in?" Before I could answer, she said, "Lina, if you and I and our friends are going to succeed, we must be very, very careful. But there are occasional moments when there is nothing to fear, and we must take advantage of them, *glory* in them, because they allow us the chance to be what we truly are: human beings." She took an apple from a basket, quickly cored it, sliced it, and gave me half. "Now let's talk about German cuisine. Meat and potatoes. All over Europe they think of it as banal. Leaden. Greasy. Olive oil for the Italians, peanut oil for the French, butter for the English, and for the Germans—bacon grease."

"Don't forget lard."

"No, we mustn't forget lard. Lovely, light, delicious lard. But what I want to show you is fine German cooking, the sort you must be doing to please the person for whom you will be working." I wanted to say something, but I was chewing a piece of apple. Margarete held up her hand. "No names," she warned, but then she flashed her fabulous smile. "No descriptions, either. Don't tell me, 'The man I'm working for is a bald dwarf who lunches with Rommel's wife every other Thursday.' The less we know about each other's . . . activities, the safer we will be." She reached into her shopping bag and pulled out a large package wrapped in white butcher paper. "Today, we are going to roast veal and prepare sauerkraut—but sauerkraut in champagne sauce." She pulled out a small bottle. I glanced at it: French champagne.

"Aren't you a little nervous about walking down the street with champagne and half a calf?" I asked. "The penalties for dealing in black market goods—"

"Lina," she said, unwrapping the meat, "I am a trusted employee of the Abwehr. My father's family has been eating fine veal since before the Hundred Years' War. And my

mother, who is very beautiful and very charming, was a
great actress. She's retired now, but in the late twenties and
thirties she was a favorite of our Führer, and his affection for
her has never diminished. Should I feel afraid?"

"No," I answered her. "I guess you should feel pretty
good."

Margarete turned to me. Her hand came out of the shopping bag, and she was holding a bunch of parsley as if it was
a delicate bouquet. "I will feel very good," she said quietly,
"when every single goddamned Nazi is dead."

All the men on the streets of Berlin were in uniform.
Those few who weren't were either doomed or people to be
afraid of; you knew instinctively to avoid both. The women
were more like me, in dreary coats of *Zellwolle*, a fake material that from a distance looked like wool but up close
looked like a scouring pad. It did nothing to keep you warm.

Now and then, one of the wives or mistresses of men in
power would glide by, wrapped in a cloud of French perfume and yards of fur; the invasions of France and Scandinavia had done wonders for the women of the powerful. In
London I'd heard that Goebbels was trying to get them to
play down their privilege; he'd even put an end to their
morning horseback rides in the Tiergarten, the park in the
center of Berlin. He didn't want the masses to be resentful.
Ha. One look at Margarete's cashmere sweater collection
and her fox coat and her gold earrings in those days of standing on line for an hour and a half just to buy a turnip should
have caused a riot of resentment. But either the Nazis'
women were the German equivalent of movie stars—they
lived sumptuous lives on everybody's behalf—or people
were too terrified to show their resentment.

I was perpetually terrified, but who—even the most innocent—would not be? The second time I left Herr
Friedrichs's house, I'd seen three Gestapo men beating up a
middle-aged man outside a bakery. The man's head was in
the gutter, his body on the sidewalk; one of them stamped
his boot down, again and again, on the man's stomach, and

his head jerked with every blow. The other two just said, "Move along," to the people on the street, mechanically, because not a single person stopped or even slowed down. Maybe no one was innocent.

I'd finally gone outside, seven days after I arrived in Berlin. All my papers were in order—my passport, my workbook and my ration card. The OSS may have sent men parachuting in the dark and going splat onto concrete highways, but everyone said they were great with documents. I hoped so. Herr Friedrichs had looked at all three of them, as well as the card I didn't have to carry, my *Ahnenpass*, my ancestry passport, which proved Lina Albrecht's Aryan descent. All he said was, Adequate. They had to be more than adequate, because there could be an identity check anywhere, anytime. It was all up to the discretion—and the mood—of the Gestapo.

The picture on my passport had been taken in England. It showed me in three-quarters profile, so if you looked close, you could really get a good idea of how stupid-looking the braids were and how washed out I looked without any makeup. Or maybe I'd just gone pale that day because right before they took the photograph, they put my right and left index fingerprints on the card. I remember I'd gotten that numb feeling again when I saw the partially filled out passport and pictured that if it had been made out to Linda Voss instead of Lina Albrecht, there would be a giant "J" stamped on the left side.

But dead Jews don't need identity cards. One of the OSS men in the boarding house in London had mentioned, quite casually, that there were still about forty thousand Jews in Berlin, but then he'd added, No. Wait a second. Probably a lot less by now. They're in the middle of another roundup. More deportations and the usual deaths. I'd asked, What do you mean by, usual? And he'd answered, Suicides. The ones from Eastern Europe don't know what's going to happen to them. The ones in Berlin are starting to understand.

I had to go to the fish store that first day. And even though I traced and retraced the seven blocks on the map and in my

mind, the walk never seemed to end. Good German that
Lina was, she kept her eyes down and minded her own business, but I worried that something in my stride, something in
the way I carried my pocketbook, something in the way I
looked at a traffic signal, would give away that I was an
American.

My heart pounded so hard I could hear it inside my ears. I
was going to meet my contact. Once I became a chef, I'd be
giving all my information to the fish man. Now I was just
going to introduce myself, to say, "Good morning. I hope
the walleyed pike is not as bony as it was last Thursday."

I tried to ease the banging of my heart by telling myself
that the OSS had chosen a reliable and cautious member of
the resistance for me to report to, and the chances of a
Gestapo agent hiding under the halibut were small. But as I
waited to cross the street, I froze. I knew that whether I
waited one second or twenty minutes, I could not take
another step forward, and that inevitably, shamefully, I'd
lose control and go running back to Rex's—giving away my
hysteria, my foreignness, my guilt just by the mere fact of
running.

But then Edward Leland stopped me. I stood there on
that corner and said to myself, Edward has gone to ground
in Denmark and in Poland and in Czechoslovakia and in
Rumania, and he can't even speak the language. Does his
heart ever beat like this? Does he ever want to turn and
run?

And then I realized how well I'd gotten to know the man
I'd worked for, because suddenly I understood that yes,
something in him probably wanted to run back to whatever
seaport he'd entered in Poland, screaming his head off. I
crossed the street and asked myself, Why didn't he run?
What made him keep going?

I couldn't figure out the answer, but it was as if Edward
was standing next to me. I could hear his voice, deep, sure,
soothing: Do it *now*, I could suddenly hear him say. Think
about it later.

So I just wrapped my ugly brown *Zellwolle* coat tighter around me and walked fast, so Rolf Vogel, fishmonger, would not run out of walleyed pike before I got to the store.

# 22

"There's an old *berlinersch* expression," I said. " *'Eine jute jebratene Jans is eine jute Jabe Jottes.'* " That was one of the nine hundred forty-two sayings that the Pohls, the awful old couple in Baltimore, had taught me.

Margarete von Eberstein, the sleeves of her red silk blouse rolled up, was showing me how to stuff the neck of a goose with a forcemeat of ground liver, pork and herbs. " 'A good roast goose is a good gift of God,' " she repeated, smiling, as she tried out my accent. She put the neck into my hands and remarked, "Here. The good gift of God needs more stuffing."

By the end of my third week in Berlin, Margarete had come to the house at least ten different times, both on weekends and after work at the Abwehr, where she was a translator. I almost laughed when she told me that: She could get along all right in French and Italian, she explained, but her specialty was English. Here we were, becoming friends, and I had to fight all my instincts and suppress the urge to turn to her and say—in English: Squishing all this slimy stuff into a goose neck is one of the most disgusting things I've ever had to do!

After all the hours I'd spent with Margarete, I could predict her reaction. Her mouth would drop and she'd stare at me, and then all of a sudden she'd burst into laughter. Not that ho-ho-ho, typical overjolly German guffaw, but the sort of laugh that's described in books as musical.

The odds on our ever becoming friends were about as

great as my becoming great buddies with one of Nan's Smith College socialites: nil, or pretty close to it. But just as politics makes strange bedfellows, war makes peculiar friendships. We were thrown together by a single common denominator: We both hated Nazism. Of course, so did Herr Friedrichs, and that certainly didn't make him my pal. But Margarete and I discovered that we had a lot in common. Not that I shared her love of literature or her passion for cooking; how much did I have to say to a woman who got all flushed with pleasure at the mention of wild mushrooms? And if she'd known about it, she definitely wouldn't have shared my appreciation or obsession or whatever it was with the movies; I'd have been willing to bet that if someone had shown her a picture of Cary Grant, she would have had absolutely no idea who he was.

But what we did share, I guess, was a hatred of grimness. Right from that first Saturday afternoon, we'd sensed a quality in each other; fun.

What bothered me was that the more fun we had together, the less fun—if you can call it that—I was having perpetuating all the lies of my cover story. She believed I was Lina Albrecht, who was twenty-eight years old and the daughter of a Berlin butcher and a housewife (both dead), who had married a man twenty-two years older, a man who worked as majordomo in the household of an Austrian playboy who lived in Portugal, and that my husband had died of a kidney disease eighteen months before.

I'd hinted that the playboy had allowed me to stay on in his house, as his cook. Margarete got the impression (and getting this impression across was as much a part of my cover story as the part I actually spoke about) that the playboy had kept me around for more than my *Eintopf*. And she got the impression that just as the playboy was tiring of me, along came his cousin, Konrad Friedrichs, who saw in me not only what his cousin did, but also a truly new face . . . and someone he could use for his own political purposes.

Margarete trussed the goose once, and then had me do it.

It took me six tries, and in comparison to hers, my results looked pathetic. "What a mess!" I said.

"Lina . . ." she began.

"What?"

"What do you think of people who intrude upon the most private part of your life?" Margarete asked.

I lifted the goose and put it into the roaster. "What do you want to know?" I responded.

"Are you in love with Konrad?"

"No."

"Good."

"Why is it good? Because elderly foreign office officials don't marry young—well, sort of young—household employees?"

"That's part of the reason," she said. "But also . . . I would feel better if I knew that what you are doing . . . you are doing out of deep conviction. Because if you do it out of love, Lina, if you go wherever you are going to please a man, then you surely won't survive. It takes a hard edge. I think—no, I *know* I have it. I don't know if you do. You seem so sweet, so vulnerable. Losing your husband . . ."

As Margarete spoke, I immediately thought of John, but I forced that picture out of my mind and replaced it with the make-believe Johannes Albrecht. Outside London, at the rooming house, the OSS people had shown me photographs of a man in his early fifties, heavyset, with a hard, bulldog face, and said, This is your late husband. You can't do better? I'd demanded. Come on, they'd said, and kept me up till three one morning telling them details about my "marriage." I told them everything, how "Johannes" liked his socks folded, not rolled, and how different he had become about sex after the first year of our nine-year marriage.

"Do you miss your husband?" she asked.

"No." I smiled a little and added, "Sorry."

"Was he bad to you? Did he beat you?"

"Margarete, your view of reality is not exactly realistic. Ordinary, working-class husbands do not routinely get drunk and beat their wives."

"They obviously lack a sense of the grand gesture. I am disappointed."

"I'll disappoint you some more. Ordinary wives do not automatically have twenty children and commit suicide by drowning themselves in a vat of cabbage."

"I never thought that." She cocked her head to the side. "But it is a magnificent image. I almost wish it were true. Not so anyone would actually suffer. But it's so magnificently German: so prosaic, so stoic. Now tell me, why don't you miss him? Did you ever love him?"

"No. I was fond of him, in the beginning. But at that time in my life, I had no one else to be fond of. I was an only child, and my father had died when I was ten, and then, when I was seventeen, my mother died. And two months later there was Johannes, on his holiday, visiting his brother, who lived in our building. Now that I think about it, he was probably looking for a wife. I guess he was tired of . . . the sort of women he could meet in Lisbon."

"Prostitutes?"

"I suppose so."

"Did you like living in Lisbon?"

"No." I put the goose into the oven. Margarete had preheated it. "We lived in a villa by the sea. It sounds very romantic, but it was just isolated. And Johannes didn't let me go anyplace alone."

"Was he jealous?"

"No. There was too much work to be done. Polishing silver, dusting books, keeping inventory of linen. He didn't trust the local girls to do it, and now that he had a wife, he was free of those chores. I suppose he thought if I caught the morning bus to Lisbon and spent a lovely, interesting day, that I'd want to go the next day, and the next."

"Do you speak Portuguese?"

"No. The man whose house we lived in—"

"The Austrian?"

"Yes. He only wanted German spoken in the house. Why he was so insistent upon that when it had been his choice to move out of Austria and into Portugal, I'll never know."

"So you've never been in love, Lina?"

"Well . . ." I remembered the OSS photos of the mythical Austrian playboy. A face that could have been on the cover of a Propaganda Ministry leaflet on "The Greatness of the Aryan." Except for the jutting chin, the man in the picture had looked uncomfortably like John.

"Oh! You were in love with the Austrian!" Her eyes brightened.

"Margarete, my life isn't a fairy tale. I knew it wasn't . . . mutual. And I knew it would only be for a short time, and that there wouldn't be a happily ever after."

"Was it worth it?"

"I guess so. I mean, I'm not like you. I don't have many opportunities to meet wealthy, educated, exciting men."

"He was very exciting?"

I looked her straight in the eye. "Yes. Exciting where it mattered most."

"Oh, my!" Margarete breathed. She took the knives, spoons and plates we'd been using and took them over to the sink. Suddenly she wheeled around. "Everyone thinks I'm a woman of the world, but I've never had anything like that."

"You'll have it," I said.

"I don't know. I've walked around the garden, so to speak, many, many times. And all I've met is . . . many boring men. Boring where it mattered most."

"I don't think . . . excitement happens that often. It's chemistry. I really believe that. You can be fond of someone. Like at the beginning, I was awfully fond of Johannes. Good, steady old Johannes. But even if I'd loved him . . . when we were together, well, there just wasn't any chemistry."

"Did you love this playboy?"

"No. He . . . he didn't have a good character, and I think you have to admire a man to really love him. He was very rich, but he never worked a day in his life. He existed only to enjoy what he was born with."

"He sounds like my father."

"Oh, I didn't mean . . ."

"No," she said thoughtfully. "That's all right. My father

wasn't . . . isn't a playboy. He's quite faithful to my mother, although the reverse, I believe, is not the case. But he's a man who rides and hunts and enjoys the fruits of his wealth, his inherited wealth, and who—" She broke off.

"What?"

"My father will do anything and everything to preserve the status quo. In 1932, there was a group of noblemen, the DAG, who endorsed Hitler. My father was one of its leaders. Hitler is anti-Communist, he said, and the National Socialists stand for a Germany that we all stand for. What he meant was a Germany where the aristocracy will be treated like proper aristocrats."

"When did he become disillusioned?" I asked.

"He didn't. If Hitler doesn't turn on you, he can be a loyal and generous friend." Her face grew somber. "The Baron von Eberstein has prospered."

"What about your mother?"

"You must be joking, Lina. My mother is an actress. Hitler was her admirer. He thought her brilliant. Do you think she could find anything sinister or immoral in such a man—or in the movement he led? No. To the contrary. My mother finds Hitler, finds Nazism, 'brilliant' also."

"Then how did you come to where you are?"

"I suppose because my parents ignored me. So I was free to look at their lives, look at their choices, and then form my own opinions."

The baron, through luck and his ties to the Nazis, had managed to keep hold of his money and his land. There were moments, when Margarete described her father sauntering out of the woods after a morning's hunting, his black rifle slung over his shoulder, that he sounded like a handsome, romantic and exciting figure: a baron but, in his daughter's eyes, something of a prince. A remote prince, though, and a prince who brought a lot of brutal, loud-mouth peasants back to the castle with him.

Margarete's mother visited her husband's estate at Christmas, Easter and for a month in the summer, but she kept her own house in Berlin. She was one of the great actresses of her day, and she performed not only in German but in English and French as well. Goethe, Shakespeare, Molière. She could do them all. That she'd had a daughter was a fact she frequently forgot. Margarete said her mother came home the summer she was ten and kept calling her "Pretty girl," as if she'd forgotten her name. Margarete said, She could memorize all of *Faust* and *Antony and Cleopatra*, but she couldn't quite remember whether I was Margarete or Margot.

So Margarete retreated to the kitchen. When she spoke about her childhood, and about the warmth and patience of the family's chef and his wife, who assisted him, you could see—in her stories about getting lost while picking white asparagus or her early disasters in learning to eviscerate a hen—not only the girl who became the laughing, high-spirited Berlin sophisticate, but also the sad child who, despite her high and comfortable niche in society, had grown up feeling that there was no place she could really feel at home. Her father would be off hunting or decanting wine for Nazis, her mother would be off emoting, and even the kindly chef and his wife—the second their work was done—would rush off to their own two children.

Sometimes, she said, she'd stay in the kitchen after all the help—the menservants and the kitchenmaids—went to bed. I'd sleep there, she told me. It was the warmest place in the house. Warm not in degrees, but in . . . Do you understand? I said yes, I did.

"Lina, I have to tell you something." I glanced up from the *Preiselbeeren*, the German equivalent of cranberry sauce, I had just started. "I have a lover." I had barely begun to smile when she added, "I hate him."

"Who is he?"

She was wearing a long white wool skirt—real wool—and she rubbed her hands up and down the front of it, discoloring it with the residue of goose grease that had been on her hands. "No one knows." She sounded edgy.

I understood. "I won't ask, then."

"Except the people in the . . . movement. They know. When I mentioned this man's interest in me"—she was talking unnaturally fast—"they wanted me to . . . they encouraged it." Suddenly her blue-gray eyes turned a shadow color and filled with tears. "He is a colonel. On Hitler's personal staff."

"I see," I said.

"No you don't. He is fifty-four years old and he is fat as"—she lifted her head and looked at the oven—"an overstuffed goose. With fat little fingers and fat thighs and breasts—like a sagging woman." She came back to the table, lowered herself into a chair and wiped her eyes with a kitchen towel. "Oh, God, I hate it."

"Then don't do it, Margarete."

"I have to."

"No. There's a limit. Tell them you can't."

She made herself smile and lifted her chin. High. Aristocratic. "Oh, but, Lina, the information I get from those fat lips. He sneaks away from his sow of a wife and I prepare Königsberge Klopse and what takes me an hour to make he sucks in less than a minute. But then, before we go . . . inside, he sits back and burps and tells me about his day. In the time it takes him to digest, I get intelligence that sometimes saves lives. You tell me. Should I give him up?"

My eyes suddenly got wet with the tears that had been in hers a moment before. "I don't know," I whispered.

"Oh, Lina, I know there is something better than this. I only pray I live long enough to enjoy five minutes of it."

If it had been up to Konrad Friedrichs, I would have visited the fish store every day. Practice! Practice! Practice!

But Herr Friedrichs was a spy only in that he gleaned information from the foreign office, flew to Lisbon on legitimate Third Reich business and, while he was there, brought in a suit to a dry cleaner, with the data written in code and folded and slipped into a minuscule slit in the cuff of his trousers. The dry cleaner would bring the suit to the back of the store, to a waiting OSS operative, and for Herr Friedrichs, that would be the end of it.

Unlike Margarete and Rolf Vogel, fishmonger, Konrad

Friedrichs was always aloof; he worked alone. The idea of
an organized German resistance cooperating on an American intelligence operation was too horrible for him to even
contemplate. But he trusted Margarete. Not because she was
trusted by Norman Weekes and not because of her bravery
and skill, but because, despite her parents' fascist views, she
came from a great family who for centuries had stood for the
best Germany had to offer. When Norman stuck me on Herr
Friedrichs, it was Margarete, his only contact in the resistance, who calmed him down, and Margarete who promised
to make sure I indeed became the great cook the OSS
claimed I was.

But Margarete had to be insulated from knowledge, protected from my operation, so it came down to me and Herr
Friedrichs working together. The two of us were not born to
sing a duet. Konrad Friedrichs did everything from bathing
to spying on a rigid, unvarying schedule. But as Margarete or
Rolf could have told him, you can't have an obvious schedule when you're out in the field. So even though it caused a
number of major nostril flare-ups, I told him I would not go
to Rolf's every day to Practice! Practice! Practice!

"Listen to me. No human being can eat that much herring," I told him, when he made one of his slippered trips to
my room. "If I go there that often, that regularly, someone in
his store is going to think it's curious. I'm a cook working
for a highly placed individual in the foreign office—*you*—
and they know you have allowances ordinary citizens don't
have. You could eat veal seven days a week for breakfast,
lunch and dinner if you wanted to. So why is your cook
hanging around the fishmonger's?"

"You're like all of them. 'Secret agents.' Enamored of
cleverness. Disdainful of hard work."

"If somehow the Gestapo gets onto Rolf, if he's being
watched, don't you think they're going to notice me?"

"Your execution of the transfer of information must be
flawless *before* you leave here and enter the household
of . . . where you are going. You must—"

"Practice!" I said. "Don't worry."

" 'Don't worry'! The vanity, the naïveté in that expression. I have been doing . . . what I have been doing for years. You . . . For all I know, they picked you out from . . . from a burlesque line. Your only credential is that you obviously grew up in a household that included a low-class individual from Berlin."

"My grandmother was German. Whatever her social class, she was a refined woman. She would never make offensive remarks about other people's families."

He stuck out his chest and took a deep, aggrieved breath. Very huffy. "You think I am arrogant, pompous. That is not the case." Boy, did this guy need a mirror! "I am not denigrating your grandmother. I am merely trying to emphasize the fact that you come to this occupation as a novice."

"You may be right, but there was only one person in the whole world who could take this job, and that was me. I have the willingness and I have the guts. And what I lack in training I make up for in common sense."

"Your common sense! You will soon be dead, or wish you were, and it will be worse, *worse*"—his voice rose to a panicked squeal—"worse for me. You are my doom!"

I could sympathize with his terror. But I was really getting fed up with his contempt for me. "Do you think I would risk my own life and the lives of other people if I felt I wasn't prepared?"

"You do not know what the word 'prepared' means!"

I got up and opened my door, which wasn't easy because the room was so small I had to practically climb over Herr Friedrichs's knees. "Please leave my room."

He stood tall. "It is *my* room. *My* house."

"Well," I said, "our conversation is over. You can either leave or throw me out. Which would you prefer?"

Maybe I should have been more understanding about his predicament, but the truth was I was so preoccupied by my own near hysteria, I didn't have patience for his.

On the plane to Lisbon, the OSS had given me a pocketbook with a tiny compartment in the bottom that opened when you pressed against a hinge. They said, When you get to Rolf's store, have a sack full of heavy vegetables, cans, what have you. When he waits on you, he'll have to help you set down your packages, and in that maneuver he'll brush against your pocketbook. That's how he'll extract your information. He'll pull out the paper you write everything on from the hidden compartment in your pocketbook. Don't worry. This is guaranteed: No one will see what he's doing. He's a real pro. He knows how to trigger the mechanism; he's used this kind of transfer technique before. You just have to look burdened down so he can get close enough to help you. Relax. It's a piece of cake.

Except the piece of cake didn't work. On three separate visits to the fish store, Rolf couldn't get the bottom of my pocketbook open. Okay, we were just practicing, and all he would have pulled out was a small piece of blank paper. But when the real time came, the paper—even with the tiny writing I'd mastered, with letters the size of commas—had to get out of Berlin. And he was the first step in its journey.

If anyone could have made that hinge work, it would have been Rolf Vogel. He was a man about my age, with thinning red hair, pasty skin, pale freckles and one arm. He'd lost the other in a motorcycle accident when he was young. But while that handicap kept him out of the army, it didn't keep him from boning a fish with amazing dexterity or lifting a wooden crate of iced fish that must have weighed pretty close to what he did.

And he wasn't a nervous wreck like Herr Friedrichs. Rolf was so calm he even soothed me. I didn't know the reasons for his willingness to put his life on the line when ninety-nine point nine percent of his countrymen cringed and cowered and *Sieg Heil*ed till the cows came home, but whatever the reasons, they were deeply felt. And because he knew how great the danger to him was, and was willing to accept it, he wasn't going to fall apart. Rolf Vogel didn't sweat. He didn't bite his nails. In fact, he behaved pretty much the way I imagined Edward Leland would have. Matter-of-fact. If it's cold, toss a wool sweater with starry snowflakes into your travel bag before you slip into Denmark. If you know you're going into occupied Poland, just say, Well, see you in a few weeks, Linda, and simply walk out the door. Casual. In control.

After the third failed attempt at making a transfer, he just said, "Perhaps you would like to see the trout today." He guided me toward the rear of the store. We were still in sight, but it was safer. "What do you think of them?" he asked, looking at the fish. His hand rested on a stack of wrapping paper. He seemed to be saying silently, maybe we can work a transfer with this paper. I sniffed. I didn't like the idea; it was too open. "They are quite fresh," he assured me. I sniffed again: Lina Albrecht, the perfectionist. "I like to see for myself."

"Please go ahead," he said, as if this was nothing new to him. At least a quarter of his customers were pains in the neck.

I lifted trout after trout, and stared into their dead eyes. Boy, were they ugly when you took the time to look at them. And resentful, with those little pursed mouths. But I had to come up with something. And then I cleared my throat. Rolf watched. I poked at a trout's mouth. It opened, and I stuck my finger down its throat or gullet or whatever it was. Well, whatever it was was large enough for a small piece of paper. Rolf barely tilted his head, but I knew he was nodding his understanding.

"I don't like these. Let me see the halibut," I said.

"Certainly," Rolf said. *"Certainly."*


On my last night at Konrad Friedrichs's, I arranged my body in its usual position: twisted right, left and sideways to avoid the jabbing mattress springs. On an earlier night, I'd tried something extra: putting my right arm over my head, my shoulder covering one ear and my hand the other, so I couldn't hear the sounds of the bombing and the antiaircraft fire. But after a minute the silence wasn't golden; I had to be awake to hear the wrong set of footsteps, or a voice asking for me.

On that last night, I lay awake, brooding over Herr

Friedrichs. I couldn't stand him, but in the end, I realized how much he'd done for me: bringing me in from Lisbon, allowing a member of the resistance to train me in his own house, hiding me, and most of all, nagging me all the time, shaking his head in disgust at my low-class stupidity, forcing me to be more frightened—and, I realized, more cautious and suspicious—than I might otherwise have been.

Two days earlier, I'd done what in England I'd been ordered to do: taken the subway all the way to Alexanderplatz, to test my ability to get around Berlin and to pass myself off as a working-class Berliner. Oh, had I been proud! I left early in the morning, and when I got to Alexanderplatz station, people were still leaving the safety of the underground; there had been an air raid the night before. I joined the crowd climbing up the stairs.

A good lesson. This was Berlin, not New York. Not a single person shoved, jostled, elbowed or thrust himself ahead of anyone else. I forced myself to walk at the measured pace of the crowd, not to try and beat it; I kept my head down, although it was as much to avoid the mass exhalation of the morning breath of people who'd slept underground as to mind my own Teutonic business.

Up on the street, the lines were already forming in front of the stores. Women held on to their pocketbooks, with their passports and ration books, more tightly than they did to their children. The people were poorer here, and at first I felt secure. I looked more like one of them, a housewife. When I walked into the fancier stores near Herr Friedrichs's, I really didn't belong. Shopkeepers eyed my knit hat, my shoes, and then realized: Of course! I was someone's servant.

I stood on a line for almost two hours. War showed on faces. People looked haggard, gray, exhausted by the effort to get through even this, the beginning of their day. That's when I realized I wasn't one of them, and I knew they realized it too. What set me apart was that I was healthy. My skin was clear; there was still a sheen to my hair. And most of all, I wasn't gaunt. Okay, I wasn't stout by anyone's standards, but I was an American: solid, comfortable, at peace. And I'd had four weeks at Herr Friedrichs's, cooking with Margarete, where—despite my nervous stomach—I'd tasted a little of this, a little of that, and though I was too overanxious and overwrought to actually eat, I hadn't lost any weight. My figure appeared less like an ordinary German's and more like an upper-class Abwehr translator's: full, well-treated.

I examined those faces in the line; they all shared the same quality: They looked out at you but they didn't see you. Well, that's not quite right. Sure, they saw me, saw my suspicious vitality, but they didn't give me a funny look: no New York "Hey, what's with her?" or even a cool, calm, collected German-style once-over, like Olga used to give me if I went off to school in a dress that she had decided was wrong.

It was not dead eyes; the women on line had dead brains behind the eyes. They had made themselves stop thinking, so no random, renegade expression could pass over their faces: not a tic or a blink that could be challenged.

The fear I felt from being just that little bit different diminished somewhat when I realized these women weren't going to call out: Hey, look at this one! She's *wrong!* If I was, they knew the authorities would find me. They would not turn me in, because they were as afraid as I was of making any kind of scene in which they would call attention to themselves.

It was cold, and my feet throbbed as I stood there in the early December cold. I thought: Would people from Queens and Brooklyn ever be like this? Could they ever be made so scared that their insides died? I didn't know. But then I looked down to the street corner from where I was standing in line and saw workers on their way to offices, stores and factories.

Not a single one of them put a foot off the curb when the light was red. New York was a city of jaywalkers, of parkers at fire hydrants. Would a cabdriver's unwritten license to say to a cop, "Up yours, buddy," protect a nation from a Hitler and his Brownshirts? Could a Hitler arise in a nation where the average citizen never thought twice about exceeding the speed limit?

To be fair, though, when you see your neighbors being rounded up and taken away and their houses and furniture and even their canned tomatoes snatched up by Party favorites, and you never see your neighbors again . . . well, it doesn't encourage a big mouth and an anti-fascist sneer.

But to continue to be fair, Hitler and FDR had come into office within months of each other in 1933. Okay, conditions were much worse in Germany; they not only had a depression, they had the heavy burden of the First World War on them. But they picked a wild-eyed, booted, hate-spewing monster who screeched to them by torchlight: You are the Master Race! And we picked a cripple with gusto and gallantry, who sat by a homey, crackling fire and urged us to have courage, to have patience, to have decency and to have hope.

I finally got into the store; it had once sold a combination of housewares and hardware, but now there was nothing even resembling the cast-iron skillet I'd thought of buying. Its inventory consisted of two items: soup bowls and potato peelers. I left with a potato peeler, but at least the store owner had not detected anything strange in my accent; I was almost positive of that. And it hadn't bothered him that I was strangely robust; when he gave me my change, he said, Here, Fräulein, and then grinned at me. I put my head down so he'd think I was blushing, slipped the potato peeler into my pocketbook and left.

I'm doing okay, I thought, and though I didn't skip down the street and whistle, I felt far more confident than when I'd left Herr Friedrichs's that morning. I was almost at the station when I saw that a side street had been cordoned off. Police. Gestapo. I didn't look. I calmed myself by thinking it was an area that had been hit the night before. Even though the bombings were getting worse, the authorities kept trying to prevent people from coming face-to-face with terrible devastation—rubble and the awful empty craters left after the attacks—especially in residential neighborhoods.

A bombing, I thought. A fact of life. And then felt a hand on my arm. I looked up. Gestapo. A face that would have been nice-looking if it hadn't been so enraptured by its own ability to terrify. "Show me your passport," he ordered.

It took me a second to open the clasp, and my pocketbook jiggled as I struggled. I prayed, Dear God, don't let that hinge work now. I handed him my passport. He examined it, and then he came up close. How had I given myself away? "Is your name Lina Albrecht?"

"Yes."

Had someone been watching Konrad Friedrichs all along? Was that it?

"Your age?"

"Twenty-eight years." He had a thick pompadour, kept high off his forehead with hair tonic.

"Place of birth?"

"Berlin." Oh, God—or Oh, Olga, Oh, Mr. and Mrs. Pohl—let him buy my accent.

Was the identity check one of those random ones they'd warned me about? I was just walking too slow for his taste, or too fast. He didn't like my looks. He liked my looks, like the shopkeeper who'd grinned. He stared at my passport, then at me, over and over and over. Was he trying to paralyze me so that when he finally proclaimed, You are *not* from Berlin! Your accent is foreign! all I'd be able to do would be incline my head in agreement.

"What are you doing?"

"I was shopping."

"Shopping?" His eyes narrowed with skepticism, and he shook his head, as if I'd told him an outrageously unbelievable lie. "What have you been shopping for?"

I started to rummage through my pocketbook, too frantically, I thought. Slow down. Find the potato peeler to show him. He yanked the pocketbook away from me. "A potato peeler," I said. "That's what I was shopping for."

Just as I uttered the words, he pulled out the peeler. "You are from Wilmersdorf," he said. "What are you doing in this area?" He pronounced every word precisely, separately, slowly, prolonging the threat. And oh, did it work! I was so scared, and he was electrified by my fear. He moved in on me, pressing his face against mine, a horrible cheek-to-cheek. Looking sideways, I could see the almost invisible dots on his skin where he'd shaved. "Well? Why are you in Alexanderplatz?"

"I heard the store here had potato peelers. The kind with the rounded top."

"What?"

"So you can scoop out the eyes," I whispered.

"And for that you came all the way from Wilmersdorf?"

"Oh, yes. I'm a cook. Please, my work passport is in there." He jerked himself up, away from me, and groped through my pocketbook; he threw my handkerchief on the sidewalk. "I work for Herr Konrad Friedrichs, of the foreign office."

He pulled out my work passport and scrutinized it as if positive that any minute he'd discover something I could be guilty of. A gust of wind came and blew away my handkerchief. He held the work passport up, so the sun could shine through it. I took a fast glance as he examined my papers. His face was in profile; he had a thick plug of yellow wax in his ear.

Suddenly he shoved the pocketbook back into my hands and slapped my identification on top of it. "All right," he said. "Get going. And no more loitering."

"Yes. I won't. Thank you."

I walked down the street, clutching all the papers that registered me as a citizen of the Reich—allowing me to work and live—tight against my chest. When I turned the corner I walked faster, but then slowed myself down. Easy. Put your pocketbook in order. Here in Germany, kiddo, neatness counts.

On that last night in the basement cell of Konrad

Friedrichs's house, I forced my mind to travel, to get back where it could be at ease for a few hours, to go home.

I thought about how my mother, who used her tweezers the way a carpenter used his hammer, had worked on her beauty, but after my father was killed in that fire, before she actually started boozing, she was never able to get the seams of her stockings straight. The first sign she was falling apart. She'd come out of her bedroom and call, How're my seams, Linda, lamb? and after a couple of times when she'd gotten so upset she'd cried, I learned to say, Straight as an arrow, Mom.

And then my mind drifted into Manhattan, and I thought about having lunch in the conference room of Blair, Vander-Graff and Wadley, with Gladys Slade controlling the gossip with the same thoroughness (but more seriousness) that Roosevelt would insist on in running a cabinet meeting. When I thought how the small talk about Mrs. Avenel's pushiness and Mr. Post's carrying on with Wilma Gerhardt and Mr. Nugent's vague resemblance to Ronald Colman had once been the high point of my days, and how lying awake and inventing moments with Mr. Berringer—who in my imagination I dared to call John—had been the crowning glory of my nights, I realized what had become of me. Well, not what had become of me, because I really didn't know, but at least that from where I had started to where I had wound up had been one hell of a trip.

And there was no return ticket. That night—and every night I was in Berlin—I had some bad moments. To be honest, bad half hours, bad hours. Lying in my bed, my motor racing, I wasn't able to concentrate on anything but one thought: I'm *stuck*. Caught. What border could I run to and say: Hey, let me across! I don't belong here! I'm from Queens! What person could I throw my arms around and cry: Oh, God, I want to go home! Help me!

I made myself get control. I thought about John. It wasn't easy. Not because it brought me any pain, but all I could conjure up as I lay in that miserable excuse for a bed was an

image: his handsome face, his remarkable body. Images.
John coming out of the shower. John's face when he glanced
up from editing a brief, or looming over mine during sex.
John with me in his arms. John with Nan in his arms.

Hey, I thought, no matter what's happened, this guy is still
your husband. That didn't help. Trying to feel something for
John was like forcing myself to fall in love with air. I
couldn't. I felt no passion, no anger, no longing, no loss.
Right before I finally fell asleep, I thought: The only thing I
really feel is curiosity; simple curiosity. I mean, how can
you love someone and feel absolutely, explicitly, indubitably
nothing?

# 23

If he'd lived in the United States, the best a guy like Horst Drescher could have done for himself would probably have been to own a small business—one renting wheelchairs and artificial legs, or manufacturing paper party favors—and been vice-president of the Lions Club; he'd never make president, because most of the members would think anyone who would wear a satin vest was a jerk and unfit for the highest office. He would live in the suburbs, because city life would be too much for his nervous-wreck wife, Hedwig, but since he fancied himself so urbane, he wouldn't want to be too far away from concert halls, the theater and expensive restaurants.

That's what he would have been in America. In Nazi Germany, Horst Drescher, at age twenty-seven, was one of the most fortunate men in the foreign office. The army couldn't go near him; he'd been born blind in one eye, and his feet pointed out so far it looked like he was doing a Donald Duck imitation whenever he walked. So he was fortunate. And powerful. Not because of the work he did, although he was chief of the British Section and worked at least twelve hours a day. And not because of his skills in diplomacy and language: anyone in the foreign service, from janitor to ambassador, could see through his so-called subtlety in two seconds flat. And the two times I overheard him speaking English to someone on the phone, it was so incredibly, stiffly German-accented that he sounded like a kid from Queens in a game of soldiers who got stuck with playing the Nazi.

But that's what he was, the Nazi. His fanatical party loyalty was the reason he had risen so high in that huge gray building on Wilhelmstrasse. That, and the fact that for one week Hitler had gone on a rampage, calling for "young men, new blood" in government. He got what he deserved: Horst.

In the same year that *Mein Kampf* was first published, 1925, when Horst Drescher was ten years old, he joined the *Deutsches Jungvolk*, the junior version of Hitler Youth, and he had been a true-blue believer ever since. He wasn't loyal for any personal gain. He believed in Hitler and in what he stood for: the Master Race. What kind of ten-year-old boy wants to spend his time glorying in Aryan superiority instead of throwing a ball? According to the OSS report, little Horst Drescher. "He is a passionate believer in Hitler's racial theories, and apparently believes himself to be an example of all that is noble, manly and cultured." The report went on to say that Horst also embraced all the other Nazi notions: *Lebensraum*, anti-Semitism, *Führerprinzip*—everything, the whole ball of *Weltanschauung*.

Well, almost. Adolf the Ethical was a vegetarian. Horst Drescher would eat anything that didn't get up and walk off his plate— as long as it was washed down with a big glass of pilsener and a little glass of schnapps.

But when I started working for him at his beautiful stone villa in the Dahlem neighborhood, I didn't know that. All I knew was what the OSS knew, and their information had come from Alfred Eckert, who had most likely dashed off something like "A callow youth who fancies old-fashioned German food, and a lot of it!" to pad out a too-short report. Some pencil-pusher at OSS naturally put a giant asterisk on that one. "Drescher, Horst: Born 1915 in Magdeburg. *Weakness—German cooking!!!" The OSS had passed on the word to Konrad Friedrichs. And when in desperation he'd gone to Margarete von Eberstein and, without naming names, described the person whose house I was supposed to slip into—and how impossible the task seemed—Margarete had declared, I can help.

Sure, but on my second night at the Dreschers', I loused

up the pheasants. Else, the downstairs maid, who did the serving, came charging in from the dining room. "You must hurry! They're waiting for the next course!" I looked at her, a little surprised. They must have inhaled the appetizer.

I opened the oven. "Oh, my God!" I had been warming the roasting pan and the vegetables on low heat, but when I'd put in the birds, I'd obviously forgotten to turn up the oven. Else sidled over and we both stared at four barely cooked pheasants; they looked like they had been hanging around a hot kitchen instead of actually roasting.

"What are you going to do?" she squeaked.

"Hide them," I said. They looked more wounded than dead; red juice was oozing out of the cavity. "And pray." I grabbed the pot of white sauce I'd planned to use on the carrots and poured it over the pheasants. It covered them like a heavy sheet. Then I decorated the platter with all the greens, lemon slices and capers I could grab, thrust the platter into Else's hands and said, "When you walk through that door, smile. And *don't* be afraid." Since she had a brain capacity equal to one of the pheasants', she did what she was told, unquestioningly, and marched toward the dining room with a wide and empty smile on her face.

As the door swung open, I got a glimpse of Horst's back, and the profiles of his wife, Hedwig, and his dinner guest, a somewhat older man, with a nose so upturned and flat that it looked like a pig's snout; the man had been Horst's beloved *Deutsches Jungvolk* leader and was now the chief Party functionary in Saxony.

"How are we doing in England?" the man was asking Horst.

"Very well, Bruno," Horst replied.

"But they are bombing us more and more."

"Desperation, Bruno." And the door swung shut.

I got busy, trying not to think about how Horst would react to the pheasant disaster. I spooned about a cup of butter over the carrots. Then I did the same with the potatoes and, as an afterthought, tossed in some dried dill that hung from the ceiling, which Else said had come from France. By the

time the Germans get through, I decided, the only thing
that'll be left in France will be the French.

Else came back for the vegetables. Her fair-skinned face
was all flushed with pleasure. Good old Bruno had probably
pinched her behind. I asked her, "What kind of a mood does
Herr Drescher seem to be in?"

"He wanted more bread." Brilliant. Some master race.
She toddled out with the vegetables.

No screams of dismay had arisen over the gloppy, white-
coated revolting mess I'd sent out on a silver platter. I
calmed myself by saying that even if the meal was the worst
thing in Horst Drescher's life, he wouldn't fire me. His former chef had been hit by a car on his way to the butcher shop
and had two broken legs. And I had come so highly recommended . . . by Konrad Friedrichs, of all people.

Originally, the OSS had hoped Herr Friedrichs could find
someone else willing to sing the praises of my cooking, but,
already frightened, he was firm: I will *not* enlist anyone else
into this foolhardy operation!

Konrad Friedrichs's office was on the same floor as
Horst's, and so, on a Monday, he'd said, Well, on Friday I
am off to Lisbon for two weeks. Then on Thursday, having
spent most of the past few days listening to foreign office
gossip, he called Horst and said, I hear your chef has met
with an accident. Most unfortunate . . . but perhaps fortu-
itous. I have a cook—nice, quiet Berlin woman, a widow—
and I've been wondering what to do with her. I travel too
much. Don't really need her. She's quite capable. If you're
interested . . .

I arrived at the Dreschers' villa on Saturday morning. It
was a graceful stone house, set behind an ornate iron fence,
on a cobblestone street. They had lived there for nearly a
year; before that, it had belonged to a Jewish family who had
owned a department store. They had "emigrated," which
meant they'd been rounded up and sent somewhere east.
Probably Poland or Czechoslovakia. No one talked about it.
Their house, from attic to basement, including the beds,

clothespins, sterling silver, couches and extra light bulbs, now belonged to the Dreschers.

According to the OSS report, Horst loved what had become his. Alfred was quoted: "He will pass through a room and stroke the wood of his breakfront. He will discuss the value of his antique Meissen porcelain." And I could just see him lifting a sugar bowl up to the light, peering at it with his one good eye, a small smile crossing his bland face. Horst looked even younger than his twenty-seven years. His face was still blotchy—although in the morning, the pimples were beige with dabs of Hedwig's heavy foundation makeup. He was round-shouldered, and had a small, almost girlish build—except for his bloated, satin-vested belly. He was not the sort who got his Aryan kicks hiking in the Schwarzwald.

But if he was young, he had the tastes of an old man: beer, politics, food, culture. Not women. The report said: "He seems immune to the charms of women other than his wife . . . and our sources indicate he may be immune to hers as well. The couple have been married for five years and have no children."

His main love was his work. Too bad for Germany. According to the briefing Konrad Friedrichs gave me just before I left, Horst was of almost no use in the foreign office because he had no ability to analyze intelligence or plan strategy. But he knew every single minuscule fact there was to know about his area, Great Britain. No report, magazine clipping, aerial photograph or coded message escaped his eye.

The problem was, once he absorbed all this data, he had no idea what to do with it. Sure, if you asked him the square footage of Windsor Castle he could tell you, and he knew the name, address and telephone number of every German agent in England, Scotland and Wales. He could choke you on facts; he just couldn't think.

Still, all this information took time to digest, but so did dinner. Horst took great pleasure in returning to his graceful

house, eating an elaborate meal and then going into his
study to read over his reports. On the nights when he went to
the opera or the ballet or the theater, where he sat in a box
reserved for the highest officials, he would return and pore
over his papers until two in the morning.

These nights of the lively arts were the best nights for
snooping. That's what my friend Alfred had related to the
OSS. Alfred, designer for the Nazi elite, had always managed to drop in to help his client Hedwig get ready—a very
intricate process. Horst would come home, put his papers in
his study, lock the room, have a lighter-than-usual supper—
alone, because Hedwig and Alfred were probably doing up
her corset—then rush upstairs and change into his tuxedo.
He'd come down later, wait and pace, until, finally, Alfred
would escort an overwrought Hedwig downstairs. She'd
plead a headache, a terrible period, a congested chest. Horst
would look to Alfred for help. Alfred would reassure her:
"My dear, look at you! I've made you beautiful. You will
*dazzle* them! Go, now. Go." The first few times, he'd picked
up his case and left with the Dreschers. But then Horst, the
gracious host, the man who knew that in Alfred he had found
someone who could truly appreciate all his fine objects,
said, "Please, stay. Have a bite to eat. And drink, if you like.
I have different glasses for red and white wine. No need to
rush."

Horst was deeply grateful for the help Alfred was giving
him. He really needed help. Hedwig was definitely not an
asset to his career—although that had been why he'd married her. Her father had been with Hitler since the early days
in Munich, and although he was too old to hold a permanent
position in government, he was a trusted—and therefore
powerful—friend. But he died six months after the wedding,
sticking Horst with a woman no other man, even the most
politically ambitious, had been willing to take. Hedwig
Drescher was lumpy, with hair so thin you could see her
scalp, and tree-trunk legs. She was twelve years older than
her husband.

She tried to disguise the age difference with heavy, mask-like makeup and bright-colored dresses, but she knew the attempt was a lost cause. She was the clumsy, chunky daughter of a dumb, jovial Munich policeman. She had nothing to recommend her, not even her father's joviality; she just had his dumbness. No one wanted her around, least of all her husband, and yet as a proper wife she had to accompany him on his social and cultural outings.

But at least Alfred, with his charming patter and inspirational speeches, had been able to lift her out of her near-constant state of nervous tension and get her out with her husband. The OSS report had quoted Alfred: "She gets hysterical because she wants to please him and can't, and so she makes herself ill. She loves him, poor cow."

Else rushed back into the kitchen, breathless. "The master says, 'My compliments to the new cook. A fine partridge.' "

Partridge? I thought. It's pheasant. But then I knew that at least I was safe in the kitchen.

The poor cow seemed to have her period three weeks out of the month. That's what Dagmar, the chambermaid, told me. "All the time cramps. But the cramps, I think they are in the head, not in the . . ." She used some word I'd never heard of, but I nodded my understanding.

The assassination of Alfred Eckert was almost as much a disaster for Horst as it had been for the OSS. Now there wasn't anyone who could rally Hedwig for a night out with the Nazis and in the next few weeks, past Christmas and into the new year, 1943, I could see his pasty face getting crimson every time he came home from work, passed the parlor and saw Hedwig curled up on a chaise, squeezing a hot-water bottle against her stomach.

Not that I saw too much. I shopped in the mornings, chopped and mixed all afternoon, and cooked into the night. After that, I climbed the back stairs to my room, a cubicle not much bigger than what I'd had at Konrad Friedrichs's. (Although at least the former owners had furnished it cheerfully: a bed with an old headboard that had a bouquet of roses painted on it, a wide strip of what—probably a hundred years before—had been a nice flowered rug, and a wood chest.)

I kept away from the Dreschers as much as possible. Once, Horst barged into the kitchen. He was giving his guest, von Ribbentrop's personal assistant, the grand tour of the house. I was juicing a lemon and stared at Horst, and then at the guest, a man so bucktoothed it looked as if he was eating his own lip. "Carry on, cook," Horst said, with a grand wave of his hand. The two of them inspected the stove and the icebox as if they knew what they were looking at. As they swept out, Horst called: "And don't forget! More of those potato croquettes!"

Other than that, I managed to avoid anything more than a chance "Good evening, sir" meeting in a hallway. But I couldn't stay away from Hedwig, because she was always around, clutching hot water bottles or ice packs, reclining in a series of robes that I bet were Alfred-designed: long, belt-less, all in shades of blue—aquamarine, sapphire, royal blue—with V necks, created to hide her formlessness and to bring out her small but decidedly blue eyes.

Her suffering room, the parlor, was right opposite Horst's study. Even if he went out at night and I was positive Else and Dagmar were asleep, I couldn't try to jimmy the lock when she was lying on the chaise—giving off occasional moans—with a full view of the study door.

How long, I worried, could I visit Rolf and stick messages into fishes' mouths saying, Sorry. Can't get into study. Wife always lying in parlor opposite. Will try again.

I got embarrassed thinking about what Norman Weekes must be saying, as he and his Harvard crew rolled their eyes in hopelessness and honked. Well, what *can* one expect when one recruits such a relentless plebian. But I got genuinely upset at the thought of Edward. On one hand, I knew my sneaking past him, collaborating with his adversary the minute he left the country, going against everything we both knew he believed in, would make him hate me. On the other hand, I still hoped for his admiration. For some reason, I wanted him to think—even if it was way in the back of his mind—that Linda was doing a decent job. She'd even picked up a few tricks from him, the champion spy.

So one night when Hedwig was sprawled out on the chaise in a turquoise robe and impenetrable makeup, having missed a Wagnerian opera because she wept and said she had the flu, I stood at the open parlor door and said, "Madam, it would please me if you would allow me to make you some tea with honey. It would help your throat."

"*No*. I don't like tea." Nasty. Pouty. Unable to get her mouth to form a "thank you." And she had an awful whine. She was really worse than a cow. I had increased admiration for Alfred, that he hadn't lost control and plunged his pinking shears into her heart.

"Milk with honey, then?" I suggested. She hesitated. "And perhaps a biscuit?"

"I'll try," she sighed.

Two minutes later, I came rushing back with a tray. "Madam, if I may suggest . . ."

"What?"

"It might help your chest if I put a bit of brandy in the milk." If I'd taken even an eyedropperful of his beloved schnapps, Horst would have known in a minute. But there was a dust-covered case of brandy in the basement, and my guess was he'd forgotten it was there. "Just a touch."

"Whatever," she murmured.

"Would you like to have it down here?" And then I tossed off what I hoped sounded like a casual suggestion. "Or up in your room?"

"Well . . ." she said, gazing out of the room, probably overwhelmed by the thought of the stairs.

"I could help you upstairs, Madam, and then come down and reheat the milk to the proper temperature."

She held out her hand for me to help her, like Greta Garbo dying in *Camille*.

Twenty minutes later, Hedwig had enough brandy in her to make her sleep until the following afternoon. And I went down and knelt before the locked study door.

\* \* \*

Horst guarded his key to the study as if it would open up the gates to heaven. Still, I solved the locked-door problem easily enough, even though jiggling the handle, a hairpin and a larding needle didn't work. I figured there *had* to be an extra key. In any well-run house, the wife isn't going to let the husband walk off with the only key in his pocket and not be able to let the maid get into his study to wax and dust and vacuum. I leaned against the locked door and asked myself, Where would a good housewife, where would my Grandma Olga, put the extra key?

It wasn't in the silver chest, my first choice, and it wasn't underneath the record player in the parlor. But finally I found it upstairs in the linen closet, under a pile of heavy damask tablecloths. Big ones, for when the table was opened to seat twenty. For their holidays. I touched the tablecloths; they were so rich. And I couldn't help thinking how little in common that nameless family of Jews had with my family of Jews. It was like comparing apples and oranges . . . or me and—I almost laughed thinking about it—somebody like Edward Leland. I closed the closet door slowly, and I was easing my way down the hall—a weird, ice-skating motion they taught us in Training School, which was less apt to make a board squeak than tiptoeing—I thought about apples and oranges. Both fruit. So maybe Edward Leland and I . . . the tablecloth family and my family . . . In a world of barbarians, the light of simple human decency is so overwhelming, so blinding, that you no longer see things like old silver and Yale and fancy accents.

I stopped thinking and went down the stairs. They taught us stairs too: Sit on the top step, brace yourself with your hands and then gently, slowly, lower your backside. If someone catches you, the instructor had said, grunt with pain and hold on to your ankle and accept any offer of help. Don't forget to limp.

Recalling it now, it all sounds easy, almost mechanical. But finding the key, getting in the study, was the easy part. That first night, I just stood beside the desk and examined the heavy cardboard envelope of papers, not daring to touch it.

I had to be careful. I didn't know if Horst's suspicions had been aroused by Alfred Eckert's death. Did he know—did anyone—that Alfred was spying on him? Deep down, I was almost positive that the traitor in the resistance had found out only that Alfred was a spy—but not where he was spying—and had passed the word on. Because if the traitor had known, if the Gestapo had known, that Horst was the subject of Alfred's snooping, that he had been bringing home top-secret papers and leaving them while he went to hear Brunhilde hit a high note, he wouldn't be in the foreign office, or in Berlin; he'd probably be dead or, as everybody liked to say, "East." But I had to be certain.

I switched on the flashlight that I'd taken from the kitchen and held it over the envelope, looking for telltale hairs, dustings of powder—any of the tricks Horst might employ to make sure his papers weren't being tampered with. Nothing.

It was lying face-down, the flap unsealed. Then I studied his briefcase. Ordinary black leather. No special locks, no small explosive devices set to blow off a busybody's hands. It looked safe. All I had to do was put on a pair of thin cotton gloves, skim through the files and copy down anything that looked important: names, addresses, statistics or lists of any sort. Get whatever you can, Norman Weekes had told me the last time I saw him. This fellow brings home prime information at least once a week. Alfred had been given a miniature camera to photograph the documents, but since I was going to be living in the house, they'd decided not to risk it.

I switched off the flashlight. Now came the part that would always be the most dangerous: getting out. What if Hedwig was a secret drinker, and after all my cleverness, the triple slug of brandy I'd poured into her milk hadn't knocked her out but perked her up? What if she had toddled downstairs and resumed her place on the chaise? And what if Dagmar had sneaked down to grab the last cherry tart, or Else, to steal a lemon to lighten her hair?

I waited as I had been taught to wait, counting, so I would be forced to remain in place for five minutes. A slow, ago-nizing count to three hundred, all the while listening for a hiccup or a footstep—any sound at all. Linda Voss Berringer, secret agent.

I got that old familiar pain in my gut, sudden, stabbing, but worse than it had ever been. Still, I kept counting. When I got up to ninety-seven, the pain became so excruciating that I had to clutch my arms around myself, hold myself tight, as I doubled over.

And then it was time. Inch by inch, I forced myself to straighten up. Slowly, I opened the door. No one was there. I took a long, shaky, deep breath and thought: Two months in Berlin, and I haven't been able to get even the tiniest, most consequential fact.

But then I thought: Look at the bright side. I wasn't dead. And the key would always be in the linen closet.

I missed seeing Margarete. My day off was every other Sunday, and sometimes we managed to see each other for an hour or two, but we had to keep out of each other's lives. Even if she'd been allowed to know where I was staying, she couldn't have gone knocking at Horst's front door, wrapped in cashmere and fur, tied up with gold jewelry, and demanded, in her elite voice, Where is my good friend Lina?

And what was I going to do? Drop in when she was visiting her cousin Countess von Dorzeck or her old pal Prince Wolfgang zu Sayn-Graetz, wave my apron over my head and holler, Hiya! I'm Margarete's buddy. Or better yet, join her at her apartment for a midnight dinner with her lover, the gross, bloated Nazi. Just for the fun of it, to see if a member of Hitler's inner circle could spot an American spy.

So we met at odd places: at a workmen's café for a beer, in a bookstore not far from Alexanderplatz that was always filled with the bohemian types the Nazis hadn't gotten to yet. In late March, when it was getting warmer, we'd go to the zoo, or the Spandau Citadel—a beautiful old fortress, complete with a tower that Rapunzel could have let down her hair from. Spandau was just far enough away from the center of Berlin that it seemed like another country. A fairy-tale country. We sat near a lake and watched people paddling around in rowboats.

Then we walked into the woods. It was so quiet. Peaceful. Safe. Still, Margarete whispered. "You know, there was terrible fighting right there during the Napoleonic Wars." She pointed through the trees at the high brick walls of the fortress.

I grinned. "Of course I know that."

She didn't grin. "I worry about you all the time. You're so naturally . . . lighthearted. You don't comprehend the danger, the bestiality of these people."

I leaned against a tree. It was covered with tight, pale green buds. "I may not know too much about what Napoleon did, but believe me, I know just how evil these people are. Why else would I be doing what I'm doing? Because I don't like their uniforms?" Margarete put her spring coat on the ground; it looked new, a light yellow, the color of pineapple. She sat on it and motioned for me to join her. "You are really crazy," I said. "It must cost a fortune, and you're going to get grass stains all over it."

"I like grass stains. Now, please, tell me how it is going with you." She smiled; she had faint dimples. "Just generalities, as usual. No details." She slipped off a shoe and massaged her arch. "You know, this is all so dreadful, this having to protect each other from . . . from knowledge. Here we are, friends, but we can't even discuss the most boring, ordinary occurrences in our daily lives. I mean, instead of just saying 'the colonel' whenever I talk about the pig, I would like to be able to say his name. And I know when you tell me about what you're doing, about where you are, you'd like to tell me . . . well, not their names, but what they are like and the degree of danger you are in and just . . . the feeling of what it's like for you."

"The feeling is, this great man I'm working for still hasn't gotten over his acne and—"

"No!" She held up her hand, like a traffic policeman. "No descriptions! Don't trust me, Lina. Don't trust anyone." She

took my hand for a minute. "I'm really being selfish, you
see. If you relax with me, I will relax with you. And that sort
of comfort is a terrible menace. Don't you see, if I, if you, if
any of us gets into trouble, we can't be in a position where
we know too much, because we might be forced to reveal it."
She let go of my hand, picked up a stone and brushed the dirt
off it with her thumb. "I think we all have an inflated idea
about our own valor. '*I* can stand up to torture. *I* would never
break down.' That's the worst kind of arrogance, because
when we think that, we're not only committing the sin of
pride, we are putting our friends' lives in peril." She looked
over at me. "Am I babbling on too much?"

"No. Of course not."

"If there can be any benefit from Nazism for me, it has
been discovering friendship. Those of us who . . . who
oppose have learned to cherish—almost worship—our
friends and colleagues. Especially someone like me. I'd led
such a pampered life, and my so-called friends were just as
spoiled and narrow as I was. One of the things I value about
my friendship with you, Lina, is that we're so different—and
we're so much alike. Women who play a man's game. But
you come from a part of Berlin I may have passed through,
but I never really saw. Now, in the middle of all this inhu-
manity, you—and all the others"—she threw the rock hard
and it ricocheted off a small tree—"have taught me what it
really means to be a human being."

"What are you thinking about?" I asked.

"What do you mean?" she demanded.

"I mean, you always seem so calm. But you threw that
rock like it was a weapon. Who were you trying to kill?"

"Them," she said, with more feeling than she'd ever
shown. "I'm so angry because . . . it has become personal.
Oh, yes, you know that eventually one of your friends in the
movement—usually the most courageous—is going to be
discovered. But when it's a *dear* friend, it's more than just
an inevitable sadness. It's more than an acceptable risk of
war. It's losing part of your life."

"They got some of your friends?"

Margarete nodded. "Yes. And among them, my dearest friend. Oh, you should have known him. What a joyous man he was!" And I thought: Oh, God, I know exactly who you're talking about. "His name was Alfred, and he was a couturier. Not a particularly brilliant one, just all right. His success had little to do with his gowns and a great deal to do with his being extraordinary company. Lina, he was so witty, so full of silly gossip and great compassion. And energy! He went *everywhere*, all over the city, and people adored him, trusted him. And he was brilliantly successful because no one suspected. No one would have believed that this homosexual who'd managed to escape the pink triangle because of his connections, this faggot who put his hair in pin curls every night and wore a hairnet, could possibly really be a traitor."

"Do you have any idea how he was found out?"

"Yes! He loved everyone in the movement. And he trusted too many of us. 'Oh, I'm going here tonight, with that big-mouth fool So-and-so.' Or: 'Our friends sent me a new camera! *So* tiny!' I took him aside so many times and begged him to be discreet. I said, 'Darling, stupid Alfred, don't you understand they are always trying to infiltrate the movement? What if they succeed? Do you think a traitor will give you a gold swastika for Christmas?' "

Margarete's voice cracked as she added, "He was my trusting and beloved friend." Once again she took my hand; she held it very tight. "Listen to me. Alfred had a talent for spying—and a genius for living. But he believed so much in the righteousness of his cause that he couldn't comprehend that anything—or anyone—bad could be attached to it. And so look what happened to him. He prattled away once too often. He was given up, betrayed . . . by one of his own, one of his *friends*. Because—and this I will tell you—we know it *has* to have been a betrayal. So please, don't become too comfortable. Because either one of us could die in just the blink of an eye . . . or very slowly and horribly. Be my friend, but don't trust me. Don't trust *anyone*."

* * *

Don't trust Rolf? Fine. I stayed cautious until the end of April. I'd visit the store, trek across the sawdust-covered floor and examine the fish like Field Marshal Rommel inspecting his troops. Finally I'd say: This one, and the one above it. No, wait. Give me that one instead.

Rolf would take the fish to a counter in the back, clean it, scale it, and somehow, with his one hand, take the paper I'd hidden and slip it away somewhere. I watched him once or twice; I never spotted a thing.

I wasn't sure how much all the intelligence I was giving him was worth. Well, I did know the OSS would get somebody hopping on security when I copied down a list, sent to the German foreign office by the army high command, of all the American aircraft on a base near Weymouth in England. And I knew they would be delirious with joy when one time the Gestapo stapled a handwritten note to their report from one of their agents, code name Elefant, a high official in the British Home Office. In the note, Elefant wrote: "If you have any questions, do *not* call me at office. It is an intolerable and dangerous intrusion! Call me at home." And then the dope gave his home phone number!

But most of the documents Horst brought home were obviously catalogs of British or American troop movements, page after page of statistics, directories of names and what I guessed were either triumphs of cryptographic genius or expense accounting by German agents in Great Britain. Shepherd's pie: 3 shillings.

Then one day I finally got word from home. Just before Easter, Rolf was wrapping the trout I was buying. It was a lot of trout, even if it was only the appetizer; Horst was planning a dinner for twelve and carrying on as if it was the resurrection: a fish course with a cream sauce! no fowl! do not buy meat! I am endeavoring to obtain a spring lamb!

"You always choose the best fish," Rolf said.

I gave him an I-bet-you-say-that-to-all-the-girls look, but I said, "Thank you."

"Your employer must be very happy with you." For a second it didn't hit me. I thought he'd meant Horst. And then I realized: It was a message.

"I hope he is," I said. "He is a fine man. I am honored to work for him."

Don't trust anyone. But at the end of February, there had been a mass roundup of the remaining Jews in Berlin. The SS called it *Fabrik Aktion*. Operation Factory. Everybody knew about it. Nobody spoke about it. Well, no ordinary people. But Horst did. After four or five pilseners, I heard him through the door, booming at his dinner guest, a Waffen SS general: I hear Goebbels is pleased with the roundup of the Jews. The general responded through a mouthful of potatoes: Not so pleased. We estimate there are still four thousand we have not picked up.

The last week of April, I couldn't stand it. I had to know about my family. I had to trust Rolf. I slipped a note into a haddock. "My friend, if you read these papers and not just pass them on, could you find out for me what has happened to two old ladies, Jews, Liesl and Hannah Weiss, who live, or used to live, on Klarrenstrasse (I do not know the number). If you tell me to try the codfish, I will know you were not able to find out any information. Please, do not put yourself in any danger. This is merely a matter of curiosity." I signed it: "Your friend."

In the next two weeks, I went to Rolf's store three times. There was no signal at all from him. And then, on a beautiful day in May when even the inside of the fish store smelled good, he told me to have a look at the turbot. While I was inspecting them, he came up beside me. I glanced at him. He picked up two of the smaller fish and said, "No good." I understood. I watched as he carried them over to a large trash can on the other side of the store and, one at a time, tossed them into the garbage.

# 24

Bombs scared me as much as the Gestapo. Maybe more, because at least with the Germans I had a chance to use whatever wits I had to save my own life. But when the Russians, and then the RAF Bomber Command, flew over Berlin and dropped a thousand tons of bombs in one day, being clever didn't help. Cowering in an air raid shelter was about all I could do.

The bombing began to grow in fierceness in the winter I first came to Berlin, 1942–43, but most of it was in the eastern part of the city, near the airport, and farther north, aimed at the tank and munitions factories. Of course I heard it. At night I'd lie in bed on the top floor of the villa in Dahlem and hear—even feel—low booms; if I'd been in my bed in Ridgewood, I could have convinced myself it was a Mack truck backfiring just across the borough line in Bushwick.

By the time I left Konrad Friedrichs, I'd learned to sleep through the attacks. Now and then, I'd wake up startled, my forehead and neck all sweaty, at the sound of the "all clear" whistle, but that wasn't exactly a shocking occurrence; sweet dreams didn't come in Germany. Still, throughout that winter, a person—like a Hedwig—could live in luxurious suburban safety and only have to put up with a little disturbing background noise . . . and the strange red haze that hovered over the city each sunrise.

Not that Hedwig ever saw a sunrise after the milk, honey and touch of brandy—a touch big enough to knock out a hippopotamus—I brought upstairs to her every night. She forgot about her periods completely; now she just whined all the time about her violent headaches. A terrible thing to do to a fellow human being, right? Making some miserable, wretched wreck of a woman drunk every night. Maybe turning her into an alcoholic. Wasn't it awful? Actually, it didn't bother me one bit.

So Hedwig slept through the winter air raids, and the spring ones too. While the SS and the police were executing *Fabrik Aktion*, rounding up Jews—maybe my two cousins with the quivering, spidery handwriting—and shipping them east, she snored.

All that spring, I kept remembering what Edward had said about Germany being hell. I wanted so much to talk to him about it, tell him he was right, that hell wasn't just here in Berlin, with its red sky. This was only headquarters. Hell was where the gas chambers were, with prussic acid filling the lungs of silly old ladies who complained about their dentures. And the tiny lungs of babies.

I wondered if the Germans had been as efficient as they'd hoped to be with their construction. Probably. You couldn't get a goddamn cast-iron skillet in the whole city of Berlin, but boy, were they productive when it came to murdering Jews.

*Judenrein*. I'd heard it six or seven times from the dining room. Jew-free. The ideal, purified German state that Horst with his satin vests and pimples dreamed of: a perfect Reich for perfect Aryans like him and Hedwig.

The bombing stayed normal all summer. Well, if you lose electricity, gas and water for weeks at a time, life isn't normal. But at the villa, where the water truck pulled up to the curb, special door-to-door Nazi VIP service, where Horst came home with boxes of candles every night, life was tolerable.

Of course, Hedwig kept whining: Cold potato salad and sausage *again?* War is heck, Hedwig.

I walked through Berlin. There were no cordoned-off streets anymore with Gestapo and Wehrmacht guards making sure you didn't see the holes where houses used to be.

You can't hide half a city. Buildings were blasted to rubble, dust. Now and then you'd come upon just a wall standing, looking like the pictures you see of movie scenery in *Life*— real fronts of Wild West bars or candy stores, but from the side, flat and false.

I tried not to think of home. New York—rude, pushy, funny: "Huh, lady? Whadaya want?" Even Washington— clean, serious, courtly: "May I help you, ma'am?" Quit it, I told myself. Don't think of life when you're in the land of the dead.

Outside Rolf's fish store, spread-out newspapers were held down by bricks. (Bricks made great paperweights, and the city had mountains of paperweights.) You were supposed to wipe your shoes on the usual phonied-up casualty lists or the radio listings, to get the shards of window glass out of the soles before you went inside. Who could blame them? The city was made of glass. The farther east you walked on Kurfürstendamm, the less you could ignore the crunch-crunch of glass under your feet; the sidewalk became a dazzling, rough, crackling-loud pathway.

You'd tread carefully, farther on, and you'd meet up with dazed strangers, who kept pointing: I live in that apartment over there—four rooms. Except they were pointing at air. People wore bandages, eye patches, slings, casts. It was horrible. People wandered around in the early morning, still bleeding from the night before.

Did I feel sorry for them? You've got to be paralyzed not to feel some pity for an old man who's standing and crying by a pile of rubble, and you see a pair of legs sticking out from under all the pulverized mortar and bricks. His wife's legs, covered with heavy elastic stockings, the kind to help with circulation problems; she probably hadn't had time to find her shoes. And you'd have to be numb not to feel for the bewildered little kids who kept calling for their dogs.

Every time I heard the unmistakable sound of an RAF Mosquito coming close—and you knew what was coming before the "take cover" whistle blew—I'd rush with the crowds, breathless, panicked, to find the nearest bomb shelter. But at the same exact minute when my heart was thudding and my mouth was dry with terror, I wanted to yell, Get 'em! Get 'em! More! More! More!

So did I feel sorry for them? These people huddled around me in an underground station or the basement of a fruit store were the same people who screamed with pride when Hitler told them of their destiny. I'd heard their screams on the radio in Ridgewood, way back in the early thirties.

Or if they weren't the screamers, they were the voters: Cast your ballot for the man who'll show the Slav and Czech scum just what German power really is!

And if they weren't the voters, they were the watchers. They watched the torchlight parades. They watched the soldiers march, the tanks and cannons roll down the street, and they cheered. They watched their neighbors lose their right to vote, their businesses, their citizenship, their houses and their lives. Maybe they didn't cheer; maybe they said "Too bad" when the Gestapo came to get Liesl and Hannah—but not too loud; someone might hear them.

They had welcomed the devil, or at least didn't say, Hey, get out of here, and he had set up business right smack in the middle of town. So let the good people of Berlin get a little taste of what hell was like. And the answer is no, I wasn't sorry.

I lost all sense of time. I was in Berlin forever. The bombing would just keep getting heavier until one day there would be nothing to bomb anymore. November 1943, a whole year after I arrived, was the last time I knew whether it was a Tuesday or a Friday. There were fires burning all the time in the city that month, immense fires; the British had bombed Berlin's supply of coal, and nearly all the fuel for winter was in flames. I'd come back to the villa and my hair would have patches of black: the huge pieces of soot that drifted down all over the city.

By December, or it may have been February 1944 . . . It was winter, anyway, and people were chopping down trees in the Grunewald to burn to keep from freezing. That's when

I lost track of the month. But somewhere in that time, the villa was hit. I could hear it coming. Walking through the city, I'd learned to judge, just by the pitch of the whistle a bomb makes, about where it was going to land.

At ten at night, I heard the whistle. I threw off my blanket, ran into the hall and screamed for Else and Dagmar. Else bolted out of her room, and together we ran down to the next floor and banged on Hedwig's door. But the bomb exploded before I could even shout, Wake up, you imbecile.

We were thrown to the floor. It wasn't a direct hit, because we would have been dead. But close. Even as I heard the blast, I felt the violent change in the air pressure. Oh, dear God! My chest kept moving in and out, but I couldn't breathe. It was like my lungs had been yanked out.

And then it was over. Absolute quiet. We pulled ourselves up, to discover that no one in the house had been killed. Horst wasn't even home; he was at the Philharmonic, getting culture. Of all of us, Dagmar suffered the worst. She'd just made it out of her bedroom when the door of the bathroom down the hall was ripped off its hinges; it went flying past her, but it managed to break her shoulder, her arm and a couple of ribs.

Else and I, lying on our stomachs, hands over our heads, were cut by slivers of flying glass. Horrible, because later you could feel them under your skin, but you couldn't see them, much less get them out. And most of them were in my back, so every time I turned or bent over, I got forty or fifty stabs of pain.

What happened to Hedwig was that her antique clothes cabinet fell down and all her blue robes spilled down on the floor.

So it didn't matter one bit what month it was, because when you alternate between being resigned to death and trembling uncontrollably at the thought, it doesn't really matter if it's Friday, March 10, 1944, or not.

When I wasn't thinking about death, I was thinking about my job—both jobs. It was getting harder to find food, even for Horst, and I worried that he'd decide he didn't need me, that Hedwig could slice a *Kochwurst* as well as I could. So far, I'd gotten reprieve after reprieve; the gas line was reconnected, so the oven worked; then someone in the foreign office flew back from Paris and gave Horst veal. So much veal! He and his friends sucked up veal roasts and veal stews and veal fricassees for a couple of weeks.

On the days I thought my job was pretty safe, I worried about the villa. Forget being a cook. I was also a spy. What if they scored a direct hit and bombed Horst's study? Then he'd have to work nights at the foreign office, and I'd be stuck in a Nazi kitchen, up to my ears in *Gefüllter Fasan*.

One of those nights in '44, toward the end of winter, wrapped up in a blanket on the cold floor of the basement, waiting for a raid that never happened, I let go of the present and thought, for a second, about going home. I realized that as much as I ached to hear English and to be back in New York, I had no one to go back to. Somewhere at OSS Training School, in a small brown envelope in a metal cabinet, was my wedding ring. Suddenly, it hit me that I hadn't thought of John for weeks—maybe months. I knew then, for sure, that the ring was going to wind up in some other cabinet, in the Unclaimed Property Office. It would stay there forever. I didn't want it, not even as a souvenir to stick in the drawer next to my 1939 World's Fair official embroidered handkerchief.

So, I thought, here are my choices: I would die, courtesy of a British bomb or German prussic acid; Germany would win the war and I'd be stuck as a cook for the Dreschers the rest of my life; or the Allies would win, and somehow, even if it took years, I'd have a shot at getting *home*.

So what if there was no one to go home to? Even if I had to start my life all over again, slinging hash in a diner in Long Island City or working for some fat-mouth lawyer on Court Street in Brooklyn, I wanted to be back in New York more than anything else.

But I didn't want to think about it too much, to picture lying on the sand in Rockaway, or drinking a chocolate malted, or ever really—being now, at last, at age thirty-five, of sound mind—finding my one true love. Because if it came down to dying, unfulfilled dreams would make death hurt even more. I'd rather check out with a few bittersweet memories: of John, of at least not dying an old maid, and of having done a good turn for the red, white and blue. I had enough regrets, like not seeing my mother before she died. And not, all those years, ever having had the guts to say, Hey, you want to know what kind of a name Voss is? It's Jewish. I hadn't even had the courage to admit it to Edward, the one person who knew me better than anyone, and knew the truth.

Edward Leland was my biggest regret. I'd slammed the door on that one forever by not resolving our fight, and by leaving that cold, typed letter on his desk: I quit. Then, just to make sure there was nothing to go back to, I'd burned my one last bridge by sneaking behind his back to Norman Weekes. So there was no chance of regaining the best . . . what? Friendship? Association? The best connection I had ever had. But, I thought, life is full of regrets. And I'll take life any way I can get it.

Because, you see, deep down I knew we were going to win the war. It was on every face I saw in the street, in the snappiness of Rolf's walk as he crossed from one side of the fish store to the other, in the ever-more-downward slump of Horst's shoulders. Sure, Berliners picked themselves up and tried to put as many pieces together as they could, but there was none of that energy, none of that quiet spirit, none of that zest for life I'd heard in British voices over the radio in those days back in 1940, during the Battle of Britain. The Germans were losers—and they knew it.

Hedwig took to bed almost permanently in the early spring of 1944, and while that may sound as if it would have been a boon for me, it was really a disaster. I found myself in the exact position I'd been in when she was sniveling away in the parlor; exposed. From her bedroom, she had a panoramic view of the linen closet out in the hall. And I couldn't rely on her stupors: One minute she'd be snoring, an awful sound, as if she was being forced to gargle with some hideous-tasting mouthwash. And then, just as I put my hand on the door handle of the linen closet, she'd call, "Lina! My milk!"

"I was coming to see if you were ready for it, Madam."

"Well, I am."

I couldn't take that chance night after night, so finally I decided to keep the key. It was a risk, but not the worst I'd ever taken; sneaking into Berlin was not what you'd call the act of a totally balanced person. Besides, I was almost positive the second key had passed from the Jewish family into the Dreschers' possession unnoticed. Horst had never invited more than twelve people, so there was no need for anyone to even breathe near those huge tablecloths. I couldn't see Horst saying, Gee, Hedwig, let's invite twenty people for a Passover dinner.

Naturally, I couldn't walk around twirling the key on a chain. I had to make sure no one could ever associate the key with me, so I prowled through the house, looking for a safe, accessible hiding place; I couldn't risk keeping it in my room or in the kitchen. Finally I found what I needed.

There was a tree right by the side door of the house—a door everyone used except for formal occasions—and on it there was a branch barely above eye level. It had a small indentation in its upper side, like a little wood saucer. I could slip out the side door anytime; it was the way to get to the shed where they kept the garbage. I made it a point to always lift the small kitchen garbage pail up, away from me, as if to keep it from dripping. Plopping the key into its tree saucer was a comparative cinch.

Did I ever need easy access to that key! The German foreign office was buzzing about an invasion of France by the Allies. There was no doubt that it would happen; the only questions were when and where. So I took to sneaking into Horst's office every night, because it was clear that the invasion would be launched from England, Horst's territory.

Going into his study was like entering a gold mine: There were reports of troop concentrations in England, a feud between the British and the Free French; there were analyses of General Eisenhower's character and intelligence, and a pile of incompatible accounts on when the invasion would take place, accompanied by maps and by weather and tidal charts.

Even reading the material the way I did—at three in the morning, while Horst slept upstairs; with a quick glance just to figure out what was worth writing home about; and then trying to write those teeny letters wearing cotton gloves and by flashlight—I knew: Not only were their agents in disagreement, but their meteorologists were at each other's throats. But the OSS could make something out of all the facts and figures, because they knew which information was accurate; the more stuff I could give them, the more they would know about what the Germans suspected.

As for where the invasion was going to take place—well, it seemed to me the allies had succeeded in baffling the Germans. There were three prime areas Horst's agents in England kept swearing would be *the* spot: Pas-de-Calais, Normandy, and running a distant third, Seine-Maritime. I'd creep up to bed by three-thirty and listen to the bombs and the anti-aircraft fire, and I'd try to conjure up a map of France, but even though I was positive I once knew which area was which, the only thing I could remember was that all three were north, across the Channel from England.

Mornings, I trudged toward Rolf's, stepping over bricks and twisted metal, moving aside for the streams of people left homeless, who wandered around with their few possessions in soup kettles or, if they were lucky, baby carriages, and I prayed that the fish store hadn't been hit.

One morning, though it had survived still another night, Rolf said, "Bad news," when I walked in. Fortunately, before my mouth could drop open, he motioned me farther into the store, and I saw what he meant. There weren't any more than ten fish in sight. That's okay if you're a cook for a foreign office big shot who brings home loins of French lamb and Polish hams, but it's not okay if you're a spy and there isn't a goldfish with a mouth for a message. "Not even a mackerel can get through."

"Too bad," I said. As usual, I was holding my tiny piece of paper between my index and middle fingers. I always took it from a slit in my coat sleeve just before I walked into the store.

Rolf looked dejected. His head was down, and even his arm hung limp. But then I realized his index finger was pointing to the floor; he'd managed to steer me to the side of the counter where he cleaned and scaled, so our feet couldn't be seen by the two other workers in the shop. I dropped the paper on the floor. "But come back as soon as you can," he said. I noticed his shoe had moved a fraction of an inch and had kicked the paper under the counter. "They say there's some nice herring coming in."

"I'll try," I said.

"Good." He guided me back toward the door. "The more you come, the better your chance of getting a nice piece of fish. It may be a bother, but I'm sure your employer will appreciate your efforts."

So the OSS wanted the intelligence as fast as I could give it to them. And a week later, I knew I had something big.

It was a translation of a report from one of Horst's agents in England, but when I shifted the paper to copy it better, I realized there was another paper stapled to it: the original report, in English. From the fold lines and the way it was curled up, it had obviously been rolled and pushed into a small space: a bullet casing, or even a pen.

*I have settled into the town of Lydd, and ensconced myself at the local pub, so much so that the Americans take me for one of the locals. One of them, a Captain Grayson, is a member of the liaison group between Eisenhower and Montgomery. Quiet chap. Quite the loner. He reads a good deal of poetry. I made his acquaintance after several nights of observing him reading from the works of Walt Whitman, the American poet.*

*"Ah," I said, "to think in this godforsaken spot there is someone else who cherishes* Leaves of Grass.*" He was stunned that the English knew of Whitman (!), but was rather thrilled. I used my cover story, and there is no doubt he believes that I am a (if not the) Royal Army expert on heavy artillery. I had "a bit much" to drink and told him all about the Gun Mark 3.*

*Last night I got him talking about French poets, particularly Verlaine. One thing led to another, and my dear Captain Grayson, responding to my passionate Francophilia, told me the invasion will take place on the beaches of Normandy and that the talk of Pas-de-Calais is a ruse! I made light of it, saying it was too painfully logical and therefore unlikely. I have invited him to dine with me Thursday, when I will show him my library and allow him to convince me that Normandy is the place.*

I copied the English word for word, put back the envelope, flap side up, then stood at the door for the longest five minutes I'd endured since I'd started poking around in Horst's study. Someone *had* to stop this Grayson guy. Or encourage him; if he was a plant, Horst's agent in England believed he was telling the truth. And by the list of names at the end of the translation, enough people in the foreign office, SS, Army General Staff and Abwehr were getting copies to show that the Germans took him seriously. If "Grayson" was OSS, he should keep piling it on.

I had to get to Rolf's, but the more I thought, the more I realized going the next day would be risky; I'd just been there and bought two carp. No one, not even someone like me, with unlimited ration coupons, could be in such dire need of fish as to come back the next day. My orders were clear: Come often, but every day is too often. I didn't want to risk arousing suspicions. I would wait one more day.

My mistake.

* * *

It was late afternoon, and I was in the kitchen seeding a cucumber, when Hedwig screamed. It was such a departure from her usual whine that it tore through the house, all the way down to the kitchen. By the time I raced up the stairs to the second floor, Else and Dagmar were already there. Hedwig stood in the dark, wood-paneled hallway in her aqua robe; it had a milk dribble down the right breast. Her hands were clenched tight on the open linen closet door.

All Dagmar could do was say, "I didn't know there was a key, Madam," over and over. But even if Dagmar had wanted to help Hedwig, she couldn't; Else had thrown her arms around the chambermaid in terror and was squeezing the air out of her, like a wrestler. And Hedwig herself was in such a woe-is-me state that, finally, all she could do was shriek again.

The three of them looked like one of those stuffed wild animal tableaux at the Museum of Natural History; they were absolutely incapable of freeing themselves from their ridiculous positions. I would have laughed, except that what was happening was so perilous and I was on the brink of hysteria myself. My voice quavered so much I was terrified that it alone would give me away. "What happened?" I asked. "Is there anything I can do?"

The actual sound of someone speaking a full sentence seemed to jolt them all. Else let go of Dagmar and began to cry into her apron; Dagmar bent over to the pile of giant tablecloths, which were now on the floor, and, clearly for the second or third time, began to open each one wide and shake it; and Hedwig said, "The key is missing!"

"Key?" I asked. I had to do four things at once: get control of myself, look more innocent and dumb than even Else, figure out how dangerous my situation was, and see if I could save myself. "What key?"

"The key to my husband's study."

I tried to look confused. "It's always locked. Doesn't Herr Drescher carry the key?" If I was nearly hysterical, Hedwig was far out in front of me. She clenched at the door even

tighter, her hands like claws, and screeched, "He called from
the office! He forgot some papers here and he must have
them. He is upset. No; angry. *So* angry. He told me I would
find an extra key under the pile of big tablecloths." She took
a huge gulp of air and then whispered: "He said, 'This is a
top-secret key. Tell no one!' " Her whisper was replaced by
a loud wail.

Else grabbed onto me; it was like being hugged by King
Kong. "We'll all look for it, Madam," I said, in the gentlest
voice possible. I pulled out of Else's strangulating embrace
and moved toward Hedwig. "Let me help you into bed. You
must rest. I'll get you some warm milk . . ." I managed to
unhook her claws from the door. ". . . and then the three of
us will find your husband's key."

She allowed herself to be led into her room. I sat her on
the edge of the bed, knelt down and took off her slippers.
"Everything will be fine, Madam."

When I stood up, I saw her hands were now covering her
face; she was sobbing. "Hurry," she begged. "He
sounded . . . like a madman when I told him I couldn't find
it. He said he'd phone again, to see if . . . but he didn't. Dear
God, he's probably coming home. You *must* find it, before
he gets here."

"I will, Madam." I shifted her bulky body into the bed.

In the five or six steps it took me to cross the room and
close the door, I realized I had to get out before Horst came
home, or I was finished. I was the newest member of the
household staff, and for that reason alone I would be under
the most suspicion. But all of us would be grilled, over and
over, first by Horst, then, if he was stupid enough to let out
the truth about his bringing papers home every night, by the
professionals. They'd check our stories, our papers, our his-
tories.

"She wants her milk," I told them. "I'll be right back." I
hurried down the hall. For a second, I glanced at the flight of
stairs that led to the third floor and my room. I should go get
my papers, I thought. A change of underwear. But I couldn't

risk letting Else and Dagmar see me go up there; even they might start to wonder.

I hurried down the stairs, through the dining room and into the kitchen, so, if they were listening, they could hear the door swing shut. I hung up my apron, grabbed my brown coat off a hook, took some loose change and an apple, and ran out the side door.

I looked up at the tree branch. Let the key stay; I wouldn't be needing it, and besides, I had to run. Except I had no sense of where to run to. I only knew that it was no more than a fifteen-minute ride to the villa from the foreign office, and Horst wouldn't be telling his driver, Twice around the Tiergarten.

I climbed the small wall in back that separated Horst's property from the neighbor's. There were sharp pebbles embedded in the stone and gravel; they bit into my hands and tore at my stockings. Just as I reached the cobblestone sidewalk outside the neighbor's house, I heard the squeal of the brakes of a too-fast Mercedes-Benz stopping in front of Horst's. The car door opened. Then came a faint but distinct cry of panic: "Hedwig!"

It was almost six in the evening. Rolf's store would probably be closed. I had been in Berlin for a year and a half—too long to gamble on going to the safe address I'd been given. So if I was going to survive, I had no choice but to jeopardize the life of my best friend. My only chance lay with Margarete; she knew the way the game was played. She could tell me what to do and, if necessary, galvanize the resistance into action. But as I stood in front of her apartment building, I wanted to cover my face and cry for what I was doing to her.

It all looked so secure, so protected, with its ornate wrought-iron door. Imposing stone urns stood on either side. They were filled with red geraniums and seemed oblivious to the war. And just my walking through the front door, showing my face, would endanger everything Margarete had.

There was one small chance. Horst might realize that his own life was in peril because he had housed a spy, and he'd keep my disappearance a secret. But I doubted it; it was too risky. He knew Else or Dagmar might talk, especially if he begged or bribed them not to; that was the beauty of his Third Reich. Or it would have to occur to him that the Gestapo might catch up with me—maybe when I was performing some terrorist act—and under torture I might cry out: Horst Drescher! Sooner or later—probably sooner, maybe within hours—the photograph on the passport in my room would be copied and sent to every policeman and Gestapo agent in Berlin.

There was no doorman, but just to be safe, I walked around the huge stone building until I found the service entrance. There was an elevator inside, a cage. It was open. The operator was gone; he'd left his newspaper on his tiny half circle of a stool. But I walked past it, over to the door to the service stairs. It was locked.

I had no choice. I got into the elevator, slammed the gate shut after me and turned the operator's wooden handle to the right. The elevator jerked and then started slowly, *so* slowly, to creak upstairs. Finally it stopped. Margaréte had once remarked that she lived on the top floor of her building; it was an endless cave of an apartment, she'd said, but it had a magnificent view of the Brandenburg Gate.

I stepped out of the elevator, into a small alcove. There was a large metal door, the back door to her apartment, and another to the staircase. I made sure the door to the stairs was open and took the elevator down three or four floors, where I left it. Then, heart in throat, I climbed all the way up again.

It was obvious Margarete's endless cave took up the entire floor of the building; besides the door to the stairs, there was only one other door in the service alcove: The area itself was all empty space, with nothing to hide behind. I crouched close to the door to the apartment and waited, knowing all the time that if anyone came up on the service elevator, I was dead.

You focus on crazy things at times like that. There I was, listening at a back door for a front door to open, my picture about to circulate all over Berlin, and I was thinking: Why did I have three cups of tea this afternoon? because I had to go to the bathroom. That's all I could concentrate on. Okay, so maybe I thought a little about the rumor of the Gestapo's latest persuasive technique: They smashed the joints of your fingers, one by one, with a hammer. And then I thought: Wouldn't it be funny if all of a sudden, after going untouched, this building gets an early-evening bomb, with me on the top floor. But in truth, those pictures of peril seemed like nothing compared to the strain on my bladder.

I must have been there nearly an hour when, through the metal door, I heard someone enter the apartment. I listened: There must have been rugs but, finally, wood floors, because there was the click of a woman's heels. The noise advanced. I tapped at the door. Nothing. I knocked. The footsteps stopped. I said to myself, Oh, God, let it be her, then I put my mouth to the door and called out, "Margarete!"

The footsteps clicked closer. "Who is it?"

"Lina."

The door was opened a slit. "It is you!" she whispered. "Why . . . ?"

"I'm sorry."

"No. You must be . . . in terrible trouble. Come in." She led me into a small vestibule between what must have been a maid's room and the kitchen.

"Do you have a bathroom?"

"Lina!" she said softly, smiling. "If that's why you came here, I shall be extremely annoyed. All right, follow me."

Some cave. We walked through hallways hung with framed paintings—a couple of old barons, and the kind of German still-life paintings of fruit bowls that somehow always have dead rabbits and candlesticks too.

There were crystal bottles of bath salts, perfumes and lotions all over her bathroom, as though it never occurred to Margarete that in the middle of the night she would hear a whistle and then her life would be reduced to shattered glass.

She took me into her kitchen and we sat together on some sort of fancy wooden bench she had along one wall of the huge room. "Let me make you something. A nice omelet?"

I said, "Please, I can't eat."

"Nervous stomach again?"

"Nervous . . . everything. More than nervous. Oh, Margarete, I've done a terrible thing coming here. I've brought you into this whole mess. If I'm seen coming or leaving, everything, all this"—I waved in the direction of the hallway, with its rich gold-framed barons—"won't do you any good."

Margarete slipped off her shoes and tucked her feet under her. For a minute she didn't say anything. She studied her hands, fiddled with the heavy gold bracelets she wore, but didn't look at me. "Lina, it is simple. If you had a choice, you wouldn't be here, so there is no reason for you to feel remorse. Now tell me what happened."

I told her all about Horst, Hedwig and the key. All about my work. Every time I added another detail, I felt as if I was digging her grave a little deeper. So, for whatever it was worth, I didn't tell her about Captain Grayson and how urgent it was that I get that message through. If I couldn't save her, at least I could try to give her a little protection, allow her to have the luxury of a little ignorance.

Both of us might be captured and forced to talk. But despite what she had once told me about how members of the resistance movement committed the sin of pride by thinking: Oh, yeah, I can withstand the worst kind of torture, I felt that I could last longer than Margarete. She had extraordinary courage and nobility, but I was afraid that the nobility might be the thing to do her in. Even though she'd talked a lot about how much she hated her pampered childhood, she had still lived it. Okay, I wasn't raised on the toughest streets in New York, but no one had ever ironed my clothes or polished my chandeliers for me. I was older, and just a little bit tougher. Looking at her perfect white hands, with their opal and gold rings, her gleaming buffed nails, all of precisely the same length, I sensed that that small difference might be important.

And there was another difference: I was half German but completely American. Even after all this time, they were foreigners to me. And if it came down to me and the Gestapo, I really believed I could hate them—and withstand them—a little better than she could. They had murdered her dear friend Alfred. Well, they'd rounded up and slaughtered my family. My people.

Margarete finally looked me right in the eye. "Is there anything else I should know?" she asked.

"No," I said. "You know everything now. How terrible does it look for me? Would it save time," I demanded, trying to smile, "if I just went straight to the Berlin police and gave myself up?"

She leaned over and adjusted a loose hairpin on one of my braids. "It might save time, but it would be infinitely stupid. Now listen to me, my dear friend. I'm going to tell you exactly what to do." She glanced at a big wall clock. It was almost seven-thirty. "You have to get out of here. The pig is due here in an hour, and he might stay the night, so I can't offer you my most choice accommodations. The first thing you must do is get to this Rolf." She paused. "But his fish store is certainly closed by now." I nodded. "So you will get to him first thing in the morning. Now, is your hair in your passport photograph braided?"

"Yes."

"All right. Let's hurry inside. You'll take down your hair and I'll give you something to put on—less domestic, more well-kept mistress. You'll spend tonight in the Friedrichstrasse underground. Get in the middle of the crowds. Stay in the middle but don't talk. Anything, even the tension in your voice, could give you away. I don't think you comprehend how frightened you are, Lina."

"Oh, Margarete, I really think I do. I'm *terrified*." She stood and led me back through the long hallway, into her bedroom. I took out my hairpins. She wrapped them in toilet tissue and buried them in a wastebasket that was full of cold-cream and makeup tissues. She handed me her brush. Silver. I brushed my hair and she said, "Don't leave the underground too early—even though there are always a few people who get up and go around dawn. Wait a little later, for the main part of the crowd to leave, and go out with them, blend in. Now listen to this: Do not take the train from that station to Rolf's. No one does that. Everyone goes home, to see if they still have a home and to wash up. Take your time. Walk to the Französische Strasse station. You should plan on getting to Rolf's between seven-thirty and eight. Even if the store is still closed, he will be there; they go to market early." I put down the brush. "How is his fish?"

"Not bad," I said, "but probably not up to your standards."

"Isn't it odd?" Margarete said. She looked in the mirror of the dressing table, picked up the brush and ran it through her long brown hair. "All these years I've never even heard there was a fishmonger in the movement."

"It's too bad you don't know him," I said. "There's something really admirable about him," I said. "I mean, I don't really know him. The only strong opinion I've ever heard him express is that it's wrong to cut the heads off fish. But I know, to me, he really represents everything good about Germany. Well, Rolf—and you."

"Oh, don't flatter me. But him. Lina, there you have it: the greatness of the common man."

"And the greatness of the uncommon woman." And then I turned to her and said, "Thank you, Margarete."

# 25

I didn't dare risk sleep, so I sat up. All night long I felt the damp chill of the wall of the Friedrichstrasse underground through my coat. I couldn't risk taking it off and rolling it into a backrest or a pillow, as I'd done in the past; the report on Captain Grayson was slipped into the slit I'd made months before, in the lining of the cuff of the sleeve.

Lives could be saved or lost; I *had* to get the intelligence to Rolf. So I leaned against that clammy wall all night, listening to the slow, heavy night breathing of the crowd, just waiting to get free, and thinking about Captain Grayson. Either he was an OSS jewel—the world's supreme conveyer of disinformation—or one selfish, rotten, weak son of a bitch. Selling his country down the river. For literature! I smiled for a second, imagining the army recruiting Nan and all the other little cerebralettes into a special WAC battalion to take care of morale for guys like him: Oh, Captain, forget the three panzer divisions. Tell me about Verlaine's metaphors.

Seven-thirty or eight, Margarete had said. Your friend should be there by then.

I half closed my eyes and pictured Rolf's store: the sawdust-covered wood floors, the scrubbed counters, the orderly rows of fish on their beds of chopped-up ice. They were all laid out whenever I got there—usually around ten o'clock. But, I thought, by ten o'clock the ice was always partially melted. I remembered it clearly then; I was careful always to lean forward, not to step too close to the counters, because the freezing, fish-scented water would drip onto my shoes. I figured they must set out the ice about five-thirty, six in the morning.

I couldn't stand the waiting. And so, soon after the "all clear" signal, just after daybreak and the end of curfew, I copied the first of the early risers; I yawned, stretched my neck and made my way on cautious tiptoes among the still-sleeping mounds.

But when I got to Rolf's, a little after six, he wasn't there. No one was. The door was locked, the store dark. I walked to the corner. The old man who ran the newspaper kiosk, a man I'd seen a million times, glanced up at me, not so much suspiciously as curiously. I couldn't afford curiosity.

"I was told to get here early," I said, to explain. "To the fish store. They might have some haddock."

"No haddock today," the newsdealer said. "The police-man told me." Oh, God, I thought. "The man who worked there was killed last night. The one-armed man."

You're effing falling apart! an instructor at OSS Training School had roared to me one time. Don't give me any of that tender-maiden crap! No flutters! No fainting! This is war, girlie.

"The one-armed man?" I showed surprise. A little regret. "How was he killed?"

"A bomb."

"Oh." All the energy I had left seemed to seep out of me. Was it horror? Relief that Rolf hadn't been caught? I felt so weak. The apple in my pocket that I'd taken from the Dreschers' weighed me down.

"His wife came first thing, the policeman told me. Before dawn. Took his knives, the kind fish people use, and some other things that were his. Said she didn't know if they would bother opening the store again."

A *bomb?* I kept thinking. But what did I expect? A special RAF note engraved on each casing: Abstain from detonating in presence of friends.

"Did he own the store?"

"Yes." He cut the cord on a pile of papers. "You know, I

never knew how he lost his arm. I couldn't ask. He was quiet, kept to himself." He looked at me expectantly. "Do you know?"

"No," I said. "I never . . ."

Out of the corner of my eye, I saw a man walking down the street toward Rolf's. Maybe it was nothing more than my own dread that made the whole world seem menacing, but I felt something was wrong about him. He looked okay, not tight, cold Gestapo. But even from a distance, his raincoat looked too clean and well-pressed. Or it could have been that his walk was not quite brisk enough for a government worker getting an early start on his day.

Maybe Rolf had been carrying something on him when he was hit, and when they found his body, searched it . . .

"Well," I said to the newsdealer. "It is sad. He seemed like a nice man."

"A good business, if you don't mind smelling like that all the time."

"Yes," I said. "Goodbye."

And then I turned the corner, out of sight of the man in the raincoat, and walked fast. Not too fast. Just the sharp pace that an energetic cook would take when she is on the trail of haddock.

I went to the zoo. There was no grass; the ground was black, and the air was absolutely still. It had been bombed a few weeks before. The cages had been so badly damaged that the police had had to shoot the animals, for fear they'd get loose and run wild in Berlin. Boy, had everyone gotten all weepy over that. Poor animals! The slaughter of the innocents! The Germans were so compassionate.

I sat on what was left of a bench. The jagged ends of the wooden slats were scorched; when you touched them, they broke off into cinders. I took the apple out of my pocket and bit into it. It's funny; when you read about people who know their time is up, they're always tasting or smelling something and going Ahh! at the beautiful sense experience they never noticed before. Don't believe what you read. My time looked like it was almost up, and what might be my last meal was an ordinary, unexceptional, mealy apple.

I put it back in my pocket. I couldn't eat. My nerves were shot, and so was my stomach. For almost two years I'd done almost nothing but sauté, roast and stew. I'd lived in the middle of abundance, and yet in all that time I hadn't been able to get down one entire meal. I'd tasted a little. I'd drunk tea. And on those nights when I didn't have to hide from bombs, I'd gone to bed with a hot-water bottle clutched to my aching belly. My clothes hung on me. My skin had turned ashen. Finally I looked as if I belonged in Berlin.

Oh, I was so tired. A couple of times I felt my head drop to my chest. I made myself sit straight, the way aristocrats do. Back at right angle to seat: like Margarete, or Nan. It was an awful, uncomfortable position for a regular person to have to stay in, but it made me breathe in deeper and kept me awake. Maybe that's why all those sleek upper-class girls had that special air about them; they just took in more oxygen. Then I wondered about what kind of jerk I was to be sitting there, on a fragment of a bombed bench, doomed in a doomed city, thinking about my not being classy. If Edward was sitting where I was, knowing the chances were pretty good he didn't have much more than a day or two to live, what would he be thinking about? Apples and stomachaches and rich girls? Concepts: good and evil; the nature of justice? Or something I never even dreamed about?

It was time to get moving. The news about Captain Grayson had to get to the OSS before he could meet that agent for a home-cooked dinner, a few poems, a couple of drinks and then a confidential chat—fascinating, old bean—about the invasion of good old La Belle France.

Except I didn't know what to do. Fifteen, twenty minutes passed. I was crazy to be staying in one spot like that. A policeman or a soldier could come along any minute and demand my papers. But I was unable to move because I couldn't think of where to move to.

Okay, I said to myself. Enough with the inaction. This is

war, girlie. Make believe you're Edward Leland and you're stuck in enemy territory and you've got an urgent message you've got to get out. What do you do? You think: Who do I know? Who can I trust? All right: I know Margarete. Oh, and I know old laughing boy, Konrad Friedrichs, the guy with the million-dollar smile.

But stop. Think like Edward. Analyze. Who has a better chance of getting that message out?

At about seven-thirty that morning, I lay behind a hedge, flat on my stomach in the dirt, and, with my shoe in my hand, hammered at a window gently, until it cracked. Slowly, patiently, I picked out the pieces of glass so the frame was clean. Then I slithered down through the narrow basement window—into my old bedroom at Herr Konrad Friedrichs's.

My number two fear was that when I showed myself to Konrad Friedrichs, he'd have a heart attack and drop dead on the spot. But number one was his housekeeper, the Wicked Witch of the West, Frau Gerlach: Just my presence in the house would probably be enough to set her warts humming. So I stood with my ear against the door of my old cubicle, going through my familiar count to three hundred, listening for any sounds. A little after two hundred, I thought I heard footsteps moving across the room above me. That would be the pantry; she was getting out dishes to set the table for breakfast.

I climbed up to the first floor and put my ear against still another door. No sound. I opened it a crack and peered out. That always works terrifically in movies, because the hero can always see the villains having a meeting forty feet down the hall and around the corner. But the only thing I could see was a tiny strip of wall. So I slid out the door and, fast, looked to the right, to the kitchen. Nothing. For all I knew, she could leap out with a skillet in her hand and attack me, but she might just be sitting and having a cup of tea; I wasn't going to hang around and count to three hundred again. I rushed off to the left, to the narrow wooden staircase, and, throwing all my Training School techniques aside, ran right upstairs, straight into Konrad Friedrichs's bedroom.

He didn't have a heart attack, although he seemed to stop breathing for at least a full minute. He just gaped at me. I gaped back. He was standing beside a high chest of drawers, wearing a starched-collared shirt and a tie, but he didn't have on his trousers. He had old man's legs; white, knob-kneed, hairless, "My God!" he said. I put my finger on my lips to signal him to keep quiet. "How dare you!"

"I don't have time to listen to you now," I told him softly. "I'm only going to stay two or three minutes, and then I'm going to get out. No one will know I've been here. But listen to me. My contact, Rolf, is dead."

Herr Friedrichs walked over to his high, old-fashioned bed and, unmindful that he was in white undershorts and black hose, sat down and shut his eyes. "They killed him?" he asked.

"No. At least I'm pretty sure they didn't. It seems to have been a bomb. But they know about me." He rolled his eyes, one of those weary, it-was-inevitable expressions. I got so mad! "Look," I said, "for a year and a half I've been giving the OSS first-rate intelligence, so don't give me any of your speeches about foolhardy amateurs. *You* try living in the same house with a Nazi like Horst Drescher, sneaking into his locked study four, five, six, seven nights a week, and see how long you'd last."

He said, "You have made your point. Proceed."

"I have a message that has to get out, and there's no Rolf anymore." He started to shake his head. "Listen, there's a German agent near an American army base in England. He's getting top-secret information about the Allied invasion of France." Konrad Friedrichs's eyes widened. "You've *got* to let them know."

"I cannot. I have just returned from Lisbon and Madrid. I am unable—"

"You don't have any choice."

"Don't threaten me!"

"Herr Friedrichs, I'm not threatening you. I'm trying to save lives—including yours. Horst Drescher is no analytical genius. We both know that. But he's no fool, either. In a day or two, maybe even today, he's going to realize who recommended me so highly." He covered his face with his veiny old hands. "You have to get out."

"If I leave my country now, I might never come back."

"If you don't leave now, you'll be dead. Please, you've got to understand how critical this situation is. For you. And for the Allies. Yes, you do have to leave, but is the Germany you're living in the Germany you want? If there's any chance of saving the country you love, it lies in its defeat." I paused for a second, but he wouldn't stop hiding his face in his hands. "Don't you want to stay alive so that when it's all over, you can come back and help your people, guide them, show them what's right?" Slowly, he lowered his hands to his lap. They were shaking. He was a man who did things by the book, and this time there was no book. He didn't know what to do. "Is there any way you can get straight to the airport now and get transport out on an emergency basis? Please, think. Help me."

"There might be." His speech was halting. "But it will be harder for you. I would have to speak to Margarete, to try and get you . . . perhaps some sort of diplomatic passport."

"No! You have to get out this morning, before Horst realizes your connection to me."

"But what about you?" Give him credit. He was a cranky, rigid Prussian snob, but he was also a man of honor. Whatever I was, I was his ally. He would therefore save my life.

I wouldn't let him. "Thank you, but if I go with you, there's no chance of getting the message out." I reached into the slit in the lining of my cuff and drew out the tiny slip of paper. I walked over and put it in his hand. "There will be copies of my passport photo at every train station, airport and border crossing in Germany. We both know that." For a long time, he didn't speak.

"What will you do?" he asked.

"Margarete's already helped me once. I think I'm going to have to go back. I hope she'll be able to help me again."

"I hope so too," he said. He showed no signs of moving; he just sat primly on the bed, the message clenched in his hand.

"Come on now, stand up. Finish getting dressed." He looked down at his bare legs in shock. "I'm afraid we don't have time for modesty now. As soon as you're ready, you'll have to go downstairs and keep your housekeeper busy so I can sneak out."

I took him by the elbow and eased him off the bed. That was really all he needed. He marched to his closet, turned away from me, stepped into his trousers and began to button them. "Poor, dear Frau Gerlach," he murmured. "What will I tell her?"

"*Nothing.*"

He spun around, all red-faced, huffy. "She's utterly trust-worthy."

"I'm sure she is." I wasn't sure at all. She'd probably sell him down the river for ten pfennigs. "But it's her devotion to you that you have to worry about. She'll fear for your life. She might call a friend of yours, a colleague, to get help for you. Promise me you won't say anything to her." He stood there, stubborn. I lost my temper. "Damn it!" I whispered. "You don't have time to be noble. Don't you want to live? Don't you want to give me at least a chance to survive? For God's sake, promise me."

"You have my word," he said at last.

A little more than sixty seconds later, I was back on the streets of Berlin.

I imagined Edward again. Think, he said. What is there besides your passport—with your photograph and finger-prints—that can be used to identify you? How would Horst describe you?

Well, he'd say I had blond hair—

Don't waste time, Linda. All that information is on your passport. What else?

One of the maids would remember I have a brown coat.

Lose it.

I took off my coat and draped it over my arm. It was warm for April. At least I thought it was April; the trees that still stood were covered with the hazy green of new leaves. I used my last two coins for a bus ride. I climbed to the upper deck, took a seat and put the coat beside me. A few minutes later, when I was sure no one was looking, I gave it a light push; it fell to my feet. The bus rumbled on for another couple of miles; then I walked downstairs and got off.

I spent the rest of the day waiting in lines. I'd asked the imaginary Edward, Where should I go? Margarete's at work.

Become invisible. There are two ways to do it. Find a hiding place that you know is absolutely secure. Or blend in with a crowd.

So at around eight-thirty or nine that morning, I joined the long line of women in front of a bakery. "Hot, isn't it?" the woman in front of me said. Her dress was gray, the color of a mouse, and it had small white spots all over it from being scrubbed too many times.

"Yes, very hot. And so early in the day."

No one had conversations that lasted longer than that. Berliners were too exhausted after a night of bombing, too wrapped up in their own hardship, to want to chat. This was a line for stale bread, not for tickets at Radio City Music Hall.

So when suddenly I said, "Oh, no!" the woman looked pained, as if I was going to try and burden her with my troubles. "My pocketbook!" Her expression changed. I saw sympathy. And fear. She understood I had lost my money, my ration books and my passport: my whole German life.

"Calm yourself," she said, and then stepped aside so I could hurry off.

I made my way from neighborhood to neighborhood all day. I stood in the longest lines I could find, waiting an hour or two, and then discovering my loss. The waiting was so miserable, I had the headache that comes from lack of sleep, and the empty, aching nauseousness that comes as you start to move from hunger toward starvation.

In the late afternoon, as the sun was beginning to lose its strength, I started to walk toward Margarete's apartment building. It must have been around six-thirty when I got there, because the streets were filled with people coming home from work. I knew my chances of slipping up the service elevator were just about zero, so I went through the front door. Again, no doorman, but there was a uniformed operator at the main elevator. He had gold-braided shoulder brushes and a cap with a huge medallion. He looked like a veteran from a much better war.

"Yes?" he challenged me.

"I'm Lina, sir. Hugo, the Baron von Eberstein's estate manager . . . Hugo told me to—"

"Get in," he said, and whisked me up to the top floor. As I got out, he said, "Just ring the bell, Lina."

"Thank you, sir." And after he disappeared, that's what I did.

"I'm coming!" I heard Margarete say. Her heels made a rapid clack-clack. She'd been busy in the kitchen. I could smell onions being sautéed. The door opened. "God in heaven!" It was as if someone had pulled a plug: All the color drained out of her face.

"Is he inside?" I whispered. "The pig?"

"No." She put her hand over her chest and took a deep breath. "Come in." She pulled me inside and shut the door. "I can't believe you are here!"

"I'll go."

"*No!* It's just . . . Oh, dear God, I have been crazy with worry about you." She put her arms around me for a second and hugged me and then said, "Come into the kitchen."

We sat at a table draped in a lace cloth that went all the way to the floor. The cabinets were all glass, but the rest of the room was a rich, dark wood. "Are you hungry?" she demanded. She had a kitchen towel tucked into the belt of her blue silk dress.

"Yes, but my stomach—"

She leapt up. "I have some lovely calves' liver."

"Margarete, please, just a piece of bread." She hurried over to the bread box, took out a loaf of dark bread and sliced it. "I can't stay here."

"Why not?"

"You know why not."

"Do you want beer?" I shook my head no. She put the bread on a plate and then went to the refrigerator and returned with cheese and a bottle of milk.

"My picture is probably all over the city by now."

"It is," she said gently. "Everyone in . . . the movement who knows about you has been so frightened. What's happened? Tell me everything." She gave me a glass for the milk. A goblet.

"Please, I need a few minutes. I haven't slept or eaten since—"

"Then you must take a rest! I'll put you into a nice, soft bed with an eiderdown—"

"No, thank you." I put a small piece of cheese on the bread. Like the apple, this didn't have any taste. Still, it was food. So I just sat there, ate a few bites and sipped the milk in silence.

Margarete was comforting and discomforting at the same time. She'd smile or pat my hand, but then there were moments when her entire body tensed, as she tried to keep her jumpiness under control. I felt she would like nothing more than to run out of the room, away from me and the danger I'd brought.

"I won't come here ever again. You have my promise."

"Lina, you are always welcome."

"I'm here to ask for your help: yours and the movement's. If you can find someone who's willing to hide me, that would be more than I could rightfully expect."

"But you would like something more." She knew me so well.

"Yes," I said. "I wouldn't even have thought of it if Herr Friedrichs hadn't mentioned it."

"Oh, how is he?"

"Out of Germany, I hope."

"I see! You saw him?"

"Yes, early this morning. When he was thinking about how he could get me out of the country, he mentioned the possibility of calling you. Maybe, with all your connections . . . in the Abwehr, all the people your family must know, even the pig . . . Margarete, is there some way you can get me out of Germany?"

She shook her head. It wasn't as much a denial as saying, I don't know. "Lina, it would be so much easier for you to stay here. With all the bombings, we're becoming a nation of refugees. Give me a day. I can get new papers for you, decent ones." Her face brightened. "I know! We can cut your hair short and dress you up in my clothes. No one would know that the girl in the photograph with braids is the same person as the stylish young woman with the smart haircut!"

It was clear she was trying to sell me something, and although I knew I would probably have to buy it, I wasn't ready yet. "Let me tell you why I have to leave Germany," I said. "I don't belong here." Margarete waited. "I'm sure you understand, being a translator, that there are some people who belong in a country—and some people who don't."

"I'm sorry. I do not understand."

And for the first time in the year and a half that felt like a lifetime, I spoke English. "I don't belong in Germany because I'm an American, Margarete." For a minute she didn't react at all. Then she began to laugh uncontrollably. But she wasn't having a good time. She was hysterical. "Margarete. Stop it. *Please* calm down." I banged my fist on the table. She jumped, and she stopped. "Are you okay?" I asked.

"You speak English so well!" I began to laugh this time, and it was only a little bit of nerves. It was genuinely funny.

And now that I was speaking English, I didn't know if I could ever speak German again.

"Of course I speak English well. It's my native language."

"And your German?"

"My grandmother lived with us. She came from Berlin."

"So you are German."

"My father's parents were born in Germany."

"Your mother's family?"

"Originally from England or Scotland."

"OSS sent an *American* in here? *Why?*"

"Because there was nobody here who could do it. Margarete, come on. You know how efficient the Nazis are. Really, how many people are there in the resistance?"

"Very few," she acknowledged. Suddenly, she asked, "How is my English?"

"Excellent."

The beginning of a smile lit up her face: the old Margarete. "Could *I* get away with what you did?" She was playing her old game; she saw the danger, but she also saw the fun. "Could I slip into Chicago or some other large city and pass myself off as an American?"

"No. You're a little too precise, too clipped. And your *w*'s . . . they're still . . . slightly German." I grinned at her. "We could work on them."

"So my consummate Berlin friend is an American!"

"From New York. Hey, can you tell I have a New York accent?"

"No." She was starting to get nervous again. She stood and paced the kitchen.

"Take it easy, Margarete."

"That is rather difficult, Lina."

"I know."

She moved away from me and sat on a long carved wooden bench. "You're not a recruit? You're OSS?" she inquired.

"I've been working for them on and off since 1940."

"Did you do this sort of work for them before?"

"No. I was a secretary in New York and then in Washing-

ton. We moved down there before the war. Well, I mean
before the U.S. got into the war. Before Pearl Harbor."

" 'We'?"

"My husband's in the OSS also. He was a lawyer in one of
those big firms on Wall Street."

"What is his name?" She crossed her legs. Then she
folded her arms and hugged them tight to her body.

"John."

"Is your name really Lina?"

"Linda."

"Linda," she repeated. "Linda." Then suddenly she said,
"Oh, God, I need a drink. A brandy. Do you want one?" I
shook my head. "Excuse me, then, I'll be right back." I
smiled as she left the kitchen. Margarete sounded almost
exactly like Marlene Dietrich. While she was gone, I let
myself relax for a minute. It must have been because I was
speaking English, but I remembered *Destry Rides Again*,
and then I began to think how terrific it would be just to sit
with a big bag of popcorn and stare up at a screen. I decided
I wanted to watch something with Bette Davis. I thought: I
bet she's come out with at least two movies since I've been
away. I was really getting punchy, trying to remember if I'd
read any story in the magazines where the reporter says,
What are your future plans, Miss Davis? Then Margarete
came back to the kitchen. She didn't have a brandy.

She had a gun.

"You will never know how sorry I am," she said, in German.

*"What the hell are you doing?"* English.

"I think it should be obvious."

And it was. "You! You're the traitor in the resistance."

"Is that what they call me?"

"You're the one who killed Alfred Eckert."

"No! Alfred was my friend."

"But you killed him, anyway."

"No! Of course not." I stared at her. "Well, finally I had no
choice but to report him. He was too talkative. Too trusting. I
tried to protect him, Lina . . . Linda. I *try* to protect my

friends. Truly I do. Most of them . . . It is easy. You yourself said it. We are quite efficient, and the so-called resistance is painfully ineffectual. I merely report what the amateurs are doing. Hardly anyone . . . gets hurt. We recognize they can do little harm, but we keep track of them. You, however, were a danger, Lina. You were good. But still, I was going to save you. I swear I was. I loved you. I did. You were dear to me, special. You were everything I admired in the ordinary German. Hard-working. Smart. With a spare, simple beauty." She shook her head in disbelief. "You *look* so German."

"So Aryan."

"Yes."

"You're really one of them, aren't you?"

"No more English." She shook the gun at me, like a schoolteacher shaking her finger at a naughty student. "German, please."

"You believe all their crap," I said, in English.

"I understand the American idiom. Do not disgrace yourself by using filthy language. Now, to answer your question, I happen to love the Fatherland. And I believe, as my family believes, that the Führer has saved Germany from—"

"I don't want to hear it, you Nazi bitch! Shut up!"

"I realize you are agitated, but you cannot speak to me like that! Now please get control of yourself. It is time to talk. What is your full name?"

"Lina Albrecht."

"*Linda*, it should be obvious by now that I am in an unbearably difficult position. I will not hesitate to shoot. What is your full name, Linda?" She put the gun to my head.

"Lina Albrecht."

"How can you possibly have any doubts about the seriousness of my purpose?"

"No," I said. "No doubts. But first tell me something. For old times' sake. Did you kill Rolf?"

The gun against my head made turning to see her impossible, but I could sense her pride. "We picked him up within a half hour after you left last night. A mere half hour. He is probably dead by now."

"Who is 'we'? Your fat pig boyfriend?" She rubbed the muzzle of the gun against my scalp. Not a gun, I thought. A pistol. A Walther.

"He is not a pig! That was my cover story. His name is Franz Sommerfeld, and he is quite, quite handsome, actually."

"Is that how you operate? Every time you feel forced to get rid of one of your dear friends, you just call up Franz and ask him to take care of things? He took care of Alfred, right?"

"Unfortunately, Alfred discovered I wasn't quite what I pretended to be. He was too much the man about town, saw me once too often with my . . . real friends. His suspicions grew. Apparently, he took to watching me from the little café across the street. He saw Franz. Leave it to dear old Alfred to notice a handsome man! And then he saw the two of us going out together. And after a few times, he realized that this"—her voice softened—"beautiful man was the person I had been calling the pig. But Alfred's downfall was his romanticism, his belief in me. He couldn't believe that the disappearance of some of our . . . mutual friends had anything to do with his lovely, elegant Margarete—who wore his clothes with such chic. 'You are having a silly infatuation,' he told me. 'Drop this man, and I won't tell anyone in the movement about him. Swear it, *ma chère Marguerite*.' But of course I couldn't trust him. He would have tattled on me. Alfred couldn't resist a juicy scandal."

You know how people say, "I almost threw up"? I almost did. I couldn't shake the sickness, the horror; when she talked about Alfred, her voice was filled with delight. He was still her darling, amusing friend.

But suddenly, all the charm went out of her voice. "There is no more time. Move along." She pressed the gun harder against my head, grabbed my shoulder and pushed me toward the door.

"You're not going to kill me here, are you?"

"Lina, you are so clever. So *terribly* clever." The pressure of the gun made the whole right side of my face throb. "I'm afraid that in the time it would take me to call Franz, and for him to send his men over, you might find a way to extricate yourself." I stopped right where I was, about a foot from the kitchen door. "Please," she said, "I don't want to do it in my kitchen." Then she tilted her head—charming. "You must think I'm terrible, saying that."

"No. I think you're a wonderful person."

"Listen to me. I am doing you a favor. Don't you dare smile! I *am* being kind." She brought herself under control; her voice became subdued, soothing. "You don't want them to get at you. We both know it would be more than you could bear. With me it will be fast, merciful." I turned my head a fraction of an inch; her eyes were actually moist.

"Please," I said, "I'm begging you."

"Move, please." With the gun at my head as a prod, she led me out of the kitchen and down the long, picture-covered hall.

"Are any of these portraits old von Ebersteins?" I asked.

"Do not attempt to ingratiate yourself. Be brave. Die like a German."

But I didn't goose-step. I picked up my foot just a little higher than I had before. And then I smashed it down on her instep.

She screamed in pain, and in that second I grabbed her hand and bit it as hard as I could. It was a good bite, except her fingers didn't stiffen the way they said they would in Training School; they contracted.

Oh, God, my arm! Then the two of us became a mess of grappling arms, fingers, faces, all covered with my blood. Margarete jerked her hand away, to put the gun back against my head, but for an instant she stared at my teeth marks, and that's when I yanked at the barrel of the gun; it was burning hot from being fired, and slippery with my blood, and maybe that's why, the next thing I knew, it was mine.

I don't know how, but I managed to get a grip on it. And I put it against her head. "Margarete, this is a Walther."

"I know." Her voice was a little higher than usual, but strong. She was being brave.

"The saftey is already cocked. It will fire automatically now."

"Are you going to kill me?" she asked.

"Yes."

"Will you at least give me the final courtesy of a few quiet moments to compose myself and—"

"No."

"Lina, let me just write a note to—"

"No." I pressed my left arm against my waist; the pain was getting worse. Blood bubbled out of a small, black-rimmed hole and dripped onto her rug. I was getting dizzy. I jammed the gun harder against her head. Carefully, I inched around her until we were face to face. "Who am I, Margarete?"

"Lina," she whispered.

"No."

"Linda." This time she whimpered.

"I am Linda Voss. I am a Jew. Do you understand?"

"Yes."

"Good." And then I shot her brains out.

# 26

The linen napkin I put over the wound was like a sponge; soon it was soaked with blood. Slowly—I was so light-headed—I stepped back to the drawer in the breakfront in the hallway, tucked the gun under my chin, and with my good hand took out another napkin. A tourniquet: They'd shown us how in training school. We'd practiced on each other. Put it on that guy's thigh, they'd said, and so I put it on a Czech, and he'd looked away from me, embarrassed.

I glanced down. Blood had spilled out over my skirt. I was feeling faint now, and my knees started to wobble, my legs to flutter, as if I was doing some ridiculous 1920s dance. If a tourniquet can't be applied, they'd said . . . I lowered myself to one knee, then sat down. I tucked the gun into the waist-band of my skirt, where I could reach it with my right hand; it had to be near.

Margarete's body was a few feet away. I'd put a napkin over her face.

Pressure. Apply direct pressure to the wound. An arrow of pain slashed down my arm and spread out through my fingers. I groaned so loud and so deep I scared myself. Keep up the pressure.

I fainted or fell asleep. I don't know how long I was out . . . not long, because from where I was, slumped against the wall, I could see the floor of a bedroom, and there was still a little daylight coming through the window. I dragged myself toward it. Just to get away, to give myself time.

If I heard the apartment door open, I would take out the

gun and do to myself what I'd done to Margarete. I would not let them get me.

I crawled into the room. A large one. A bed with a footboard loomed in front of me, gigantic. If I could just lie in that bed . . . and drink a Coca-Cola from the bottle and listen to George Fisher from Hollywood on WOR . . . But I wasn't going to get home. I knew that. Until the end, though, I had to make it harder for them.

I looked around. Lace curtains, lace bedspread, a lace skirt on a vanity table covered with makeup and bottles of nail polish, which reflected in a gold-framed mirror. Margarete's room. I pulled myself along the floor near her bed, toward her night table. I couldn't get up to see what was on it, so I took a deep breath and pushed. It crashed down to the floor. The neighbors, I thought. But if they missed two gunshots . . . There was a telephone. I put the receiver back on the hook. Then I went through the drawer in the table.

Earrings, maybe twenty pairs. Gold, gold, opals, garnets, diamonds. She'd tossed them all in. Hand lotion. A diaphragm and a tube of jelly. A leather-covered telephone book: dark red leather, with tiny flowers tooled in gold.

I had to make it harder. I picked up the phone and dialed a number from the phone book. Under S. Let it not be him, God. I really prayed. It rang just once. "Colonel Sommerfeld." But a woman's voice, thank God.

"Listen to me," I whispered.

"I can't hear you."

"Margarete von Eberstein." This was it. No more *berlinerisch*. I put on the accent I'd heard but never spoken: John's, Herr Friedrichs's, Margarete's.

"I am sorry, it is difficult to . . ."

"Is the colonel . . ."

"He is not here, Miss."

The bleeding had stopped. Maybe it had been some sort of release, because now the pain was unbearable. The whole inside of my arm was trying to shove its way out of the tiny bullet hole. . . . I wanted to howl. I covered the mouthpiece the best I could with my one hand, and a small, terrible sound came out.

"Miss?"

"I must send word to him." I breathed into the phone. "Urgent. Lina is just inside. Good news. I have convinced her to take me to meet her contact. In Potsdam . . . Do you hear?"

"Yes, Miss. I will convey the message."

"I will ring him tomorrow. As soon as I slip away from her. Do you understand?"

"Oh, yes. Shall I try—"

I hung up. I curled up on my side, closed my eyes. If the pig would believe what his secretary told him, I had eight, twelve hours. I opened my eyes and thought: Stay awake. You'll be dead a long time. It would be a shame to spend the rest of your life sleeping.

Maybe I should say some prayer. Or think of all the good things that have happened to me.

Or just think of one wonderful thing for eight hours. Every detail. Something to treasure, to take along with me. Remember the time . . .

A few minutes later, I passed out.


I woke up because cold water was spilling down my neck. I opened my eyes. Someone was pressing a glass to my mouth. Dear God. As I reached to my waistband, for the gun, I saw that the man bent down before me was Konrad Friedrichs. Oh, did I smile! Who cared if he'd never crack a smile back. Was I glad to see him!

"Drink," he said.

"What time is it?"

"Sixteen hundred hours." Four in the afternoon. The next day. "Drink, please." He angled the glass to help me, and some water dripped onto my blouse. "Then you must tell me about Margarete. What horror is this? Such a beautiful—"

"We have to get out," I told him.

Suddenly I realized! Konrad Friedrichs had understood

the consequences of staying in Berlin; that's why he'd been
willing to steal away, without even telling his beloved witch
of a housekeeper. He'd known his choice was Lisbon—or
death. So now, if he *was* in Berlin, it was because he felt
safe. Oh God, he was one of them.

And then I was sure: I glanced beyond him. He was no
friend. In the doorway was a man in uniform. SS; high rank,
from so far away; all I could see were the boots, the trousers,
the holster. But that's all I had to see. With what was left of
my strength, which wasn't much, I shoved away the glass.
The water spilled over Konrad Friedrichs, and as he gawked
at his soaking wet shirt and tie, I went for the Walther.

The boots rushed across the floor. I yanked the gun out of
my waistband, raised it toward my head, and as I cocked the
safety, the SS man grabbed my wrist. I screamed. I tried to
bite him, but he twisted my arm. The gun fell into his hand.

"Linda." The man knelt over me. He was going to take me
away. "*Linda*, look at me." English. I lifted up my head. And
I saw Edward Leland.

I couldn't speak.

"Linda, are you all right?"

"What are you doing here?"

He lifted me so I was sitting up, resting against him. "I
thought I'd just drop by and say hello."

I tried to laugh, but instead I started to cry.

He put his arms around me. "It's all right. I've come to get
you out."

"It's too late." He didn't answer. Instead, he stood and
hauled me up.

Herr Friedrichs was sitting on the bed, staring at us, as if
we were some terrible show he'd been dragged to. "Did you
go to Lisbon?" I asked him.

"I do not speak English," he said in German.

I felt so woozy. I must have swayed for a second, because
Edward grabbed me and held me up.

"What happened to poor Margarete?" Herr Friedrichs
demanded.

"I'll tell you later," I said to him. Then I switched to Edward, to English. "Can we make it out of here?"

"We're going to damn well try. Can you walk?"

"Yes. I don't know how steady I'll be, but I can walk."

"Tell Friedrichs to wait here, that I'm taking you to the bathroom to get you cleaned up."

I stared at Edward. "He doesn't speak English at all?"

"No. It's been quite a pleasure, traveling with your friend. Such a pleasant, relaxed fellow."

"You were in Lisbon?"

"Yes. Come on now: Get a grip on yourself, Linda. Don't start crying again. We don't have time."

I told Konrad Friedrichs to stay put, and Edward helped me out into the hall. I stopped short. Margarete's body was still there, the linen napkin over her face. Her hand, with its ornate gold ring and ruby nails, rested on her chest. Her fingers looked stiff. Edward tried to lead me away; I couldn't move.

"I killed her."

"I assumed that. Let's go."

"I can't." I started to shake, seeing her there.

"You had a reason for killing her, didn't you?"

"Yes! She was the one. The traitor in the movement. And she was going to kill me."

"Well, you did what you had to." That didn't help. "Do you want to stand here and wait for her friends to show up so you can tell them how abhorrent you find their political philosophy? Or are you a professional?"

"Sometimes I can't stand you."

"I know. Let's move now, Linda."

He took me into the bathroom, filled the sink with warm water and gently lowered my arm into it, to soak off the napkin. The water turned dark pink. I guess I turned green, because Edward began to talk. "Two nights ago, we got word that your contact, Rolf, had been taken. I took the next plane out to England. When I got there, there was a message about Friedrichs. I flew to Lisbon right away."

"Why?"

"Why do you think?"

"I don't know."

"Look, this cloth isn't going to come off without some pulling. Shall I do it, or do you want to?" I reached into the water, pulled, and let out a scream of pain. Edward clapped a hand over my mouth and, with the other hand, lifted my arm out of the water, grabbed a towel and patted the area around the wound. "It's infected," he said, and he opened the medicine cabinet. No iodine. A lot more makeup. "I can't read the German. Is there anything there with alcohol?" I pointed to a bottle of astringent.

As he uncapped the bottle, I said, "You're going to tell me, 'This is going to hurt, Linda. Be brave.'"

"It's nice to see you haven't changed."

"Just pour the whole thing over, fast." It was so bad. I kept my teeth clenched together, and all that happened is I started crying again.

"I'm sorry I hurt you."

"It's okay."

"There's a train leaving at six tonight. We have to be on it, so we ought to put some speed on. Are you up to it?" I nodded. "All right, let's wipe your eyes, and then you'll put on some makeup."

"Are you kidding?" He reached inside his uniform pocket, pulled out a passport and held it up before me. A blonde, about thirty. Very pretty. Round face. Short hair with a wave that fell over her cheek. I looked at her name: Ingeborg Hintze. "Ingeborg?" I said. "*I'm* supposed to look like that?"

"You've got three minutes."

Edward left the bathroom, and with one hand and my mouth, I opened a box of mascara. I wet the brush, put on a few coats, then went on to rouge and lipstick. I looked into the mirror and then slumped against the sink. I looked lousy. No one would ever look at me and then say, Hi, Ingeborg.

Edward came back in less than three minutes. He was cutting a pillowcase into strips. "You'd probably be better off without a bandage, but I don't want to risk your bleeding."

"Ed, cut my hair."

*"What?"*

"Look at that passport picture. Come on. We still have about forty seconds left." So Edward Leland gave me a haircut. Not a good one, but at least I looked like I could be Ingeborg's plain, distant cousin. "Why did you pick her?"

"Most blondes have blue eyes. This passport had brown. I wasn't in a position to be fussy." He threw the hair down the toilet, flushed it, then put the makeup away.

"I didn't know you were such a neat person."

"When her friends get here, should they find a display of cosmetics and evidence that a blond woman cut her hair short? Do you think that would make an interesting dispatch to send out to the army and the Gestapo?"

He bandaged my arm and led me into the hall again, past Margarete's body, back into her bedroom. Konrad Friedrichs was where we'd left him, sitting on the bed, looking exhausted, almost lifeless. Edward motioned him to leave; he didn't understand.

"Herr Friedrichs," I said, "please wait outside."

"She is there. The beautiful—"

"The beautiful Nazi." His mouth dropped. "Please," I said, even though I wasn't sure why Edward wanted him out. He couldn't understand English. He got up from the bed and slowly, like a man of eighty, shuffled out of the room.

"Take off your clothes," Edward said. "For God's sake, Linda. You're a bloody mess. You're going to be passed off as my mistress, and—"

"Again? Can't I cross a border as something else?"

"What the hell do you want to be? A goddamn cowgirl?" He stood in front of me and unbuttoned my skirt.

"I can manage."

"We don't have time."

"I can—"

"Do you think my goal in life is to see you in your underwear?" My skirt fell to the floor.

"Why are you being so rotten to me?" He took off my blouse. I wasn't wearing a slip, just an ugly German brassiere and pants. He turned away and went to Margarete's clothes cabinet and took out a black silk dress with long sleeves. "It's too somber for this time of year," I told him.

"This isn't a fashion show, for Christ's sake. If you start bleeding again, it won't show up on the black." He held the dress so I could step into it, then eased the sleeve over my arm. "You need some jewelry or something."

"You just said it wasn't a fashion show."

"You don't want to look like you're going to a funeral. Where would she keep necklaces and things?"

My dress wasn't buttoned, but I walked away from him, to her bureau, and opened her top drawers. In the left one I found boxes. More earrings. Bracelets, probably more than fifty, beautiful, expensive ones, tossed into a box. Necklaces.

"I can't wear these."

"What are you talking about?" He came over with a pair of black shoes. Heels, with a big grosgrain ribbon. He put them on the floor beside me.

"The jewelry has to be from her boyfriend. It's probably taken from . . . from people they sent away."

"Do you think the people who owned these things would begrudge you? Or do you think they'd want you to look like a proper concubine who's going over the border to Switzerland with her married SS boyfriend to have an abortion?"

"That's my cover?"

"Yes. If they call the clinic, they will be assured Ingeborg Hintze is coming in to take care of a female problem. Let's get going." He grabbed my good arm and slipped on three or four bracelets. Then he handed me a heavy gold necklace. "Friedrichs has a car downstairs. Oh, by the way, he has new papers. He's Werner Reinke now. He's going to put us on the train. Big send-off for the general and his floozy."

"Why don't you just lay off!" I blurted out.

"Why don't you keep your mouth shut! Do you want the whole building to hear you yapping away in English?" He was pulling out underwear, stockings, sweaters. "Go find a suitcase. Fast." I stood there. "Come *on*, Ingeborg. Move!"

* * *

Konrad Friedrichs sat in the front with the driver, a man in an army uniform who was so tall his hat touched the roof of the car. Friedrichs twisted around to speak to me. "I will be putting you on the train, Lina. The conductor knows he will be taking care of a very important officer and his lady. He understands the general's disability and will not embarrass him."

"What disability?"

"He is mute." I turned and stared at Edward. I couldn't tell if he had arranged this chat in German or whether his mind was someplace else and he wasn't listening. Herr Friedrichs continued: "When he came under fire in Russia last year, they shot him in the chest; the bullet lodged in his throat. If they ask questions, you will, of course, answer for him. He is General Manfred Steinhardt, First SS Panzer Corps. He replaced Dietrich and Peiper. Dietrich's now with the Sixth, and he is a close friend of General Steinhardt—"

"Isn't a general too high a rank? Won't they be suspicious?"

"They may, but there was no time to create papers for a colonel. He was quite insistent—perhaps that is too mild a word—about getting to you; you were in mortal danger, he was going in to get you, and that was that. I had the interpreter tell him that he could not manage alone, not knowing the language. I would accompany him."

I didn't know what to say, but I figured Herr Friedrichs could live without a speech. "Thank you."

"You are welcome. Now I will see you onto the train. Then I will say goodbye."

"Where are you going?"

"I am going to stay here."

"Are you crazy? Herr Friedrichs, you're the one person in Berlin they want more than me. You've got to come with us, or—"

He held up his hand. Then, almost kindly, he asked, "Don't you long for your America?"

"Yes. I long for it."

"Then you will understand that I cannot endure being

away from my country. I will stay. Your gentleman here has arranged sanctuary for me. I will do what I can to help others here to get rid of the pestilence and, later, to help begin anew. But if I die . . . I would rather go down in flames in Germany, for Germany, than live anyplace else."

As we got to the train, an army officer saluted Edward. He saluted back and then handed over our papers and train tickets; we would not get them back until we reached the Swiss border. They would have sixteen hours to examine our papers, to discover us.

The officer opened my passport, looked at the photograph, then at me. "I know," I told him. "I've lost some weight. All of us in Berlin have."

He looked back down at the travel documents. "You are going to the clinic in Basel?" I nodded. He glanced down at me; the clinic must be a popular one. Official Nazi policy did not discourage illegitimate children; the more Aryans to carry guns, the better. But apparently, upper-echelon officers, married officers, were allowed to make sure their mistresses kept their trim figures. The way the officer had said "the clinic" had a nasty, knowing edge.

Konrad Friedrichs, standing behind us, inched forward. He gave the officer a "watch out" look. With reason. Edward looked displeased; he glared at the officer. It worked as well in Germany as it did in the United States. The officer turned pale, then quickly stepped back, allowing us to board the train. Edward took my arm. For the first time, I noticed he was wearing a white silk scarf around his neck, tucked into his general's uniform. A scarf to hide his mute, injured throat.

"Goodbye, General. Miss Hintze," Herr Friedrichs said. He inclined his head, and then simply walked off, to disappear into Berlin.

Edward helped me up the stairs onto the train. On the door was an official SS notice, with the death's head insignia. It said: "Reserved. Do not enter." We entered. It was for us. He closed the door behind us.

The sleeper was large, but it was hard to see what it looked like. The blinds were drawn, and there was only one dim light on. I sat down on a couch. It was a hard, scratchy velvet.

Edward sat beside me and put his mouth to my ear. "How are you?"

"Okay," I whispered.

"In a lot of pain?" I nodded. "I have some morphine with me, but if you can hold off, I'd like to wait until we're under way. They may have questions, and you'll have to answer . . . and I have to take my signal from the way you behave." He was businesslike. Professional.

"I can wait."

We sat in silence, listening to the activity outside on the platform. Then, without saying anything, he put his arm behind me and eased me down, so I was stretched out, my head in his lap. "It will look good for the conductor and give you a chance to rest."

"Thank you."

"Every once in a while, say something to me in German. 'Are you all right, darling?' 'Can I get you anything?' That sort of thing." I nodded and closed my eyes. A minute later, he started to stroke my hair. "I gave you a damned good haircut, Ingeborg." I kept my eyes closed. He turned my face toward him. I looked up. "Linda, I'm sorry."

"Really? What for?"

"For the way I behaved before."

"Actually, it felt like Old Home Week."

"I was never that rough on you in Washington."

"Want to bet?" He knew what I meant. Suddenly, he became absorbed in studying the medals on his uniform. "You know, you can be the coldest, most heartless . . . Sometimes, when I was working for you . . . Oh, never mind. It wasn't that often."

"I'm sorry for all those times."

The train jolted, then started to move. No toots, no whistles. It just eased out of the station, through the city.

"Would you like me to help you off with your jacket,

darling?" I asked, out loud, in German. Then I whispered. "Are you saying you're sorry because you think we won't make it?"

"Shhh. Relax."

"What are our chances? Twenty-eighty? Sixty-forty?"

"I'd say about fifty-fifty. That's being objective. Subjectively, I wouldn't have come in if I didn't think I had a good chance of getting you out."

"Or just getting me before the Gestapo did."

"If that was all I could get, I would have settled for it." The train picked up speed and we rushed through the countryside. "Linda."

"What?"

"It's been eighteen months of hell for me. Ever since I came back and found out you'd gone in, I've been ... Quick! Say something in German!"

"I love it when you do that to my hair," I said. As I was saying it, there was a knock on the door. I tried to grab Edward's hand, to squeeze it; I was so scared. But he just shook his head and put his hand on my shoulder. Possessively. "Come in," I called out.

The door opened, and there was a conductor in a white jacket. He bowed. "General! Miss. I am Martin. I am at your service." I lifted my head from Edward's lap, sat up slowly and curled up against him. He gave me an icy look that said, This is inappropriate behavior. I expect more from my mistress! I pulled away. I lowered my head, ashamed. The conductor took it all in.

"General Steinhardt would like some brandy or aquavit," I said. "And some tea for me."

"Will you be going to the dining car, Miss? Or may I bring you something? Bread, perhaps some cheese or cold cuts?"

I looked at Edward, expectantly. So he nodded. "Some bread and cheese. The general is tired. He does not wish to be disturbed again." Martin clicked his heels and closed the door.

"What was that all about?" Edward whispered.

"You don't wish to go to the dining car. He's bringing some stuff in for you. You don't wish to be disturbed."

"Speak German again!"

"Should I have ordered coffee, darling?"

We sat silent for twenty minutes, until Martin returned with a tray on a cart and set it before us on the couch. After he left, Edward reached into his pocket and came out with two white pills; I poured some water and took one. "I'll tell you if I need the other one. I don't want to get too fuzzy."

"All right."

"Edward . . ."

"Yes?"

"I'm sorry I did what I did. Sneaking behind your back to Norman Weekes the minute you left the country."

"Are you really sorry?"

"I'm sorry about what I did to you." I took a slice of cheese and made a sandwich. "How mad were you?"

"Very. And terrified. I'd read the reports on the RAF attacks on Berlin and—" His voice broke off. He ignored the brandy but took a piece of cheese. "There wasn't one damned day that I didn't . . . fear for your life. Even after the intelligence you were getting started coming out. Especially then. I knew you were in that house all the time."

"I was a cook. Did you know that?"

"Yes. Were you a good cook?"

"Of course I was a good cook, but that creep had no taste buds." I took some more bread and cheese. "Ed."

"What?"

"I just want to tell you . . . I don't think there was ever a day I didn't think about you. Whenever I got scared, and that was almost all the time, or whenever I didn't know what to do, and *that* was almost all the time too, I'd ask myself, What would the great Edward Leland do?"

"If the great Edward Leland were living in Horst Drescher's house, stealing state secrets, being bombed every night, I think . . . I know he wouldn't have made it."

"Sure you would have."

He took my hand for a minute. "I'm glad you thought about me, Linda."

The train sped on.

I thought I was being professional, alert, but I woke up later and my head was in his lap again. "How long did I sleep?"

"About three quarters of an hour."

"Could I have the other pill?"

He leaned over, got some water and gave it to me. "How bad is it?" I tried to sit up by myself. I needed his help.

"Bad."

"Do you want a shot of brandy?"

"No, thanks." I touched the silk sleeve. At least it was dry. "I'm not bleeding."

"That's good. I wish I could do something more for you."

"Ed. What if we make it out and they have to amputate my arm?"

"Stop it!"

"Rolf, my contact, only had one arm. You should have seen him clean fish. But who's going to want a one-armed typist?"

He smiled, then sat back. "Are you planning to go back to work?"

"Can you think of another way to earn a living?"

"Well, you're a wife." I didn't say anything. "You haven't asked me about John."

"I guess that's because I'm not really interested in John."

"He's your husband."

"Not for much longer. Death or divorce, whichever comes first."

"Linda . . ."

"Ed, in all those months in Berlin, when I was holed up in bomb shelters waiting to die, I thought about him, oh, maybe two or three times. But never: Oh, my dear beloved, how I yearn for you. Not even: Gee, I wish John was here to hold my hand." I peeked through the blinds. It was dark outside. "He didn't love me. You know that. And I didn't love him."

"You gave a fine imitation of it."

"Well, I loved what he was. His intelligence, his looks, his classiness. I thought: Here is what I should love. So I loved it. It was like I was reaching out for something beyond me, something better. But he wasn't better."

"He's waiting for you in London."

"He went with you to London?"

"Yes."

"How come?"

"He knew . . . we all knew your life was on the line. You're our hero, you know. Heroine."

"They must be hard up for heroes."

"You know what you did. Living there all that time. And finally, giving up your chance to live so you could get the Grayson report to us. They confronted him, you know. He tried to commit suicide, but they caught him in time. Now he's feeding false information to the German agent—just slightly false, so everything he says becomes suspect and the Germans will decide he's a plant. Linda, what you did was so important, and so brave."

"But I didn't do it out of bravery. I did it because I was stuck there, in Berlin, and it was my job. What else could I have done? Run? Where could I run to?"

"That's pretty much what happened to me in the last war. I was crawling on my belly, they started shooting, and I kept crawling. Where could I run to?"

"But you *are* a hero. You've gone in again and again, knowing how dangerous—"

"So did you."

About an hour later, I said, "I feel giddy. Not silly. I mean, the pills. I'm having a lot of pain, and I feel it, but it's like my mind is somewhere else, looking down at the pain. I had that same feeling when I was in the hospital, when I lost the baby." Edward looked as if he wanted to say something, but then he just nodded. "You know, John never came right out and said he didn't want it. He said it would have been inconvenient. We'd have to move. Good old honorable John."

"Don't be so hard on him."

"Why not?"

"Because he does the best he can with very little."

"He's not much of a man, is he?"

"Linda, my guess is that if we make it to Bern—that's where we're headed, actually, not Basel—you'll recuperate for a week or so and take the first plane out to London, back to him. So let's stop the discussion right where it is. It's gone too far already."

"I don't want him."

"Whatever you say."

"Well, I say that if he wants me now, it's because I'm the Sweetheart of OSS. All of a sudden I'm a hero. He can take me to dinner parties and not cringe over my accent. And you know what else I say? I say, if he was a man who wanted his wife, he'd have come and gotten me. He's fluent in German, for God's sake. But he left it to you."

A timid knock. Martin. "Forgive the intrusion. Shall I make up the bed, General? I don't wish to disturb you again, but . . ." I looked at Edward, as if asking what I should do, and then I told Martin to go ahead.

When he left, I asked Edward, "When do we get to the border?"

"About ten tomorrow morning. Go to sleep."

"I can't."

"Go to sleep."

I got into the bed. They gave the SS such soft sheets. "Ed?"

"Yes."

"How is your daughter?"

"Well, she's going to make me a grandfather."

"From her . . ."

"Yes. She went back to him soon after you left. Well, back and forth. Nan seems to thrive on marital crises, and her husband puts up with them. She goes off to think things over and then comes back. The last couple of times, at least, her

distress was genuine. She didn't run back to John. She had a
lot to think about, and it seems that for the time being she'll
stay with Quentin and be a wife and mother."

"Well, congratulations, anyway."

"Thank you."

"How old are you?"

"Fifty-five."

"I thought it would be about that."

"Rapidly approaching fifty-six."

"I hope you live to see your grandchild."

"Linda, go to sleep."

The awful thing was that right from where we were sitting, we could see the Swiss flag. But we were inside the
German customhouse, with an army officer at an official
desk, across from us. He had a thin face, like a hatchet. "I
am sorry, General Steinhardt, but we have been ordered to
stop all women of the description of Miss Ingeborg Hintze."
Edward stared at him. The officer inched back in his chair,
uneasy but not afraid. "And if *you* will be so good, General,
could you please unwind your scarf so I might take a look at
your wound."

Edward just kept eyeing him. And with the officer eyeing
me, I couldn't even move my finger to my neck as a signal.
But just then, Edward sensed what was expected; he opened
his collar. He kept the scarf tied, but slowly he unbuttoned
three buttons and pulled open his uniform. As the officer
tensed, his chair squeaked. Short, thick red scars covered
Edward's chest and shoulder. A livid one, like a crater, was
dug into the top of his chest; the surgeons who had put his
face back together hadn't even tried with the rest of him.

The officer averted his eyes—not enough to seem
unmanly, but enough so that he was looking just beyond
Edward's shoulder. He was a deskman. Edward began to
unwind his scarf.

The officer said, "Please, that is not necessary, General
Steinhardt. I hope you will accept my profound apologies."
Edward began buttoning his uniform, ignoring the man,

which only made his apologies more profuse. "It was simply that your not being able to speak . . . I—we—there was some concern that perhaps you were hiding a foreign accent."

Beyond the small window, the Swiss flag fluttered in the breeze. A perfect spring day over there. "Can we go now?" I asked.

"The general can go, Miss. I am afraid we must detain you."

I got emotional. Well, I was. To see the flag, no more than a couple of hundred feet away . . . "*Please*. I have an appointment at the clinic in Basel. I must be there. Some . . . some surgery."

"I am sure it can be postponed a day or two."

"It's really very important, and the general has been kind enough to accompany me. I can't ask him—"

"I am afraid you will have to." He reached under his blotter and offered me a sheet of paper. A handbill from the Gestapo. Attention! it said. And beneath it was Lina Albrecht's passport photo. I took it and handed it to Edward. He glanced at it, made a face—such a dreary little girl—and threw it back on the officer's desk.

"I regret to say, General, there is a certain vague resemblance." He wasn't sure; the general, with his perfect papers, perfect uniform, perfect bearing and perfect scars, wouldn't . . . but any man can be duped. "You, sir, are free to go, but I must phone my superiors and ask that they send an investigator to scrutinize Miss Hintze's documents."

Edward nodded, as if he understood completely.

"May I see you out, General?"

It couldn't just end. I looked over at Edward and remembered when I thought it was all over for me at Margarete's apartment. I'd said to myself, Remember one wonderful thing. And what had comforted me, and then flooded me with pleasure, was the memory of sitting in the Packard beside Edward on an ordinary day, almost touching, having a long conversation comparing Churchill and Roosevelt, and his brilliant half smile when I'd said, "Ha! Got you!" after he admitted the two men had a lot in common. I remembered his suit, the smell of starch on his white shirt, his hands resting on his briefcase, and I remembered not letting myself think about how I felt about him.

The officer shrugged his apologies to Edward. And Edward seemed to understand. He put his hands on the desk and pushed himself up from his chair. As he did, the officer leapt to attention. Edward smiled. The officer moved to go to the door, but Edward put a hand on the man's shoulder: Stop. The man's pale, thin face began to darken at this abuse of military etiquette. But suddenly the face brightened.

Sticking out from under the blotter was a souvenir from Edward: a thick wad of cash. As they used to say in Ridgewood, enough to choke a horse. Enough to buy a German officer, plus, I thought, some extra. The officer reached out for it and stuffed it into his pocket.

Then he picked up the handbill with my picture, crumpled it, and stuffed it in his other pocket. "So many people pass over this border. Naturally, we are always besieged by papers such as these. The dull, bureaucratic mind at work." The officer smiled. Edward turned toward the door. "Please, allow me, General! Miss Hintze. If you will follow me, I will escort you to Switzerland."

# 27

My bed was like a crib, with high white railings on four sides. When the nuns in their white habits and their head coverings that looked like upside-down canoes came sweeping in to change my bandages or give me pills for the pain and the infection, they'd lower the side, go about their business and then raise it again. If I hadn't been so sick, I probably would have thought of it as a prison, but with my fever at a hundred and four for a few days, I was a baby again, and all those German-speaking nuns were like sugar-coated Grandma Olgas, straightening my blanket, feeling my forehead, making sure I was all right.

I wanted all the comfort I could get.

Edward came to visit me, and he brought me American presents: a Hershey bar, a Coke and, on the third day, an Eveready flashlight. He said the only other American object he could find was the American consul's Oldsmobile, and he couldn't fit it into the elevator.

I asked him how much it had cost to get me out of Germany. About twenty thousand dollars—in Swiss francs.

I know we talked now and then, but I don't remember what we said. The second afternoon, he brought in the head of the OSS in Bern, and they asked me all about Margarete. I guess I was speaking for a while, because finally Edward turned and said, "Really, this is too much for her." I hadn't thought it was, but I must have fallen right asleep, because I never saw them leave.

He came at night, and he'd sit in a chair next to the bed.

When I'd wake up, he'd ask me how I was, and I'd say fine. I could have said a few things more, but what was I going to say? I love you? I love you now, and to make it worse, I probably loved you for ages and didn't even know it? Somewhere between New York and Washington, my awe turned into understanding and my respect into love? On the third night I asked, half hoping for something, "Aren't you bored, sitting here?"

"Yes. Excruciatingly. If you go back to sleep, I can leave."

On the fifth day, my fever was down. The doctor took off the heavy bandage and covered my wound with a gauze pad. I ate boiled eggs and toast for breakfast. And at ten o'clock, Edward Leland came to say goodbye.

"I'm going to Madrid later this afternoon. And then back to Washington."

It had to happen. I knew it. I was prepared. "Well, have a good trip. I'll see you in Washington or, more likely, New York."

"Yes. I'll look forward to it."

"Edward."

"Yes?"

"You're really going?"

"You'll be fine. In a few days, you'll be out of here. Back to . . . wherever."

"And you? You'll be back to wherever?"

"Yes."

It still wasn't easy for me to move, because of the intravenous needle, but I edged over to the side of the bed and managed to grab a lever; the bedrail came crashing down. "Sit down," I said. He sat beside me, all dressed for the plane. Suit, striped tie, wingtip shoes, a gray felt hat in his hands. "Your Republican uniform."

"Better than SS."

"You look nice."

"Thank you."

"Very businesslike." He rotated his hat on his lap. "You want to get out of here, don't you?" He didn't answer. "Why? Why do you want to leave me?"

"Linda, I have to—"

"You love me, you know. I figured it out last night."

He stood up. "Please don't do this. There's no point—"

"I love you too."

"No you don't." He sat down again and took my hand. "Any feelings you have for me are just an outgrowth of our . . . adventure."

"I've loved you at least since Washington. Maybe even in New York."

"Linda, don't subject both of us to—"

"When did you start loving me?"

He lifted my hand and kissed my fingers. "In New York, I suppose."

"You suppose? Come on, Ed. We're having a crucial conversation."

"In New York!" he boomed in his deepest, loudest voice. "Is that better?"

"Yes."

"There were at least twenty bright, German-speaking lawyers I could have asked to come to Washington and work for me. Why do you think I chose John Berringer? I came to your apartment that day, a Saturday or a Sunday, telling myself how stupid I was, that I should just get the hell out of town and forget about you. It was right before Christmas. You were wearing a yellow robe when you answered the door. A fluffy sort of thing, beautiful, and your hair was so soft . . . I desired you. And I desired your company."

"Last night," I said, "lying here, I was thinking how much I want you. Not only that way. Every way. I wish you could take off that suit and just lie under the covers with me and hold me for a while. Wouldn't you like that? To feel each other—"

He got up. "No!"

"No?"

"I think this should end now."

"Edward, I love you. You love me."

"I'm twenty years older than you are."

"Big deal. Sit down."

He sat, but stiffly, on the very edge of the bed. "I want to tell you something," he began. "Something . . . humiliating, but I want you to understand. In Washington. It was one of those times I'd blown up at you: just being next to you in the car all day, joking about something, talking . . . and then the frustration of knowing you were going home. So I behaved badly. You left. I knew you were upset. I sat at my desk trying to understand myself: I don't attempt to captivate her and I can, on occasion, be captivating as hell. But instead, I don't even try. I alienate her. It's certainly not because of my belief in the sanctity of marriage, or at least not that marriage, because it's a sham. I push her away whenever she gets too close because I know she can never love me—"

"But I do."

"—never love me as I love her. Passionately. Obsessively. That night, and several other nights . . . I called a man known in Washington. A procurer. I arranged for a room at a hotel and asked him to send me a woman. I described her. I described you. What he actually sent me was someone with bleached hair and an overripe figure, but I paid her twice what she had expected, on the condition she didn't say a word. And in that dark room . . ." His eyes filled with tears. ". . . I pretended she was you. I made love to her and called her Linda. The next day, I said, Good morning, Linda, and gave you a list of telephone calls to place."

I reached out for his hand and put it against my cheek. "But now you can have me."

"It won't work out."

"Why not?"

"Because you can never feel about me the way I feel about you."

"This is the first time in all the years I've known you that you've talked down to me. What's the matter? You think I don't feel passion for you? You think I'm not capable of the same deep, true love you're capable of feeling? Damn it, I want you!"

"I'm going to be a grandfather."

"How about being a husband?"

"You need someone—"

"Why won't you marry me? Because you went to Yale and I went to Grover Cleveland?"

"Linda!"

"Because I'm a Jew? You're afraid to say to your partners, 'Here's my wife, the lusty Jewess'?"

"You're a Jew now?"

"Yes. You called me that, and I said I wasn't, but I changed my mind in Germany. Listen, if I can love a Republican, you can love a Jew."

"This is a ridiculous conversation."

"Is it because of John, Nan, that whole business?"

"No!" But he was starting to smile. "Although you must admit it might make for an awkward Thanksgiving dinner."

"Just the first year."

"And after that?"

"Nan, Quentin, the baby. You, me . . . and maybe the baby."

He lifted up the cover and, wing-tips and all, got under the covers and pulled me close to him. "The man is supposed to propose to the woman."

"But he's not going to be able to if he's crazy and hysterical that she doesn't love him enough. So let her do it for him. Edward, will you—"

"Quiet! Things should be done properly. So I am going to make a short speech. My dearest Linda, you and I, we're two of a kind. I think . . . no, I truly believe we were made for each other. Will you marry me?"

"Oh, Edward! Yes!" And I kissed him. What a kiss!

"I love you."

And God, what a man!